SHIELD AND SPLINTERED OATHS
THE ENERGY OF MAGIC
BOOK THREE

J.E. NEAL

Copyright © 2023 by J.E. Neal

All rights reserved.

No part of this book may be reproduced in any form or by any electronic or mechanical means, including information storage and retrieval systems, without written permission from the author, except for the use of brief quotations in a book review.

To Becca — For explaining the magic

CONTENTS

1. Pretrial Motions — 1
2. Lawson v. Lawson — 9
3. The Tally — 35
4. Things to Come — 37
5. Family Ties — 45
6. Bitter Taste — 53
7. Sweet as Heaven, Sexy as Hell — 59
8. Hunger — 71
9. Saturday — 75
10. Birthing Hips — 81
11. The Eye of the Beholder — 87
12. Beautiful — 93
13. 1964 and a 1/2 — 97
14. Shattered — 101
15. To Save a Life — 105
16. Hold Steady, Then Run Like Hell — 109
17. Battle Lines — 119
18. Politics — 123
19. Garrett — 129
20. The Thin Line — 135
21. Needs — 145
22. Brothers — 151
23. The Devil You Know — 159
24. Every Step of the Way — 167
25. Good Night, Son — 181
26. Animals — 187
27. A Receiver — 191
28. Intelligence — 195
29. In The Reflection — 197
30. The Price of the Priceless — 203
31. What Remains — 209
32. Only Job — 217
33. Escape — 221
34. Emily — 225
35. Take Care of Her — 231

36. His Father's Son	237
37. Fortune Teller	241
38. Adeline	247
39. The Pain	255
40. Fire Watch	259
41. Mr. Lawson	263
42. The Performance	269
43. The Fifteen Beacon Hotel	273
44. Fionna Styler	281
45. Action!	285
46. Those That Know the Least	289
47. Challenge	297
48. Gala Ball	301
49. Tell the Tales, Listen Close	307
50. Only Fools	311
About the Author	315
Also by J.E. Neal	317

CHAPTER 1
PRETRIAL MOTIONS
RAINER LAWSON

By Sunday evening, Emily was a nervous wreck. Rainer walked her all over Parks Mall. They were both trying to locate clothing that made them look refined and classy, but still young, per Stariff's instructions.

"I don't want you to think I care about the money," she fussed as they sat down in the food court.

As this was the tenth time she'd made this vow in the last hour, he sighed. "Baby, I know. Please, don't let this get to you. It'll all be over tomorrow, then we'll go to Governor Carrington's wedding this weekend, and *then* we're going to the beach," he tried to remind her of the pleasant things on the horizon.

"What if we lose?" She worried her bottom lip constantly with her teeth.

Rainer squirted out ketchup for his fries. "Then that's it, and I will work my ass off for the rest of my life to restore everything to the Lawson family trust that I lost, but I really don't think that's going to happen."

"If you lose, it will be my fault."

"That isn't true, and I have a hard time believing my uncle is going to say or do anything that's going to suddenly make the Senteon or the governors want to give him half of the Lawson estate. That would be like spitting on my father's grave." His body gave an involuntary shudder. Oddly, that sentiment seemed to be the one that brought her peace.

"How do you think it happened that your dad and your uncle are so different? They were brothers and only a few years apart." She dipped a chicken nugget in the ketchup Rainer had supplied her.

Thankful that she seemed to be distracted from the trial, Rainer decided to embrace the subject change.

"I don't really know." He took a long sip of his Dr Pepper. "My grandparents died way before my dad, so I didn't really know them that well. My dad used to say that his parents weren't really fair with my uncle."

He thought back to him and his father falling on the sofa in their living room to talk after a particularly harrowing evening where they'd gone to visit Stan, and he'd ended up throwing them out. Rainer had been eleven or twelve at the time.

"Not fair, how?" Emily looked intrigued. Her thirst for knowledge always made him grin, so he beamed at her as he slid his sneaker up and down against her foot to make her giggle.

"I think they preferred my dad. You know, he got straight As, was head of Ioses, wanted to change the world, so I kind of think they compared Stan and my dad all the time, and obviously Stan came up short."

He wondered if his grandparents realized the destruction they were causing when they were raising their kids.

"Your uncle was never married, right?" Emily continued her inquisition as they ate. Rainer tried not to laugh as he hesitated to envision any woman unfortunate enough to have to put up with his uncle.

"No, and since this will be discussed tomorrow at the trial, I only feel a little guilty saying this in front of you, but the only women who ever engaged in anything with my uncle were being paid for their services."

"Rainer, I'm a big girl. I do know that exists. You don't have to shield me from it."

He smiled at her and tried to ignore the photographers who had just located them in the food court. He shook his head. "I want to protect you from everything. That's my job."

Emily rolled her eyes but grinned at him just as several of the cameras clicked. She steadfastly ignored them. "If women want to do that, it should be their choice." She threw another nugget in her mouth. Her eyes goggled a moment later. "What if you and Adeline were cousins?" She seemed thrilled with the notion.

Rainer laughed as he considered that. He kept his gaze locked on Emily as they ate. He refused to do anything that would make fodder for the papers.

"If I had to give over half of my estate to Adeline, that would be perfectly fine with me, but my uncle is most definitely not British." He pointed out the logistical problems with Emily's wonderings. The only thing Candy Parker ever told Adeline about her father was that he had a British accent.

"You know, they're going to report that we were out shopping the night before the trial." Emily made certain not to glance at the photographers or to let on that they bothered her in any way.

"I doubt what they take tonight will make it to the papers by the morning. So, they can say whatever they want. I don't care anymore." This was the conclusion he'd come to after hours of abusing himself over the pictures of the belly shot.

"As long as you know how much I love you, and I know I haven't done anything wrong, as long as I've done everything in my power to do right by you and your family, I don't care anymore."

A broad grin spread across Emily's beautiful face. "I really like that." She reached across the table and took Rainer's hand. As this was the most they'd touched since they'd entered the mall, the cameras clicked feverishly.

"Are you ready to go?" After they threw away their food wrappers, he laced his fingers through hers, and they walked away. They were perfectly aware that the cameras were eating it up. He tried to do just as he'd said and not care. He wanted to hold her hand. She was the love of his life, so he did.

After picking out several conservative ties and a new dress shirt for Rainer, and several skirts for Emily to choose from that all fell below her knee, they headed home. The press swarmed as they moved to the Mustang.

"Any thoughts on the trial tomorrow, Rainer?"

"Do you think the bar photos will cast you in a negative light at the trial tomorrow, Rainer?"

Rainer opened Emily's door for her and refused to answer. He moved to the driver's side as the questions grew more vicious.

"Do you think Emily is really the woman for you? She seems to be bringing you down," spat a woman dressed in a vibrant red suit, who narrowed her eyes in on Rainer.

"Will Samantha Peterson be testifying for you tomorrow?" called another.

It took everything in him not to tell them exactly what he thought of both questions, but he drew a steadying breath, slid into the seat, and shut the press out.

As Rainer had, on numerous occasions, thrown the Mustang into reverse and not cared which particular person from the press might be behind him, they scattered as he turned on the engine.

Emily giggled as she watched them disperse. After he decided to channel his newfound, more mature attitude, he backed the Mustang out safely and headed home.

Mr. Stariff had already told Rainer and Emily that they would have to arrive at the Pentagon early, just to make their way through the sea of press that was expected to be awaiting their arrival for the trial. The governors were being brought in by helicopters, because of the danger the huge crowd could pose.

Everyone was still on edge after the Crown Governor's girlfriend Serena's capture. Iodex was providing Emily and Rainer security into the courtroom. When he had asked about his uncle, Vindico and Stariff had chuckled.

"If somebody shoots him, we wouldn't really see that as a loss," Stariff had sneered.

Rainer tried to hide his shock at the sentiment. The term cutthroat lawyer seemed to describe Jack Stariff to perfection.

Stariff had called in character witnesses from all over the Realm on Rainer's behalf, and the trial was expected to go on for hours.

They'd learned the night before that Samantha Peterson was on the witness list for Stan. This had only added to Rainer and Emily's anxiety.

After fixing Emily a cup of tea, Rainer grabbed a beer from the fridge and settled on the couch with her.

"Okay, you know you have Governor Carrington's votes, so that's two, and Governor Vindico's, so there's three right there," Logan began strategizing.

"Yeah, and Governor Willow and Dad are really good friends, and he was friends with Governor Lawson, and he's over all of Iodex," Emily stated hopefully.

"So there's four," Logan urged. As he'd already been over all of this with Stariff, Rainer was growing weary of the logistics of the trial.

"Yeah, but your dad has to recuse himself, and if Samantha has her way, Peterson will vote against me," Rainer reminded them.

In the case of a governor's recusal, when the Crown Governor stepped in, the defendant had to have five votes, including the two carried by the Crown in order for the trial not to be open for appeal.

Only carrying four votes from the governors meant his uncle could make another claim. As it had been pointed out to Rainer repeatedly by Stariff, his and Emily's fate stood in the hands of Governor Sapman. He'd only served as governor for a little over seven years. He came into office when Governess Mitchell retired.

He was a quiet, withdrawn man, but had run his entire campaign stating his adoration and deep respect for Rainer's father.

Emily was a friend of his daughter, Becca, but Governor Sapman was also extremely conservative. The belly shot photos could certainly change his vote, as that kind of thing generally had him up in arms.

"Do you know what kinds of things they're going to ask you? How's it going to work?" Adeline quizzed quietly. "My trial with my mom won't be for several more months, because the Non-Gifted courts work much slower."

Emily nodded. "Mr. Stariff says that they'll let his uncle make his claim that Rainer isn't responsible enough to have the entire estate, and that his lawyer will try to play to the Senteon's sympathies." She rolled her eyes before continuing. "Then Mr. Stariff will basically try to prove that Rainer's uncle is a good-for-nothing jerk by questioning him."

"That shouldn't be hard," Logan quipped.

Rainer grinned, despite everything racing through his mind and weighing heavily on his heart.

"Then, you, Logan, and Mom, and Dad, and Mentor Sullivan, and Will, Garrett, Connor, and I think the entire Elite Iodex team, will go on the stand to tell everyone what an amazing man Rainer is."

"Pretty much anyone with the last name Haydenshire," Rainer explained.

"I'll be sure to say just that," Logan teased. "Rainer Lawson is the most amazing man I've ever shared a bedroom with."

"Shut up," Emily retorted. This only served to make Logan and Rainer laugh harder.

"Anyway," she huffed, "then I go up for questioning, and then Rainer, and then the Senteon gets to question Rainer, and then they vote. Then the governors vote."

After taking another sip of his beer, Rainer took Emily's hand and kissed her cheek.

"You forgot that my uncle gets to bring in witnesses to prove that I'm a complete loser, baby."

"I know. I don't like that part."

This made Rainer laugh again. He decided to fill in a few of the gaps she'd left open.

"They'll ask everyone things about how I managed my monthly allowance from the estate when I was growing up, and talk about the things I've purchased since I received the inheritance, what kind of guy I am. Stuff like that." Rainer sighed before admitting the final piece of the trial.

"The focus is on the lack of a prenup." He hated the pained expression that formed on Emily's face whenever anyone stated anything about the prenup.

"I'll sign one," she vowed for the hundredth time.

"No, you won't," Rainer insisted, just as he had every time she'd offered.

"You could tear it up after the trial."

"Emily, please." Rainer couldn't have this conversation again. He just didn't have it in him. "I have been in love with you since I was, like, four years old. Your mom tells that story all the time about how I toddled over to you when you were newborn and sat with you and cried when my parents took me home. So, if you've been lying to me since you were a toddler, and your plan from kindergarten on was to trick me into marrying you so you could have the estate, then you can go ahead and take it, because I don't want to go on anyway."

She wrapped her arms around him and squeezed him tight.

Logan chuckled and shook his head. "All I'm saying is, once Mom gets on the stand, it'll pretty much be over. I'm one hundred percent sure the rest of the governing board is just as afraid of her as Dad is."

His prediction had everyone laughing again.

CHAPTER 2
LAWSON V. LAWSON

The alarm went off at five, and Rainer's heart raced. He moved slightly but kept Emily cradled in his arms where he'd soothed her to sleep the night before. He kissed her forehead as she began to stir.

"Hey there." He refused to start this day differently than any other. He wouldn't let his uncle have any power over his life. She smiled against his chest. "We have to get ready."

She whimpered and shook her head against his chest. She always made him smile.

"I was having a really good dream," she fussed.

"What were you dreaming about?" He decided he wanted this moment with her before the world crashed in around them. He wanted just a few peaceful moments of the two of them alone and safe in the serenity of their bed.

"You," she giggled.

He was intrigued. "Me?"

She sighed and then yawned deeply. "Yes, and I was just about to the best part."

Rainer chuckled and then slipped his hand from her back. He massaged his way to her right breast.

"What's the best part?"

She gave him a delicious grin. "I'll show you later."

"Is that a promise?"

She nodded and clung to him. "Guess we should get this over with first, though."

"Over with sounds good to me."

"And after it's all over,"—she ran her hands over his chest and made the electricity arc between them—"I'll bring you back here."

He kept one hand kneading her right breast and slipped the other to her backside. He cupped and squeezed her lush cheeks.

"And…" he urged.

"And while every form of media in the entire Realm searches high and low for us after the trial, I'm gonna take you to bed and take care of you." Her voice was raspy and excited.

It made him ache. "I can't wait." He kissed her heatedly as he dipped his tongue into her mouth, giving them a few minutes to enjoy one another.

Emily worked carefully on her makeup, and Rainer emerged from the shower.

"What do you really think Samantha is going to do? Why is she testifying? She hardly even knows you." Emily mouthed this just before she puckered her lips and applied lip gloss. She'd been instructed not to wear lipstick.

Rainer shook his head as he began pulling his brush through his hair. "I have no idea. What could she possibly say? She'll be under oath, and I can count on one hand the number of times we've even spoken."

Emily brushed a kiss in the air beside Rainer's jawline. She didn't want to coat his cheek with the lip gloss.

Images of his father hard at work, and thoughts of his ancestors working and saving to amass the sheer amount of money that currently sat in his many bank accounts made him slightly queasy.

"Do I look okay?" Emily quizzed. Nervous energy rolled off of her in waves. Her entire body was drawn taut.

"You look beautiful, baby. You always do." She'd chosen a navy blue pencil skirt that fell to her knees, and a dressy button-down silk blouse. She'd decided to wear the blue and teal scarf she'd purchased at the beach when she and Rainer had visited at the beginning of summer. She'd declared that she wanted to wear at least one thing that was actually her choice.

Though the skirt was made of a heavy material, she'd donned a slip she borrowed from her mother. She'd always refused to wear them in the past.

"I hate panty hose." She stepped into a pair of very low heels.

As Rainer retied his tie, he smirked. "How about as soon as I get you home, I'll take them off of you?"

"That's what I'll say on the stand. Hi, I'm Emily Haydenshire, soon to be Lawson. I've been crazy over Rainer since I was born, so if you all could get this ridiculous trial over with then I'd like him to take me home and take off my panty hose." She rolled her eyes at her own joke and effectively cracked Rainer up.

"We need to get going." He took her hand.

The trial was set for ten o'clock, and it was barely seven when they left. The traffic around the Pentagon was gridlocked between the press and Gifted and Non-Gifted people alike trying to get to work.

Rainer's jaw clenched until he was concerned his molars would disintegrate as he navigated his way through the cars and eventually pulled up to the large front entrance of the Pentagon.

Iodex moved in. They kept the press behind the ropes as Portwood moved to the driver's side door. After Rainer emerged, he climbed in to move the car to the secured Iodex parking deck.

After straightening his jacket, Rainer tried to draw steadying breaths as thousands of cameras clicked feverishly. He opened Emily's door for her as Vindico and Tuttle cast and tried to shield them from the cameras as best they could. Ramier and Ericcson did the same for Logan and Adeline as they raced up the stairs.

"What do you think your father would say if he were here, Rainer?" dozens of reporters cried.

"How do you and Emily plan to celebrate if you win today?"

"Do you feel Jack Stariff will ensure you a win, Rainer?"

"Emily, who's that skirt by?"

"Great scarf, Emily, could you turn so we could get a shot?"

"Are you feeling nervous, Rainer?"

"Have you seen your uncle since he filed the suit?"

"Are you hoping for reconciliation?"

"Is that Armani you're wearing today, Rainer?"

The endless questions sounded distant, though the reporters were less than four feet away. His heart was beating in his throat as Vindico held the door for them. They rushed inside just before the reporters broke through the barricades and swarmed the entrance.

Stariff met them at the door. He shook his head at the press. "I have never been asked so many times who designed my tie."

"Sorry," Rainer offered. The sea of people they'd just shut the doors on astounded him. The last time he'd experienced so many reporters all at once was the day of his father's funeral.

"Don't apologize. I've just never seen anything like it." Stariff escorted the four of them into the elevator. They stepped out on to the Senate floor.

"I'm going to put you in one of the witness rooms. A few news sources have given their reporters a press pass, so they'll be entering in a little while. It would be best if they didn't have access to you until the last possible moment."

Rainer ushered Emily into the small room near the courtroom that held a coffee maker and a soda machine. Logan and Adeline made everyone coffee, but no one spoke. The nervous energy in the room was palpable.

A few minutes later, Rainer heard the choppers begin landing on the helipad of the Pentagon. His heart raced as he tried to recall everything Stariff had told him to do or not to do, or to say or not to say.

Emily took his hand and willed calm into him.

"You're gonna be fine, man," Logan vowed. Adeline nodded her agreement.

"Thanks." He wondered if it was odd that thoughts of losing the money didn't bother him, in terms of him not having it to spend. It was the thought of losing what his mom and dad and all of his ancestors had worked so hard for that made him nauseous.

Time seemed to be moving too quickly, and Rainer's heart raced as he watched the hands on the clock spin.

"Let's do this." Stariff gave Rainer a soothing smile as he gestured them from the room.

"Logan, you and Adeline will go in first. Join the witnesses on the benches in front. I'd like you and all of your brothers to sit together, as a show of solidarity."

"Emily, you'll be next. Just another minute or two," he explained.

Logan slapped Rainer on the back and Adeline brushed a tender kiss across his cheek before making their exit.

Emily trembled as she hugged her brother goodbye.

"Hey." Logan hugged her tight. "Have I ever let you down?" She shook her head as Logan smiled at her. "Then don't worry."

Rainer was unable to sit still. He began to pace. His brain was frenzied. He couldn't order his thoughts. His father, his childhood, the money, Emily, his uncle, the abuse he'd suffered the few weeks he lived with Stan, the Haydenshires, the Realm, the farm, his father's grave—it all swirled in a volatile, confusing mass that robbed him of breath.

Stariff returned a minute later for Emily. She clung to Rainer as he whispered how much he loved her. Stariff smiled and gave them a minute.

"I love you, and if he wins then I will help you replace every single penny. I promise you." She brushed a quick kiss across his lips. Rainer squeezed her hand as she turned to follow Stariff.

He broke out in a cold sweat. Anyone who might've been able to console Rainer was seated in the chamber room, and he'd never felt so utterly alone.

How could my uncle do this to my dad? How could he do this to me? Fury and anguish consumed him. He fought the ache in his heart. Why couldn't his dad have been there? He needed him.

A knock sounded on the door, and he swallowed the bile that flooded his throat.

"Are you ready?" Stariff inquired.

"I don't know." Rainer wiped his hands on his suit pants.

"You'll be fine. Just let me do what I do," Stariff assured him as they entered the chamber.

Rainer locked eyes with Emily as she mouthed, "I love you."

Rainer hoped she knew he loved her too, as he was unable to say or do anything but force himself to put one foot in front of the other until he'd seated himself at the table beside Jack Stariff.

Governor Haydenshire offered him a reassuring smile from the raised governors' bench. Rainer accepted it gratefully, especially considering the way the week before had begun.

He glanced to his right and took in his uncle. Stan was seated, with his lawyer, in a cheap brown suit that appeared to be several sizes too small. He was giving Rainer a simpering glower. Contempt and fight lit through Rainer in heavy doses as he returned the glare.

Donald Mulligrew was serving as his uncle's attorney. His reputation for being a slick ambulance chaser was well-known throughout the Realm.

Mrs. Haydenshire looked furious as did Will and Garrett. Logan, Levi, Patrick, and Connor were all shooting Stan glares that said he'd better hope he never ran into any of them in a dark alley.

Chancellor Wilshire and Mentor Sullivan, the mentor in charge of Ioses order at Venton, both gave Rainer encouraging nods. All of Iodex offered Rainer smiles as he was seated.

The governors were all in their seats, though none of them looked at Rainer or his uncle.

Samantha Peterson was preening and applying lipstick on the witness bench for his uncle. Rainer shook his head and stared back at the table. He didn't want to see who else might be testifying against him.

Governor Carrington banged the gavel, and Rainer flinched at the sound. The Crown Governor stood and shook his head. "I would never want anyone to say this wasn't done in accordance with the law. So, today, we're here to try Rainer Emory Lawson, on his character, to determine whether he is deemed worthy of the estate left him by his father, Joseph Emory Lawson, the most beloved Crown Governor of our Realm."

He was unable to keep his anger out of his tone. "The plaintiff today is none other than Stan Leroy Lawson, brother of our dear Joseph, and Rainer's uncle. Stan is asking that the Senteon consider assigning him half of the Lawson family estate, as he feels Rainer is unable to use the money responsibly, and he feels that he was cheated out of it as a young man when his brother was awarded the entire estate upon their parents' death. So, Mr. Mulligrew, I give you the floor for your opening arguments."

Mulligrew stood. His beady eyes landed on Rainer. They were full of mocking disdain.

Rainer resisted the urge to flip him off by folding his hands in his lap. His father had often sat with his hands folded in his lap, and he had to hide a smile as he considered that, perhaps, that was why.

"Thank you so much, Crown Governor," Mulligrew drawled. "Most esteemed governors and members of the Senteon, I intend to prove today that Rainer Lawson isn't the clean-cut kid we all loved to admire. As most of us saw in the papers last week, Mr. Lawson just isn't the man his father was, and for the Realm to make such an error in judgment as to award him the entire Lawson family estate would, in my client's opinion, be an egregious mistake. Lascivious behavior, lies, cheating, squandering, all of these concerns swirl rapidly around Mr. Lawson, and I believe, after we leave here today, we'll all have a much clearer picture of just who the son of our great Governor Lawson really is," he vowed before he reseated himself.

Rainer wanted to scream, but he drew a deep breath and clenched his jaw as Stariff stood.

"Governors, members of the Senteon," he greeted the power players respectfully before he stood in front of the raised desk the governors were seated behind.

"Mr. Mulligrew is correct," he stated as all those in the courtroom furrowed their brows. "We don't really know Rainer Lawson. Well, not most of us. We love to snatch up papers full of half-truths or just out-and-out lies about Rainer and his fiancée, Emily Haydenshire," he gestured his head toward Emily, who gave him a sweet smile. "I would, however, like to know when, in this Realm that Rainer's father gave his life to preserve, did it become unlawful to inherit hard-earned money and use it as we see fit? I would like to bring light to the fact that anyone voting against my client today is taking Crown Governor Lawson's final wishes and throwing them away flippantly, like he didn't matter at all.

"The people I've brought in for testimony today do know Rainer Lawson. They know him better than any of us do. These are not people who have flipped through a tabloid and formulated an opinion of a man they've never even met. So, I agree with Mr. Mulligrew. I do believe that, at the end of the trial, we will all know Rainer a little better, and we'll be proud that we do. He is a fine man who has already given everything to this Realm, at a very young age, and now some of you want to deal him a final blow, it seems." He narrowed his eyes at Stan.

"I believe Rainer has given us enough. You see, it wasn't just his parents he gave us. He's given us his service in his work for Elite Iodex. He's given leadership and mentorship as head of Ioses Order at Venton Academy. But there's so much that's been taken without his permission—his privacy, his childhood, his fiancée, they've all been up for grabs, it seems." Stariff grew angrier the longer he spoke. "Rainer couldn't even take Miss Haydenshire away after their graduation to ask her to marry him without the Realm feeling they should be invited along, via harassing photographers and reporters. I think, when we're finished here, we'll all agree that what Rainer hasn't willingly given us, we've simply taken, and that needs to stop here and now."

Stariff returned to his seat. Rainer was thoroughly impressed.

Mulligrew stood again. He begrudged Stariff a simpering huff as he called Stan Lawson to the stand.

"Let's do this," Stariff huffed under his breath as Rainer felt the electricity crackle around him. The courtroom had Jack wired. He was ready to fight, and Rainer finally drew a full breath as he understood what made him the best lawyer in the Realm.

"Mr. Lawson, could you please tell the court when it was that you became so concerned about the inheritance left to your nephew?" Mulligrew's voice was overly sympathetic.

"I read in the papers that Rainer had asked her to marry him." Stan pointed his finger at Emily. Nodding, Mulligrew waited. "And, listen, we all know women are trouble," his uncle spat stupidly, as over half of the Senteon were female.

Stariff chuckled, which he turned into a cough. Mulligrew grimaced but said nothing.

"I'm just trying to protect my nephew. He didn't even make her sign one of them prenup things to protect the estate. He didn't even tell me he's gonna propose, even though I'm his only living relative." Stan pretended to be devastated as Rainer rolled his eyes.

Mulligrew turned to the Senteon and shook his head. "Now, for the record, the approximate value of the estate is close to a billion dollars. Can any of you imagine having that kind of money at twenty-one years of age and then not having your girlfriend sign a prenuptial agreement?"

This went on for several long minutes, with Mulligrew hammering home the fact that Rainer hadn't asked Emily to sign anything before their engagement.

He took his seat, and Stariff was vibrating in his dogged desire to tear Stan apart. Rainer watched as Stariff moved fluidly in front of the Senteon and the governors.

"Mr. Lawson, could you tell the court the circumstances under which custody of Rainer was taken away from you and given to Governor and Mrs. Stephen Haydenshire?" Stariff demanded. "I'll remind you that you're under oath." He narrowed his eyes in on Stan.

"Uh well," Stan stammered as everyone in the courtroom braced. "Like I said, Rainer never liked me. My brother turned him against me, so he went off crying and wailing to them." He gestured to the mass of Haydenshires seated on the benches. "And next thing I knew, he was being taken away. Just like that."

Stariff nodded and moved back to the table where Rainer was seated. He withdrew several papers from a folder.

"Governors." He raised the papers and asked that they be admitted. Governor Carrington nodded his agreement. "Mr. Lawson, what I'm holding in my hands is the custody hearing for Rainer when he was fourteen years old. The date on this document is just six weeks after his father's death. Rainer had shown up at school with a black eye and badly bruised face left unhealed.

"He'd spent one night outside on the stoop of your apartment because you'd locked him out. Upon walking home from middle school one day, as you'd failed to pick him up, he found you stealing money from his room. This was part of his monthly allowance left him by his father until his coming of age. You were using it to pay the prostitutes who were leaving your apartment," Stariff shot furiously. "And you pled guilty to all of these charges, in hopes that custody would be taken away, did you not?" Stariff held Stan's eyes. He refused to allow him to drop his gaze.

Rainer's uncle didn't answer, so Stariff continued.

"Governor and Mrs. Haydenshire demanded an emergency trial and were awarded full custody by the Senteon and governors. Many of them are the same people seated in this room today."

He turned to face the Senteon again and urged, "For those of you who weren't at that trial, or who might've forgotten, that was Governor Lawson's son, just six weeks after his father's death, at barely fourteen years of age who was abused, neglected, exposed to prostitution, and being robbed by the man seated before you now. Things Stan Lawson pled guilty to, not so many years ago. That's how we allowed Governor Lawson's child to be treated."

A slight murmur broke out in the Senteon, from people either recalling the custody trial or horrified by the information they'd just been given.

"Objection!" Mulligrew called.

Governor Carrington's brow furrowed. "On what grounds exactly?"

"Relevance."

After shaking his head, Governor Carrington huffed, "You're here to put a price on this young man's character, so as I understood it, this entire trial is to determine who is fit to handle the Lawson estate. Anything regarding Stan Lawson's character that can be proven is allowable. The court records clearly show that what Mr. Stariff has stated is true and therefore allowable."

"Thank you, Governor." Stariff nodded his appreciation. "May I?" he quizzed. All of the governors nodded for him to continue.

"Mr. Lawson, could you tell us what you do for a living?" he asked contentiously.

"I work off and on. I haven't had a lot of work lately. I've been worrying about Rainer," Stan vowed.

Rainer tried hard not to laugh at the "Pfft!" that echoed from Mrs. Haydenshire. Governor Haydenshire shot her a pleading look as he shook his head minutely.

Stariff continued, "Well, when you're not consumed with worry over the nephew you abused and neglected—"

"Objection!" Mulligrew screeched again.

"Withdrawn," Stariff immediately offered. "When you work, what is it that you do?"

"I work the party circuit." Stan puffed himself up importantly.

"The party circuit?"

"Yeah, I do magic tricks and stuff for Non-Gifted kids' parties. It's not easy. Sometimes you have two parties in one weekend."

A titter broke out around the room, but it was quelled quickly.

Any Gifted person using their energy for cheap thrills for the Non-Gifted was heavily frowned upon. If a Gifted person was flaunting their abilities in a way that would make the Non-Gifted assume there were people with abilities, they could be arrested.

Stariff pretended to be concerned. "So, you, Stan Lawson, brother of the greatest Crown Governor of our time, perform magic tricks for Non-Gifted children's parties?"

"That's what I said."

"And what do you plan to do with the money if you should receive half of the estate today?"

"Retire."

"From your weekend job?"

"Yeah," Stan huffed as if that would be the natural course of action.

Stariff pulled another document from one of his folders. "This is the withdrawal document from Venton Academy where you dropped out of the academy during your freshman year." The governors nodded their allowance of the documentation. "Why did you decide to quit your education, Mr. Lawson?"

"I've never needed it," Stan stated firmly. "My brother wanted the education. Not me."

Stariff nodded. "I've certainly found mine to be useful. I imagine most everyone in the room would agree, especially Rainer. Wouldn't you agree, Stan, that a person with a completed education might be better able to manage an estate than one who decided at eighteen years of age that they just didn't want to study?" Stariff shrugged as he awaited an answer.

"No, not necessarily."

Stariff nodded again and then delivered a blow. "Seems to me, if you'd completed your education, you would've known that you could've signed custody of Rainer to the Haydenshires immediately following Joseph's death. You would never have had to be bothered with him when you were named his guardian."

"Yeah, but I thought I was gonna be getting money for him," Stan explained, as the eyes of everyone in the courtroom goggled.

"No further questions." Stariff nodded to the governors who tried hard not to look amused.

Several witnesses took the stand. People Rainer had never seen before all claimed his uncle to be a good person who had been treated unfairly by his parents in light of his brother.

Stariff discounted their testimonies by reminding them that they were under oath and asking how long they'd known Stan. He would then point out to the Senteon that three weeks seemed a relatively short time to plead someone's good character.

Samantha Peterson was called to the stand. She droned on and on about how Rainer and Emily hung all over each other at the academy, with Stariff objecting on relevance numerous times.

"And could you tell the courts about your relationship with Rainer, Ms. Peterson? I think, since we are all concerned over Rainer's ability to make responsible decisions regarding Miss Haydenshire, that any of Rainer's indiscretions should come to light." Mulligrew patted her hand consolingly as Samantha wiped away fake tears.

Emily scowled, and Rainer's molars ached from clenching his jaw. He'd had enough. He leapt from his seat and sent it sailing backwards. He narrowed his eyes at Samantha while Stariff attempted to pull him back into his seat. "Are you really going to just keep lying, Samantha? Perjure yourself? Are you going to sit there under oath and tell everyone, including your father, that we had some kind of relationship? We were never even friends."

"Rainer, sit down!" Stariff demanded heatedly.

"Rainer, sit down now, son." Governor Haydenshire shook his head as Rainer reseated himself fitfully. He glared at Samantha.

"If I may," Mulligrew drawled contemptuously. "Miss Peterson, please tell the courts when Rainer Lawson first approached you," he urged.

Rainer's blood boiled as Emily huffed audibly.

"Well, I wouldn't necessarily say he approached me," Samantha hemmed. Mulligrew looked disheartened. "I could just tell, you know, in school, the way he would look at me like he wished he were with me instead of Emily, but you know he had to stay with her because the Haydenshires adopted him or whatever."

Rainer rolled his eyes, and Logan laughed out loud. Governor Haydenshire shot Logan another look that said for him to pipe down.

"And when you and Rainer were at school together, what kinds of things did you discuss?" Mulligrew asked with a pitying tone.

"Well, Rainer was obsessed with being head of Ioses, and what he would do with all of the money he was going to get. He bragged about it all the time." Samantha gave Rainer a haughty glare.

Rainer turned to Stariff, and growled, "That is a lie," under his breath.

"I know. Just sit back and let her hang herself. She's giving me plenty of rope."

"Oh, and his car—he told me about it constantly," Samantha drawled and rolled her eyes. "I just don't think Emily ever listened to him, and she was always with other guys, so it was natural he'd look at other options."

Emily's mouth dropped. Her mother and Will had to physically keep her in her seat.

"Objection, relevance. Miss Haydenshire is not on trial here," Stariff boomed.

The Crown Governor agreed and had the last statement redacted. After a few more outright lies about where Rainer and Samantha had hung out, and how Samantha would've most certainly signed a prenup had Rainer asked her to marry him, instead of Emily, Mulligrew sat down. He looked very pleased.

Stariff smiled as he rose. "First of all, Miss Peterson, I would like to remind you that you are, in fact, under oath, and that the penalty for perjury in the Realm is a minimum of twenty-five years in Felsink Prison. This Realm takes lying under oath very seriously." This seemed to shake Samantha. "Now, you're claiming that Rainer Lawson cheated on his lifelong girlfriend, now fiancée, Emily Haydenshire, with you?"

"Well, not exactly cheated." She gave a fake smile to Stariff and then the Senteon.

"Okay." Stariff nodded. "Why don't you tell the court if there was ever any kind of romantic involvement between you and Rainer Lawson?" Stariff demanded. "Twenty-five years, Miss Peterson," he reminded.

"Not romantic, per se," Samantha hemmed.

"Interesting."

"And how many classes did you and Rainer have together at the academy? He's in Ioses Order and you're an Adminis Predilect. How many times a day would you say you saw Rainer?"

Samantha paused. She was getting flustered. She turned to her father. "Is he allowed to ask me stuff like that?"

"Yes, Samantha." Her father glared at her. He looked thoroughly nonplussed.

"We didn't really have many classes together. I don't guess I saw him all that much, since he didn't live on campus."

"So, in all of the time you were not seeing one another, Rainer discussed his car?" Stariff repeated her earlier statement.

"Well, whenever we talked, he talked about his car."

Never breaking his rhythm, Stariff continued. "Seeing how much Rainer clearly meant to you, would you mind telling me what kind of car Rainer drives? It seems it's in the paper on a regular basis. This shouldn't be a difficult question."

"Uh," Samantha furrowed her brow as Rainer grinned. "It's old, and red with white stripe things."

"Old?" Stariff nodded. "Is that what Rainer said when he discussed it with you?"

"I don't know. I mean, I just heard him talking about it a lot. You know, with Logan and stuff."

"Have you and Rainer ever *actually* had a conversation, just the two of you?" Stariff narrowed his eyes.

"We talked at a wedding a couple of weeks ago." Samantha grinned.

Stariff nodded. "And could you give us any details of the conversation? Remember, Miss Peterson, I will be putting Rainer on the stand to corroborate your recollections, as I will Miss Haydenshire."

"We talked about him moving in with Emily."

"What was Rainer doing when you were talking to him at that wedding, which I, and most of the governing board, attended, I might add."

"Getting Emily food." Samantha rolled her eyes.

"And you approached him?"

Samantha glanced around uncomfortably.

"Miss Haydenshire was also in attendance at the wedding then, as you stated that Rainer was getting her food."

"Yes, of course. When is she not with him?"

Unable to hide his grin, Stariff feigned confusion. "It seems to me that trying to start a romantic relationship with someone you barely know might work better if you weren't on a date with your fiancée. Please correct me if any of these statements are false, Samantha, but you and Rainer never had a single class together all six years you were at the academy. You never attended a sporting event or formal or any other thing that might be considered a date together. The closest you came to having a conversation with Mr. Lawson was when you overheard him discussing his car with his best friend. Yet, you phoned tabloids to fake a relationship with Rainer, though one never existed.

23

You approached him while he was with his fiancée at a friend's wedding. He turned you down. You got your feelings hurt and decided to testify against him. That all seems a little petty, don't you think?"

Samantha looked mutinous. "My feelings were not hurt. It's his loss."

Emily beamed as Rainer tried not to laugh. That was the only part of the statements she'd denied.

"That's all, Governors." Stariff chuckled as he returned to his seat.

Samantha stormed back to her seat in an embarrassed huff. But Mulligrew wasn't finished. He stood and carried a handful of photographs with him toward the Senteon.

"As they say, pictures are worth a thousand words. I'd just like to share a few of Rainer Lawson from last weekend alone."

He then proceeded to go over, in great detail, shots of Rainer sliding his hands up Emily's skirt and licking her stomach. Rainer willed it to be over soon. The photos were passed to each of the governors and around the Senteon. Vomit swirled in his throat as he stared steadfastly at the table in front of him.

"Now, I ask you, do these photographs make us feel like Rainer is an accomplished young man, capable of making wise decisions with the Lawson estate? I don't believe that they do."

After several long minutes with Rainer willing his coffee to stay in his stomach, Mulligrew sat down, and Stariff was up.

"May I address the photographs, Governor, before I call my first witness?" Stariff requested.

"Certainly." Governor Carrington looked morose, as the photos didn't leave much to be defended.

"Ladies and gentlemen of the Senteon and governors, this trial is to determine whether or not Rainer Lawson has proven himself irresponsible, and therefore unable to manage the money he's been bequeathed by his late father.

"We're not here to judge what Rainer and Emily did last Saturday night, but I would like to point out that it wouldn't appear from the pictures that Rainer is cheating on Miss Haydenshire, nor she on him. I would also like to say that I know I'm extremely thankful, and I'm certain most of our esteemed governors feel the same, that there was no one around photographing or videotaping me and all of my many indiscretions when I was twenty-one years old.

"But there's the rub, the reason we all feel inclined to either defend or attack this man's character. Can Rainer, at twenty-one years of age, manage his father's estate?" Stariff hemmed.

"His father believed he could. Should we doubt Joseph Lawson? Rainer spent no money on the night those pictures were taken. He'd been invited to a private party that turned out not to be so private, and now I'd like to prove to this court that Rainer Lawson is a fine upstanding man, who is more than capable of managing his estate, despite thoughts otherwise based on those photographs. So, I'd like to call Governor Stephen Haydenshire to the stand."

Governor Haydenshire told the courts that Rainer had always worked very hard on the farm, had always gotten good grades, had been respectful of him and Mrs. Haydenshire, and thankful for what they'd done for him.

When Mulligrew asked about the belly shot photographs, the governor nodded. "I suppose that I'd have to agree with Jack. I'm glad no one was photographing Lillian and me when we were twenty-one, and though Rainer knows my feelings on what happened, I really can't think of a finer man for Emily."

Emily beamed at her father, as did Mrs. Haydenshire. The governor elaborated on Rainer's biweekly trips to check on his uncle, despite the filth he would find when he arrived.

After the governor, Mrs. Haydenshire was called.

"Lillian," Stariff greeted her after she'd taken the oath, "could you tell the court how long Emily and Rainer have been dating?"

Mrs. Haydenshire smiled. "Emily informed me when she was four that she was going to marry Rainer. She dared him to kiss her on the cheek when she was seven, and I suppose the rest is history. I'd say at least sixteen years, but probably more. They were raised together." She dared anyone to object.

"That's longer than most marriages last," Stariff commented. "And, in your vast experience, Mrs. Haydenshire, and we are all aware of your knowledge of children, would you tell me how likely it would be for a four-year-old, or even a seven-year-old, to decide that they would spend their entire life pretending to love someone, and convince them to marry them, so that when they turn twenty-one they could walk away with their fortune?"

"Not very likely," Mrs. Haydenshire chuckled.

"Objection. She's not an expert witness!" Mulligrew spat.

"The woman has raised, or is in the process of raising, ten children, all of whom are more productive in this Realm than your client," Governor Carrington huffed. "Her statement stands."

"Can you tell me when Emily learned of Rainer's inheritance and her reaction to it?" Stariff never missed a beat.

"Neither Rainer nor any of my children were aware of the inheritance, obviously, until after Joseph was killed, but several years after that, Stephen and I sat down with Rainer to explain what it would all mean for him.

"Emily didn't seem to react at all, and I firmly believe that Emily would still love Rainer and want to be with him if he hadn't a penny to his name."

Emily nodded adamantly though she wasn't supposed to.

Logan was called next. He confirmed that Rainer's uncle's apartment was always in a state of filth whenever he would go with Rainer to check on Stan.

He was followed by all of the other Haydenshires.

Vindico gave a long diatribe about what an outstanding man and officer Rainer was, much to Rainer's shock.

All of Elite Iodex pled Rainer's good character, and all said that they believed Rainer would do anything necessary to serve the Realm, and that they were all proud to serve with him.

They were followed next by Mentor Sullivan and Chancellor Wilshire. Shocked embarrassment rocked through Rainer to have so many people herald his good deeds.

A moment later, Stariff gave him a sympathetic smile. "Next I'd like to hear testimony from Miss Emily Haydenshire."

Rainer hated that he was doing this to her. He brushed her hand with his own as she passed, and she turned and smiled before being sworn in.

"Miss Haydenshire, how long have you and Rainer been involved in a romantic relationship?"

"I guess that depends on what romantic means to you. Like my mom said, I've wanted to marry Rainer since I was four and began to understand what being married to someone was. I told him he was my boyfriend when I was five. He kissed me when I was seven. We called each other boyfriend and girlfriend in elementary school, so at least sixteen years."

"If I may, I'd like to ask Miss Haydenshire and Mr. Lawson a battery of questions about one another to prove the depth of their commitment, even if the questions themselves don't pertain to the case at hand."

"As the trial hinges on whether or not we believe Rainer should have obtained a prenup, then I'll allow that," Governor Carrington agreed.

"Thank you, Governor." Stariff moved back to Emily.

"Objection! How does this prove anything? These questions were rehearsed," Mulligrew huffed indignantly.

"Okay, how about this? I'll allow Mr. Mulligrew to ask any question he'd like, as long as it pertains to how well Rainer and Emily know one another. The governing board may ask as well."

He offered the questioning up to the court just as he'd told Emily and Rainer he would. Mulligrew delightedly agreed and began.

"So, Miss Haydenshire, what kind of car does Mr. Lawson drive?"

Stariff was a genius. This was precisely how he'd told Rainer this would work.

Emily was trying not to laugh as she readily supplied, "It's a 1964 and a half Mustang convertible. It was released late in 1964 as an early 1965 model. They were originally constructed as pace cars in the 1964 Indianapolis 500. It's crimson, not red," she huffed at Samantha, "With Le Mans stripes. Rainer installed an enhanced screaming V8 engine and then installed an air conditioner and an FM radio, because I asked him to. He put in ivory leather seats that I picked out, and it has a Haartz Pinpoint Vinyl ivory soft-top. He also had the rear fold down seats replaced with permanent seating so it would seat four instead of only two."

Rainer's heart swelled with love and pride. He beamed at her.

"Wow," Stariff commented as Mulligrew looked thoroughly shocked. Mulligrew moved to the table where Rainer was seated.

"May I see your phone, Mr. Lawson?"

"Are you submitting that for evidence? It wasn't in the docket," Stariff challenged.

"Fine. Rainer, would you mind giving your phone to your lawyer for just a moment?"

Rainer shrugged and handed his phone to Stariff.

"Now, Emily, could you tell us which phone numbers Rainer has called recently?" he quizzed with a gotcha grin.

Emily was visibly loving this. She tittered on the stands.

"My cell about a dozen times, Logan's cell, Garrett's cell, and probably Mom and Dad's house number." Stariff beamed as he held up the call list for the governors to see.

"What was Mr. Lawson's worst subject at the academy?" Mulligrew huffed furiously.

"Creative writing," Emily came right back.

"What music was Rainer listening to the last time he listened to music not in your presence?"

"He's been worried about the trial, so I'd say Radiohead. If I had to guess, either 'Creep' or 'House of Cards.'"

Emily glowed in her knowledge as Rainer laughed. Stariff held up the phone again, displaying the Best of Radiohead album cover and pointing to "Creep," which was highlighted as the last song played.

"Don't we believe that a woman after a man's money would make it her business to know everything about him?" Mulligrew returned to his chair dejectedly.

Stariff stood again. "I don't believe so," he stated firmly. "These two people are in love and have been since they were too young to even understand it."

Stariff turned back to Emily. "Miss Haydenshire, remembering that you are under oath, please tell the courts if you have any intention of divorcing Rainer and taking the money in his estate."

Emily looked appalled. "No. Never!"

"You see, folks, I don't believe that we're so callous, that we're so full of scorn, that we can't recognize love when it stands right in front of us. For all that Rainer has been through in his relatively short life, I'd still call him very lucky to have what he has in Emily, and for her to have the utter love and devotion she has from Rainer. No further questions for Miss Haydenshire."

"Mulligrew?" Governor Carrington urged.

Mulligrew leapt up with a sickening smile.

"Do you and Rainer ever argue, Emily?"

"Sometimes—not very often, though," Emily's voice shook slightly.

"Has Rainer ever done anything without your knowledge? Gone anywhere that you weren't aware of?"

"Only for work. Sometimes I'm not allowed to know where he's going until later, because he's an Iodex officer, but I trust him completely."

Her vow soothed Rainer's soul, and her quick thinking had saved him once again. The only place he had ever gone without her knowledge was The Tantra.

"Have you ever spent money without Rainer's knowledge?" Mulligrew continued.

"No, not that I recall, except maybe for a gift for him. I don't always tell Rainer if I purchase food or a cup of coffee or something. I do have a job, Mr. Mulligrew. His inheritance aside, I actually make significantly more money than Rainer."

Stariff had instructed Emily to point that out any chance she had.

"So, you would say that purchases are made without Rainer's knowledge?"

"Donald," Governor Carrington reprimanded before Stariff could object. "Stop being argumentative. Withdraw that question and move on."

"That's all I have for Miss Haydenshire." Mulligrew returned to his seat.

"I'd now like to call Rainer Lawson to the stand," Stariff stood.

Rainer was sworn in and sat down. He was feeling somewhat calmer. He could now look into Emily's eyes as he was seated in front of her.

"Rainer, would you please tell the court the last three major purchases you made with money from your inheritance?"

"Let's define major, Jack," Governor Haydenshire demanded.

"Yes, Governor. How about over $250?"

The governors nodded their agreement.

Rainer swallowed. "I purchased Emily a Hummer H3 before she started work. I financed the remodel on a guesthouse on the Haydenshires' property, and I gave a friend of mine some money a few weeks ago. I can't think of another purchase over that amount other than we stayed at the Gansevoort hotel a few weekends ago, but Emily and I share a bank account. She's on a professional Summation team. She could've just as easily been the one paying for that."

"You have millions upon millions of dollars at your disposal, Rainer. Why live in the Haydenshires' guesthouse? You could buy a mansion anywhere you want."

"I didn't want to take Emily away from her family. I didn't want to be away from the Haydenshires either. We're just starting out. We don't need a big mansion."

Stariff shot a goading grin at Mulligrew. "Sounds almost thrifty to me. And have you and Emily ever fought about money? Has she ever spent more than you were comfortable with?"

"No." Rainer shook his head. "Usually, I can't get her to buy anything."

"Sounds like a gold digger to me," Stariff quipped.

"Watch it, Jack," Governor Carrington admonished.

Stariff asked him a few more questions before turning him over to Mulligrew. Rainer felt momentarily like he'd been thrown to the wolves.

"Mighty expensive automobile for your girlfriend, Mr. Lawson. Care to explain that?" Mulligrew sniped.

Rainer drew a deep breath. "Emily was very nearly killed in a car accident just after her sixteenth birthday. Photographers were chasing her, and they ran her car off a bridge. As the press seems to be ever-present in my life, I wanted her in something safe."

"And you felt a Hummer would keep her safe?"

"I offered to get her a Porsche Cayman, but she felt it was too expensive and wouldn't allow me to spend that much on her." He narrowed his eyes and smiled. Mulligrew had no comeback for that.

The Senteon was visibly impressed, and Rainer's chest unfettered slightly.

"Could you elaborate on your and Miss Haydenshire's physical relationship, please, Rainer?"

His eyes goggled. Stariff hadn't mentioned anything like this.

"Uh, no, I couldn't!" Rainer snapped furiously.

Stariff leapt from his seat. "Objection!" he screamed.

Mulligrew turned his snide grin to the governors.

"Wouldn't we all agree that men can often be turned by a pretty head and a little promiscuity?"

"Are you calling my daughter promiscuous?" Governor Haydenshire demanded hatefully.

"Do I need to get the photos back out, Governor?" Mulligrew came right back.

"Crown Governor, please," Stariff huffed. "Rainer and Emily's physical relationship has nothing to do with his ability to manage his assets, and is certainly no one's business, save Rainer and Emily's."

Governor Carrington considered for a moment.

"Objection sustained. Stick to the topics at hand, Donald." Governor Carrington looked disgusted as Mulligrew huffed indignantly.

"Any future purchases in mind, Rainer, say, if you win here today?" Mulligrew tried again.

"Objection, subjective!" Stariff called again.

"Sustained." Governor Carrington was getting impatient.

"Mr. Mulligrew, do you have any further allowable questions, or can we proceed?"

"I would like to ask Rainer about the ring that he so flippantly gave to Miss Haydenshire. Some believe its value to be priceless, yet he decided, just one day after receiving his inheritance, to use it as an engagement ring. I think we would all agree that something of that value should be sealed away permanently for its safety."

"What is the question?" Stariff demanded.

"Do you feel that giving Miss Haydenshire the Lawson family ring was irresponsible?"

"No." Rainer shook his head. "As far as I know, every wife of a Lawson man for the past several generations has worn that ring, my mother included. Since I have every intention of making Emily my wife, I wanted her to have the ring. To my knowledge, the ring isn't priceless. Other than its antiquity, it's a diamond engagement ring and nothing more." Rainer tried not to think that he'd just perjured himself.

"That's it, Governor," Mulligrew spat and then returned to his seat.

Stariff went on for thirty minutes in his closing arguments about what a fine man Rainer was, and urged the Senteon and the governors to think of what Joseph would've wanted them to do.

Mulligrew continually referred to the photos of Emily's belly shot, and stated that Rainer had pulled the wool over everyone's eyes including the governors. He insinuated several times that Emily was nothing more than a gold digger. Rainer ground his teeth in his fury.

"We've heard Mr. Lawson's character be both defended and attacked, and now it's time for us to level our wisdom mindfully and with awareness of the gravity of the task at hand," Governor Carrington instructed. "Does any member of the Senteon have a question for either Rainer or Stan?"

"Rainer," called a middle-aged man seated in the second row of the Senteon.

"Yes, sir," Rainer answered respectfully.

"I'm Ben Hendrix, the Senteon Representative from Iowa, and I would like to know if you have any reaction to the photographs of you and Miss Haydenshire at the party over the weekend. I've never seen such a thing. What would you call that, exactly?" He did look thoroughly confused.

Rainer stood, swallowed down his shame, and explained. "I would call it a mistake, sir. My dad used to tell me that we are more than the tally of the mistakes we've made, so I guess I'm hoping that you'll give me this one, because Emily and I both know we screwed up. I really can't tell you how sorry I am or how ashamed I feel."

"Well said, son," the Senteon member complimented.

Rainer offered the man a kind smile and sat back down. Stariff slapped his shoulder in a gesture of approval.

"Any other questions from the Senteon?" Governor Carrington urged. Silence fell over the courtroom as Governor Carrington gave any of the governors a chance to ask either Rainer or his uncle a question regarding the case.

"Then we'll have the Senteon vote. The governors will take their recommendation into account as we decide the fate of the Lawson family estate."

Rainer's pulse raced as he waited. He shared a desperate glance with Emily.

"Crown Governor," Governor Haydenshire drawled, "I'll be recusing myself, due to an obvious conflict of interest."

Governor Carrington agreed. The motion surprised no one.

"Members of the esteemed Senteon of the American Gifted Realm, in the case of Lawson vs. Lawson, if you deem Rainer Emory Lawson unable to properly attend to the estate willed him by his father, Crown Governor Joseph Lawson, and believe that his uncle, Stan Leroy Lawson, should be given half of the current value of the Lawson estate, including the Lawson family ring and any additional assets, please say aye."

Five people out of the fifty on the Senteon said "aye," and Rainer allowed himself to breathe.

Governor Carrington turned to the governing board.

"With the recommendation of the Senteon, we'll adjourn for a few minutes and then return with our decision. Governor Haydenshire, we'll bid our farewells to you now."

Governor Haydenshire removed his long black robe and went to take the seat beside Mrs. Haydenshire.

CHAPTER 3
THE TALLY

Rainer couldn't recall a time when the clock had moved slower. His fate hung in the eerie stillness that permeated the silence of the room. His stomach churned as he willed the governors to return.

He decided he just wanted to know. The waiting was unbearable. No matter the decision, he just wanted the answer.

It felt like he was in some kind of nightmare where he could see and talk, but everyone around him was unaware of his presence. The silence loomed. It pressed in around him.

Finally, the governors returned and everyone stood.

"Please remain standing for the vote," Governor Carrington ordered. Rainer's heart raced as his body cinched tightly, as if he'd been preparing for battle.

"Governor Vindico…?"

With a kind smile, Governor Vindico soothed, "I vote in favor of Rainer Lawson keeping the estate fully and intact."

"Governor Willow…?"

"I too, vote in favor of Rainer Lawson keeping the estate fully and intact."

Rainer had to place his hand on the table as relief washed through him. With Governor Carrington's vote, that was four.

"Governor Peterson…?"

"I vote for the estate to be divided between Rainer Lawson and Stan Lawson," he stated defiantly.

"And Governor Sapman…?"

Governor Sapman studied Rainer for what seemed like an eternity before he drew a deep breath and cleared his throat.

"I vote in favor of Rainer Lawson keeping the estate fully and intact."

Rainer heard Emily's gasp of relief.

"And, as the Crown Governor of this Gifted Realm, I, Regis Carrington, vote for Rainer Lawson to keep the Lawson family estate as a whole and intact."

Governor Carrington completed his final act as Crown just before he moved to shake Rainer's hand. Emily pushed through the crowd, descending on Rainer. She threw her arms around him. He lifted her off the ground in the exuberance of his embrace.

"This isn't over," Stan sneered. He glared furiously at Rainer as he was escorted from the courtroom.

CHAPTER 4
THINGS TO COME

Despite his utter elation, chills shot down Rainer's spine. He wrapped Emily up in an all-encompassing embrace. He was desperate to shield her, but from what, he wasn't certain.

People surrounded them. They wanted to shake his hand, but he refused to let go of Emily.

Something in his uncle's threat had him reeling. His Uncle Stan had never sounded so determined or so vengeful.

Emily studied him. "You won, Rainer. Don't let him get to you." She leaned up and kissed his jaw. He stared after his uncle and watched him until he'd disappeared onto the elevators. He kept a firm hold of Emily's hand while he shook Stariff's and thanked him profusely.

"Jack, you're coming for dinner, yes?" Mrs. Haydenshire urged.

"Oh, please join us, Mr. Stariff," Emily added.

"As much as I hate to turn down both of the Haydenshire women, I have a late meeting tonight, but"—Stariff leaned in as Rainer, Emily, and Mrs. Haydenshire all followed suit—"I did hear that I should start kissing up to the new Crown Governor."

"That's not out yet, Jack," Mrs. Haydenshire reprimanded, but she was unable to hide her broad grin.

37

"Well, I'm in, and I'd say this trial could be very useful for your upcoming campaign," Stariff insinuated.

Everyone nodded, though they tried not to look too pleased. Lachland Peterson voting against the Crown Governor, and against Joseph Lawson's last wishes, had the potential to be very detrimental to his upcoming bid for Crown.

After a few more congratulatory handshakes, the Haydenshires moved as a unit toward the front of the Pentagon.

"All right, Rainer," Stariff directed. "Here's your chance to show a little class. Perhaps erase some of the damage from last weekend."

"Okay, anything." Rainer was pleased to hear there was something he could do to make up for all the damage he'd done.

"There are several reputable papers out there. If you and Emily answered a few questions, you could show a great deal of maturity," Stariff explained. "Don't say anything about being pleased you won. Show concern for your uncle. That kind of thing."

Emily and Rainer shared a nervous glance. Rainer's policy had always been to ignore the questions, but that was before there'd been pictures of him licking Emily's stomach in the papers.

"Logan, you and Adeline can walk with Rainer and Emily, or you could fly back with the rest of your family," Stariff explained.

A broad grin lit Logan's face. "Have you ever been in the helicopters?" he quizzed Adeline.

She shook her head.

"We'll fly." Logan looked pleased. "Governor's son and all that goes with it, that was the deal," Logan reminded her.

"Have fun." Emily waved to her family.

"Are you ready?" Rainer's nerves set back in as he took in the throngs of reporters.

"I guess." Emily wrapped her hand tightly around Rainer's bicep. He placed his hand over hers, secured her to him, and opened the door.

"Rainer, tell us what you're feeling after your victory," screeched a reporter to Rainer's right.

"Uh, I'm thankful it's over, and hopeful that my uncle and I can find peace at some point."

Emily gave him a reassuring smile as they stepped down a few steps.

"Emily, are you planning any shopping trips soon?" called a young female reporter very near Emily. The reporter was from a style magazine, and the question didn't seem judgmental in any way.

Emily smiled. "No, I'd really just like to spend some time with Rainer and my family."

Reporters frantically scribbled down her quote.

"Rainer, will you do anything to prevent your uncle from making further claims against the estate?" called a reporter from Wall Street.

"I have complete faith in the governors' decision, and I trust the individuals that I have managing the estate." Rainer nodded in the reporter's direction as dozens of flashbulbs went off in his face.

"Any ill will toward your uncle, Rainer?" a reporter from the *Times* asked.

Though he wasn't entirely certain this was the truth, Rainer shook his head. "No. I hope my uncle will find someone or something that fulfills him. I'm very blessed to have both." Rainer gestured to Emily. The crowd swooned.

"When's the wedding, Rainer?" After chuckling at the education they were receiving, Rainer tread carefully.

"I think we'll be keeping that information to close friends and family for now."

"But you've set a date?" They became frenzied, and he sighed.

"No more questions." He cut them off and rushed Emily into the Mustang that had been brought around for them.

"Well, that was different," she commented as he drove away.

The air that had been pent up in his chest for days finally began to release. He was able to think about something besides the belly shot and the trial.

He slowed the car. He just wanted a minute with her. She beamed at him with a tranquil smile, one he hadn't seen in quite a while.

"Thank you for loving me through all of this. I don't deserve you," he vowed suddenly.

"Are you kidding me? I almost lost you half of your family's estate.

I can't believe you didn't dump me the first chance you got," she sounded truly shocked.

"Em, *I* almost lost half of the estate, and I would never dump you for any reason. I'm the luckiest guy in the Realm. Trust me."

"I've kind of wanted to ask you something, but I don't want it to upset you or for you to think it's like the belly shot," she started hesitantly.

As Rainer pulled on to the interstate, he waited for more. "You can ask me anything. I won't be upset, and what on earth could be like the belly shot?"

"Well, not like the belly shot exactly, just like it in terms of the Angels doing it, and it being kind of wild, I guess."

"Okay, I'm going to go ahead and say if there are cameras involved in any way then no, whatever it is. Just please, no."

Emily laughed and shook her head. "No cameras. I swear."

"Why don't you just tell me whatever it is?"

Emily seemed to have to steel herself. It made Rainer insanely curious.

"Em, just tell me."

She drew a deep breath. "Dana's husband is coming to practice Wednesday."

As this did nothing to help Rainer understand what she wanted, he prompted, "And?"

Emily bit her lip nervously.

"Come on, it's me. I've gone to the store on multiple occasions to buy you tampons and Midol. Nothing about you will upset or embarrass me. Whatever it is, just tell me."

"I know. I just usually know how you're going to react, and I can't quite figure this one out. It's weird for me. Dana's husband is a Gifted tattoo artist. He does all of the Angels' tattoos, and I kinda want to get one. But I don't want an Angels tattoo. I want something different, but I was worried after the mess I caused with the belly shot and with Dad and everything, that you would freak." She stated all of this in one long gush, without taking a breath. "What I want is really what *I* want, not because all of the Angels have them."

Rainer tried to consider every possible scenario involving Emily getting a tattoo.

"How do you know it won't end up in the papers?"

Emily seemed relieved to be discussing it. "Paran is doing them at the stadium Friday evening after practice. Only the Angels, and I guess anyone who might be picking one of us up," she indicated Rainer, "will be there. So, it wouldn't be like somebody got a shot of me going to a tattoo parlor or anything." Emily hemmed for a moment. "Do you like them? Do you think they're sexy?"

"I'm sure if it's on you, I'll think it's sexy," he answered truthfully. "You're an adult, and I'm sure as hell not your dad. You don't have to ask my permission. If you want a tattoo, get one."

"I know, but if you hate them I don't want to do it."

"Your dad will flip." Rainer glanced over at her as he turned down the two-lane road where the farm was nestled.

"No, he won't. Will has Brooke's name on his chest, and Brooke has their birth dates and wedding date done up on her ankle, and Patrick has the Duco crest on his arm, and Garrett's covered in them."

"Yes, but Garrett is Garrett, and you're his baby girl."

"Daddy will be fine. I want to know if you like them."

"So, you aren't doing the double A or the lightning bolt and halo thing?" Rainer tried to envision that somewhere on Emily's body.

"I want it to be a surprise." It was in that moment that Rainer could tell how badly she wanted the tattoo.

"Why didn't you say anything about this before? I thought we weren't doing the not telling each other thing again?"

"I'm sorry. I don't know. I had to think about what I wanted and where I wanted it, and we were so stressed about the trial. Then the whole thing with the belly shot. I just wouldn't even let myself really think about it until this was over."

Rainer nodded his understanding. His mind was full of Emily's body inked with a tattoo.

"Are we going home first or on to your parents' house?"

"I'm changing first," Emily informed him.

Rainer turned toward the guesthouse. He studied her, dressed in an extremely conservative, navy blue stiff skirt and low matronly heels. There was nothing about what she was wearing that was her save the scarf she was running through her hands.

Though she never wore anything too revealing or inappropriate, she definitely had a style all her own. Her uncle Tad was right. The things she picked out were all her, and her style was deeply engrained in her personality.

Rainer understood in that moment that it was one of the many things he loved about her. He regretted that his being Joseph Lawson's son had stifled her for the past week as they'd worked to appear to be mature and overly responsible for the sake of the lawsuit.

Emily's favorite high heels, scarves, and her signature jewelry that she usually purchased at antique stores had been put away. She'd very willingly put away a part of herself for his sake.

"Em, baby, if you want a tattoo then it'll be sexy as hell." He knew that's what she wanted to hear. "Can I bring you dinner or something before you get it?"

Her entire being lit with excitement. "Really?" She looked like he'd just made her entire week.

Anything that made her smile like that, he wanted her to have. He nodded as a sudden thought occurred to him.

"Isn't that going to hurt, sweetheart?" He tried not to sound like he didn't want her to have the tattoo, but the thought of her in pain for any reason set him on edge. He was her Shield, after all.

"Probably a little, but Fionna says that whenever she and Chloe get one they cast each other and keep it from hurting. Dana says Paran is really good at making the redness go away when he's finished."

Rainer tried to hide his disdain that some other guy was going to be casting her. Since Paran was not a medio, then he would be using his own energies to help her heal.

"Or you could heal it for me, I guess." Emily sounded disappointed.

"No, it's fine. If you want it to be a surprise, then I can't wait to see it. Where are you going to put it?" He suddenly thought of a whole other reason that he might dislike Paran.

"I haven't decided yet."

"But it won't be photographed and put up over the bar at Anglington's, right?"

"Uh, most definitely not. I think the patrons at Anglington's have seen quite enough of me."

Emily rushed to change clothes, and Rainer suddenly remembered something.

"Hey, Em, baby, I should have told you this, and honestly I just forgot with everything we've had going on."

"What?"

"Your dad thinks your mom might be pregnant again."

The hairbrush hit the dresser. She stared at him in wide-eyed bewilderment.

"What?!"

"Your dad thinks your mom's gonna have another baby," Rainer eased. He wasn't certain how to handle her reaction.

"Rainer! She's over fifty. She cannot have another baby."

"Maybe your dad was wrong, but I doubt that." He didn't point out that she was also over fifty when the twins were born.

Emily shook her head and stomped into the closet. "I'm just not thinking about this right now."

"Got it."

CHAPTER 5
FAMILY TIES

Rainer glanced at Emily nervously as he pulled the Hummer into the barn.

Grandpa Haydenshire's Buick was parked nearby. Rainer prayed there wouldn't be an incident with Logan and Adeline.

As they all entered the kitchen, he inhaled deeply of Mrs. Haydenshire's homemade marinara sauce and meatballs. His mouth watered.

Emily went to help her mother and grandmother as they formed the meatballs and chatted placidly. Upon Emily's arrival, talk turned to weddings, much to her obvious delight.

Rainer took a haphazard glance around, but didn't see Grandpa Haydenshire in the kitchen or family room anywhere.

He offered hellos to Will and Brooke.

Garrett was having dinner in DC. Patrick was seated on the window bench, scowling. He'd had another fight with Lucy. The twins were zipping around the kitchen, causing general havoc.

"Rainer, sweetheart, do you think you could take them outside for a little while?" Mrs. Haydenshire requested.

"Of course."

"Do you need some help?" Emily offered. Rainer knew she was having fun with her mom and grandmother, so he shook his head.

"Nope, Logan's coming."

She and Mrs. Haydenshire laughed as Logan rolled his eyes and threw a few grapes from the bowl on the counter into his mouth.

"Okay, fine."

"Adeline, sweetheart, just grab some meat and start rolling it," Mrs. Haydenshire instructed.

Logan cracked up. It seemed the trial being over and the promise of copious amounts of food had him in a great mood. He waggled his eyebrows at Adeline and gave her a wry grin. She turned the shade of the marinara.

Rainer slapped him on the back of the head. "Are you twelve?" He carried Henry out the back door and headed toward the swing set. They set the twins in the baby swings and began pushing them and listening to their squeals of delight.

Logan turned to ask Rainer something when, "What the hell?" spat from his mouth.

"What?" Rainer glanced around and then saw Governor Haydenshire and Grandpa Haydenshire on the dock fishing. "Logan, man, I think your parents are trying to make peace before the election, maybe?"

"If he says one word to Adeline," Logan threatened.

Rainer certainly couldn't promise Grandpa Haydenshire wouldn't be rude to Adeline, so he offered Logan a sympathetic gaze as they released the twins from the swings and watched as they ran around the yard.

∼

Everyone settled at the large table in the dining room. The air vibrated with nerves and hostility as Logan glared at his grandfather while seating Adeline.

Levi slapped Logan on the back and simultaneously pushed him into his seat. He seated himself between Logan and Rainer in a show of solidarity.

Brooke half walked, half waddled to the table. She fell into her seat with Will right behind her. Governor and Mrs. Haydenshire followed everyone in and set down pasta bowls of spaghetti while Paps Anderson carried in the large pot of sauce. Emily's grandmother brought in baskets brimming with garlic toast.

As everyone was seated, the Haydenshires held hands and beamed at one another. Rainer took Emily's hand. It seemed most everyone at the table knew what was coming.

"Oh, for crying out loud. You cannot be serious! Do you two even know what causes this? My word, son, you're a Realm governor. Certainly you can cast her!" Grandpa Haydenshire bellowed. He threw his hands toward Governor and Mrs. Haydenshire in acrimony.

"Dad." Governor Haydenshire glared at his father. "First of all, we wish Garrett were here, but he already knows that I am officially going to run for Crown Governor. The campaign will start as soon as we get back from the beach, a week from Monday, so we're going to need a lot of help. I expect all of my children to pitch in."

Everyone, save Grandpa Haydenshire, vowed to help in any way that they could.

Mrs. Haydenshire glowed as she stepped forward slightly. "And," she drew an excited breath.

Logan and Levi both squeezed their eyes shut.

"I haven't seen a medio yet, but we are expecting again." Tears formed in her eyes as mixed reactions went around the table.

"Congratulations, sweetheart." Nana Anderson stood to embrace her daughter.

Adeline looked overjoyed. "Oh, Mrs. Haydenshire, I'll help any way I can, and I can check you anytime you'd like."

"Well, if that don't make the daisies rise up and sing in hell then I don't know what might," Grandpa Haydenshire huffed furiously, though no one was entirely certain what he meant.

"So, I'm going to have a brother younger than my kid?" Will seemed stunned.

"You could have a sister," Emily pointed out.

Will shook his head. "One out of ten isn't good odds, Em." He still looked thoroughly put out. "What if we need you to help us?"

Mrs. Haydenshire took her seat and patted Will's hand. "Sweetheart, your little one will be here several months before ours.

By the time the newest Haydenshire comes around, you'll have everything down pat. Now everyone dig in so I don't have to reheat everything."

Rainer studied Emily. He tried to be nonchalant. She didn't seem to have had a dramatic reaction to her parents' news, but as he rubbed her leg he felt her energy swirling rapidly.

He concentrated and tried to determine what he was feeling from her. Tension and worry rose like gathering storms just under her skin.

Grandpa Haydenshire jabbed his fork Rainer's direction. "What the hell was that you were doing to Emily in the papers the other day? Looked like you two were advertising for a cathouse. She go into heat or something?"

Rainer clenched his jaw. He had no real defense for what Emily's grandfather had seen in the papers.

"Dad, please," Governor Haydenshire sighed. "I would like Lillian to just relax and take it easy. We're going to be on the road campaigning, and I don't want her to have any more stress than is absolutely necessary."

"Well, son, it seems to me that you can't leave her the hell alone long enough for her to not be in a condition where she doesn't need stress. If you want her to relax, why don't you two try separate beds?"

No one spoke for several long minutes. Everyone focused on their pasta and willed the dinner to be over soon.

Mrs. Haydenshire was steadfastly ignoring her father-in-law as she smiled. "I set up the ice cream churns on the deck, so after we're finished you can all get them going. I put the hand crank one out as well. One of you just cast it and let the twins help."

"We'll do it, Mrs. Haydenshire. You just rest," Adeline urged sweetly.

"Oh, honey, I plan to." Mrs. Haydenshire laughed. "I'm going to sit out on the swing and let you all bring me a bowl when it's ready."

"We'll take care of the dishes, Mrs. Haydenshire," Rainer offered.

"Yeah, we'll help, Mom," Will and Levi joined in. Mrs. Haydenshire nodded her appreciation as Nana patted Rainer's hand sweetly.

"Yeah, let's serve up ice cream along with our pipe dreams, and pretend that Peterson's not gonna eat you alive for this litter you've already got, and now another one on the way, not to mention that he's decided to turn your daughter into a stag film star," Grandpa threw at Rainer. "And then let's just pour some hot damn cherry sauce all over the fact that *he's* gonna put his leash on a stray cat." His hand shot outwards toward Logan. He knocked over two glasses of tea in the process.

"You know what, Grandpa, you can go straight to hell." Logan's chair flew backwards into the sideboard as he leapt.

"I'll meet you there, son," Grandpa Haydenshire fired back. His eyes were furious as he glared at Logan.

"Logan." Adeline pulled Logan back into his seat as Emily, Rainer, and Patrick cleaned up the tea.

"Why do you have to be like this?" Logan demanded.

"Because you all have no idea what kind of shit storm you're stepping into with your dad running for Crown. Everything you do will be scrutinized, and they've had you living in la-la-land your whole life. You don't have a clue what the cold, cruel world is like, and it's high time you learned."

Logan shook his head defiantly. "You're wrong. Just look at Rainer —his parents died for the Realm, so people like Dad could even have the opportunity to run for Crown Governor. He knows what it's like to hurt and to lose everything.

"And all the rest of us, we all stood there in the pouring rain the day we buried Cal. We all cried so hard we couldn't see. We know pain like that, and Adeline, my gosh." He turned to Adeline and gazed at her adoringly. "Her mother's in prison. She never had a dad. She took care of her mother. Paid the bills, cooked the food, what little they had, since she was tiny. It's not all great and wonderful and idyllic, but we're a family, and we fight for what's right, and for what's good, in the hopes that we won't have to lose anyone else. Why can't you just see the good for once?" With that, he took Adeline's hand and pulled her toward the kitchen.

"We'll start the ice cream, Mom." He sounded very much at peace as stunned silence echoed very loudly around the table.

Emily gave Rainer a horrified expression. "Rainer, go talk to him," she pled under his breath.

"He's right, and I don't know what I would say to get him back in here." He was well aware that everyone at the table could hear him.

Emily nodded and then stood and addressed her family. "Rainer's right. Everything Logan said is true, and I don't understand why you two continue to put yourselves through this." She threw her hand out toward her grandfather. "We're going out with Logan and Adeline. When everyone's finished, we'll do the dishes, Mom."

"Because we are a family, Emily," Mrs. Haydenshire replied suddenly. Her fervent tone halted Emily in her tracks. "The very same reason your father and I choose to see what wonderful children, what wonderful people, you and Rainer are instead of focusing on the times you might not have shown the best judgment. The same reasons that Logan just listed for all of us. We don't get to just pick the best qualities in one another to love. We have to love each other for who we are, mistakes and all. This is your grandfather." She made the same gesture toward Grandpa Haydenshire that Emily had just given in her diatribe.

"He helped create and raise your father, the most wonderful man I've ever met, and in turn your father created and raised ten phenomenal children with one on the way." She narrowed her eyes at Grandpa Haydenshire then glanced back to Emily.

"He served this country and our Realm nobly, and he is certainly entitled to his opinion."

She turned her determined gaze back to Grandpa Haydenshire. "However, I am also entitled to mine. You've always been very willing to let Stephen and me know that you disagree with the way we've chosen to live the life that we've created together, which is fine. But, we've never asked you for help. We've never needed you to bail us out of a situation we created. Stephen has always and will always take the very best care of me and of our children." She placed her hand tenderly on her stomach.

"And I do understand that not everyone accepts the way we've chosen to do things, or why we've continued to add to our family, but you see, sir, we feel that children are a gift and that, though ours certainly have executed their fair share of mistakes,"—she winked at Rainer with a wry smile as he let his head drop in shame—"that what they add to our Realm is so much more than what they take from it. I appreciate your part in making Stephen into the wonderful man, wonderful husband, and phenomenal father that he is, but I don't feel you've ever just stepped back and taken a look at what you've created." She reached and took Governor Haydenshire's hand as he gazed at her with rapt adoration.

"And you've certainly never taken a real look at what he's created and what he's giving to the Realm," she concluded with a peaceful smile at her husband.

"Here's to Dad." Will raised his tea glass.

"The next Crown Governor," Rainer vowed as Governor Haydenshire swallowed harshly.

"Here, here!" Logan, who had returned to the dining room in time to hear his mother's diatribe, joined in the toast.

"Yeah, he's pretty much the greatest dad ever." Emily beamed at her father.

Soon Connor, Levi, and Patrick had joined in and, after noticing everyone's raised glasses, the twins dropped their sippy cups from off of their high chair trays with delighted laughs.

"I think the sentiment is the same." Rainer chuckled as Adeline picked up the juice cups.

With that, everyone, save his own father, toasted Governor Haydenshire. He shook his head and fought the sentimental emotion that must've settled thickly around his throat.

"I know I was never good enough for you, Dad," the governor finally spoke. His voice was rough in his vow. "But, let me tell every child in this room, I may not always like everything you choose to do, but I couldn't be more proud of the people you're becoming. Growing up, I don't think I ever really knew if I was loved, but I don't ever want any one of you, whether we gave birth to you or not, to doubt how much we love each and every one of you."

"Daddy." Tears poured down Emily's face as she moved to her father. Rainer watched him stand and embrace her. Tears of his own fell into her hair.

Mrs. Haydenshire wiped her eyes. "I know that growing up,

Stephen worried if he did something you might disagree with that you would throw him out."

"There's nothing certain in this world. I tried to teach him that," Grandpa Haydenshire combatted.

Mrs. Haydenshire turned to her children. She grinned at Emily, who was still tucked safely in her father's tight embrace.

"I want all of you to know that your father isn't giving up his position as governor for the election. It seems Governor Peterson has decided to give up his seat as a show of certainty that he's going to win. However, your father and I don't need to show the Realm certainty. We want to show all of you that, whether he wins or loses, this farm will be here. You will always have a home here. We will be here, and there is nothing you could do that would make us decide we didn't love you anymore or that would make us deny you your home."

Governor Haydenshire chuckled as he wiped away Emily's tears. "I can't give up my job. I have a few more mouths to feed than Peterson, and a daughter who's engaged to be married who has extremely expensive taste."

Emily squeezed her father tighter as she laughed.

"Let's go have some ice cream, baby girl." He took Emily's hand, just as he had when she was four years old, to lead her out onto the deck. "Dad, we'd love for you to join us," he extended the invitation.

CHAPTER 6
BITTER TASTE

Connor and Logan were supervising the five ice cream churns. They were summoning and pushing them to full tilt, so the ice cream would be ready faster.

Emily and Rainer helped the twins slowly turn the hand crank on the ice cream maker that was many decades older than either of the boys. Rainer harnessed the potential energy in the crank and casted it forward whenever the twins wanted to turn.

"Keaton, no sir." Rainer shook his head as Keaton stuck his hand in the ice just as Emily helped Henry turn the crank.

Emily beamed at him. "I think you're gonna make a really good dad, yourself." She leaned her head on Rainer's shoulder.

They laughed as Keaton narrowed his eyes determinedly and pulled his hand away with a round piece of ice. He kept his eyes locked on Rainer's in a show of fiery defiance. He brought the ice to his mouth.

Rainer waited patiently. He matched Keaton's gaze and continued to chuckle. Suddenly Keaton's entire little body shuddered as his face contorted in protest as he tasted the ice mixed with salt.

"I told you."

Keaton dragged his tongue under his teeth and scowled just before he burst into tears. Rainer shook his head and lifted him into his arms. He fell onto his back and hoisted Keaton up in the air and let him pretend to fly as he quickly dropped the ice. Henry immediately wanted a turn, so Levi joined in, and everyone laughed as the twins made airplane noises.

When the ice cream was ready, everyone was served a bowl and scattered out on the large deck and across the Haydenshires' backyard.

Rainer couldn't find Emily. He knew she'd made a bowl of vanilla ice cream just moments before. Patrick hit him on the arm and gestured toward the barn. "She looked upset."

Rainer thanked him and tried to make his way to the barn without anyone but Patrick noticing his disappearance.

He climbed up into the loft to find Emily tucked in the back corner. She was eating her ice cream in minuscule bites that barely covered the tip of her spoon.

"Hey there." He studied her as he tried to determine what might be wrong. She smiled at his customary greeting.

"Are you okay, baby?" He seated himself beside her. She nodded her lie. "Em?" He set his Styrofoam bowl down and put his arm around her. "Come on. Why are you up here?"

She shrugged and began biting her lip.

"Did I do something wrong?" He tried to think of something he might've said or done in the past five minutes that could have upset her. She shook her head and suddenly tears pricked her eyes.

He wrapped her up in his arms. "What is it? Just tell me."

She shook her head defiantly but then buried it in the crook of Rainer's neck and began to sob. "Em, baby, I'm usually pretty good at figuring you out, but you've lost me on this one. Did one of your brothers upset you?"

She shook her head again and let him wipe the tears from her cheeks. "Come on, no secrets. Remember?" He cradled her face in his hand. "It breaks my heart when you cry. Tell me what's wrong."

"He's right." She shuddered in Rainer's arms. He caressed her back and face.

"Who's right?"

"Grandpa is right. Governor Peterson is going to say horrible things about them because of us, and now Mom's pregnant again."

Rainer's heart fractured. He knew she was right. "If Peterson attacks your family, that only shows what kind of man he is, and it says nothing about what kind of people your parents are. The Realm will see that." She was still sobbing, and Rainer knew there was more. "What else is bothering you?"

"I can't tell you." Her entire body trembled in her emotion.

"Baby, you can tell me anything."

"I'm a terrible person for even thinking it. It's so selfish. I'm ashamed."

"Okay, how about this?" He noted how her rhythms calmed slightly when he spoke. "Because you are one of the most selfless people I've ever met, I give you a pass to be really selfish for a few minutes, and whatever it is, I'll do my best to make it better, okay?"

Her shame wouldn't allow her to speak.

After her clue that whatever had upset her she deemed as selfish, Rainer at least had a decent assumption. "Can I take a guess?" Her eyes held his, and he saw the plea in them as she nodded hopefully.

"I think maybe you're a little bit upset about the new baby. And I know that you're really scared about everything that happened to Serena, and now your dad's running for Crown. But Em, I don't think either of those things is selfish." He refused to break her gaze.

"What if something happens to one of them? What if something happens to Mom? He took Serena and now he's going to be even angrier because Daddy's going to run. He already killed Cal. I can't..." she broke down completely.

Rainer let her cry. He had no reassurances for her. He didn't know what was going to happen, and so much had already been taken away.

"And then there's going to be the campaign, and the twins, and then the new baby, and I'm getting married. And the press, and now it won't just be Rainer Lawson's getting married. It will be the new Crown and the former Crown's kids are getting married, and it's going to be horrible."

After several long minutes, her sobs eased. He kissed her head.

"Feel a little better now?" She gave a reluctant nod. "Look at me."

She lifted her head.

"Baby, Vindico and Iodex, and all of us are aware of what we're up against. Governor Peterson is an ass, but he's not in the Interfeci so, either way, I think we'll be able to handle Wretchkinsides."

They were actually waiting to see who Wretchkinsides was planning to finance so he could control the board.

"And, I know you wanted your mom to help you plan the whole wedding. I think she wants that too. So, why don't we give it a little time? The campaign is only two months. We can delay the wedding a little more if you want. It doesn't matter to me. If you don't want the press involved, I'll do my best to make it as private as we can. All I want is to be married to you, so,"—he brushed an errant hair behind her ear—"if you want to leave right now and fly to Vegas and have Elvis marry us, then I'm game, or if you want to wait until after the baby is born, then I'll be okay with that too."

He was pleased when a slight giggle escaped her. He studied her beautiful emerald eyes, and he saw hope start to swirl in their depths.

"Whatever you want, Elvis or the whole Senate affair, or anything in between, I'm fine with. I promise you I will do my best to give you whatever you want, but all I want is to watch you walk down an aisle, in a white dress, on your father's arm, and then I'll vow to love you and cherish you for the rest of my life, okay?"

"I'm sorry," she lamented.

"For what, baby?"

"For being stupid and selfish and..." She tried to come up with another name for herself in that moment, but Rainer halted her progress.

He kissed her tenderly and then continued to soothe her with long, languid kisses. He let his mind whirl with images of her in a wedding gown and then him getting her out of it.

She gave a heady groan. It spilled into his mouth, and he increased the intensity of his hungry kisses. They broke apart when they heard one of the twins squeal as he ran by the barn. They panted for breath.

"Are we gonna go on a honeymoon?" Emily wondered.

Rainer gave her an incredulous stare. "Are you kidding me?"

"I'm serious. We haven't really talked much about the wedding, and you haven't said anything about the honeymoon. We just joked about it a few weeks ago."

"Believe me, baby, we're going on a honeymoon. A nice long honeymoon where I can spend weeks doing nothing but worshipping your gorgeous body from sun-up 'til sundown."

Emily's tears had dried, and she looked extremely pleased with his answer. "And where might you be doing this?" She sounded much more like herself.

"You plan the wedding. I'll take care of the honeymoon." He knew exactly what he was looking for in a honeymoon locale. He just hadn't really begun to search.

There were a few places that intrigued him. If it were up to him, they would go to some private island where they saw no one but each other for an extended vacation.

"But you're going to need my help." She refused to relax.

"Nope, I will take care of everything, and if you need any help with the wedding, I can do that too." Since she seemed to have decided that with her mother expecting her eleventh child she was going to have to plan the wedding on her own, this seemed to bring her a great deal of peace.

"Thank you," she whispered. "I guess we'd better get back."

"Whenever you're ready." He knew the world had been a little too much on this particular day. He wanted her to stay wherever she felt safest. He was just thankful that he got to stay with her.

"But if, at some point over the next few months, I decide that I do want to do the Elvis-Vegas thing, will that still be okay?"

"You call me. I'll book one of the jets."

"But what if I want to know where we're going on our honeymoon?" She began her descent down the ladder.

Rainer waggled his eyebrows. "Then you'll just have to be patient, Miss Haydenshire."

She raised her eyebrow in intrigue as she sassed, "Once you've planned it, I'll be able to get it out of you if I want."

"Doubt it." He took her hand and led her back toward her family on the deck. "But you're more than welcome to try," he baited her flirtatiously.

When they returned, Mrs. Haydenshire was on the phone with Tad, sharing the family news.

"Well, there they are. Hang on, Taddy." She stood and handed Emily the phone.

Governor Haydenshire had seen Emily's red, swollen eyes and gave Rainer a quizzical gaze.

Rainer shook his head and tried to indicate that she was fine, and her father needn't worry.

With a wistful gaze, the governor gave Rainer a nod. Rainer understood that he was letting go just a little at a time and letting Rainer take care of his baby girl.

Emily ended the call and sported a broad grin. "Uncle Tad and Nathan are going to be here Friday, because they're planning Governor Carrington's wedding. He says they'll have most everything done Friday, and that they want to take me wedding-dress shopping all day Saturday and Sunday morning."

"Well, can I come?" It seemed Mrs. Haydenshire knew at least part of why Emily had been crying.

"If you feel up to it." Emily nodded hopefully.

"There is nowhere else I would ever be, sweetheart."

Emily seated herself on the swing beside her mom and hugged her tightly.

CHAPTER 7
SWEET AS HEAVEN, SEXY AS HELL

Friday afternoon, Rainer and Logan helped work on a harrowing case where two Gifted teenage boys, who'd just become freshmen at the academy, decided to draw energy from power lines. The results had been deadly.

"Why would you do that?" Logan shuddered as he and Rainer got ready to leave for the evening.

"Because drugs are bad, particularly for Gifted children." Vindico shook his head. "There's a reason Venton does drug tests so often."

Iodex had been called in because of suspected foul play, but upon interviewing friends of the victims at the academy, they discovered that the boys had been bragging about doing it for a while. They'd also been using methamphetamines for the same length of time.

"I'm taking Em out. We probably won't be in until late," Rainer phrased the lie he'd concocted with Emily. She didn't want Logan to know about her tattoo plans.

"Okay, have fun," Logan called as he headed to the Accord. Rainer waited a few minutes and then followed Logan's path. He headed to Alexandria to pick up dinner.

He tried to stop thinking about the day he'd had while trying to calm his nerves over Emily getting a tattoo and the inevitable pain.

He reminded himself that Emily was really excited and wanted to do this and that Fionna wouldn't let it hurt her.

When he arrived at the arena, he summoned twice and flashed his badge, per the new security protocol at the stadium, before he was allowed inside.

Security was much tighter since Emily's incident in the parking deck. She met him at the entrance to the field.

"Hey there." He willed his nerves not to show. She was on to him instantly. She took their drinks from his hands so he could carry the rest of the food.

"I think it's really sweet that you're more nervous than I am."

"I don't handle you in pain all that well."

"I'll be fine." She popped a kiss onto his cheek. He followed her to a small room near the Angels' vast locker rooms that had several soda machines, enhanced water dispensers, a massive snack bar, and a few tables.

Chloe and Fionna were in there as well. They were sitting at a table with Connor and Katie.

"Hey Rainer," Katie leapt. "I'm taking a vote." She lifted her shirt slightly and yanked down the side of her shorts, revealing her right hipbone. "Here?"

Rainer turned his head away instinctively.

Katie and Emily giggled. "Or here?" She spun and lifted up the back of her shirt to reveal the lower portion of her back.

"Uh," Rainer stammered uncomfortably. He had no idea what an appropriate response would be.

Connor laughed. "He's not going to answer that. Just get it wherever you want."

"What do you think?" Katie urged.

Rainer shook his head. "I think that I have no opinion on that, and that you should put it wherever you want."

"I told you he wouldn't vote." Emily laughed. As she spread out their food, Chloe and Fionna picked their previous conversation back up.

"All I'm telling you is that's what Garrett said," Chloe vowed.

Fionna rolled her eyes in an irritated huff. "He is not dating anyone, Chloe. I didn't feel that he was into anyone when I was around him last time."

"He's Daniel Vindico. He's never into anyone. He bangs them and moves on."

"Hmm, sounds a little like Garrett," Fionna sneered. "Oh Emily, I'm sorry!" Fionna's eyes goggled.

Emily gave her a consoling smile. "No worries. I grew up with him."

With a slight giggle, Fionna nodded.

Chloe scowled. "Why don't you just volunteer to be his fuck buddy for a while and get him out of your system? I'm sick of hearing about him. It's been, what, like ten years now?"

"You don't know what I know," Fionna fired back, and Rainer saw the hurt in her eyes.

Paran arrived a few minutes later, and Dana introduced him to Katie and Emily. Rainer shook his hand. He bit his tongue to keep from threatening to do him physical harm if he hurt Emily.

"I've got all the pens set up in the locker room, and my assistant is here, so who's up?" Paran quizzed with a kind smile.

"Here, I'll go," Fionna stood. "I just want my lightning bolt and halo touched up a little and my surfboard."

Paran smiled and gestured for her to head to the locker room.

"Come on, Chloe. You're casting me," Fionna demanded.

"Fine." Chloe threw away the wrappers from her dinner and followed Fionna out.

"Vindico is dating someone?" Emily asked.

"I have no idea, baby. I kind of think he is, but not because he wants to, as odd as that sounds. He doesn't really share much about his personal life with me though."

"I think I need to talk to my big brother." Emily pulled her phone from her purse and touched Garrett's name on the list of favorites.

"Hey Em, what's up?" Rainer could hear Garrett's voice clearly and realized that Emily was amping the signal on the phone.

"I was just talking to Chloe and she was telling me about Vindico." She bent the truth slightly.

"What about him?"

"That he's started dating someone new."

"Oh, yeah. I guess he's been casually dating that stripper we met at The Tantra that day you flipped because Rainer had to go, remember?" Emily seemed to steel her resolve with an eye roll. "She's been keeping tabs on Wretchkinsides's men for us, and she asked him out. He went. As long as she doesn't get hurt, I guess it's not a big deal."

"Except to Fionna," Emily urged.

"Yeah, well, Dan's still a fucking disaster. Fi needs to find somebody else. She doesn't need to get involved in his shit."

Emily begrudgingly agreed and then got off the phone with her brother. When Fionna returned, Rainer was relieved she didn't seem to be in any pain.

"Okay, Em, you ready?" she urged.

Dana followed Fionna into the room. "Come on, while Paran's doing Emily's, Marc can do yours." She tugged on Katie's hand.

"Okay, wish me luck." Emily drew a deep breath.

"Good luck, baby." Rainer tried to breathe calm from the air around him.

"She'll be fine." Fionna had immediately sensed Rainer's nerves.

"I've gotta stop hanging out with Receivers all the time."

The girls laughed then waved to him as they left.

"Does Dad know Em's getting a tat?" Connor quizzed.

Rainer shook his head and awaited the inevitable response. A low slow whistle slid between Connor's teeth. "Damn, she's got nerve. I'll give her that. He's gonna blow."

"She says he won't because Will and Garrett and Patrick and Levi all have them."

Connor shook his head. "Not a chance. She's Emily, the baby girl."

"I know," Rainer sighed.

"Is she getting it somewhere only you'll see it?"

Rainer appreciated Connor trying to think of a way for Emily to stay out of trouble with their father.

"I don't know. She wouldn't tell me what she's getting or where. She wants it to be a surprise."

"I'm sure she's getting the Angels logo. Maybe with her number or some twist, but that's what they all have."

Rainer considered that, but prior to the belly shot he'd never known Emily to do anything because everyone else was doing it, especially when it came to her style or a look.

"Maybe." Rainer glanced at his watch and wondered how long it would take. "Do you have one?"

Connor shook his head. "Nah, never really thought about it, I guess. Garrett's are cool, but that's his thing. I don't really want one."

Rainer considered all of Garrett's tattoos. They covered his bulging biceps and his back. He had dragons in flight on his chest. They were breathing flames that appeared to be scorching across his pecs. There were music notes with lyrics and several others. He wondered momentarily if Chloe had summoned for him to keep the pain from being too intense.

"Are you okay, man?" Connor's brow furrowed.

"Yeah, I'm just worried about her."

"I figured. Just wanted to make sure."

Rainer appreciated that he hadn't chided him for his overprotectiveness of Emily.

"She'll be all right. She's a lot tougher than you and Dad give her credit for being."

"Yeah, I know." He just didn't want her to have to be so tough.

"Hey, I heard Dad tell Mom that Peterson's already printing up Wyvern shit for the campaign, even though they're not supposed to do any of that 'til after Labor Day." It seemed Connor was trying to get Rainer's mind off of Emily.

Rainer nodded. He'd already seen evidence of it at the Senate. "I'm not surprised."

The Peterson's family crest was of a wyvern over the widespread falcon's wings. Rainer knew that one of the meanings of the wyvern was revenge and retribution, so he thought it was fairly apt.

He considered the Haydenshires' lion crest, and his own, with the phoenix over the falcon's wings. Emily wanted the crests on the wedding invitations.

"Are you excited about the new baby?" Rainer was desperate to talk about anything besides Emily and the tattoo.

"I guess. They can't keep their hands off each other, so it was inevitable. Are you and Em gonna have twenty kids too?"

"Whatever she wants, I'm game, but I'd also be good with, like, two or three."

Connor nodded his agreement.

"How's it going with Katie?" Rainer asked.

"Okay, I guess." Connor sighed. "I'm not looking for anything too serious. I'm really not that interested. I told her if we had to hang out, it'd have to be at her place because I can't move out. Mom and Dad need my help with the election and everything, which she thought was sweet. So, I'll work that angle until I'm out." Connor clammed up when Katie emerged.

"Do you wanna see it?" she asked.

"Sure." Connor smiled.

She giggled and then spun and lifted her shirt tail. Connor looked momentarily disappointed with the newly acquired double A logo, with a lightning bolt and halo that was now situated a few inches above Katie's tailbone.

"Nice," he commented.

Rainer knew something was up with Connor, but he clearly wasn't ready to talk about whatever it was.

"Really?" Katie spun back around.

"Definitely."

"Where's Em?" Rainer asked Katie before they headed out. He assumed she should be finished as well, if she was getting a similar tattoo in a similar location.

Katie beamed. "It took Paran a while to draw hers up. She'll be out in a little while. I think you'll really like it."

"Are you ready to go?" Connor looked mildly bored and a little anxious to take Katie wherever they were planning on going.

"No, I wanna see Em's. Let's wait."

Connor shrugged and then pulled Katie onto his lap as he sat back down at the table. They chatted for a little while longer until Rainer grew frantic.

"Are you sure she's okay?"

"She's fine, Rainer. Chill." Katie laughed at him outright. Another half hour passed, and Katie and Connor were making out in the chair. Not wanting to see the show, Rainer began pacing in the hallway outside of the snack room.

A few minutes later, Fionna emerged and grinned broadly.

"Paran's casting her, then she'll be done. You're gonna flip." Coming out to tell Rainer that a guy he barely knew was casting his fiancée did nothing to quell his frantic worry.

Fionna furrowed her brow. "Are you okay?" She knew perfectly well he wasn't. She could read his emotions in his energy. "Did you not want her to get one?"

"Oh, uh, no." Rainer shook his head. "I was just worried about her."

"I think that's sweet. I wish some guy cared about me that much."

Before Rainer could comment, Emily emerged from the locker room with Paran and Dana behind her.

She was giving Rainer a decidedly naughty grin. Not certain if he should ask to see it, Rainer allowed himself to breathe as she appeared to be perfectly fine.

"I think it's some of my finest work," Paran commented.

"How'd it turn out?" Katie and Connor joined them in the hallway.

"Just like I wanted it," Emily stated with a knowing grin. Curiosity was getting the better of him, though he tried to be patient.

"Do you wanna see it?" She gave him a come-get-me grin. Still trying to wash away his case of nerves, he nodded.

She lifted her shirt slightly and pulled the right side of her jeans down to reveal her hipbone.

Rainer's mouth fell open. "Wow, uh, I thought you were probably getting something with the Angels logo or something?"

He tried not to pant, but was completely unable to take his eyes from her hip. She was clearly pleased by his expression.

"I know." She moved closer to him as he continued to study her abdomen unabashedly. "But I didn't want something everyone else had. I liked this better."

Branded across her right hip just below the waistband of her jeans was the Lawson crest. His crest duplicated to perfection on her gorgeous body.

Rainer moved closer to study the tattoo. The wings and the flames below the phoenix were actually formed out of smoky, swirling letters and numbers. In the falcon spread below the phoenix was a lightning bolt and halo. The feet of the falcon formed the Angels' double As.

"See,"—she pointed to the phoenix's chest—"those are our initials all together, and here's the Auxiliary crest." She pointed to one of the phoenix wings.

As he studied it closer he noted his birthdate and hers intertwined in the phoenix's legs. Cal's initials and birth and death dates were there in the flames along with the Haydenshire lion.

Every event that meant something to her, everything that made her who she was, was swirled beautifully inside of his crest. And he was inexorably moved.

"Wow," he said again. Lust was evident in his tone. The tattoo was somehow deliciously sexy and incredibly sweet all at the same time.

It represented her perfectly. He'd always known she was the perfect combination of hellcat and heavenly angel, all swirled into one beautiful package, and he was extremely turned on looking down at his mark branded across her gorgeous hip.

Connor laughed, which Rainer assumed his expression must've warranted. "Are you trying to kill Dad?"

"No," Emily huffed.

"Yeah, well, I'm thinking you putting his crest inside your panties might just do that."

"Shut up, Connor," Emily spat. "So, do you like it?" Rainer almost laughed at her complete change of tone as she turned back to him.

He swallowed down the lust that had come on quite suddenly and nodded. "Uh, yeah."

Everyone was still laughing at him.

"I like a happy customer," Paran joked.

"Oh, will you pay him? I'm just gonna grab my bag."

Rainer pulled his wallet from his pocket and watched as Emily walked back into the locker room.

He couldn't pay for the tattoo and get Emily out of the arena fast enough. Raw need and primal lust made his head spin.

After giving quick waves to everyone, Rainer half dragged her toward his car. He grabbed her bag and threw it in the back seat. He spun her up against the passenger side door and pinned her body against his.

She was shooting him wanton, needy gazes. Hunger quaked in his rhythms. His body was hot-wired to take her.

"So, I take it you really like it?"

A hungry groan escaped him. "That doesn't even begin to cover it."

She panted. It set him on fire as he sucked her bottom lip and let his hands brush across her chest and then down her sides. He growled in desperation. She took in his covetous need evident in his rhythms.

"Take me home," she pled in an aching whisper.

"Get in the car, baby. I don't know how much longer I can wait." He popped open the door for her.

Her eyes lit in thrilled desire as she settled in the car. He crawled into the other side and pulled her back to him.

"When I get you home..." he warned before devouring her mouth again. He slipped his hands up her shirt and groped her heatedly.

"I need you, but someone might see us out here. Please just take me home." He reminded himself that the faster he got her in bed the faster he could have her. He backed the car out and flew home.

Thankful that it was almost ten and it appeared Logan and Adeline had gone to bed, Rainer parked the car, exited, and had her out and in his arms in a matter of seconds.

Before he opened the door to the house, he spun her again and pressed his now-straining erection against her abdomen. He listened as she gasped from the force.

"Take me to bed," she demanded. He nearly lost it. He unlocked the door and kept his lips locked on hers as they stumbled into the kitchen.

"What the hell?" Logan was laughing at them.

Rainer jerked away and ran the back of his hand over his mouth. "I thought you were in bed," he huffed.

"Because my new bedtime is 9:30?"

"I didn't see any lights on."

"Yeah, we're watching a movie here." He moved to the kitchen, handed Rainer a beer, and then pulled another for himself. "We're almost done. You can watch Carlo bite it."

Rainer took a sip of the beer but nearly spat it out. That wasn't at all what he wanted to taste or what he wanted in his mouth.

"Why are you watching *The Godfather* again?"

Emily shot Rainer needy, pleading gazes that made him reel.

"It's a classic, and how freaking many times have I watched *The Fast and the Furious* with you? Where'd you go, anyway?"

Emily drew a steadying breath and swallowed down her need as Rainer reached for her.

She moved in front of Logan and Adeline, effectively blocking them from the TV. Logan huffed and grasped her waist. He moved her to the side slightly.

"Well, do you wanna see what I got?"

"No." Logan seemed irritated that no one wanted to see *The Godfather* again.

"Yes." Adeline elbowed Logan.

Emily bit her lip. The motion had ardent desire surging through Rainer's veins. She pulled up her shirt and lowered the right side of her waistband to reveal the tattoo.

Rainer's pulse raced and desire slammed through his veins. He stared at his brand on her body. Desperation permeated every inch of him.

"Wow." Adeline sat up off of Logan and studied the Lawson crest.

Logan choked on the long sip of beer he'd just taken. When he regained the ability to breathe, he shook his head. "Dad is going to lose all of his shit at least twice."

"No, he's not," Emily insisted. Logan doubled over laughing at her.

"That's really cool. I like how you did all the initials and the Auxiliary crest and everything," Adeline admired.

"Thank you. I showed him the crest and told him the stuff I wanted in it. He drew it out perfectly."

"Yeah, because Dad's gonna love Rainer's mark right beside your crotch." Logan rolled his eyes.

"When will he ever see it?"

"Uh, next week at the beach, genius."

Emily wrinkled her nose and did look momentarily concerned. She shook her head just as suddenly and put her hands on her hips.

"Who cares? I'm grown. Will, Garrett, Patrick, and Levi all have them. He'll get over it."

"Uh-huh, sure he will, *baby girl*."

Emily glanced back at Rainer and noted the volatile storm still swirling in his dark, hungry eyes. She gave him another longing look and then glanced at their bedroom door.

Only too eager to have her anywhere alone, Rainer yawned deeply and feigned exhaustion. "I'm kind of tired."

Emily nodded, fully aware that they might be going to bed, but they were most definitely not going to sleep.

"Me too. Come on, Logan. You can quote this movie in your dreams," Adeline pled, much to Rainer's delight.

"Fine." Logan's grin said he clearly hoped she was going to entertain him more than *The Godfather*. He took her hand and led her to their room.

CHAPTER 8
HUNGER

Rainer moved to Emily in three long strides. He pulled her against his body, braided his fingers through her hair, and crushed her mouth to his.

He used one hand to grip her backside as he guided her body in rhythmic circles around his straining length.

She panted deliciously. Using every ounce of restraint in his body to remember that Logan and Adeline were only one room away, and that as soon as he got her in their room he could have her, Rainer pulled away and led her to their bedroom.

He kicked the door shut and continued to consume her mouth. All restraint was gone. He grabbed her hand and pressed it to the fly of his pants. He forced her to grasp him as a loud needy moan escaped her.

"Feel me," he commanded. "Feel how hard you make me, baby."

Her eyes flashed with hunger and excitement. She slid her hand up his zipper line and then plunged it into his boxers. She kneaded him. She squeezed and traced him until his cock wept for her affection. She spun her fingers over his head until he thought he would lose his mind, and then she broke away from him.

Greedy, hungry lust coursed through him. His eyes flashed wildly as she backed away.

"Where do you think you're going?"

With a decidedly wanton grin, she told him to wait for her.

"I don't want to wait. I've waited too damn long already." He attempted to catch her.

She licked her lips seductively and slipped into the closet. Rainer felt like he was being strangled. He wanted her, raw and primal. He wanted to own her, to claim her, and he wanted it now.

She'd put his mark on her, and he planned on taking what was his. Moments later she emerged, wearing a black lace bra and matching, barely there panties that framed her newly inked abdomen to perfection. She'd added a pair of sky-high stiletto heels to complete the provocative picture.

His eyes were dark and ravenous as he took her all in. Her energy swirled in fervent anxious need. His shield gave constant craving pulses.

The thought of what her father would say about the wanton sex kitten, fresh with his mark, standing before him hot and wet, flashed through his mind as he caged her between him and the closet door.

If the governor didn't like what he saw in those pictures, he sure as hell wouldn't like what Rainer was about to do to her. Rebellion mixed itself into the potent cocktail in his mind.

Clearly her hellcat side was coming out tonight, and he planned to be the one to tame her.

He devoured her mouth then trailed hot kisses down her neck until her head fell back. She panted as he nipped her breasts.

With a quick flick of his hand, he removed her bra and threw it on the floor. He caught her right breast in his mouth and sucked and licked with ferocity.

A stuttered moan escaped her, and he moved on to the next obstacle in his path to getting inside of her. He jerked the scrap of lace between her legs to the side and shoved his fingers in her.

He needed her ready. She was hot, wet, and swollen. She throbbed around his hand, so he moved his mouth back up her neck.

"Em, baby," he choked in a feral growl as he dragged his teeth over the hollow of her throat. The heavenly liquid form of her energy dripped down his fingers, and he was done for. "I'm about to throw you on that bed and have my way with you, rough and dirty, so if you want me to stop, or you need me slow down, you need to tell me right now."

In a fevered moan, her body tensed and pitched. Fire lit from her soul and flamed in her eyes.

"Don't stop." She stared at him as he took in her kiss-swollen lips and ravenous eyes. "Take me."

"Did you set the cast?" He forced himself to wait until she answered.

"Yes, just take me now. I want to feel it," she purred.

The electricity between them sparked in a heated red glow.

A low, rapturous, growl thundered from his chest as he grabbed her and spun her until she was on all fours on their bed, and he let his eyes rake over her as she shook her backside for him.

In that moment, he knew that removing the G-string was not as important as being inside of her. He pulled it aside and drove into her as she gasped from the force and then moaned her adamant approval.

"Take it, baby. Just like that," he commanded and she trembled around him.

She convulsed and moaned and begged him for more. True to his warning, he pulled her back until she'd taken all of him. He thrust into her, driving her hard and fast and watching as he entered her fully.

She panted and moaned, then called out his name in lust-filled greed.

"That's what you needed, isn't it, baby? Feels good, doesn't it? Show me how much you like it."

She was on the edge. Her rhythms spiked harder with each of his ragged thrusts. She swelled around him. Her fingers clawed at the sheets. Her back arched low, and she pressed back in an unspoken request for more. He indulged.

Her luscious body drowned him in hot liquid silk. She pulsed around him faster and harder as her rhythms arced wildly.

Her breath caught suddenly, and her orgasm consumed her. With a final ragged push, he fell on top of her as she screamed out in ecstasy, and he filled her with all of him.

He surrendered to the primal lust that had overtaken them. His release had him reeling. The ardent desire she built in him was all-consuming, and some of the things he'd said and done filtered back through his bliss-filled stupor.

He withdrew gently and moved off of her. He held her as she moved to lie on his chest. He concentrated on her rhythms. They were languid and fulfilled. She was happy and content, so he allowed himself to revel in everything they'd just done.

"I really, really like it when you're like that." She was still panting slightly.

"Do you?" He ran his hands over her back. He pushed out his shield. It settled over them.

"That was amazing. I also love the slow, sweet, you keep me casted the whole time kind of sex, too, but that…that was, wow."

"I don't ever want to make you uncomfortable or do something you wouldn't like." He felt suddenly inept where moments before he'd felt quite skilled.

She smiled against his chest. "How about this? I promise to tell you if I don't want to do something, and we just keep having fun and trying out new stuff, because we've been together since I was a toddler, and I plan on being married to you until I'm at least 112, so I don't want you to get bored."

"You have never, ever been boring, Miss Haydenshire, and I'll agree to that deal if you promise that if there is something you want me to do or you want to try, you'll tell me."

He wished at that moment that he could read her mind. He wanted to know what thoughts his part of the deal might've elicited.

"Deal," she agreed. The curious grin on her face had him thinking they needed to talk a great deal about what kinds of things she might like in bed.

CHAPTER 9

SATURDAY

As sun poured through the windows, Rainer let his eyes blink open.

He glanced down. Both he and Emily were still naked, and she was lying on his chest. Her right leg was slung out of the covers and over him. His arms were wrapped around her, and her newly acquired tattoo was on full display.

Rainer let the night before replay in slow detail through his mind. He chuckled. His tawdry sex kitten had turned right back into his sweet baby tucked up in his protective embrace.

Suddenly remembering that they had plans, he glanced at the clock and resisted the urge to curse. He and Logan were due at the farmhouse at eight to help the governor finish the work on Levi and Cal's old room. They hadn't quite finished the weekend before. With the new baby coming, they needed the twins out of the Haydenshires' bedroom and in a room of their own.

Emily and Adeline were going wedding-dress shopping with Tad, Nathan, and Mrs. Haydenshire.

Governor Carrington's wedding was the next day and then, Rainer thought with a smile, the entire family was leaving for the beach house Wednesday after work for an extended trip before the election began.

Governor Haydenshire had marched into Iodex and informed Vindico that Garrett, Rainer, and Logan were to be given vacation from Thursday through Monday. That had been the last thing Vindico wanted, but he certainly couldn't argue.

A knock sounded at the door. Rainer raised his head and chest. He carefully kept Emily tucked next to him as he pulled the covers over her completely. He was certain it was Logan.

"What?" he tried to be loud enough for Logan to hear him but not shout in Emily's ear. Logan pushed the door open. "Hey," Rainer wrapped the covers tighter over Emily.

"Ah geez." Logan stepped back out. "Sorry, I thought you were up. Uncle Tad and Mom just called. They're on their way, and Dad's wondering where we are."

"Shut the door."

"What time is it?" Emily whimpered. Rainer chuckled at her. She sounded like an adorable frog. He kissed her forehead.

"Hey, there. We overslept. It's almost eight." He cleared his throat and ran his hands down her soft, smooth skin until he'd reached her backside, which he took several long moments to massage.

She wriggled beside him. Rainer watched eagerly as she stretched, and the quilts and sheets fell to her waist. He gave her a shuddering growl much to her delight.

She crawled out of bed and began getting ready. Rainer dressed and headed to the kitchen to fix coffee and find something to eat.

Rainer made them both coffee and bagels.

When he returned to their bedroom, Emily was gnawing her lip. Something was very obviously on her mind, and when he was with her like he'd been the night before, her energy remained on his skin. He could read her with ease. "What's wrong?"

"Nothing. I was just trying to figure out if there was some way only Adeline could help me change into the gowns."

"So your mom doesn't see your new ink?"

"I'm debating, actually. If Mom sees it, then she can do her whole 'Emily, your father is under a lot of pressure right now, and I can't believe Rainer would like something like that' thing."

"Oh, believe me, baby, it drives me wild." Rainer let the image of her in a thong and heels shaking it for him on their bed remain in the forefront of his mind.

"I noticed, but if she sees it today, maybe she could break it to Dad before we get on the beach."

"I thought you said he wouldn't be mad?" Rainer wondered if she'd finally seen the flaw in her plan.

"I don't think he will, really."

"Uh-huh, sure."

She giggled and stuck her tongue out at him. He gave her a decidedly naughty grin, which made her laugh.

Soon Tad, Nathan, and Mrs. Haydenshire were spilling into the kitchen. "Em's almost ready," Rainer assured them as Adeline appeared.

She looked thrilled. "I'm so excited!" She grabbed her purse and her new sunglasses, a recent gift from Logan. "I've never been to a wedding before. I watched a few on TV when we had enough money for it."

Logan and Mrs. Haydenshire shared a pained expression.

"And, obviously, I've never been shopping for a wedding dress. I've never even seen anyone in one in person. So, I get to do all of that in one weekend."

Before anyone could respond, Emily stuck her head around their bedroom door.

"Uncle Tad, come here a sec." Her mischievous grin gave her away. Tad looked thrilled.

"Oh, whatever this is, it's going to be good." He whisked into Rainer and Emily's room.

"What is that all about?" Mrs. Haydenshire asked.

"She's probably showing him her new…" Logan started, but Rainer threw his elbow out hard and caught Logan in the gut. A hissing groan escaped him as he glared at Rainer.

Rainer shook his head minutely and let his eyes goggle. Logan rubbed his side.

"Her new what?" Mrs. Haydenshire quizzed Logan again.

"Uh…ear…things." He pointed to his own earlobes.

Adeline tried hard not to giggle as she supplied "Rings."

"Yeah, earrings." Logan was still glaring at Rainer. Mrs. Haydenshire hadn't bought that for a moment, but to Rainer's relief, she decided not to interrogate them.

Tad and Emily emerged thick as thieves. Emily was beaming, and Tad was shaking his head.

"Well, let's see it then," her mother demanded.

"See what?" Emily had never been a very good liar, and her pleading glance at Rainer immediately sold her out.

"Ten children, Emily Anne. Ten. Eventually you will learn that you can't put anything past me. Now show it to me."

Emily hesitated for a moment.

"Please, child, tell me it is not somewhere that I used to cover with a diaper."

With an audible huff and a dramatic eye roll, Emily pulled down the waistband of her jeans and lifted the right side of her shirt, revealing the phoenix crest tattoo.

"Of course, Rainer's crest. How did I not see that coming?" Mrs. Haydenshire quipped before she scolded, "Emily Anne, your father is under enough stress. Did you have to do this right now?"

"Mom, it's no big deal. Just don't tell Daddy."

"Oh, I'm not," Mrs. Haydenshire assured her. "You are."

"It really is a work of art, Lill. You should see everything in it," Tad urged his sister.

Mrs. Haydenshire turned her glare on Tad.

"You know," Nathan stepped up to bat for Emily. "I just saw a new line of gowns that have sheer fabric detailing here." He moved to Emily and slid his hands from the bottom of her rib cage to the top of her hips. "You could show it off in the gown."

"Uh, no," Emily, Tad, and Mrs. Haydenshire stated at the same moment.

Rainer momentarily tried to envision Governor Haydenshire escorting Emily down the aisle in a see-through gown. He was simultaneously turned on and confused by the image.

"We should probably go." Adeline effectively rescued Emily.

"Yes, let's." Mrs. Haydenshire guided everyone out into the garage.

Rainer brushed a kiss across Emily's cheek. "Good luck."

"She'll be fine."

Rainer let his hand slide across her backside as she moved away from him. She giggled and blew him a kiss as he closed the door.

CHAPTER 10
BIRTHING HIPS

Rainer and Logan got ready quickly and rushed to the farmhouse. Connor and Levi had volunteered to help. Patrick informed everyone that he and Lucy had something they really had to do that day, and that they wouldn't be back until late. He seemed quite agitated and nervous, so no one argued.

They spent the day tediously steaming off wallpaper, stripping the walls, sanding, and painting. Everyone took turns looking after the twins while the others worked. When the last coat of paint had been applied, Governor Haydenshire called it a day and told everyone to shower and change so they could make dinner.

Governor Haydenshire manned the grill to prepare dinner in his wife's absence. Rainer and Logan looked after the twins.

Just before six, Emily and Adeline appeared, followed by Tad, Nathan, and Mrs. Haydenshire. Emily fell onto the couch with a dejected huff. This was not at all what Rainer expected from her after a day of wedding-dress shopping with her uncles.

"What's wrong?" He carried Keaton in and set him in front of his toys in the living room.

Tad sighed. "We must've seen every bridal salon in a fifty-mile radius."

"She's going to be the Crown Governor's daughter, and she's marrying Joseph Lawson's son. They're practically royalty. She needs Paris, Milan, Madrid," Nathan gushed exuberantly. "We have DC."

"It's just the first day. Isn't it supposed to take a while?" Rainer pulled from what little knowledge he had about wedding gowns as he sat beside Emily and hoped she'd let him cradle her into a better mood.

"You come back to the city next weekend. New York won't let you down," Tad vowed. "And Vera still wants to meet with you, but she'll be in Paris for the next two months."

"I have a challenge next weekend, and New York isn't going to make me tall and thin."

"What?" Rainer's brow furrowed.

Mrs. Haydenshire shook her head. "She tried on a few gowns that would be better suited for girls with quite a bit more leg and with a little less..."—she gestured to her own breasts while stating—"curves."

"Honey," Tad tsked, "women pay thousands of dollars every single day to have installed what God saw fit to supply you with from the get-go."

After a distinct eye roll, Emily sulked. "Yeah, birthing hips," she quoted Mrs. Peterson's insult.

Rainer was completely stunned. He tried to figure out a way to explain to her how drop-dead gorgeous he thought she was, and how much he adored all of her luscious curves while in the presence of her mother and uncles.

Mrs. Haydenshire drew a deep breath. "I think I'll just see if Stephen needs any help. Trust me, Taddy, Rainer is the only person on the planet who can get through to her once she's like this."

Adeline looked devastated.

"Mom's right. Why don't we take the twins back outside?" Logan suggested.

"Good luck," Tad whispered as he and Nathan joined everyone else on the deck.

"Em?" Rainer tried to determine what to say first.

"What?"

"I'm sorry you didn't find a dress today, and I'll take you anywhere you want to go to find one, but, sweetheart, you are stunningly gorgeous."

They'd been through this before, and Rainer tried to remember everything he'd said back in school when she would go through this same funk. She would obsess that she was short and that her chest and backside made her look fat.

"Em, baby, do you remember last night?"

With a half smile she huffed, "Yes."

"Uh-huh, that's what you do to me. Your curves,"—he slid his hand over her breasts—"and, baby, that ass, my god…it drives me wild. Seriously, I almost broke my own rule and took you in my car at the arena last night. That's how hot you are."

She rolled her eyes but couldn't hide her grin. "Okay, but curvy is not what's in style."

Rainer moved until his mouth was right beside her ear. "I don't give a damn what's in style. Your body makes me ache. I drool just thinking about it." He felt her energy begin to spiral, and he couldn't quite hide his wry grin. "I need something to grip and something to pound into when I take you."

She laughed and rolled her eyes. "But we went to a million stores, and there was nothing even close to what I want. This is my *wedding* dress. It has to be perfect. Everything has to be based on the dress."

"Okay, so the next weekend that I'm off and you don't have a challenge, we'll go back to New York."

"Maybe." She shrugged. He kissed the side of her head and let Nathan's words and Emily's worries run through his mind. An idea came to mind, but it would take a great deal of planning, and he wasn't certain he could pull it off.

"Let's try New York. If you don't find anything there, then I might have a few ideas up my sleeve." He knew she loved a surprise. Her eyes lit.

"Like what?"

"That is for me to know and you to find out."

She beamed and he relaxed.

He'd just pulled a new record time in getting her out of a funk. But he questioned his abilities again as her face fell once more.

"But will you still love me if I gain a bunch of weight when we have babies?" She looked truly terrified. "You know, I'm kinda short like Mom and she gets kinda big," Emily whispered uncomfortably.

Sam's voice seared through Rainer's head suddenly. *You got to make her understand that it's her soul that drives you wild, not her body, Rain Man.*

Immediately thinking that he was going to visit Sam soon, Rainer gazed at Emily with rapt adoration.

"Emily, I love you. I don't care what you look like, or how much you weigh. And when I think about you carrying my baby, it drives me wild. I can't imagine anything more beautiful than that. Please don't let one day of shopping get to you. When I look at you, all I see is perfection. You're everything I've ever wanted. I'm the luckiest guy in the Realm."

"So, you don't think I would be prettier if I looked more like Adeline?"

"Em," Rainer shook his head. Adeline was very attractive in a thin, willowy kind of way, and clearly she got Logan going. As happy as he was for Logan, she definitely wasn't Rainer's definition of sexy.

"I couldn't be happier for Logan, and clearly Adeline is his one and only type, and that's great for them. But you…you drive me wild. I've never ever seen anyone sexier than you." She still didn't look certain, so he decided to turn the tables on her.

"Would you be more attracted to me if I were a few inches taller and built like Garrett or, hell, Vindico?"

He tried to fathom being built like that, but he was several inches too short and couldn't build mass like Dan was able to no matter how much he lifted.

"No. If you were any taller, I couldn't kiss you."

He smiled at her wryly as he kissed her head.

"Then, I guess we're perfect for each other because, believe me, baby, all of your delicious curves make me crazy wanting you."

She watched as his eyes fell to her cleavage. He stared at her luscious tits and made sure she watched his eyes as he let his mind fill with what it felt like to squeeze and grope her and then lick and suck them.

She shivered slightly and caught the erotic energy that began rolling off him.

"They're all exactly where I want my hands to be." To illustrate his point, he slipped his hand to her backside. He grasped it and massaged before quickly pulling his hand away.

He wanted her to want more. She grinned at him and seemed to finally believe what he was saying to her. But she still wasn't the confident girl he knew and loved.

Something else had happened.

CHAPTER 11
THE EYE OF THE BEHOLDER

Dinner was served, and Rainer continued to watch over Emily. She seemed almost back to normal, but he caught the slight changes in her energy when he would rub her leg or touch her hand.

As Governor Haydenshire began plying everyone with root beer floats and urging them onto the back porch to enjoy watching the summer begin to give way to fall, Adeline motioned to Rainer discreetly.

Emily helped the twins with their drinks, but didn't fix one for herself. When she was distracted with Keaton, Rainer followed Adeline into the front hall.

"Emily didn't want me to tell you this." Adeline cringed.

"I knew something else happened." Rainer hoped to alleviate any guilt Adeline had and to get her to talk to him. She looked pained.

"We went to this really sort of expensive, exclusive shop that Nathan had to get us into, and the saleswomen were so rude. Really, really rude. They only had like ten gowns, very exclusive one-of-a-kinds. I don't know why we even went in. Anyway,"—Adeline looked devastated—"Nathan wanted her to try on this gown that wouldn't have been right for her at all, but he insisted, and she did, and while I was putting it on her the saleswoman told her that she was too…" Adeline blushed violently.

Rainer squeezed his eyes shut. He knew where this was heading.

Adeline seemed to slip into medio mode. She became very matter-of-fact. "Well, she said that if Emily wanted to wear a designer gown, she was going to have to lose some weight and she said her breasts and hips were too large and that since you hadn't set a date yet, that she should spend some time reducing her size."

Rainer found it odd that the conversation didn't make him uncomfortable. His concern over Emily was the only thing that mattered to him at the moment.

Adeline drew a deep breath. "Well her exact words were, 'Your breasts are just too large for our gowns, and you're carrying too much weight in your hips. We cater to a much slimmer physique.'

"I told her that I was a medio, and that Emily was perfectly healthy and that weight really isn't a great indicator of anything at all because the body adapts to size. That didn't really help though."

Rainer was seething. "That's the biggest bunch of bullshit I've ever heard. So, they didn't have the gown in her size, and they decided to take it out on her?"

"Exactly. We told her that, but she wouldn't listen and then it got worse."

"How could it have gotten worse?"

"You know Emily's size, right?"

Rainer nodded and hoped Adeline would get on with it.

"The lady told Nathan they only stock dresses in a two or smaller. She said it really mean and right in front of Emily. So, we left and Emily was crushed and then we went to some really nice bridal salons, but several of them were run by Gifted saleswomen. They were only interested in selling one of their gowns to Governor Haydenshire's daughter, and to your fiancée, because you know the publicity and all. So, they just told her everything looked good, and sort of smothered her to death while they had other salespeople calling up the papers to get pictures of her leaving their stores. It was a disaster."

Rainer fought the deep desire to drive to the exclusive bridal shop and give the owner a very large piece of his mind.

He decided he would make his plan work, because the scenario with the press was only going to get worse once Governor Haydenshire announced his bid for Crown.

Elections in the Gifted Realm were only allowed to go on for eight weeks. They typically began right after Labor Day, and the election would be held at the end of October. The Inaugural Ball would be held Halloween night.

"Thank you for telling me. Could you do one other thing for me?" He glanced around to make certain Emily wasn't coming to look for him.

"Anything." He could feel the love Adeline had for Emily as it swirled in her rhythms, and it warmed his heart.

"Could you distract her? I need to talk to Will."

Adeline didn't ask any questions. She just nodded.

"Yeah, of course. I know just the thing."

"Thanks. You're the best."

"There you are." Logan moved into the front hall looking concerned. "Is everything okay?"

"No," Rainer sighed. "But I plan to fix all of this." He left Adeline and Logan in the entrance and headed to the kitchen. He fixed a root beer float and added two straws, then headed to the back deck.

His irritation chafed his shield. He didn't want her to look like those stick figures she always compared herself to in magazines.

He'd always thought he'd won some sort of fantastic lottery when it came to Emily's body. He couldn't fathom her thinking she was fat, or a saleswoman informing her that she needed to lose weight. It made him furious.

"Hey there, gorgeous." He put his vengeful thoughts aside. He didn't want to sell Adeline out, and Emily could read him easier than she could read anyone else.

He took a seat on one of the wooden benches that ran the length of the deck. Rainer put his arm around her and held up the float. She smiled at the two straws but shook her head.

"Come on, Em. You love root beer floats."

She shrugged, took a tiny sip, and then pulled away. The saleswoman had done a real number on her, and it was going to take Rainer a few weeks to put his plan into action. He just had to keep reassuring her until then.

Mrs. Haydenshire looked extremely concerned as she noted Emily refusing dessert.

It appeared all thoughts of outing Emily's new tattoo to the governor were forgotten in light of Emily's faltering self-esteem.

"Mrs. Haydenshire?" Adeline called.

"What, sweetheart?" Mrs. Haydenshire answered kindly, but she was still studying Emily.

"Could we look through your and Governor Haydenshire's wedding pictures?"

Mrs. Haydenshire beamed. "Of course, but he wasn't the governor then. He was but a lowly aide to the Senteon," she teased her husband.

"That's true,"—Governor Haydenshire laced his fingers through his wife's—"but somehow, I convinced her to marry me anyway."

"You know, he kept telling me he was going to be Crown Governor someday, but I just thought he was trying to get me to come back to his apartment with him." Mrs. Haydenshire laughed heartily as the governor turned red.

"Hey, look at that," Levi goaded. "Dad had moves." Everyone cracked up as Governor Haydenshire shook his head and laughed.

"Oh, he had moves, all right," Tad chimed in, to all of the kids' delight.

"Careful, Taddy," Mrs. Haydenshire warned, but Tad wasn't going to be dissuaded.

With a delighted grin, he continued, "First, Lill gets in trouble for signing her junior premise, Lillian Haydenshire, instead of Anderson, and turning it in that way. This was before they were even engaged. She almost failed because she refused to change it."

Emily's mouth dropped open as she giggled. Rainer's heart swelled just to see her beautiful smile.

"Wait, it gets better." Tad laughed and shook his head. "So, the academy calls Mom and Dad that Friday to tell them that they felt Lillian wasn't taking her education seriously, and if she didn't rewrite her premise they were going to fail her. Dad comes home from work early that same day. He planned to chew her out, but he finds Stephen and Lillian in the pool. It seemed that at some point the top of Lill's suit just fell off," Tad continued to goad. "That's what she told Dad. That it just fell off of its own accord, and that Stephen was trying to help her find it." Tad could hardly finish the story. He was laughing hysterically.

Whistles rang from Levi, Will, and Connor. Everyone cracked up at the mental picture Tad had painted for them. Governor Haydenshire looked momentarily like he might kill Tad if given the opportunity, but eventually he and Mrs. Haydenshire were laughing over the memory as well.

"Yes, and I now understand all of the things that your dad threatened to do to me if he ever caught us like that again," the governor retorted. This brought on renewed laughter.

"I just can't see Paps yelling at you." Emily shook her head.

"Oh, baby girl, trust me," Governor Haydenshire assured her, "he was very frightening before he became a grandfather. He kept thinking I was corrupting his little girl, but she was the wild one."

The governor winked at his wife.

The laughter continued as Rainer nodded. "Yeah, I wouldn't know anything about that."

Governor Haydenshire nodded his reluctant agreement that Emily and her mother were very much alike. Emily and Mrs. Haydenshire laughed over the assessment, and Emily hid her face in Rainer's chest as he cradled her to him. He kissed her head sweetly. The governor smiled as he watched Rainer soothe her.

The laughter and the retelling of stories seemed to calm Emily's soul, much to Rainer's delight.

"Well, on that note, I think we'll just go inside and go through our wedding album." Mrs. Haydenshire's face was crimson in her embarrassment. "If you want to try on my gown, sweetheart, you can, but it would have to be taken in. You're a few sizes smaller than I was then." She winked discreetly at Rainer.

"Really?" Emily seemed thoroughly shocked.

Rainer beamed at Mrs. Haydenshire.

"Yes." Mrs. Haydenshire acted like she didn't understand why that would surprise her. Emily followed her mother back into the house with Adeline and Brooke following after them.

As soon as they were out of sight, Rainer moved to the space Brooke had previously occupied beside Will. Tad and Nathan leaned in as Rainer began discussing his plan.

CHAPTER 12
BEAUTIFUL

Emily seemed almost back to normal by the time Rainer drove her home.

"I tried on Mom's gown."

"And?"

"It was a little too big, but she was pregnant with Will." Emily was still slightly shocked by this.

"She wasn't pregnant with Will when your grandmother made the gown, Em, and she was, like, one month pregnant when she got married."

"That's true."

"So, do you want to have it taken in and wear it?" He secretly hoped she wouldn't. He was getting more and more excited about his plan. She laughed.

"Uh, no. It has a decidedly early 90s big puffy-sleeved vibe. That's not really the look I'm going for."

Rainer laughed and tried to envision that. "Is there anything you want special for your birthday?" Rainer wished he hadn't said that as soon as it leapt from his mouth. He wanted this to be a big surprise.

"My birthday isn't for, like, five more weeks."

"As I have been at every single birthday party you've ever had, including being at the hospital when you were born, I am aware of when your birthday is."

"What are you up to?"

Rainer commanded himself not to say anything else about this year's birthday until he talked to Vindico.

"You'll have to wait and see, baby doll." Flirting his way out seemed like the only option.

"And you were not there when I was born."

"Actually, Miss Haydenshire, my parents helped your grandparents keep all of your brothers when you were born, and then they brought all of us to the hospital to see you." He had no actual memory of the event, since he was just over a year old, but he'd heard the story most of his life.

She giggled as he continued.

"I distinctly remember thinking how sexy you were lying there, in those little glass tray bed things in your pink hat. I wanted to unwrap your blanket."

She guffawed.

"But, you know, I played it cool. I decided to wait until we were toilet-trained before I asked you out."

"I love you," she gushed.

"The feeling is definitely mutual." He leaned in and brushed a sweet kiss across her lips as he pulled the car in the garage.

He guided her into the house, laid back on the sofa, and pulled her onto his chest. He cosseted her to him. He let his energy soothe her as he reached under her shirt to massage her back.

"I don't want to go wedding-dress shopping again tomorrow," she admitted in a pained whisper. Her plea stabbed through him.

"We don't have to be at the wedding until seven. Do you want to go somewhere just the two of us, or hang out with Logan and Adeline or something?"

"Can we just hang out, just you and me, until Governor Carrington's wedding?"

"Of course. Anything special you wanna do?"

"I just want to stay with you." She clung to him.

"With you is my favorite place to be."

She smiled against him.

Rainer closed his eyes and tuned into nothing but her rhythms. Her energy was ragged and weary. Disappointment and desperation ran deep as well. She was fighting them, but they were making a valiant comeback.

He couldn't stand it. He couldn't believe she couldn't see how beautiful she was and what she meant to him. Determined to prove to her how much he loved her and how badly he wanted her always, he decided to act. "Let's go to bed, baby."

Logan and Adeline had stayed at the farmhouse, involved in a game of cards, but Rainer knew Emily wanted to leave, so he'd feigned exhaustion to bring her home.

He leaned and lifted her into his arms.

"What are you doing?"

"Carrying you to bed," he stated as if that should have been very obvious.

"I can walk." Her fear that she had somehow become too heavy for him since the last time he'd done this was evident in her tone.

"I don't want you to walk. I want to carry you." She smiled hesitantly and tucked her head under his chin as he glided to the bedroom.

"Are you tired, sweetheart? Because there are a few things I really want to do before we go to sleep." He let his voice take on a raspy, lust-filled tone.

"Like what?" Her energy leapt.

"Don't worry, I'll show you. I have several things to show you, actually. The first,"—Rainer set her on the floor and began undressing her—"is how incredibly sexy I think you are."

CHAPTER 13
1964 AND A 1/2

The next morning, Emily had packed and casted a large picnic basket, and they'd stopped by the nearest gas station to get enough Dr Peppers to last for the day.

Rainer grabbed her a sack of cinnamon discs and a ring pop. Emily giggled as Rainer paid the tab and walked her back to the car. Before he cranked the car, Rainer grabbed one of the Dr Peppers and chilled it for her, which made her beam.

"Ready, baby?" He smirked and revved the engine for her, as the top lowered.

She pulled her hair up in a ponytail and nodded. "I take it you like it when I ask you to take me on a drive up the ridgeway, then?"

"I rank you asking me to take you out driving for the day right up there in the list of sexiest things ever to come out of your mouth. It falls right under you telling Mulligrew that my 'Stang is a 1964 and a half."

She laughed as he drove away and headed up the parkway. They watched as the rolling hills turned into higher and higher peaks ahead of them.

As the curves grew tighter, Rainer slowed enough that they could talk as they left Arlington behind them with all of the stress and the worry that had forced its way into their lives in heavy doses as of late. He was glad to let it fade away.

The drive was serene and restorative. The knowledge that no one knew where they were, and that they were deliciously alone, made Rainer's heart swell.

He had to force himself to watch the road instead of staring at her. As they drove farther away from their problems, Emily began to unfetter. Her shoulders relaxed and her sweet smile seemed permanently affixed to her beautiful face as she breathed in the cleaner air.

"Having fun, baby?"

She beamed. "I've missed just being with you so much."

She made his heart ache momentarily, and he nodded his agreement.

"Kind of nice to leave everything behind for a little while." All of the responsibilities, all of the tension, Wretchkinsides, her father's campaign, wedding dresses, Iodex, the press, the trial, the belly shot—Rainer felt it all slip away as he edged the gas pedal with a little more force.

They talked endlessly about nothing specific. They reconnected and restored each other.

"Can I switch gears?" Emily asked. Rainer glanced at her, and he saw it in her eyes. She just needed a day for the two of them to slip back into slightly younger versions of themselves. She needed to be rescued and soothed from all of the stress that awaited them a few miles the other direction.

"Sure, baby. Go for it." He took his hand off the gearshift. He'd given her a few lessons on driving a stick. She'd gotten pretty good, but after the wreck, she'd refused any more instruction.

"You'll tell me when?" Her excitement turned nervous.

"You can do it, Em. You don't need me. Just feel it." She switched to third when she felt the engine start to edge as he engaged the clutch. "See…?" He winked at her as she'd just proven his point.

"I always need you."

Since he didn't have to shift, he slid his hand to her thigh and massaged it.

They stopped at a park off of the ridgeway. Rainer parked the car under the dogwood trees that overlooked a secluded mountain lake.

"This is the best day ever." Emily's rhythms were languid and happy. Rainer beamed as he lifted the picnic basket out of the back seat and opened her door for her.

She spread a quilt on the ground under the trees, while he unpacked their lunch. Rainer reclined on his side and situated Emily so she was seated against him while they ate the sandwiches she'd made.

They talked and laughed throughout the meal. Afterward, Rainer threw away their wrappers and then engaged her in slow sensuous kisses, with no intention of them leading anywhere else.

Everything in Rainer's world in that moment fell into thoughtful perspective. Making love to her was an extremely important part of their relationship, and it was far too special, too vital to them, to allow anyone else to ever intrude.

Leaning her over a bar or groping her on a quilt in a public park, even if they were alone at the moment, was something he would just never do. He'd learned his lesson.

He made out with her, enjoying the way her body felt beside him. He formed her lips around his own and occasionally slipped his tongue in her mouth, but nothing more. He allowed them both to remember what their relationship had been not so many months before.

He slid his hands to her legs and massaged her thighs suggestively, but never slid them higher as memories continued to form in his mind. The first time he'd kissed her. The first time he'd felt her breasts, plied them in his extremely inexperienced hands. The first time she'd slid her hand over him. She'd admitted later that night that she'd been surprised by his length and the rigidity.

When he'd backed her up to the pier at Buoy's. The feeling of the slick heat her body made for him. Taking her, making her all his on graduation night at the beach house. The first time he'd tasted her, her first release. The first time she'd slid him into her mouth and licked and sucked. It all flooded through his mind as he kissed her heatedly. She pulled away after a long while.

"We'd better go." She cuddled closer into his embrace.

"I don't want to go." He didn't want to return to the chaotic, stress-filled world that had come on so suddenly. He thought back to everything that had happened since the night they'd both given graduation speeches at Venton. It was overwhelming. "I just want to stay here with you. Let's just run away. We've got loads of money. Just stay here with me."

He kissed her passionately and rolled her to her back so he was positioned over her. Her soft, sweet moan had him backing away, but stopping was the last thing he wanted to do.

She grinned up at him. "This is a public park, so I'm pretty sure even you can't build us a house here. Plus, I think, even though everything is kind of crazy right now, there's a whole lot worth fighting for back down there."

He knew she was right. He just didn't want to give up the peaceful solitude their day had provided them. He stood and reminded himself that he wasn't a kid anymore, and that there was a life out there he was meant to live. He took her hand and helped her up.

He felt the spark that always ignited when he touched her. The spark he'd felt for the first time when he was eight years old and brushed a kiss across her cheek, when their Gifted energies were still completely undeveloped but there, just under the surface.

He was aware at times it lost its novelty, but he decided to always pause to feel the spark between them. His entire world rose and set with that spark.

It was getting late in the afternoon, and they needed to get home to get ready for Governor Carrington's wedding.

"Do you want me to put the top up, sweetheart?" He didn't want her to get cold as they drove back. She shook her head.

"No, I want to feel it when we drive. I want to enjoy every moment of this day with just you." He understood precisely how she felt.

Rainer grabbed the quilt they'd eaten on and shook it vigorously. She slid into the passenger seat, and he covered her up in it. She laced her fingers in his.

"Let's go home."

CHAPTER 14
SHATTERED

They were two of the last people to arrive at the wedding. Rainer and Emily quickly eased into seats beside Logan and Adeline. Rainer took in the porcelain tiling of the floor in the governor's mansion. Serena had designed the opulent villa that was tucked away in Bethesda, Maryland.

There was no wedding party, so as soon as Governor Carrington and the minister entered, the bridal march swelled from the six-piece band, and everyone stood.

Rainer leaned forward and wrapped his hands around Emily's waist. "Are you ready?" he whispered as he tried to envision her in a white gown walking toward him, the way it would feel to join their futures, solidly, as one. He felt her energy swirl rapidly as she nodded. Thrilled excitement spun in her rhythms.

He beamed at her as they turned to watch Serena glide down the aisle. She was dressed in a skin-tight white gown with a coral overskirt train, a reflection on her Jamaican heritage. She looked stunning. No one would ever have guessed that two weeks before she'd been beaten, bloodied, and broken. The coral showed off her dark skin beautifully, and Governor Carrington blinked back tears as she entered.

The vows were simple, and there was only one song, a Jamaican hymn, but the love between the governor and Serena was palpable in the room. Whistles rang from several of the guests, and Governor Carrington dipped Serena in a hot and heavy kiss when he was instructed to do so.

The wedding bled smoothly into the reception, per Nathan's instructions. He opened all of the doors on the lower level of the expansive mansion and out onto the large lanai. Everyone enjoyed jerk chicken, curry lamb, coconut rice, and the spiced rum cake that was the centerpiece of the outdoor decor.

Emily, Mrs. Haydenshire, and Serena were in deep conversation before too long.

Governor Haydenshire made his way over to Rainer and Logan. They were discussing the security for the upcoming election with Vindico.

Governor Peterson and Yvette were in attendance, though they would only speak with a few other guests.

"I probably don't want to know what you did to make my baby girl smile like that again, but I suppose I'm glad you did it," Governor Haydenshire allowed.

Vindico and Logan both chuckled as Rainer smiled. "I took her on a drive up the ridgeway, sir."

Both Vindico and Governor Haydenshire looked impressed.

"You have always had a way of making her smile when no one else could, even when you two were toddlers. I guess I can't really ask for more than that." He bowed his head to Rainer.

"He's a pretty decent guy, Governor," Vindico allowed with a slight chuckle.

The band set up and began playing as Governor Carrington stole Serena from Mrs. Haydenshire and twirled her around the center of the lanai that had been designated as the dance floor.

Soon Governor and Mrs. Haydenshire joined them, along with several other couples.

"Could I maybe get a dance, Miss Haydenshire?" Rainer quizzed flirtatiously.

"I thought you'd never ask." The way she was gnawing her lip made him wonder what was on her mind.

Rainer led her onto the dance floor and spun her into his arms. The slow sultry tones of the island band, the lanai lit by tiki torches, and strung lights that Nathan had casted to glow different colors over the massive pool, gave the entire evening a warm island feel.

Rainer twirled Emily around the dance floor and whispered how much he loved her as he slid his hand farther down her back.

"Watch your hands there, Mr. Lawson," Governor Haydenshire teased as he danced Mrs. Haydenshire beside Rainer and Emily.

"Yes, sir." Rainer slid his hands back up, making everyone laugh.

Logan cut in, and Rainer danced with Adeline. He took a break and got himself and Emily some punch, while Governor Haydenshire danced with Emily. He set the punch back at their table. As the song neared its end, Rainer edged back onto the dance floor toward Emily and her father.

"May I cut in?"

"No," Governor Haydenshire quipped.

Emily giggled. "Aww, please, Daddy. He's really cute."

Governor Haydenshire shook his head with a wistful grin. "I never have been very good at telling you no."

He kissed Emily's cheek and handed her back to Rainer.

A slight breeze picked up as the night wore on. A chill shot through Emily. "Rainer, something bad is going to happen. I can feel it. I kept telling myself I was being crazy, but I can feel it." The hair on the back of his neck stood. He took in the guests as they laughed, danced, and all enjoyed the party.

"Tell me what you feel," he urged.

Suddenly everything shifted. Emily froze on the dance floor. She shivered and clung to Rainer. Her rhythms plummeted.

He searched the area frantically as Emily's hands flew to her head.

"Dan!" Rainer shouted. The black energy was too close. She could hardly breathe. One of the waitstaff was handing Mrs. Haydenshire a cup of punch.

"There's someone here who's not supposed to be. I feel them." Emily gasped for breath.

He watched Vindico's eyes goggle as he raced toward them, and he shoved two men out of his way. He knocked the glass from Mrs.

Haydenshire's hand just as she'd taken a small sip. It shattered on the tiled floor.

"That's Vasquez!" he shouted. He threw his arms out toward the member of the waitstaff who was fleeing the scene. They hadn't recognized him in the catering disguise, complete with hat and glasses.

Mrs. Haydenshire began to tremble violently. She grasped the table for support.

"Lillian!" Governor Haydenshire rushed to her.

"Get him!" Vindico demanded.

Portwood and Ericcson took off while everyone else rushed to Mrs. Haydenshire.

Vasquez lept over the low terracotta planters that fenced in the lanai. He summoned a magnetic cast and harnessed the stacked silverware on the table near the cake. With one flick of his hand, he managed to fling the cutlery daggers through the air and back at Portwood and Ericcson. He forced them to use their shields on themselves and other guests while he escaped. The screeching sound of tires filled the air.

"The chopper's outside. Get her on it!" Governor Carrington demanded. One of the enhanced helicopters had been loaned out to Governor Carrington to take him and Serena to their honeymoon destination. It was waiting on the front lawn.

Vindico caught Mrs. Haydenshire as she collapsed.

"Dan, she's pregnant!" Governor Haydenshire was terror-stricken.

"Mom!" Emily began to sob.

"Let's go!" Vindico lifted Mrs. Haydenshire and sprinted to the chopper that was already spinning, per the Crown Governor's orders. "Georgetown Hospital, now! Tell them we're coming!" Vindico demanded as he and Governor Haydenshire climbed onto the helicopter.

"Rainer," Emily begged. Rainer swallowed down the abject terror that pulsed through his body.

"Come on." He pulled Emily back to the Mustang as all of the Haydenshire children in attendance sprinted to their cars and raced to Georgetown Hospital.

CHAPTER 15
TO SAVE A LIFE

The waiting was endless. They sat in a huddled mass in the trauma waiting room of Georgetown Hospital. Rainer was sick. The smell, the sights, it was all too familiar. Every time he inhaled, he was thrust back to the hellish nightmare of watching as medios worked tirelessly on Emily. There'd been nothing he could do except watch and pray for a miracle then either.

Adeline had scrubbed instantly and rushed back, but she hadn't returned. That was two hours ago.

Rainer glanced at his watch as he held Emily tightly. She'd cried herself out. She had switched from Rainer's chest to Logan's, and then to Garrett's shoulder.

Mr. and Mrs. Anderson arrived soon after everyone else.

Will was there before Rainer and Emily. He'd come from the farmhouse instead of the Crown Governor's mansion. Brooke had stayed with the twins, but Rainer and Emily were heading back there as soon as they'd heard anything, to spend the night with Keaton and Henry.

Vindico and Governor Carrington sat in one corner with Serena. They whispered about how one of Wretchkinsides's men had managed to get his way in the house, along with the waitstaff, without anyone noticing.

Levi and Connor paced, just as they had when everyone had awaited word on Emily. Vindico was on his cell frequently. He called into Iodex and to key people around the world who knew of Wretchkinsides's whereabouts. The first question had been how Vasquez had gotten out of prison.

It was quickly determined that Wretchkinsides wanted to scare Governor Haydenshire out of running. They clearly wanted someone who would be easier to manipulate and would look the other way when their heinous crimes were committed.

Further research was done, and Ericcson called a little after midnight to inform them that Vasquez had been paroled with Governor Peterson's signature on the release papers.

Finally, at a quarter to two, Adeline rushed back into the waiting room. "She's going to be okay." Logan wrapped her up in his arms. Air filled Rainer's lungs as Emily began to cry tears of thankfulness instead of those of horror. "We were able to remove all of the poison."

"Is the baby...?" Will choked as Adeline shut her eyes. She grimaced and pulled away from Logan.

"She hasn't lost the baby, but something is wrong. Oh, and it's a little girl. I think she's still likely to miscarry though." Adeline's chin trembled. "It's too early to tell what might've happened. We have the heartbeat, but her Gifted rhythms are gone."

Emily broke down in Rainer's arms as he held her to him. She couldn't seem to stand on her own.

"Em, shh, shh, it's going to be okay," he soothed repeatedly, but it wasn't true and everyone knew it.

He knew she thought it was her fault. She'd been upset about the baby, and now she was blaming herself for whatever the complication might be. This was on top of being able to feel every single emotion from every person in that waiting room. It was more than she could handle.

The fear, the terror, and the sadness—she could feel all of it all around her constantly.

Logan looked like he was going to be sick as did Connor. Garrett sank back in the chair, too stunned to speak. Tears sprang to Will's eyes as he let his head fall into his hands.

"When can we see her?" Levi asked. Patrick looked horrified as he began to pace once again. Adeline let Logan wipe away her tears as she drew a shuddering breath.

"Your dad's coming out in a few minutes, but she can't have visitors until tomorrow." The terror of everything she'd seen and helped heal swirled rapidly in her eyes.

Governor Haydenshire appeared a short while later. Rainer had to look away. The pain etched in every hollow of his face was too much, too deep.

The governor's face was swollen. His eyes were bleary and a horrifying red. Never in the twenty-one years of his life could Rainer recall ever seeing Governor Haydenshire sob.

"Daniel," Governor Haydenshire demanded.

"Sir." Vindico snapped to immediately.

"You will find the man who did this to my wife and to my little girl, and we will end this for good."

"Yes, sir." Vindico gave him a single nod.

After allowing himself to draw a steadying breath, Governor Haydenshire pulled Adeline from Logan's grasp.

"Thank you. You saved her life," he choked, with tears marring his face once again.

He took in all of his children standing and awaiting his calm, buoying force in their family. He was the anchor that held them all securely in this life.

"She kept your mother's heart beating while they got the poison out of her blood stream. It took hours. She never stopped. She saved her life." Tears coursed down each and every face that stared back at the governor.

"No, sir." Adeline shook her head adamantly. "She saved mine."

After a few minutes, when tears subsided somewhat, Will whispered. "What about the baby, Dad?"

"I don't know, son, and we won't know anything for several more weeks."

"Daddy," Emily choked as her father wrapped her up in his arms. He held her tight.

"My sweet baby girl. Looks like, if God's willing, I might get another baby girl." Governor Haydenshire rocked Emily in his arms.

"She has to be okay. She just has to be." Emily convulsed as her father reassured her.

At 3:45, Rainer half walked and half carried Emily to his car.

Will took Brooke home after he awakened her, and Rainer carried Emily into the house. He settled her in her old bedroom and went to check on the twins before falling asleep.

CHAPTER 16
HOLD STEADY, THEN RUN LIKE HELL

Rainer awoke just a few hours later as a tiny, cold, wet hand smacked his face. With a groan, he turned over and lifted Keaton into bed with him and Emily.

"Hi, Wainer," Keaton announced. He was still patting Rainer's face rather forcefully.

"Hi, Keaton," Rainer sighed.

"Where's Mommy?"

Rainer's heart ached as he tried to think of what to tell Keaton that wouldn't frighten him. Emily rolled over and blinked heavily.

"Hey there, baby. Guess who learned to get out of his crib?"

"Hi, EE." Keaton wriggled between Rainer and Emily and then fell back dramatically against the mattress.

"Hi, Keaton." She slid over so he would have more room.

Rainer studied her. Her face was still swollen and red. Her eyes were exhausted. It had been just over three hours since Rainer had carried her to bed.

"Where's Mommy?" Keaton quizzed Emily. He held out both of his hands in a gesture of curiosity.

"Um," Emily choked, and Rainer reached for her hand.

"She's with Daddy, and they'll be back in a few days. Em and I are going to stay with you."

Keaton seemed to consider this for a moment before poking out his bottom lip. "I want Mommy," he huffed.

"How about some breakfast?" Rainer knew distracting Keaton was the way to go.

"I want Mommy to make me bef-fast now," Keaton demanded shrilly. Henry began crying from the Haydenshires' room.

With a deep sigh, Emily stood. She took a moment to steady herself and then moved to her parents' room to remove Henry from his crib.

They each carried a twin to the kitchen and placed them in their highchairs. Emily perked coffee while Rainer put Cheerios on the twins' trays until he could locate something to fix them for breakfast.

"Duce!" Henry commanded.

"Got it." Rainer poured apple juice mixed with water in their sippy cups and supplied it to both boys.

Emily chased a mug of coffee with a Dr Pepper and then began scrambling eggs.

Rainer answered Logan's call. "How's your mom?"

"Better." Logan sounded thoroughly relieved. "They just moved her to a regular room. Dad's pissed off about half of the staff, so I'd say things are almost back to normal," Logan chuckled, though he sounded exhausted. "Per Dad's orders, Adeline's going to be Mom's in-room medio, so that means she won't be leaving until Mom does." A deep yawn overtook him as he tried to recall everything that had happened in the last few hours. "And Mom's insisting that we are all still leaving for the beach Wednesday night. She says we can all just wait on her hand and foot there, instead of at home."

Rainer laughed. That sounded precisely like something Mrs. Haydenshire would insist upon. Rainer glanced at Emily and wondered if she knew how like her mother she really was.

"So, basically, once the poison was out, she was just weak. Medio Sawyer healed her liver last night, and some kickass cardiac medio team healed her heart. The poison they used affects the heart and liver so…" Logan's voice edged toward fury, and Rainer braced for the vengeance, but it never came.

"They're keeping her here to watch the baby and to let her rest. She wants you and Em to bring the boys up here."

"Okay." Rainer began thinking through the logistics of doing just that.

"The press is swarming, though, so be careful." With a resentful sigh for the media in general, Rainer assured him that he would.

"Dad's gonna announce his candidacy today. He's gonna do it from here, in front of the hospital. He's planning to slam Peterson for releasing Vasquez." Logan's voice dropped and Rainer had to cast his phone to hear him.

"Wow." That wasn't a move he'd expected from the governor right out of the gate.

"Yeah, he's pretty pissed."

"He should be."

"I know, but this is gonna get ugly quick."

"Yeah, it is." Rainer tried not to think of all of the horrors that could come out of this campaign.

Logan clearly needed to talk, and Rainer felt bad he hadn't been there when all of this had come to light.

"Hey, let me go help Em get the twins ready. Then I'll go switch the Mustang for the Hummer. Do you or Adeline need anything from the house?"

Logan sounded thankful as he moved the phone from his mouth slightly to ask his mother and Adeline if they wanted anything from the house.

"Yeah, I'll get Em to get that," Rainer assured Logan as he heard Adeline's request. She'd informed Logan that she'd be wearing scrubs the entire time she was at the hospital, but that she could use clean underwear, a bra, and her toothbrush.

"Thanks, and could you bring me a suit and tie? Dad wants us all out there when he makes the announcement."

"Of course. Anything else?"

"Yeah, hang on," Logan moved the phone again. "Mom wants her robe, some thick socks, the book on her bedside table, and those two new cookbooks she bought. She says they're on the island."

"Got it." Rainer slid the cookbooks to the end of the counter so he would remember.

"See you in a little while."

When Rainer hung up the phone, he recounted everything Logan had explained to Emily. Her brow furrowed when he told her the governor's plan to announce his candidacy from the front of Georgetown Hospital.

"I guess the battle's on." She shook her head.

"Yeah." Rainer prayed that they all survived the next two months.

∼

After switching the cars, Emily packed for Adeline and Logan. She laid out a suit for Rainer and picked out a tie that would complement the dress she'd put on.

Rainer secured the car seats in the Hummer and put the sunscreens in the windows, more to block the twins from the press than from the sun's rays.

By eleven, they were heading back to Georgetown. The first obstacle would be to keep the press at bay long enough for them to get Keaton and Henry into the hospital without anyone snapping photos of their faces.

The governor had been debating them being in the press during the campaign, but after last night he was adamant that the twins were not to be photographed.

Rainer phoned Vindico and explained the problem. Vindico seemed pleased Rainer had called to ask for help rather than trying to deal with the press on his own. He'd stated that Rainer was thinking like an officer and not like a student and assured him that he would take care of everything.

When they arrived, Vindico was directing the dozens of police and Iodex officers who were setting up barricades for the press. Rainer parked the Hummer and edged out of the car carefully, to determine the best way to proceed. A million flash bulbs went off as he emerged.

"Rainer, how is Mrs. Haydenshire doing?"

"How's Emily taking her mother's near-death experience?"

"Is Emily with you? Where is Emily?" The questions rang endlessly.

Vindico magnified his voice as officers surrounded the press.

"Mr. Lawson and Miss Haydenshire will be bringing in the Haydenshires' youngest children. Anyone who photographs them will be arrested as the governor has made it perfectly clear that they are not to be in any form of media until they are of age." His voice was menacing.

The crowd edged nervously, and Rainer felt the defiant energy buzz from the assembly. Debate whispered through the crowd as to whether or not arrest would be worth having the first shot of the Haydenshire twins in their credentials.

"Six of us are running beside you, but you're going to have to keep them covered and run like hell," Vindico explained in a furious whisper.

Rainer had already assumed that. Garrett and Logan appeared a moment later, having seen the Hummer arrive.

"I told you it was a freaking zoo," Logan spat.

"Let's get them in before any more arrive." Vindico shook his head.

Rainer, Vindico, Garrett, and Logan all rushed back to the Hummer as Rainer released his cast from it. They were joined by numerous other officers who circled the car to keep anyone from getting too close.

"We're gonna have to cover them up," Rainer explained.

Emily slid out of the passenger side, and Garrett blocked her face from the long-range lenses.

"Okay, we're going to play a game." Emily forced her voice to take on a happy, excited thrum, but Rainer knew she was exhausted.

"Yay!" Keaton clapped.

"You hide under your blankets and then when Rainer and I pull off your blankets, you can see Mommy, but you have to leave them on until we take them off or you'll be out."

The boys nodded their instant understanding.

"No out," Keaton instructed Henry who nodded vehemently. The boys were elated. Rainer, Vindico, and her brothers stared at Emily in stunned disbelief of her genius.

"Let's throw a little wrench in their plans, actually." Garrett gave a wry grin as everyone waited to hear his idea. "Logan, you run in with Emily. I'll take Keaton with half of the escorts. You two bring Henry with the rest. That way they're never together, and it won't be what they're expecting."

"Let's get it done," Vindico agreed.

The boys had already pulled their blankets over their heads, eager to begin the game.

Rainer and Vindico released Henry from his car seat but kept the entire doorway blocked with their bodies as Logan and Emily sprinted into the hospital. The press stirred. The confusion tactic had worked.

"Ready to play, Keaton? If you lay your head on my neck, I can run faster, and we'll beat Henry," Garrett whispered to Keaton.

"Yay!" cried from under the blanket as Keaton tucked his head onto his big brother's massive chest.

"Let's move!" Garrett shouted to his escorts as he flew through the barricades and up the steps into the hospital. He kept Keaton surrounded by his hands and arms.

"I want to play," Henry demanded a moment later.

"Okay, let's go." Rainer scooped him up and gave him the same promise Garrett had just given Keaton. He hid his blanketed face in Rainer's neck as Vindico and the rest of the officers circled around Rainer and Henry in a furious sprint. Henry began to cry as shouts from the press frightened him.

"Shh, buddy, it's okay. We're almost there." Rainer took the steps two at a time and kept his hand over Henry's face.

Henry's tiny fists formed tightly around Rainer's shirt. He shook in his terror. The press continually called out both of the twins' names, not certain which one Rainer had, in an effort to get them to lift the blankets.

They made it to the elevators. Henry was sobbing, and Vindico was furious.

"It's okay, buddy. We're almost to Mommy." Rainer continued to talk to him through the blanket.

"I want EE." He kicked his legs as tears soaked through his blanket.

Rainer understood only too well. He wanted Emily to soothe him. He was terrified, and Rainer, of all people, knew how incredible it felt for Emily to dissolve the terror and fill the recipient of her cast with her tender love.

"She's with Mommy. We'll be there in just a minute."

Vindico shook his head. His face was drawn in disgust. "This is sick. His mother's in the hospital, and she wants to see her kids. He wants his big sister. It shouldn't be so freaking hard to get them to her."

Rainer knew that freaking wasn't the word Vindico would've used normally, but he'd reined it in for Henry's sake. The elevator doors opened and they were met by another throng of cameras.

Vindico, Portwood, Ericcson, and several other Iodex officers all flashed their badges. They looked quite fierce as they ordered the press away. Rainer kept Henry concealed tightly in his arms and raced to Mrs. Haydenshire's room.

Two guards stepped aside to allow Rainer entrance, then blocked the door way as Rainer slid himself and Henry in through the tiniest opening he could manage.

"I won!" Keaton announced as Rainer finally removed Henry's covering.

"I want EE!" Henry wailed.

Emily rushed to him. He laid his head on her shoulder, sucked his thumb, and hid his face again.

Rainer finally took in Mrs. Haydenshire. She was propped up in the bed. She looked tired and worn, but her face held some color as she grinned at him.

"How are you?" Rainer was terrified to touch her lest he hurt something, somehow.

"I've been better." She beamed as Keaton crawled up on her chest. "Actually, now I am better." She kissed Keaton's cheeks and laughed as he leaned back to kiss her as well.

The room was full to bursting with the governor and most of the Haydenshire family, along with Adeline, Rainer, Lucy, and now the twins.

"Levi and Connor went home to change," Emily informed him.

"Mrs. Haydenshire, I'll just keep the twins in here with you, while everyone goes out for the announcement," Adeline revisited a conversation Rainer had missed.

"It's a disaster out there." He hoped to help Adeline's case.

Mrs. Haydenshire sighed. "Yes, but I don't know if we'll be able to keep them out of the cameras through the whole election."

"Lillian, I am not doing this. I'm not risking your life or theirs so I can be Crown." He gestured to all of his children.

"Stephen, please. I don't have the strength to argue with you anymore. You are running, and you are going to win, because this Realm needs you more now than ever before. I will be fine. Our children, including this one,"—she gestured to her stomach—"will be fine. I know it. I can feel it, and I'm never wrong, so please."

No one argued. They all knew it would fall on deaf ears. Patrick began pacing. Lucy eyed him nervously.

"Uh, Mom, Dad," he stammered. Governor and Mrs. Haydenshire shared a concerned glance.

"Yes, son?" Governor Haydenshire drew a deep breath. Patrick reached to take Lucy's hand.

"Well...we, uh, we..." What little color had returned to Mrs. Haydenshire's face quickly faded as everyone waited with bated breath.

Patrick gave a determined nod. "We eloped Saturday."

No one spoke, though everyone's mouths fell open.

The governor's eyes closed in defeat. He rubbed his temples. "Was there any particular reason you chose to get married without your family being there?"

Rainer braced as Emily continued to sway Henry. They shared a knowing glance.

"No, sir," Patrick answered the unspoken question of whether or not Lucy was expecting.

"Okay." Governor Haydenshire looked somewhat relieved.

"Patrick!" Mrs. Haydenshire looked stunned. "Son, I would like to have seen you two get married. You're my child."

"I know, Mom," Patrick offered apologetically. "But, Friday, I was finally named partner in the Senate Housing and Realtor office. And actually, I'm planning on going into business on my own. I've been handling yours and Dad's rental properties for several years now, and I needed to grow up. We wanted to start a life on our own. I'm going to start buying my own properties. I've been planning to do this for a while. You have enough to deal with without me still living at home, and we didn't want a media circus." He gestured to the crowd out the tiny window in Mrs. Haydenshire's room.

"We just want to be married," Lucy whispered. "I'm sorry, Mrs. Haydenshire."

"So, the renters in the house on Davenport Lane moved out Friday, and we're going to move in there. Saturday morning, we got Governor Vindico to sign and cast the certificate for me, but he said that I had to tell you by tomorrow or that he would tell you, and now we're married." Patrick looked relieved to have admitted all of this.

"You stayed at Mom and Dad's alone on your wedding night?" Garrett stared at Patrick like he'd grown four heads.

"Garrett," Mrs. Haydenshire scolded.

"What? I'm just saying…who does that?"

"Well, congratulations, I suppose," Governor Haydenshire offered, though he still looked shocked.

Lucy smiled timidly. "We still want to help out with the election as much as you need us to. We just thought we'd been mooching off our parents for long enough."

Levi and Connor returned at that moment. They took in everyone's stunned expressions.

"What?" they quizzed simultaneously. Patrick retold the story. This time, he looked at peace with his decision as he gazed at Lucy with a grin.

With that, they each pulled wedding bands from their pockets and slid them onto their fingers.

Rainer smiled at Patrick as Lucy added a large diamond ring to the wedding band. They hadn't even really been engaged.

Governor Haydenshire slapped Patrick on the shoulder as he phoned his press agents to tell them to address Lucy as Patrick's wife when she was introduced during the press conference that afternoon.

CHAPTER 17
BATTLE LINES

By noon, the entire front parking lot of Georgetown Hospital was crawling with press from all over the Realm.

Non-Gifted people began wondering what was going on and were informed that a major celebrity was being treated in the hospital and for them to stay out of the way.

This only succeeded in keeping most of them milling about inside the hospital waiting rooms in hopes of viewing the nonexistent celebrity.

Governor Carrington, who'd decided to postpone his honeymoon until he'd joined with the Haydenshires for the announcement, was positioned at the podium.

The Haydenshire children and their significant others were arranged around Governor Haydenshire. Mrs. Haydenshire had finally agreed that she didn't want the twins exposed just yet, so Adeline stayed with the boys and tended to Mrs. Haydenshire while everyone else posed for the cameras.

Vindico, Stariff, Governor Willow, Neil Glenridge, the head of the Senteon, Anna Eleanor, the head of the Auxiliary Department, Patrice Vanzlant, the head of Senate Housing office, Medio Sawyer, the chief of staff at Georgetown, Governor Vindico, and several heads of the Senate Bank were all situated alongside the governor to show that the heads of all of the most vital Senate Departments would be supporting Haydenshire in his run for Crown.

"Logan! Logan! Logan!" rang from the press in every direction. Logan raised his eyebrows and cupped his ear indicating that he would answer a question.

"Where is Miss Parker? Have you broken up? Did your father feel that her reputation might mar his image in the upcoming election?" shouted several reporters.

"She's taking care of my mother," Logan spat. This very effectively ended that line of questioning.

A hush fell over the crowd as Governor Carrington began his speech. "As most of you know, I have decided to end my term as Crown Governor," he drawled in his deep, smooth intonation. He went on to announce that he would be supporting Governor Haydenshire in his hopes to replace him as Crown, then handed Governor Haydenshire a check for a great deal of money to go toward the campaign.

The governors were photographed repeatedly as they shook hands. Governor Haydenshire took the podium and reminded the press why he was making the announcement from Georgetown Hospital. He then publicly renounced Governor Peterson for allowing a murderer to walk the streets of the Realm. When he'd finished his speech, he introduced all of his children and their significant others.

The press went wild when he called Lucy Patrick's wife. They were visibly infuriated that they'd somehow missed one of the governor's son's weddings.

For a moment, Rainer thought that eloping seemed like a great way to go. He reminded himself of how much Emily loved to play wedding and that she had binders full of items for their ceremony that she'd been making since she was about fourteen years old.

Governor Haydenshire returned to the podium to inform the press that the family would answer a few questions.

"Where are the twins, Governor?" asked a tabloid reporter.

"The twins are safe, and I would appreciate your discretion and your help in keeping my children safe during this election process."

"How is Mrs. Haydenshire doing? Governor Peterson informed the press this morning that you're expecting another child."

"My wife is recuperating from her ordeal. She's obviously still here, or I wouldn't be making this announcement from the steps of Georgetown." He was hoping to dodge the question about the baby.

"Is she pregnant again?" called another reporter.

The governor forced a smile. "Lillian and I are expecting another addition to our family in March."

The crowd buzzed as they wrote furiously.

"Was the fetus harmed during the attack on Mrs. Haydenshire?" a reporter from *The Senteon Sentinel* shouted.

Governor Haydenshire gave a slight headshake and called, "Next question."

"Rainer, who do you think your father would back if he were alive today?"

Rainer edged forward. He kept Emily's hand in his own.

"Governor and Mrs. Haydenshire were dear friends of both of my parents, and there is no one else my dad would want to replace Governor Carrington. There is no question if he were alive today that he would fully back Governor Haydenshire, as I will do in his absence."

"Will you be contributing to the campaign, Mr. Lawson?"

"I will support Governor Haydenshire in any way he'll allow me," Rainer vowed. He'd never given much thought to financially supporting the governor's campaign. He smiled as he realized that he'd stumbled upon a way to repay the Haydenshires that they couldn't refuse.

Governor Haydenshire gave Rainer a kind smile and a nod of appreciation.

"When was the wedding, Patrick?"

"Saturday," Patrick answered. He stepped forward and pulled Lucy with him as Rainer and Emily stepped back. Lucy looked terrified, but a reporter from the *Gravity* looked extremely pleased.

"When's the baby due, Patrick?"

"We won't be starting a family anytime soon."

All of the Haydenshires couldn't quite hide their chuckling grins as the press in a collective group began erasing their plans for the next day's front page.

Several more subdued questions were asked of the governor before he declared it time for him to get back to his wife.

He asked the press to give the family a little time for rest and relaxation before they began his campaign.

Rainer noted that he skirted questions of whether or not the family would be making the annual Labor Day trip to Virginia Beach.

CHAPTER 18
POLITICS

The next day the battle lines were firmly drawn. Rainer awoke once again to Keaton's voice. This time, however, Keaton had taken the liberty of going to the kitchen first and bringing a box of Cheerios up, which he was eating by the fistful.

In effort to share with Rainer, he'd begun placing them on Rainer's forehead while he slept. Emily laughed as Rainer removed them.

Mrs. Haydenshire was to be released that evening at five and was still insistent that they were all leaving for the beach the next day.

Rainer needed to go into work to ask Vindico for the favor he needed in order to give Emily the birthday present he was planning.

Emily had insisted he go and that she could look after the twins while she got everyone packed for the beach.

Rainer had disagreed, until Lucy and Brooke had informed him that they were already off work for the Labor Day holiday and would be at the farmhouse all day to help Emily prepare for Mrs. Haydenshire's return.

Patrick and Connor had also taken the day off and would be helping out as well.

After his shower, Rainer dragged down the stairs. He let the memories wash over him. He'd showered and come down those same stairs his entire adolescence.

Emily, Brooke, Will, Patrick, Garrett, Lucy, and Connor were staring at a newspaper on the kitchen table.

"Oh no," Rainer sighed. Will moved so he could see.

Do We Really Want to Trust the Realm to Someone With so Little Self-Control?

was the bold headline. It was a quote from Governor Peterson's announcement speech. The point was illustrated with a large picture of the Haydenshire family and Rainer, minus the twins, as it had been taken many years before they were born.

The paper had purchased the photo from the professional photographer who had taken the shot. It showed the family in a state of relative discord.

The kids were looking away or giving each other bunny ears, and it was obviously not a shot Mrs. Haydenshire would ever have purchased.

Only Governor and Mrs. Haydenshire were looking at the camera and smiling. It made them appear slightly dimwitted and indicated that the children were overwhelming.

The governor's speech was printed, and he'd taken numerous swipes at Governor Haydenshire's inability to keep his hands off of his wife.

He'd gone so far as to state that Governor Haydenshire had no abstention and would therefore be ineffective and worthless as the Crown. He'd even joked that the Realm would have to add a personal staff member to the Crown whose sole job would be to pull Governor Haydenshire from the bedroom when he needed to try a case.

Sickening fury washed over Rainer as he shook his head.

"Dad's speech is here," Emily pointed to another page. The headline read...

Do We Want a Governor who Allows Murderers to Walk the Realm?

"And someone handed me *this* when I went into the Senate this morning to get a few things from my office." Will slapped down a brochure printed up by Peterson with shots of the Haydenshire children in many varying, compromising positions.

Rainer and Emily's belly shot was in there along with Connor's reprimand by the academy governing board for saran-wrapping the Auxiliary Order's campus building.

Will and Garrett's photos were in there from more than a decade before. They were stumbling out of Anglington's Bar and attempting to fall into a cab. Will had missed and landed on the concrete just in time for a reporter to snap the shot.

Pictures of Levi's mug shot from when he'd been arrested for his car being clocked going over a hundred and thirty miles an hour.

There was another of Garrett surrounded by bikini-clad women at the beach, all admiring his vast ink work.

There was an ultrasound photo of a fairly developed fetus, obviously not the Haydenshires' eleventh child, with the caption, "And another on the way."

The implication was the same. If Governor Haydenshire can't control his children, how can he control the Realm? The last photo was of Samantha, holding up her academy diploma and smiling in her cap and gown from graduation.

"Lachland Peterson, a man with the right kind of family values," was the caption.

"The polls still have Dad ahead by a good bit, so I guess we'll see," Will concluded.

"I knew he would do this. I knew Grandpa was right." Furious tears threatened Emily's eyes.

"Hey, we have the court documents where Stariff nailed Samantha for lying to the press and the courts about having a relationship with Rainer. If Peterson wants to treat Dad like a game, we'll show him how it's played," Garrett snarled.

Rainer nodded adamantly. The need to defend the governor washed over everyone in heavy doses.

"No, we need to wait this out. Save some stuff for closer to the election," Emily strategized. "The whole thing is going to be vicious, obviously."

She turned and laid her head against Rainer's chest. He kissed her forehead and inhaled the scent of her. He missed their bed, their home, and being alone with her.

He allowed himself a minute to feel the spark again. He would never let the Haydenshires down by not helping when he was needed, but he hoped to get to spend a little time alone with Emily during their beach trip.

He knew he would be stuck in a room with most of Emily's brothers, and she with their girlfriends, so Rainer doubted if he'd see much of her at all.

∼

Garrett and Rainer decided to ride into Iodex together. Rainer still needed Will and Brooke's help with the present he was planning, but their Monday evening plans had obviously fallen to the wayside the day before in light of Mrs. Haydenshire's hospitalization.

Vindico seemed pleased Garrett and Rainer had come in. Though he offered for them to return home, they both said they needed to get some work done since he'd given them Thursday and Friday off.

"Any word on the baby?" Vindico asked Garrett quietly.

Garrett shook his head. "It's still too early, way too early to tell if she'll be able to keep it. It'll be weeks before they know anything. Mom keeps insisting that she and the baby are fine and, I mean, she's birthed ten and miscarried three, so she would know."

Vindico looked truly devastated for the Haydenshires. An Iodex officer, not from the Elite force, walked in studying one of the brochures Peterson was handing out.

Vindico's eyes narrowed. "Steadman, I sure as hell can't tell you who to vote for, but I won't have that kind of shit in my office." He pointed to the offending brochure.

Steadman's eyes goggled. "I'm not voting for Peterson. Are you crazy? He tried to have me kicked out of the academy because my parents couldn't afford it, and I went on scholarship. Some idiot just handed me this on my way in." He tossed the brochure into the trash.

Rainer couldn't quite hide his smile as he wondered just how many toes Governor Peterson had stepped on in his belief that the Gifted with money were somehow better than those with less, and that even those with less were somehow more valuable than any Non-Gifted person.

Eventually Rainer worked up the courage to go into Vindico's office and present him with his request. By five o'clock, Rainer was ecstatic that Vindico had not only agreed but had struck a deal that seemed to please them both.

"Em's gonna flip." Garrett grinned as Rainer explained the deal he'd worked with Vindico. He was too excited not to tell anyone.

"That is definitely my plan." Rainer chuckled as he drove toward the hospital to help the security team get Mrs. Haydenshire out without incident from the press.

It was after seven when they all arrived at the farmhouse.

Emily was glowing. She and Connor had cleaned the entire house. Lucy and Brooke had fixed a tremendous meal while Levi and Patrick had entertained the twins outside all day and brought in the last of the garden harvest and then prepared it for fall and winter. The Haydenshires were visibly moved by their children's efforts.

Governor Haydenshire settled Mrs. Haydenshire into her recliner and made her a tray of food while all of the children did everything they could to make her comfortable.

"I clearly should visit the hospital more often," she teased, but everyone saw the worry and the fear in her rhythms that she tried to cover in the joke.

CHAPTER 19
GARRETT

The next afternoon, Rainer, Logan, and Garrett glanced at the clock constantly. Five o'clock seemed elusive. The clock moved slower with each passing minute. They were all eager to get away from Arlington and to get to the beach.

Even if Mrs. Haydenshire was still tired and weak, they were all desperate for a change of scenery and to view their respective significant others in nothing but bikinis and cutoff short-shorts for the next five days.

Rainer and Logan had debated renting their own condo, so they could sleep with Emily and Adeline, but Mrs. Haydenshire had teared up the night before and gone on and on about how happy it made her to have all of her kids back under one roof at the beach house again. They'd quickly nixed the idea.

Vindico emerged from his office at a quarter 'til.

"I still think you're crazy, man," Garrett goaded. Vindico rolled his eyes. "Think about it. Labor Day weekend with dozens of strippers on Chincoteague." Garrett was in awe of what Vindico had turned down, even if he couldn't reconcile Vindico dating Bridgette just for information.

She'd invited Dan to go with her and several of the girls from The

Tantra for the weekend in a hotel on Chincoteague Island. He'd turned her down hard, according to Garrett.

"Yeah, a weekend getaway is a little more commitment than I'm looking for. Trust me, I spend as little time with all of that as I possibly can."

"You could come with us. Chloe's usually up for several rounds." Garrett gave a macho laugh as Rainer and Logan's mouths fell open in shock.

Vindico shuddered. "First, I don't mess with Gifted girls. You know that. Second, that's sick, man. If you want to share her, dump her. And third, I sure as hell don't want your sloppy seconds."

"Dumping her would indicate that I'd made some kind of commitment to her, and I am not about that life." Garrett shuddered as if the idea disgusted him. "So, you're just gonna work the last weekend of summer?"

"That's my plan. I get so much done when you yahoos aren't here getting on my nerves."

"Whatever. Some of us have better priorities—like getting laid this weekend."

Vindico looked amused. "Yeah, because a family vacation to Virginia Beach with your entire family, which no offense, is *huge*, is a great way to get lucky."

"Dude," Garrett scoffed, "I've been on this trip with my folks every year of my life. I've also gotten laid every Labor Day weekend since I was sixteen years old, and every year it's been a different girl, or girls, so…" He waggled his eyebrows and held his hands out as a mock scale. "Work," he lowered his right hand slightly. "Or tapping several hotties in bikinis?" He lowered his left hand significantly. "Yeah, I'll take the beach."

"It is astounding to me that any woman would ever sleep with you, honestly."

Garrett laughed. He didn't seem to mind the assessment.

"You two have fun," Vindico offered Logan and Rainer who were still reeling from everything Garrett had just informed them of.

"You,"—he gestured to Garrett—"try not to get a venereal disease while you're there, or at least acquire one that won't require you to miss work while you're being healed."

"Yeah. Been there done that. It sucked."

Rainer couldn't believe what he was hearing. He'd always known Garrett was wild and liked to play fast and loose with women on a regular basis. He'd just never heard him discuss it so flippantly.

∼

On the way home, Rainer still shuddered anytime any of Garrett's stories filtered back through his conscience. He walked Emily out to the Mustang after their final practice until after the holiday.

"What's wrong?" Emily immediately sensed Rainer's disgust.

"Your brother is kind of a jerk, no offense."

"Garrett? Oh, yeah, I know."

"You have no idea," Rainer assured her. He was beyond certain if she knew half of what he'd just heard, she would've told him.

"I bet I know more than you think because Chloe enjoys telling all of us about their wild sexcapades on a regular basis, but what did he say?"

Rainer shook his head. He couldn't repeat half of what he'd heard. Not to Emily, anyway.

"Come on, I'm a big girl, and I've heard some extremely disturbing things from Chloe already. So tell me."

Rainer filtered through all of the information Garrett had shared with such ease.

"Did you know Garrett's been banging different women every Labor Day weekend that we've gone on this trip since we were, like, six?"

"No, but that doesn't surprise me."

"I don't even know how that happens. I couldn't even,"—he stopped himself from stating what he'd tried to do to Emily on the beach at Buoy's—"without getting interrupted," he picked back up. "How is he having sex-fests the entire weekend without your parents ever figuring it out?"

"That's what he does whenever he's not with us, and if you think about it, that's a lot of the time. He shows up wherever Mom and Dad want us to eat dinner, but he's not with us on the beach most of the day. Then he disappears right after dinner and then sneaks in late at night."

"Did you know he got some kind of STD while we were there a couple of years ago?"

Emily rolled her eyes. "I certainly hope Peterson doesn't find that out, but Chloe's coming with us this year, so he won't be out banging anyone who'll lie still for him this time at least." Rainer couldn't tell her what Garrett had said about Chloe.

As Rainer exited the interstate, he turned back to Emily. He didn't want to think about Garrett anymore.

"Are we going to our house or the farmhouse, sweetheart?"

"I talked to Mom a little while ago. She sounds much better. She said for us to go home and finish packing and then head on. She and Dad left a few hours ago."

Rainer turned down their driveway. Logan and Adeline were loading the Hummer with their bags. They'd decided to drive down together, since there were so many cars going. As Rainer helped Logan load up his and Emily's bags, they talked about Garrett.

Disappointment rocked through Rainer. He'd known for a long time that Garrett was a bit of a womanizer, and he'd heard the tales of his escapades on more than one occasion.

But Garrett was an outstanding officer and always there when his family needed him. He was fiercely protective of Emily and always took excellent care of all of his siblings. He helped whenever his mother needed help.

Rainer couldn't seem to reconcile the two sides of the one guy who'd been one of his heroes since his childhood. He'd taught Rainer to drive a stick and had gotten Logan, Rainer, and Emily out of trouble on numerous occasions. He was doing an outstanding job training Logan and Rainer in the ways of the Elite Squadron.

He'd healed Emily's hickey for them and never told her parents. He'd covered for Rainer and Logan on a campout once when they'd had a little too much to drink and were too young to be drinking in the first place. Of course, he was also the one who'd supplied them the beer, Rainer recalled wryly.

"Do you want me to drive the first half?" Logan's offer shook Rainer from his reverie.

"Only if you won't flip if we make out in the back," Emily teased.

Adeline laughed as Logan rolled his eyes.

Rainer threw Logan the keys. Even if they didn't make out, he wouldn't mind just hanging out with Emily, and he knew she liked to sleep in his lap on a road trip.

Emily added her makeup bag to the stack of luggage, and Rainer slammed the back door.

They checked the guesthouse to make certain they'd turned off all the lights and had everything they would need, and then they all piled into the Hummer.

CHAPTER 20
THE THIN LINE

Logan pulled through a drive-thru and ordered everyone dinner, then went to the gas station. He sat in the driver's seat once he'd turned off the car.

"What, you're not filling my car up for me even though I'm letting you drive it?" Emily teased.

"Tell your sugar daddy to get your gas."

Rainer laughed as he climbed out and filled up the Hummer. He and Logan went into the gas station to stock up for the drive. They set off listening to the radio and talking.

Rainer supplied Emily with all of the pickles from his chicken sandwich.

"Aww, you deserve a kiss." She leaned and brushed a sweet kiss on his cheek.

"I think I deserve more than a kiss," Rainer teased, just to annoy Logan.

"Okay stop, and on that note," Logan huffed, "am I the only one who thinks Patrick and Lucy got married just so they can have the other bedroom?"

Governor Haydenshire had allowed all of the Haydenshire boys to bring their significant others with them on this trip for the last several years. He'd also given them strict room assignments.

Will and Brooke got one of the rooms with a king-size bed. The Haydenshires and the twins were staying in their usual room. The room with a double bed and a foldout was given to Patrick and Lucy.

This meant that Logan, Rainer, Garrett, Levi, and Connor were sharing one room and that Emily, Adeline, Katie, Sarah, and Chloe were sharing the other.

The girls were excited about this. Emily had informed Rainer that they viewed it as an extended sleepover. The boys, who all were rather accustomed to sleeping with one of the girls on a regular basis, save maybe Connor, were not. Rainer wasn't certain how far Connor had gotten with Katie yet.

Rainer and Emily had discussed spending some of their time on the long weekend looking for a beach house for the two of them to purchase. They were going to try to be discreet, since Mrs. Haydenshire's emotional state had been fragile since she'd come home from the hospital.

Emily curled up in Rainer's lap after they finished their dinner, and he played with her hair and grinned at her as she discreetly caressed him and then pulled her hand away so Logan and Adeline never knew what she was doing.

Rainer ached for her, but would never ask her to stop even though he knew there was no way he would be able to be with her for the next several days.

That knowledge combined with her hand tracing over his crotch was incredibly frustrating. She fell asleep after a little while, and Rainer reclined slightly and let his eyes close as well.

He awoke after a while and offered to drive. He felt bad he'd fallen asleep. Adeline was out in the front seat and Logan had no one to talk to.

"No, it's okay," Logan whispered. "Why don't you just keep Em asleep if you can. That way she won't freak on the bridge." Emily's near-fatal car accident on a bridge in Arlington tended to make her extremely nervous on bridges in general.

"Thanks. You're the best." He draped a quilt over Emily and cossetted her tenderly in his lap and sent soothing pulses of his energy through her bare shoulder. She sank into a deeper sleep.

"She's still exhausted from staying with Mom so long." Logan gestured his head toward Adeline.

"What she did was incredible," Rainer vowed.

Logan's immense love and pride settled in his eyes. "Yeah, she is pretty incredible."

Logan pulled up to the beach house just after ten, and Rainer woke Emily.

"Hey there, baby. We're here." He ran his hands under the quilt he'd covered her with. He let them caress and explore until she was grinning broadly.

"I didn't mean to sleep the whole way." She yawned.

"S'okay," Rainer assured her as she sat up and they began unloading. Connor and Katie had already arrived, as had Will, Brooke, Patrick, and Lucy. Levi, Sarah, Garrett, and Chloe were still en route.

Mrs. Haydenshire and the twins were already asleep, and Governor Haydenshire demanded absolute silence.

Rainer and Logan threw their bags into the boys' designated room without any real enthusiasm.

"It's gonna be a long, long weekend," Logan lamented.

Garrett and Chloe arrived a few minutes later. They were already planning on everyone going to a dance club in town. Connor and Katie agreed. Rainer studied Emily. He wondered if she'd want to go but hoped she wouldn't.

"If you want to go, you can, but I'm going to need to wake your mom up to do her blood pressure and to cast the baby in a little while," he heard Adeline inform Logan. Rainer couldn't get over how confident she sounded.

Logan gave her an adoring smile. "I really don't think either of us need to be in too many bars or clubs until we get everything settled with your mom. It's not you alone on anything ever again." Her entire being glowed as she beamed at him.

"Let's just stay here with Logan and Adeline. We can go hang out on the beach," Emily urged.

"That sounds perfect." Rainer was relieved.

Governor Haydenshire listened as plans were made. Levi and Sarah joined the dance club crowd as soon as they arrived.

Garrett tried repeatedly to get Will to go along, since Brooke had fallen asleep in one of the recliners. He called them old just to goad his big brother.

"Yeah, that's what I'm going to do. I'm going to leave my wife, who is completely exhausted from being six months' pregnant with my child, to go to a dance club with hundreds of drunk women so that I can make her feel insecure and unstable as she continues to expand because she is bringing my daughter into this world." Will rolled his eyes. "Seriously, you can't be that much of a moron."

"This is why I will never get married. It clearly sucks all the fun out of everything."

Soon, Logan and Rainer were carrying quilts out to the beachfront, as the girls donned cut-offs and T-shirts.

"This is way better than some smoky bar." Emily lay down on the quilt beside Rainer. She cuddled up next to him and stared up at the moon.

"Definitely." Logan rolled slightly with Adeline on her back and began making out with her.

Rainer turned on his side as he didn't really want to watch the show, but he also didn't mind engaging Emily in a few kisses either.

"Hey, man, you know there's a whole wide beach out here," Rainer hinted. Logan rolled back.

"Yeah, I know, but this is the beachfront that we own, and I don't plan on giving Peterson any other pictures for his brochures, so looks like you'll be cleaning your own pipes this week," Logan huffed.

"Geez, really? You kiss your mom with that mouth?" Rainer was truly irritated with Logan's rather rude insinuation in front of Emily and Adeline. Emily knew Rainer was mad, and she tried to hide her giggle.

"I don't know what that means or I'd yell at him," Adeline offered as an apology. This only served to make Logan chuckle more.

"Okay, okay, I'm sorry," Logan offered in a halfhearted apology after a few minutes. "This is just weird." He pulled himself up into a seated position. Rainer followed suit. The girls turned and reclined in their laps.

"What's weird?" Emily quizzed, and Rainer caught the concern in her voice. Both of them were aware that something had gotten to Logan.

"I don't know."

"Come on, it's us," Rainer urged.

"I don't know. Mom just got out of the hospital, and we still don't know if there's anything else wrong," he stumbled over the words, unable to elaborate on what might be wrong with the baby. "And Peterson, and Garrett, and I don't know. I just don't really want to be here bunking with you and my brothers, no offense."

Rainer certainly wasn't offended. Adeline sat up and kissed his cheek.

"It's like everything's different." No one spoke and Logan continued, "We shouldn't be here vacationing. We should be out hunting down the cumsack who did this to Mom."

And there it was. The fury Rainer had been expecting for days had finally erupted. Logan was trying to sort through everything that had happened, and he needed help.

"You know Vindico did everything he could to track him down. He fled the country. He's back in Monterrey. Mexican Iodex had eyes on him, and they're moving in once he surfaces again. We don't have any authority there," Rainer repeated everything he'd learned from work.

"Logan," Adeline soothed, and Logan instantly turned to her. "This is what your mom wanted, sweetheart. Medio Sawyer said it would be good for her and the baby to relax. I know this is all different from the way it's been the past few years that we've come, but it means so much to her for us to be here. I think she just wants this little bit of peace before she and your dad start traveling for his campaign."

"I know."

Rainer watched him let guilt mix into the volatile cocktail of regret and remorse and the bitter feelings that came from trying to walk the thin line between being his parents' son and being his own man.

The thoughts swirled so apparently in his mind. Rainer brushed Emily's arm, then squeezed it lightly until she looked up at him. He gestured back toward the beach house. She got up off of his lap and kissed his cheek.

"Hey, Adeline, there was a product rep at the arena today, and I got some of that new coconut milk mask we saw in that bridal magazine. Come on. We can try it out while all the other girls are gone." Adeline glanced at Rainer and then back to Logan. She was on to Rainer and Emily's plan. Logan, however, looked confused that the girls were leaving after he'd just poured his heart out to them.

Adeline stood and kissed Logan's cheek. "Come kiss me good night in a little while."

Understanding shadowed Logan's features as he realized that Rainer wasn't going anywhere.

Logan nodded. Lost desperation settled harshly in his eyes as he let her hand drift through his. He watched her as she walked away.

Rainer stared up at the star-strewn sky and tried to think of where to begin. Logan was refusing to meet his gaze.

"So, not to go all Oprah on you, but it's kinda been a hell of a week or two. I know we broke up and all, but if you want to get together for coffee and talk, I think I'm probably ready for that now," Rainer teased.

Logan finally broke. He began laughing as he lay back on the quilt.

"Okay, but just coffee. You're not coming back to my place." He folded his hands behind his head. "I can't believe Garrett." He pricked the surface of the tightly strung vault of hurt and disappointment he'd been carrying.

It'd had him bound and shackled since the night his mother had been rushed to Georgetown. "He goes to Brazil all the time and works with orphans. He was named officer of the year last year when he pulled that guy out of that burning car, and that's the third time he's gotten that award. And then he comes home and bangs whoever he wants and passes his girlfriend around for other guys to do whatever they want with?"

Rainer knew that, as much as he'd always thought of Garrett Haydenshire as the coolest guy he knew, and as much as he'd looked up to him as a kid, it was nothing compared to Logan's admiration of his big brother.

He wasn't certain which was worse—to watch your parents falter, to know that they're mortal and that they can't always make everything better, or to watch your childhood heroes fall from the pinnacle of nobility erected in your mind.

Deep within Logan, in a place he kept locked tight, Rainer knew he felt his parents had let him down. They'd faltered, and nearly fallen, and the disappointment in his brother was bitter and devastating as the cold cruel world threatened to overwhelm Logan Haydenshire.

"Maybe he was just bullshitting Vindico. I know Garrett likes to party, but…" Rainer offered though he knew Garrett had done everything he'd said he had, and that everything he'd said about Chloe was true.

Logan shook his head. He knew as well.

"Okay, so he's a man-whore, but that doesn't mean he doesn't do all of those great things or that he's not a great brother." Rainer willed Logan to believe what he was saying. "Doing all of that might not be what we'd ever do, but it also shouldn't be a judgment call on his character. Everything he's doing to the women he's with, they want too." Rainer shrugged.

"I'm just in a bad mood," Logan quickly shut Rainer back out.

"Yeah, I got that much." Rainer wasn't letting him dodge it anymore. He wasn't going to stand back and watch reality eat Logan alive.

"Come on, man. It's me. I already know half of what's wrong with you. I talked you through your first time. Just spill it." Rainer reminded Logan that he'd never let him down, and he had no intention of starting now.

"It's just been a while, and everything with Mom, and work, and the election. It's getting to me." Logan stared at the sand as if it had wronged him in some way. "What if something is wrong with the baby? That's my little sister. I don't know what to do with that. I know she's had miscarriages before, but I didn't know she was pregnant until she lost them." He folded his legs in front of him and kept his gaze steadfast on the ground.

"If there's something wrong then they'll heal her, I guess. I mean, it might be rough at first, but she'll get the best medical care there is. You know that."

"If she makes it here. If Mom loses her on top of everything that happened on top of the election, I'm worried it would really do Mom in. And what if Peterson wins? What if he becomes Crown?"

There was so much Logan hadn't stated but that Rainer derived from his sentiment. He thought it was cowardly that Carrington had stepped down, and he was angry with him as well.

"I really don't think that's going to happen," Rainer eased. "Peterson is going to keep up this shit about all of us, your whole family, and I think he's digging his own grave."

"I hope."

He wondered if he should comment on Logan's admission that it had been a while.

"How long's a while?" Rainer stared out at the restless sea.

"Uh, the last time was that time we were drunk," Logan choked. He clearly wanted to talk about it, though neither of them had any intention of meeting the other's eyes.

"Is everything okay?" Rainer swirled his hand in the sand beside the quilt just to have something to do.

"I hope," he shrugged. "She works all the time and she's had some problems...like when she thought she was..." His explanation drowned in his anguish and in his embarrassment. "The medio who's gonna deliver Will and Brooke's baby is going to examine her when we get back. Vindico gave me a couple of hours off to go with her."

Rainer's heart ached. He hadn't known any of that. He'd assumed Logan and Adeline were just as active as he and Emily.

Whatever had made Adeline late a few weeks before was affecting their sex life, and Logan was lost and scared and, from the looks of it, doubting his abilities on top of everything happening with his family.

"I'm really sorry."

Logan finally met Rainer's gaze. His expression held a mix of terror and grief.

"Thanks. It was rough for a few days last week, and then she was at the hospital with Mom, but she's kind of better now." He seemed to hope Rainer would find the answer for him somewhere in the distressing details.

"And now you're stuck in the room with me."

Logan chuckled, though Rainer knew the laughter was to cover the pain.

"It just makes her kind of weak and really tired. It comes and goes, but it seems like it's happening more than it isn't. I'm really worried about her."

"I'm sure." Rainer wasn't entirely certain what Adeline was experiencing. "But she's becoming an obstetrics medio, man, so I'm betting if it was really bad she'd know what was causing it."

The fact that Adeline was a Valeduto Predilect with the power to heal her own body rapidly did make the problem all the more concerning. Whatever was causing this wasn't being healed.

Rainer was desperate to find some way to soothe Logan. He glanced back at the house as a slight grin spread across his face.

"So, whatever it is, it's gone right now?"

Logan nodded. "Yeah, she hasn't had it since the wedding, but she was with Mom in the hospital and then we were just completely exhausted when she finally got home last night after checking on Mom at the house."

"Okay, well, as romantic as I'm sure it would be to spend a little time with Adeline in a room with four sets of bunk beds, if you want to, Em and I could hang out in the living room and keep everybody out of there, if they come home anytime soon, which I seriously doubt," Rainer pointed out. "Your mom and dad are already asleep, and Will just took Brooke to bed." He pointed to the darkened living room. "It's barely eleven."

"She'd freak if she ever knew I told you any of this."

"She'll tell Em. They're probably talking about all of it right now, and I'd never ever say anything. But I saw the way she was looking at you earlier. I don't think she'd mind spending some time just the two of you."

"That'd be nice." Logan glanced back at the house eagerly.

"Go on." Rainer brushed the sand off his hands.

"If you ever say anything about how freaking fast I'm about to run into that house, I will hit you."

"I will never tell Adeline that you were jonesin' so bad for her you fell all over yourself to get back inside." Rainer cracked up as Logan hurdled over a pylon and sprinted up the planked boardwalk that led back to the Haydenshires' beach house.

CHAPTER 21
NEEDS

A little while later, Emily and Rainer were snuggling on the couch watching TV. They were both hoping Logan and Adeline were enjoying their time alone. Adeline had talked to Emily about the past few weeks as well.

She'd been worried Logan was somehow losing interest and that her health problems were making her unappealing. This made Rainer all the happier he'd made the suggestion.

But he'd probably meddled enough. Logan would soothe Adeline and vice versa while he concentrated on Emily.

Though it certainly hadn't been several weeks, the world seemed so much heavier that night than it had a week before. He finally allowed himself to admit that he needed to feel the sweet pulse of her release around him as he filled her with everything he was.

Emily was on her back. Rainer was lying on his side on the wide couch. They'd been making out rather heatedly with only the flashing images of the old TV set as their company.

She moaned as her body rolled under his. Hunger tensed in her waves. The sound set him on fire.

"What do you want, baby?" he rasped in her ear as he traced his hand under the T-shirt she had on. He caressed her stomach and felt it clench tightly and quiver in anticipation.

He slid his hands higher. She was wearing nothing but his T-shirt and a pair of thin, white, cotton panties with delicate lace detailing. The very air around them was thick with need and memories. Their energy and love spiraled in heat-filled waves around them.

"Tell me. I know we can't do anything, but, god, I want to hear you say it." He couldn't help himself. He so desperately wanted to hear her.

A loud moan echoed from her, and he quelled it with his mouth. He captured the desperate hunger with his lips.

"I want you," she panted. "I want to feel you deep inside of me. I want you to grab my hand and make me feel you throb." Her entire body trembled in her need. "I want you to touch me. I want to come in your hand. Then I want you to pound into me hard and fast."

A heavy growl tore from Rainer. He'd asked, and she'd supplied the fantasy in rapturous accord just as she always did.

No one was around. Her parents were exhausted from the hospital. No one would be getting up, and her brothers wouldn't be home for hours. The press hadn't even figured out the Haydenshires had come to the beach.

They were all alone in a house that was going to hold eighteen people. There were no cameras and no prying eyes.

Rainer finished his justifications and then let his mind fill with nothing but Emily. The heavenly way she felt when she tensed around him, milking his cock. The silken column of paradise that enveloped him, so hot and wet, that he owned.

If she wanted it then he was giving it to her. He grabbed her hand and forced her grab his steel-hard cock. Her eyes lit as she unbuttoned his shorts and slipped her fingers through the slit in his boxers.

His breath gasped from his lungs as she massaged and caressed him. He kissed her again and let the exquisite feeling of her hand on him drive him wild. She drew from his cock, pulling directly from the source of his erotic energy.

In a heated moan, he continued to whisper in her ear as she spun her fingers over the pearly need leaking from his head. If she kept it up, he was going to explode in her hands.

"I'm gonna take these off, baby, and I want you to show me how wet you are."

Her eyes flashed in deep desire as, "Yes," quaked from her lips.

He pulled off the virgin-white panties and shoved them into the pocket of his shorts. He didn't want them to be left on the floor if he should need to cover them up quickly. He traced back over her lips, swollen and tight, needing to be penetrated. He spun his finger in her opening as she bucked in need.

Her body clenched, desperate for him to push deeper, but he didn't comply.

He traced her again and felt her plump, fevered flesh. She spread her legs farther, showing him what she wanted. Her body tensed and pitched as she arched her back deeply.

"Please," she begged, and he pulsed hot and heavy in her hand. "Take me, please. I don't care who sees us. I need you."

He harnessed her erotic energy and closed her off quickly. He raised his head to make certain no one was coming from any of the doors in the house. He pulled his shorts and boxers down just enough to get the job done and hoisted her shirt up.

"Please," she continued her heated pleas. Simply unable to stop, Rainer rolled so she was under his body.

"You sure you're ready, baby? This is gonna have to be hard and fast. I don't want to hurt you." His body pleaded for hers.

"I want it hard. Just give it to me."

With that, he slipped his hand under her backside, lifted her body slightly, and pounded into her. He could recall only one other time she'd felt so tight as she took him in. And as the first time he'd had her, here in the same house, flashed through his mind, he plunged her depths.

She'd needed it for some time. She was fevered, hot, and dripping wet as he pulled away slightly and then pounded into her.

"Give it to me," he commanded in a low, fervent growl.

She clenched her jaw in effort not to scream, her back arched again as her body tugged him rhythmically, nursing away every stress they'd endured.

He threw her shirt upward and caught her breast in his mouth. He sucked in rhythm to his penetrating thrusts. She swelled, and he couldn't fight it. It had been too long.

With a final, driving, ragged plunge, he buried himself deep inside her. He slid her nipple between his teeth, and she spiraled out of control.

She clawed his back and buried her screaming moans in his chest. She convulsed and he slipped out quickly. He hoisted his shorts back up and snapped them. He pulled her shirt back down and held her tightly to him.

"Feel better, baby?" He kissed her cheek as she giggled and gave him his favorite mischievous grin.

"Oh, yeah." She made his entire month.

A moment later, she was gasping in the middle of their afterglow.

"Yay," she trilled as Rainer whimpered.

"Watch them with me, please." *Father of the Bride* with Steve Martin, Emily's all-time favorite movie, had just started on the small TV screen in the living room. The commercial preceding it stated that Part II would be on next.

Rainer had watched these movies with her dozens upon dozens of times. He chuckled as he recalled Emily asking him what a condom was and how you fastened one, a decade before when they'd watched it after their exams on the last day of school that year.

"And do I need to remain awake for it to count as watching with you?" He turned her on her side in front of him so she could see better, and he could hold her back to his chest.

"Yes, but if you're good and watch them with me, I'll make us popcorn, and I'll even let you play during the commercials." She thrust her chest out, showing him what she was offering. He cracked up as he agreed to the terms.

She scooted to the kitchen and grabbed a bag of microwave popcorn, then returned to the living room with a large bowl as the champagne bubbles began floating to the top of the screen.

"Here, you watch. I'll pop it." Rainer took the bag.

"Aww, you're the best."

"I know." He laughed as he summoned the radiant heat energy from the air around him and used the electromagnetic energy from his body. He heated the bag until all of the kernels popped, then opened it and dumped it into the bowl. "And I will not even point out how many, many, many times I have watched this movie with you."

She giggled. "All of the times I made out with you through it don't count. And,"—she threw popcorn in her mouth and swallowed before she continued—"I would like to remind you, Mr. Lawson, of the sheer number of times I've been forced to sit through *Redline* and *The Fast and the Furious* and then all of the endless others with you and Logan."

Rainer wrapped his arm back around her and waggled his eyebrows. "Hey, baby, it's not how you stand by your car. It's how you race your car."

"Would you shut up? I'm trying to watch the best movie ever."

"Oh, so sorry. Don't worry, if you missed anything, I can quote it to you." He kissed the side of her head.

CHAPTER 22
BROTHERS

As it turned out, neither of them managed to stay awake through Kimberly Williams and Diane Keaton giving birth on the same fateful night.

Rainer awoke to someone shaking him. He blinked confusedly, lifted his head, and stared into Garrett's eyes.

"Hey, man, you might want to get your hand off her ass and put her to bed. I don't think you want Dad to walk in and find you two like this with these in your pocket." He pulled Emily's panties out of Rainer's pocket. The white lace had been peeking out when they'd fallen asleep. He dropped them in Rainer's face.

Rainer sat up, grabbed her underwear, and pulled the T-shirt back down over Emily's backside where his hand had been fully on top of her exposed right cheek as they'd moved in their sleep.

Garrett chuckled and shook his head.

"Baby." Rainer kissed Emily's cheek. She stirred but grabbed his hand and wrapped it back over her. This time she landed it on her breast. "Em." Rainer jerked his hand away. Half of her brothers were watching the display.

"Ok, I will never be able to sit on that couch again." Connor pretended to gag.

"Em." Garrett leaned down and whispered sweetly in Emily's ear. "Let Rainer take you to bed before Mom and Dad get up, okay?"

She sat up with a deep yawn. Katie, Sarah, and Chloe headed to the girls' room.

"Wait!" Rainer yelped. He nearly leapt off the couch as Emily tried to determine what was happening.

Garrett started laughing again. "Em, go get Logan out of there. I don't know what Adeline's wearing."

Garrett was able to think much clearer than Rainer at the moment. Emily stood with Rainer's help and moved to the girls' room.

Logan appeared a minute later. He looked as bedraggled as Rainer felt and stumbled into the room he was supposed to be sleeping in. He collapsed on the bunk nearest to the door.

"Thanks," Rainer sighed. He owed Garrett big time.

"No problem." He followed Rainer and Levi into the boys' room. Garrett switched on the light. Logan groaned as he'd been awoken again.

Garrett shook his head. "It's like Mom and Dad have sent me to summer camp in hell." He pulled off his clothes and climbed up to the bunk above where Logan was attempting to sleep.

Rainer, Connor, and Levi laughed as they disrobed and each took another top bunk. After glancing at the clock just before he fell back asleep, Rainer noted that it was almost four in the morning and that he still had Emily's panties in his hand. He stuck them under the covers and decided to return them in the morning.

He awoke several hours later to the smell of bacon, sausage, and eggs frying. He inhaled deeply, and a broad grin spread across his face. It was the way he'd awoken the first morning of every Labor Day weekend at the Haydenshires' beach house.

For that one moment before he let his eyes drift open, it was easy to pretend all of the troublesome worries that surrounded the family he loved, the family who had made him who he was, didn't exist at all.

If Emily had been tucked up beside him—naked, he allowed, since this was his fantasy—it would have been utter perfection.

He let her words and everything that had happened the evening before on the couch reel slowly through his mind. *I want you to take my hand and make me feel you throb. I want you inside of me.*

Rainer turned quickly on his stomach as he ran her telling him exactly what she'd wanted over and over in his mind. He stifled a groan. *Take me, please. I need it.*

His heart raced. His stomach clenched tight as he gripped the corner of his pillow. The memories made him ache to feel her again. He tightened his jaw and forced himself to remember that he was in a room with four of her brothers, all in varying states of waking up.

He begrudgingly shut down the lurid fantasies of him ripping her clothes off and lowering her down onto him as she went for a ride.

Logan sat up and nearly clocked himself on the bunk Garrett was groaning in. Logan leaned out of the bunk, stood, and stretched. He yawned and shook himself slightly.

"Okay, none of you are really who I want to wake up looking at."

Rainer let his eyes open. He noted that Logan looked much more relaxed, and he was sporting his signature wry smirk.

He tried not to chuckle at how simple guys really were. Good food, good sleep, and good sex in one night, and Logan was out of his depressive doldrums and back to himself.

"Aww, come here, I'll snuggle with you," Levi mocked. He rolled his eyes at the announcement. Everyone laughed, including Logan.

Rainer debated hanging out in his bunk. Maybe if everyone else headed to the kitchen, Emily would come attempt to get him out of bed.

"All of you leave. I want Sarah to come wake me up," Levi commanded. The audible huffs from around the room let Rainer know everyone had the same basic plan.

"Whatever, man, I'm the oldest. You leave. Chloe has an insatiable sex drive. She gets cranky," Garrett bragged as gagging groans issued from the bunks.

"Obviously," Levi huffed.

Rainer wondered what he'd witnessed. Levi pulled up on his forearms.

"You two got lucky last night, so out." He pointed to Rainer and

Logan. "You and Chloe got us thrown out of The Cave last night for doing it in the women's restroom," he spat disgustedly.

"And you and Katie haven't been dating long enough for you to be doing her yet," he commanded Connor. "So out, and tell Sarah I miss her."

"Geez," Connor quipped. "Chloe's not the only one who gets cranky."

Connor, Rainer, Logan, and Garrett slid from their bunks. Levi didn't appear to be joking. After throwing on swim trunks and T-shirts, they traipsed out of the bedroom and headed down the long hallway into the kitchen.

Mrs. Haydenshire looked thrilled to be cooking breakfast for her family, though exhaustion still plagued her eyes.

Governor Haydenshire was beaming at her, but he was also hovering close and helping at every turn.

Emily was mixing batter for pancakes. She glowed as Rainer made his way to her and kissed the top of her head. Katie and Adeline were setting the table.

The twins were watching cartoons in the living room.

It was idyllic, and Rainer felt his shoulders lower and his breaths ease. He hoped against hope that the Haydenshires could have their usual vacation to relax and be restored before the impending storm crashed in again.

Mrs. Haydenshire grinned at the boys as they moved into the kitchen. "Where's Levi?" she asked as she flipped bacon and sausage with ease.

Sarah and Chloe must've still been sleeping, Rainer assumed, as he heated the griddle for Emily with his hand.

Connor slapped Logan on the arm with a delighted smile. "He's still in bed, Mom. I don't think he was feeling all that well last night."

Logan coughed to cover his laugh.

"Please tell me he's not hungover," Governor Haydenshire demanded. "The press will eventually figure out we decided to come down here. I need you all to stay out of the papers."

Garrett joined in. He feigned concern.

"Oh no, Dad. We didn't have but a few beers. No one overdid it, but Levi looks rough."

"Yeah, I think he might be coming down with something," Logan sealed the deal.

Concern colored Mrs. Haydenshire's face as she wiped her hand on a dishcloth and moved from the stove. "Honey, watch that bacon. I'll check on him." She headed down the hall as Governor Haydenshire took over.

Rainer, Logan, Garrett, Connor and eventually Patrick and Will, who followed the boys having figured out that something good was going on, edged down the hallway a few paces behind Mrs. Haydenshire.

She knocked on the door to the boys' bedroom but then opened the door without waiting on a response. Everyone took a few more steps toward the door and strained to hear.

"Hey, baby, come here. I have something I need you to take care of for me," Levi drawled. His voice was low and excited.

"Oh, really, and what might that be, son?" Mrs. Haydenshire spat as everyone in the hallway fell over laughing. Rainer heard the mattress on Levi's bunk squeak quickly as he turned and gasped, "Mom!" His voice quickly turned to stunned mortification.

Logan and Rainer held onto the wall. They were laughing so hard they were blinking back tears as Will and Garrett began whistling and applauding. The raucous laughter had Chloe and Sarah emerging from the girls' room on the other end of the hall, bleary-eyed.

Garrett choked back laughter as he grinned wryly. "Oh, good, Sarah, apparently Levi has something he needs you to take care of."

The hall echoed with hysterical laughter again.

Mrs. Haydenshire issued farther into the boys' room.

"Levi Evan Haydenshire, get out of the bed and come have breakfast with your family…now!"

Everyone had moved to the hallway to see what had half of the house in hysterics.

To Rainer's horror, Mrs. Haydenshire emerged from the room with her jaw cocked to the side, glaring at him. She glided down the hallway until she was standing right in front of him with her eyebrows raised in a knowing gaze.

"I assume you were probably the person last in possession of these." She dropped Emily's panties, the ones Rainer had completely forgotten about when he'd thrown the covers back in his bunk, into his hands. His eyes goggled and blood pooled violently in his cheeks.

"If you'd just return them, sweetheart, I would appreciate it if Emily wore underwear while she's here." Mrs. Haydenshire turned her glare on Emily, who was glowing crimson in her embarrassment. With that, Mrs. Haydenshire stalked down the hallway, shaking her head.

All of Emily's brothers turned on Rainer instantly. They were still laughing.

"Man, you took her panties to bed? That's just sad." Garrett slapped Rainer's shoulder consolingly.

Rainer squeezed his eyes shut as Connor harassed, "So, is it 'caught red-handed' that I'm looking for?" He pitched the ball, and Patrick knocked it out of the park.

"No, no, I think purple-headed is what you're actually looking for."

"Shut up." Emily jerked the panties out of Rainer's hand and stalked quickly into the girls' room.

"Dude, most guys use a sock," Garrett upped the ante.

Rainer wished he could melt into the floor. Mrs. Haydenshire returned to the hall.

"All of you come and eat!" She sounded highly irritated.

Emily's brothers weren't dropping either joke as everyone found a place at the table.

Connor lifted one of the large platters of sausage and bacon at one end of the table. He handed it to Rainer. "Here, when you're done with the sausage, why don't you give some to Em?"

Emily glared at her big brother, but Rainer just shook his head. He knew if he didn't act like it bothered him they would eventually stop.

Levi sank into his chair, scowling. This made him the more appealing target for the moment.

"And is the chief of staff feeling better, or did you still need Sarah?" Garrett chanted as Chloe cracked up.

Sarah was still running several shades of red. She glared at Garrett, which only added to Levi's fury.

The Haydenshires chose to ignore the incredibly stupid comments being thrown around the table. It seemed Mrs. Haydenshire had reached her limit when Garrett informed Emily she'd need to wash Rainer's sheets for him.

Rainer rolled his eyes. He was growing weary of the insinuations. The comment was meant to trap Rainer into either demanding that he would wash his own sheets, therefore admitting that he'd done what they were teasing him about, or to say nothing, and imply that he was a complete jerk who made his fiancée do his laundry.

"Garrett Alexander Haydenshire, you may be thirty years old, son, but I can still make your life miserable, so if I were you, I'd shut it," Mrs. Haydenshire declared.

Emily shot Garrett a goading smirk and stuck her tongue out delightedly.

Garrett rolled his eyes. "I'm sure he's got something he'll let you lick, Em."

"What was that, son?" Governor Haydenshire demanded.

"Nothing, Dad," Garrett piped down and began devouring his breakfast.

CHAPTER 23
THE DEVIL YOU KNOW

Soon, everyone was out on the beach either building sand castles with the twins or playing volleyball.

Rainer and Emily were in the water riding the waves when they weren't involved running their hands all over each other or locked in a kiss.

Logan and Adeline joined them as did Connor and Katie. Connor attempted to push Emily under, but Rainer shoved him into the incoming waves instead.

Most of the families out on the beach were friends of the Haydenshires. They'd been beach neighbors for years. Some were Gifted, some were not. Many of their Gifted friends wanted to shake the governor's hand or check on Mrs. Haydenshire. They all pledged their votes to the Haydenshires, for which they expressed their deepest appreciation.

Rainer noted that Garrett and Chloe left soon after breakfast and hadn't returned. Rainer and Emily headed back to the shore to lie out and help keep up with the twins, as the Haydenshires were attracting more and more company.

The twins were chasing the outgoing tide and then squealing with delight as it washed back over their feet. The water was churning with more vigor, and a wave headed toward Henry that Rainer knew would knock him over.

Rainer sprinted through the sand and hoisted Henry into the air just before the water reached him. Emily beamed, and Mrs. Haydenshire gestured to Rainer after she placed her hand on her husband's arm to show him what he'd done.

Henry was getting tired, so he laid his head on Rainer's shoulder and began sucking his thumb though it was covered in sand.

Emily and Mrs. Haydenshire swooned, but Rainer wasn't certain what had elicited that response.

The sweet smiles disappeared as Rainer quickly tucked Henry's face into his neck. Cameras began flashing furiously.

Fury lit the governor's features as he stalked to several photographers positioned just outside the private beachfront that belonged to the Haydenshires.

With a long-range lens, they could've gotten Henry's face as he'd edged farther down the beach than Keaton.

The governor let the photographers know precisely what he thought and then ordered them off the beach.

After hearing his father shouting and being wary of the cameras after the incident at the hospital, Henry began to cry as he clung to Rainer.

"Wanna go inside, buddy?"

Henry nodded. He lifted his little head as he yawned deeply. And in that moment, they had it. They had his sweet little innocent face and then the photographers sprinted away.

Rainer threw his hand over Henry's face, but he just hadn't been quick enough.

"Take him inside," Mrs. Haydenshire demanded.

"I'm sorry."

"It certainly isn't your fault. They would have gotten him alone and falling into the water if you hadn't saved him. Imagine what Peterson would've done with that," she sighed.

He rushed Henry toward the house with Emily close behind him.

Rainer saw something move, and his head snapped to the side. His training kicked in instantly. A man dressed all in black sprinted from one of the large sand dunes near the Haydenshires' house.

Rainer summoned and threw his shield over Emily and Henry as he let his eyes sweep the house and beachfront. His heart thundered as he methodically tracked the man in black.

"Do you want me to take him in?" Emily's voice shook.

"No, there may be someone in the house. Will," he shouted as Will and Brooke and Patrick and Lucy were on the beach but still close enough to hear him.

They all turned as Rainer wrapped his arms around Emily and Henry. His shield cast spun furiously around them. It glowed a fierce green.

Will and Patrick saw his cast and sprinted up the planked walk.

"Follow that guy," Rainer ordered.

They dodged around Levi's car parked on the street, and the chase was on.

As soon as the governor reached the house, Rainer put Henry into Emily's arms. He demanded that she stay in the house, and he joined in the chase.

The man seemed to have disappeared into thin air.

They all returned to the house several minutes later, still panting.

"Who the hell was that?" Patrick demanded.

Emily was pacing and bouncing Henry. She was trying to console him, but when Rainer entered the room he threw his hands out.

Rainer's brow furrowed as he took Henry from Emily. Henry buried his face in Rainer's chest and began to calm.

"He wants you to cast him again. That's where I feel safest too." Emily kissed Rainer's cheek. Unable to determine what to do next, Rainer sank down into one of the recliners and tucked Henry safely in his shield.

An hour later, they were both asleep when an afternoon storm blew in, and everyone cleared off the beach.

Emily and her mother prepared huge pots of gumbo for dinner.

Logan, Adeline, Levi, Sarah, Connor, Katie, and Patrick all headed to a movie. Lucy wanted to stay and learn to prepare Mrs.

Haydenshire's gumbo. Nothing unusual had happened since Rainer had seen the man.

The governor paced the house and called Vindico repeatedly.

Vindico suspected that Governor Peterson had hired private detectives to follow the Haydenshires, but someone with more sinister plans was certainly another possibility.

Governor Haydenshire phoned the Gifted Associated Press and every major news source. He informed them that if any pictures of Henry's face were printed, he would make certain the cost associated would bankrupt the paper, magazine, or website.

Brooke took a nap as Will tried to track down Garrett and Chloe to warn them about the intruder. Garrett hadn't been answering his phone. Everyone who was awake checked on Keaton constantly as he napped in his crib. Rainer dozed with Henry. He was in and out as everything was going on.

When he woke, Henry was tucked up safely on his chest. Neither of them was wearing a shirt, and Rainer was fascinated to be able to feel the little guy's burgeoning energy. It was just barely noticeable as he slept.

Henry wouldn't be able to access it for many years, not until he'd gone through puberty, but it was there, slowly developing beneath the surface.

Rainer wondered if Emily had ever noticed it, but realized that she would have. She picked up on energy more readily than anyone else.

He let his mind wander, and considered what it would feel like to hold their children, to nap with them laid out on his chest, or bring them to the beach to let them feel the sand and the ocean for the first time.

Henry shifted slightly. He located his thumb again, and held it in his mouth without sucking. He wasn't awake enough for that.

Emily appeared beside the chair Rainer was reclined in. She placed a mug of coffee beside him and smiled.

"You can go put him in his crib if you want." At that moment, a clap of thunder rent the sky and shook the beach house windows. Henry tensed and clung to Rainer. He trembled in his sleep.

"Shhh," Rainer soothed. "It's okay. I've got you." Emily covered them in a quilt. A moment later, Henry's body relaxed as he continued his nap.

"I'm jealous." Emily gave Rainer an adoring grin as she sank down in the other recliner beside him and sipped her coffee.

Rainer gave a whispered chuckle and started to offer to hold her while she slept later but wasn't certain if the governor was up to hearing that kind of joking.

Knowing how much Emily hated storms, Rainer wondered if there wasn't a little bit of truth behind her joke. He felt bad that he didn't know how to soothe both of them. He could take them to one of the big beds in the house with him and hold them both, but he didn't think the Haydenshires would appreciate that either. As everyone returned from the movie, Henry stirred and sat up.

"Hi, Wainer," he beamed.

Rainer grinned at him. "Hi, Henry."

"I to ride." He pointed to the front door, ready to go to the boardwalk.

"It's raining, buddy," Rainer lamented with him, "They don't run the rides in the rain. Maybe we can go tomorrow?"

He hoped they would be able to get the boys to the boardwalk safely at some point.

"So, we were photographed going into the movie and then leaving the movie." Patrick rolled his eyes and then wrapped his arms around Lucy.

"Yeah, it's so scandalous that the Haydenshire children watch movies," Logan sounded thoroughly annoyed. "Yum, gumbo." He was distracted from his irritation as his mother piled bowls and serving spoons by the large pots of soup and told everyone to eat when they got hungry. She was putting her feet up for a little while, which everyone encouraged her to do.

Governor Haydenshire entered the living room. He was carrying Keaton who'd just awoken as well.

Henry scrambled out of Rainer's lap as Keaton met him on the floor in front of their toys. Emily fell into Rainer's now-vacant lap.

"Yeah, this is way better." Rainer listened to her giggle as he cradled her to him. She laid her head on his shoulder as most everyone lined up to fill their bowls with gumbo.

"You know," she drawled in his ear. "Guys who are so sweet and good with kids are kind of a major turn-on."

"Really?" Rainer let his hand slip up her backside.

"Really."

"I might have to cash in on that later," he explained in a low, husky, growl.

"I was hoping you would." She brushed a kiss across his lips.

"Wanna go out later?" He noted that the rain was ebbing, and being alone with her was the only thing he really wanted.

A few minutes later, Governor Haydenshire's cell phone rang, and Chloe and Garrett returned from wherever they'd been all day.

"What'd you find out, Dan?" the governor demanded.

Garrett and Chloe fell onto the couch. Emily got up and got herself and Rainer some gumbo as Garrett began his story.

"Peterson has hired private detectives to follow all of us." He rolled his eyes. "I cornered the guy, flashed my badge, threatened to arrest him for invasion of privacy, and he coughed up the goods on Peterson. Oh, and as irony for you all, he said to tell you he's voting for you, Dad," he called as Governor Haydenshire rolled his eyes. "But he's still being paid to follow all of us."

"How would you arrest him? Hiring a private detective to tail someone isn't against the law," Logan asked.

"No, but following my date into a drugstore and then threatening the sales clerk if he doesn't give you a copy of the receipt, showing what she bought, is against the law. And it just so happened that Chloe felt threatened," he mocked as Chloe poked out her bottom lip and laughed at her own dramatic abilities.

"Anyway." Garrett tousled Chloe's hair and grinned at her. "Making an Elite Iodex officer's girl feel threatened tends to end badly, so the guy was fairly forthcoming."

A minute later, Governor Haydenshire hung up the phone. "We're all being followed. Seems Peterson's hired not one but four PIs. They're assigned to all of you kids and even to your mother and me.

So, I'm begging all of you, please don't do anything you wouldn't want to be on the cover of the *Times*."

Everyone agreed that they would play nice. Rainer was relieved that it wasn't Wretchkinsides's men following them. Compared to that, he decided, private investigators really weren't so bad.

"Okay, so let's all go out and be good at the Hornbeam Festival tonight," Chloe urged.

Emily's eyes lit. She loved going to the Hornbeam. It had been a year or two since they'd attended.

The Hornbeam was a huge open beach concert that featured relatively new bands from the area, but the stage was set well out in the water and the audience situated themselves on the vast Virginia Beaches. Most of the enthusiasts brought quilts and blankets and bottles of wine or beer, and cuddled up under the stars to listen to the music.

As the bands weren't headliners by any stretch, there was usually room for each couple to have their own comfortable space on the beach without encroaching on others.

When Rainer had gone with the Haydenshires in years past, they'd always had a great time. Even Brooke seemed excited about going.

Governor and Mrs. Haydenshire shared a sweet smile.

"You all go on. We'll put the boys to bed and turn in ourselves."

Rainer doubted they would be going straight to bed, but he tried to hide his smile.

"It's really fun. No partying crowds, no bar, just a good concert out on the beach. Very subdued," Logan explained to Adeline. Emily and Rainer agreed, and Adeline seemed excited to go.

Everyone quickly helped do the dishes. They ordered Mrs. Haydenshire to remain in her chair and rest while the governor gave the twins their bath. As soon as everything was cleaned up, they began getting ready for the concert.

CHAPTER 24
EVERY STEP OF THE WAY

Emily packed several quilts while Rainer piled Dr Peppers and a few snacks into one of the coolers.

"Okay, I'm going to go change. I'm so excited!" Emily was bouncing in the kitchen. Rainer caught her hand and pulled her back to him.

"Don't be gone too long. I'll miss you." He wrapped his arms around her and kissed her until Connor and Logan began making gagging noises.

"Reminds me of the first time I kissed her...when I was eight." Rainer rolled his eyes at them, only making them laugh harder.

Emily was still beaming as she scooted off to join all of the girls in their room. "Rainer?" she called.

"Yeah, baby?"

"Can I borrow one of your white button-down shirts?"

"Uh, if you packed me one." Rainer was mildly ashamed he hadn't packed for himself and didn't really know what Emily had packed for him.

"I did."

"It's yours, sweetheart." He grabbed the quilts and cooler and headed out to the Hummer. He was growing weary of the relative immaturity that came from having all of the Haydenshire brothers together in close proximity. Apart they were all mature, respectful men. Together, they tended to revert back to their horny, teenage revelry.

He let his mind drift back to the first week of summer with just him and Emily, alone in the beach house. As much as he loved all of the Haydenshires, he wanted Emily all to himself—no private detectives, no big brothers, and, though he felt mildly guilty thinking it, no parents.

He sighed and dutifully ignored the PI parked across the street snapping pictures of him loading blankets into Emily's car.

He returned to the house and moved out of the way of Will and Patrick as they loaded their own blankets and food into their cars.

As he returned to the kitchen, he listened to Garrett explain what he was calling "the tactical maneuvers for their evening" to his younger brothers.

"Okay, so they can't take all our pictures at once, a big advantage to there being eight of us, so thanks, Mom."

Mrs. Haydenshire was lying in one of the recliners with her eyes closed. "Yes, well, that's why I did it, dear."

"So, we're going to use a breakthrough and flank maneuver," Garrett explained.

Logan rolled his eyes. "You have been hanging out with Grandpa way too damn long."

Levi nodded his agreement. "So, you don't want us all to sit together. Done. Let's go."

According to Emily, Sarah was mortified, not only with what Levi had inadvertently said to Mrs. Haydenshire that morning, but angry that Levi believed she would've done that with his entire family waiting on them to eat breakfast.

She'd been giving Levi the cold shoulder most of the day, and it appeared that cuddling her into a better mood at the concert was his only concern.

He'd gone to Emily for advice on how to do just that, and in exchange, he promised he would not join in with Connor and Garrett's continued jokes about Rainer sleeping with her underwear.

Emily had given him clear instructions on how to get Sarah to forgive him. Rainer and Logan had also paid close attention for future reference.

Governor Haydenshire returned to the living room with the twins. One was dressed in Superman pajamas, the other in Batman. They began running around the living room, making the attached capes whirl out behind them.

Governor and Mrs. Haydenshire chuckled as they continued to gaze at one another adoringly.

Governor Haydenshire's smile faded as soon as Emily entered the living room, accompanied by Adeline and Sarah. The girls had all been planning on going out while on vacation and were dressed thusly.

Rainer's mouth watered as he took in Emily. She, however, looked terrified as her father glared at her outfit. Rainer assumed she'd planned to slip out while he was still giving the boys their bath. He just couldn't seem to remember how to speak as she was standing there in a gorgeous black bikini that had her ample cleavage on full display.

She'd added Rainer's white button-down, only it was open and the tails were tied up under her breasts, adding to their heft.

Her midriff was bare and the black bikini bottom was covered in a white eyelet skirt. Though it came almost to her midthigh, the patterned eyelet holes throughout the fabric made it an entirely see-through bathing suit cover.

And to her father's horror, her tattoo of Rainer's crest was on full display, accented quite nicely by the black bathing suit, juxtaposed with the white shirt and skirt.

Rainer fished around in his head, trying to remember how to make his lower jaw reconnect with his upper. He braced for the incoming fury.

It hadn't been lost on him that Emily had worn a one-piece swimsuit when they'd been on the beach earlier, but he hadn't commented. He didn't want her to ever think she had to wear bikinis for him, though he knew they were her preference.

With everything going on, he'd decided she could show off the tat whenever she was comfortable with it. As long as he got to see it on a regular basis, that was all that mattered to him.

"Damn, that's just mean." Garret slapped Rainer on the shoulder, clearly hoping Chloe was wearing something equally as revealing.

"What...exactly...is that?" Governor Haydenshire demanded. Gall burned in his eyes.

"Stephen," Mrs. Haydenshire warned, though it didn't appear the governor could even hear his wife.

"Rainer, stop drooling and go help her." Will shoved Rainer forward with an urgent whisper.

Rainer moved to Emily's side.

"I asked you a question, young lady," Governor Haydenshire snarled.

"What is what?" Emily's temper flared as quickly as her father's. Rainer shuddered and took her hand.

"Emily!" The governor moved inches from her face. "What is this right here on your hip?" He drove his index finger into Emily's hipbone. Rainer's shield pulsed in fury.

Without really thinking, he caught the governor's hand. "Sir, please."

Governor Haydenshire seemed to realize what he'd been doing, and he forced his own hand down in a tightly clenched fist.

"And for that matter, why can I see your hip bone, young lady?" he continued fuming.

Emily's eyes narrowed. "That is the Lawson crest. I believe you've seen it before. You know, it used to hang all over the Senate when Rainer's dad was Crown."

"Emily," Rainer warned through his teeth. He prayed she would calm down.

Governor Haydenshire's eyes flashed dangerously. "Yes, I have seen it!" He turned his glare momentarily on Rainer. "My question is, why is it on you?"

"Because I had it tattooed there."

Mrs. Haydenshire sighed as she moved to her husband's side. "Stephen, she will be twenty years old in just a few weeks. She can tattoo anything she wants, anywhere she wants."

"I don't give a damn how old she is. She will not tattoo his crest on her...body," the governor choked back what he was about to call the part of Emily that bore the tattoo. "And she will leave this house dressed in that outfit over my dead body."

Taking a moment to draw a steadying breath, Mrs. Haydenshire tried to negotiate.

"Emily, honey, I don't think that outfit is appropriate for the Hornbeam concerts. You can wear it as a cover-up for the beach, but not for a concert."

Governor Haydenshire spun and glared at his wife. "She will wear that never." He turned back to Emily. "And I still want to know what possessed you to brand his family crest right beside your..." He gestured his hand to Emily's crotch, still unable to think of a word for the exact placement of Rainer's crest. "There," he fumed.

"Dad, come on." Will stepped in. He took Governor Haydenshire by the shoulders and ushered him away from Emily's face. "I have Brooke's name on my chest." He pulled down the deep V-neck of the T-shirt he was wearing to bare a large tattoo of Brooke's name and their wedding date, done very artfully across his left breastplate.

Rainer debated asking Emily to change. He hoped her giving in on the outfit might make her father get over the tattoo, but the governor had pushed her too far.

He saw the defiant determination flare in her eyes. She wasn't backing down. Her fingers customarily slipped her hair over her right ear and she narrowed her eyes.

"Brooke's got all of our dates on her ankle and my name on her..." Will halted abruptly. His eyes goggled in the effort. Wherever Will's name was, it wasn't somewhere any of the family had seen. This, however, did nothing to quell the governor's fury.

He glared angrily at Rainer. "What? It wasn't enough to put your ring on her and take her innocence. You had to brand her too?" Disbelief rang through the room. Rainer felt like he'd been punched. His stomach clenched tightly as if he'd actually been hit.

"Daddy!" Emily gasped.

"Come on, Dad." Connor moved into the room to step in for Rainer. His expression was irate. "Rainer didn't even know what she

171

was doing. This was all Em. She designed the whole thing. Rainer had nothing to do with it."

Governor Haydenshire rolled his eyes in mocking disbelief.

Garrett stepped up to bat next. "That was low, Dad. I know you're stressed, and that Em's your baby girl, or whatever, but lay off Rainer. He's never done anything to her she didn't ask him to do. He's a good guy, and he takes excellent care of her. She's not a baby anymore. You didn't freak like this when I had my whole chest inked all at once."

"That is different!" Governor Haydenshire spat. "You are not Emily, and all Rainer has done is force her into his bed."

"Right!" Emily shoved Rainer and her brothers out of her way. Furious tears pricked her eyes. "It's fine for Will and Garrett and Patrick and Levi to have them wherever they want them, but not me because I'm your baby girl. And if I decide I do want one, then it must be Rainer's fault because I'm not intelligent enough to make my own decisions about my body. Well, guess what?" Her eyes flashed heatedly inches from her father's face. "I am not your *baby*! I'm all grown up, and I can have sex, and I can get his crest tattooed on places I let him see, and touch, and feel all the time, whenever I want him to. And I can wear whatever I want, whenever I want to, and you can't stop me!"

Governor Haydenshire staggered back. He looked as if Emily had just backhanded him. Everyone in the house was absolutely silent. Rainer was reeling from the things she'd just informed her father of.

Emily took another step toward her father, utter hatred etching her face as she dealt the final blow.

"And do you know what we're going to do right now? We're leaving and we won't be back." She grabbed the keys to the Hummer and flew out the door.

"Emily, wait!" Rainer ran after her but halted abruptly in the kitchen. "Sir, if you ever want to see her again, you need to go apologize and make this right, because I've never seen her so angry. You had no right to say what you said to her and to treat either of us like this. And if she asks me to take her away,"—Rainer wasn't able to believe what he was about to say to the people who had raised him and given him so much, but he continued in a heartbroken whisper—"then I will."

With that, Rainer shook his head and focused on Emily as he rushed to the garage. She was leaning against the door of the Hummer sobbing.

"Baby," he wrapped her up in his arms and let her cry as he tried to soothe her. "Shhh, it's okay. You know he didn't really mean any of that." He held her tight, well aware they were being photographed.

"I want to leave and never come back." She convulsed in Rainer's arms. She was crying so hard Rainer could no longer see the individual tears. They fell in vicious waves. She could hardly breathe.

"Okay, I'll take you anywhere you want to go. Just give me the keys," he instructed in a soothing intonation.

She thrust the keys into his hands as he tried to think of some way to make her and her father see eye to eye, on something that just didn't seem like it should divide a family.

He continued to hold her, in no hurry to drive her away. He desperately hoped her father would come to his senses. The door from the house opened, and Rainer turned as Emily buried her face farther into his chest.

Logan stalked out and shared a knowing glance with Rainer.

"Is she okay?"

Rainer gestured his hands to her sobbing in his arms. The question didn't really require any other response.

"Dad wanted me to see if you'd come back inside, Em." Logan seemed worried that he was about to be the recipient of Emily's next infuriated rant. She shook her head combatively into Rainer's chest.

"Logan, man, he went way too far this time. He needs to come to her."

"Yeah, that's what I told him, but I don't want you to leave. Please, you're my favorite sister," he tried for a joke but it was too late for that.

They could hear shouting coming from inside the house. Rainer held out, hoping that Governor Haydenshire would come around. Currently Will, Garrett, and Mrs. Haydenshire were letting him know what an absolute ass he was being.

"Em, please," Logan begged. "Listen, I don't know what's gonna happen with the election, or the baby, or with Adeline. I don't know anything. But I do know that I don't want you and Rainer to leave. I told you Dad would flip. You wouldn't listen, but he'll get over this, and, believe me, you definitely made your point. You need your family, and if you don't need us, we do need you and Rainer. You're not just my sister," he admitted with a hint of disdain, "you're one of my best friends."

With that, Emily pulled away from Rainer and fell into Logan's arms still sobbing. Her tears didn't just wound Rainer. The look on Logan's face was sick as well.

"I'm so sorry, Emily Anne." Logan, Rainer, and Emily all spun, shocked to hear the harrowing pain in Governor Haydenshire's desperate plea. "Please, baby girl, please, come back inside and hear me out. I can't tell you how sorry I am, and then if you want Rainer to take you away," he choked as tears fell from his eyes as well. He clenched his jaw and willed them away. "Then I won't try to stop you." The excruciating offer seemed to rob the governor of breath.

"I'm not your baby girl!" Emily screeched. Her voice echoed around the garage in harrowing repercussions.

"Em," Rainer soothed. The horrific pain on her father's face made his heart ache.

"Okay, I know," Governor Haydenshire stammered. His voice was distant and terror-filled. "You're a grown woman, and I know that."

"Do you?"

"I do. It's just not the easiest thing for me to remember, mainly because I'm just so afraid of losing you."

Logan kept his arms protectively around his little sister.

"Please, believe me, I heard and understood everything you just shouted at me, and all I'm asking is for you to let me apologize and try to explain why I acted that way."

"Fine." Emily spun out of Logan's arms and edged toward her father. "But we're not staying here tonight."

"Okay," Governor Haydenshire stated calmly, "I understand."

Rainer and Logan shared a nervous glance as they followed Emily back into the house.

Everyone but Mrs. Haydenshire made a quick exit, either back out to the beach or to one of the bedrooms.

"I'm just gonna..." Logan pointed to the beach where Adeline was waiting. Rainer nodded as he sank onto the sofa beside Emily to await her father's explanation.

Her fury seemed to come in waves. Renewed sobs shattered through her. She fell back onto Rainer's chest as he wrapped his arms around her. He doubted explaining that the Lawson ring made her feel everything even stronger than she normally felt things would help, so he remained quiet.

He couldn't quite help the aggrieved glare he threw at Governor Haydenshire. His fury over the way her father's words had hurt Emily cut him to the quick.

"Rainer, I owe you an apology too."

Rainer nodded, and the governor began to pace.

"Emily, when I look at you," he shook his head and choked, "When I look at you, I still see my sweet little girl with bouncing red pigtails who wants me to read her a story or have a tea party with her. It feels like just yesterday I was picking you up out of your crib and pouring cups of water down your hair because you wouldn't let your mother wash it. You said I was the only one who didn't get the water in your eyes." The pain in his expression was so deep it was clearly a physical pain, not just an emotional one.

"And then you were four years old and telling me that you were going to make Rainer Lawson marry you, and I nodded and chuckled and agreed because he was a great kid then and he's a fine man now." Governor Haydenshire nodded humbly to Rainer.

"And then you were seven years old, and precocious, and adorable and full of wonder and spite in equal measure, and I'd never had a little girl before you. You amazed me every moment of every day. I stood on our back deck and watched you dare him to kiss you. It was like being able to see into the future. I saw the look in his eye and the love and the fascination in yours. I knew right then, one day I was going to lose you, and that I was going to lose you to him." He drew a deep breath and continued.

"So, you see, sweetheart, I'm not even certain I was consciously aware of it then, but I've been fighting that battle for thirteen years now, terrified that one day you were going to slip through my fingers and be gone.

"Then you were almost thirteen, and that was the year everything changed. Then I was fighting a whole new war. That was the year the world fell apart at my doorstep. The Crown Governor, my best friend, was found murdered in his office, his son an orphan." Governor Haydenshire shook his head in disbelief.

"I went to get you from school. Remember?" Rainer nodded. "I pled with the board to give me full custody that moment, but they had to let your uncle try. He showed up with those damn papers." Anger, from years before, perforated his tone.

"But a few weeks later, I moved you into my house, bruised, battered, and terrified. It killed me what he'd done to you. I couldn't stand it. The night I moved you in was the first night that I'd slept since your father's murder because I knew you were safe. I don't ever, ever want you to think that I begrudge giving you a place to live or what little I did to raise you. Joseph did all the hard work. You were already a tremendous kid." He gave Rainer a kind, sincere smile.

"But then I saw it again. I saw you and Emily. The way she could make you smile when none of us could. The peace that settled in your frightened eyes whenever she rushed into a room wherever you were. You finally let Garrett heal your physical bruises, but I watched Emily heal the much deeper emotional ones. She made you whole again. She could pull you out of the despair that was threatening to take you under, son. When neither I, nor Regis, nor Lillian, nor any of the boys could get through to you, Emily always could. And I'd moved you into my house with my little girl." He swallowed hard and the past seemed to shape his eyes and face.

"So, I just decided to fight harder, because I wanted you there with us. I fought much harder than I even needed to, because you would never have pushed anything on her, no matter how badly you hurt or how much she offered to ease your pain. But I told myself I had to remain vigilant. That one day you two were going to decide you were old enough to do something I knew you weren't old enough to do. And then you got a car, and she decided, come hell or high water, she was graduating with you, and I knew it was done, and I had lost. But you shocked me again." He offered Rainer a broken half grin.

"I knew you weren't planning on going to see a movie and get a pizza that night, Emily." Emily's head shot up in utter shock. "I was sick. I was furious, but your mother kept telling me Rainer Lawson wouldn't do what I knew you'd gone out planning to do that night."

He shook his head in disbelief. "And an hour later you came flying in the house, slamming the doors and stomping up the stairs, furious and stinging with rejection. Rainer moved through the kitchen in tears. He looked terrified and heartbroken, and I knew your mother was right." He reached and took Mrs. Haydenshire's hand. "She always is right. But you see, sweetheart, that just made me feel all the worse.

"I kept telling myself he wasn't going to turn you down forever. That he loved you too much, and that if he thought he was hurting your feelings he would relent. So, I kept up the fight, and you graduated, and I felt like I could breathe, just a little, for the first time in about eight years, I guess. But you see, baby, your mother told me he was bringing you here, all alone, and that I had to let you go," he choked back renewed tears.

"And, I didn't know how to let you go. I still don't know how, and I didn't just start fighting to keep you from the day Rainer kissed you on the cheek. I've been fighting it for the past twenty years, from the moment they handed you to me, right after you were born, and you screamed, and I saw those precious red curls you used to have. You looked up at me, and you stopped crying, and I was done for. You were it, my little baby girl. And then I was furious all over again." He shook his head. "Who did Rainer Lawson think he was taking my baby girl to my beach house and then climbing into bed with her?

"And I know all of your brothers have done that. I knew when their first times were as well, even though they tried hard to hide it. For some reason I couldn't let go of all of those years of fighting to make certain you were ready and that you wouldn't have any regrets. I fought to make certain your first time would be with someone who loved and adored you almost as much as I do.

"And somewhere in my heart I knew Rainer did, and that he would take care of you. That he would never hurt you, but it was just so much easier to hate him and hate what he was doing to you than it was to know that it was something you'd decided together and something that you were ready to do. Because I wasn't ready for it. I knew as soon as you'd given him that, it was all over. That you were his, and I'd lost my precious little girl. As hard as I'd tried to hold on to you I just couldn't. It wasn't even that I watched you slip right out of my hands. It was that I had to let go of your hand and had to watch him catch you." He shook his head again and more tears leaked from his tired eyes.

"I think I just tried to hold on to you so tightly that no one could get to you, not even Rainer, and I took my anger and my hurt at the inevitability of life out on both of you, and I'm so, so sorry. You know, when I was yelling at you earlier, I heard my father in my own voice, and that isn't something I ever want to hear again. So, I understand if you can't forgive me right now, and I understand if you two want to go somewhere else, but I just need to know that you know how sorry I am."

"Daddy." Emily stood up from the couch and threw her arms around her father as he wrapped her up in his protective embrace.

"I spent my whole damn career fighting for women's rights, and I didn't ever extend them to my own daughter. I'm disgusted with myself."

Emily squeezed him tighter. "But don't you see? You taught me how I should be treated, and I knew when I was four years old that Rainer would love me and take care of me the way you always do, and I know that he always will because you taught him to do that."

Air finally filled Rainer's lungs again. He gazed at Emily in her father's arms. He was so thankful that she had a dad who loved her like that, even if it made the road rocky at times. He knew Governor Haydenshire was a huge part of what made Emily who she was, and he couldn't love anything more than the girl wrapped up in her daddy's arms.

Garrett pushed the sliding glass door open. Most everyone had been watching from the beach.

"Is it safe to come back in?" He smiled at the scene before him.

With an adoring smile for her father, Emily wrapped her arms around Garrett.

Garrett hugged her tight and kissed the top of her head.

"She'll always be my baby girl." Governor Haydenshire winked at Rainer.

"I know, sir, and I'll always take care of her."

"I know, son."

Emily was smiling as Garrett released her.

"Em, if you still want to go, the concerts are just starting," Garrett urged. Emily turned to study Rainer. He drew her back into him.

"I told you, baby, I'll take you wherever you want to go." He ignored the twinge of pain that etched her father's face.

"Okay." Emily nodded. She took Rainer's hand but then turned back to her father. "He caught me, Daddy. He caught me in his arms. He kept me safe, and he'll never let me go."

"I know," her father choked. "But, you see, that split second that you were falling through the air, when I watched you two walk out of the kitchen that night and get in his car, I have never been so terrified in my entire life."

"I know." She kissed his cheek. Governor Haydenshire turned to Rainer.

"I love you just like you were one of mine. Please tell me my actions over the last few months haven't made you doubt that. I cannot tell you how sorry I am."

"I know, sir, and just so you know, I'd never been so terrified as I was that night that I put her in my car and brought her here either."

A broad, knowing grin spread across the governor's face as he extended his hand to Rainer. He shook it and then Governor Haydenshire pulled him into an all-encompassing hug.

CHAPTER 25
GOOD NIGHT, SON

By the end of the night, Emily was lying under one of the quilts with Rainer. She was curled up on his chest as they listened to one of the front men work his way through popular covers.

Her eyes were still swollen and red, and Rainer kept her casted through most of the evening. Her energy seemed placid and calmed when she was wrapped up in his protective embrace.

She was exhausted. He could feel that too as he held her tenderly and brushed sweet kisses in her hair.

He was thinking about everything she'd shouted at her father and everything her father had known about him and Emily that he'd never even realized.

As most of the female concertgoers were dressed in nothing but the bikinis they'd worn that day on the beach, Emily actually had on more clothing than most of the women at the concert. Not that this information would make Governor Haydenshire like her outfit any better.

A deep yawn shook through Emily as Rainer beamed at her. "Do you want to go home, baby?"

She nodded and began packing their things. They moved quickly to keep from blocking the view of other reclined couples.

It was almost one when Rainer lifted Emily from the car and carried her into the house just to make her giggle.

She tucked her head under his chin, and he felt her energy leap. He held her while she unlocked the door with both of them laughing.

When she finished, Rainer threw her over his shoulder so her backside was right beside his face, which he slapped repeatedly as she kicked her legs and squealed.

She shook her hips as he held her, then leaned and extracted his wallet from his back pocket.

"Ha!" she declared.

Rainer still refused to release her. "It's all yours anyway, baby."

They continued to laugh as he headed through the kitchen, but they met her father in the living room. With a slight grimace, still not certain quite where the governor stood on their physical relationship, Rainer set her on her feet.

Governor Haydenshire was chuckling and shaking his head. "You brought her home early."

Rainer smiled. "She was tired. She wanted to come home." He would never let the governor down. He would always take care of Emily, just as he'd promised.

"I'm just glad you're here." The governor slapped Rainer on the back and moved to the kitchen to pour a glass of milk. With a smile, Rainer walked Emily to her room.

"Do you think I'm allowed to tuck you in and maybe get a good night kiss?" He was really only kidding, but Emily beamed and tugged him in the room.

Makeup, hair care products, brushes, two opened boxes of tampons, clothes, magazines, candy wrappers, fingernail polish, bras, beach towels, and bikinis covered almost every surface and hung from several of the bunks.

"I feel like I'm having some kind of horrible nightmare where I'm trapped in a Sephora, and I can't escape. Where do you sleep?" He reached and guided her to his chest. "Here, I need to protect you. I'm afraid you may be eaten alive by beauty products."

"Aww, I'm just proud you knew the name of the store is Sephora."

Rainer gave her a cocky grin. "Well, you see," he swayed her gently as her body melded into his, "There's this really smoking hot girl I'm after who keeps dragging me in there with her every time I take her to the mall."

Emily stepped away from Rainer and slid the lace sarong off and let his shirt hang down open over the bikini before she moved back into Rainer's chest. He growled in her ear.

"But," she sassed, "whenever I drag you in there, I always reward you when we get back home."

"That's why I keep going with you, baby, for the rewards," he flirted shamelessly and listened to her sweet giggles.

She lifted her head, and he stared down into the depths of her emerald eyes. He watched her exhaustion play on the edges of desire, fear, love, and trust.

Full of wonder and spite in equal measure was Emily to perfection. The traces of her father's little girl mixed in with his baby. It was all there swirling in the most beautiful eyes he'd ever seen.

"I love you more than life itself." He cupped her cheek tenderly in his hand and brushed a soft, lush kiss across her lips.

Slowly, he turned his head to the other side and added to the intensity as he mated their mouths. He let the love, the passion, the desire, and the lust between them build.

She braided her hands through his hair and pulled him harder into her. With a soft groan, he devoured her mouth as she began to pant.

Rainer slipped his hand under the back of the shirt she was using as a cover-up. He dipped it into the bottom of her bikini and kneaded her backside.

She trembled and began grinding her hips into him as he hardened against her abdomen. Her breath stuttered, but she stepped back, still panting slightly.

He fought with every fiber of his being not to jerk her back to him and remove her bikini altogether.

"I should probably go." He let his eyes close for one brief moment. He couldn't watch her eyes darken or follow the curve of her kiss-swollen lips down to her deliciously enticing breasts.

She gave a devastated nod, only making the act of turning away from her so much harder. He turned slowly to open the door.

"Rainer," she whispered, and his heart sped.

He spun back around to face her. *Tell me you don't want me to go. Tell me you want me to stay with you, to make love to you, to be inside of you, to hold you all night long.* His mind whirled from desire and need as he waited on her to speak.

"I love you so much."

He stepped back to her and wrapped his arms around her.

"I love you too." Her energy calmed as soon as he wrapped her up in his embrace.

"I don't think I've ever been here and wanted to go home so badly," she admitted.

"Yeah, me either. I'll take you back if you want, sweetheart."

"No." She shook her head. "But next summer when we come back, we're kicking Patrick and Lucy out of the other bedroom."

"Or we could go out tomorrow and look for a beach house of our own."

Her eyes lit as she nodded. He brushed a sweet kiss across her forehead and then gave her a wry grin. "You want some help with this?" He tugged on the clasp of the bikini.

She giggled. "If you take that off, I'm going to want you to keep going, and I kind of think I might've put Dad through enough for one day."

Rainer begrudgingly agreed. "I'll see you in the morning." He turned and opened the door before he added, "I love you."

"I love you too." She blew him a kiss and then pulled off the bathing suit top and flashed him before he closed the door. He stifled a groan just in time to notice her father returning to his bedroom. Governor Haydenshire shook his head and chuckled.

"You're a strong man, Rainer." He sighed over the image Emily had chosen to leave him with.

Rainer wasn't certain how to respond so he offered a nod.

"It's been a while since you took a cold shower after leaving her room once you thought Lillian and I were asleep."

Beginning to wonder if there was any part of his and Emily's relationship that her parents hadn't figured out, Rainer didn't deny the accusation.

"Yeah," he agreed. The curiosity got the better of him. "So, you knew about all of that?"

With a wry grin, Governor Haydenshire confided, "I used to leave the Andersons' house in the evenings and go to the Non-Gifted high school about a block away. I'd run the track around the football field, oh, say, fifty or sixty times, before I got back into my car and drove home."

Rainer laughed with the governor. He understood only too well.

"Get some sleep, and trust me, it only gets better with time."

"Good night, sir."

"Good night, son."

CHAPTER 26
ANIMALS

"To ride!" was the demand that awakened Rainer the next morning.

"Keaton, geez!" Logan grunted. Being the only guy in a bottom bunk, he was the one Keaton had chosen to climb up on, sit on his stomach, and broadcast his demand.

"There you are," Mrs. Haydenshire scolded. "Come here, little one." She lifted Keaton off of Logan's gut.

No sooner had she gotten her hands on him than Keaton scampered away. He raced down the hall and flung open the door to the girls' room.

Rainer heard several high-pitched shrieks, and every male's head that had previously been buried in pillows in the boys' room shot upward. They all wondered what Keaton was getting an eyeful of.

"Lucky kid." Garrett grimaced.

"Yeah, but it could've been Em," Logan warned. Rainer laughed as each of Emily's brothers shuddered in horror.

"To ride, EE!" Keaton continued his quest.

"Yep, that's what Rainer wants too, little man." Garrett laughed.

Emily fumed. "Keaton, okay. Let me get dressed, please."

"Aww, now I am jealous," Rainer's whimper made everyone laugh.

"Keaton Isaac Haydenshire, we do not go into rooms when the door is closed," Mrs. Haydenshire scolded.

"Why?" Keaton demanded.

"That's what *I'm* saying." Garrett jumped off of his bunk.

"That's the best time to go in," Levi agreed as chuckles spread around the room.

After breakfast, Rainer, Emily, Logan, Adeline, Garrett, and Chloe all took Keaton and Henry to the boardwalk.

Mrs. Haydenshire thanked them profusely for volunteering to look after the boys for the day and for insisting that she rest and relax.

Garrett and Chloe informed them that they were going to meet some friends, but that they would catch up with them later.

Emily and Logan glared at him.

"There are two of them and four of you. I think you'll manage." Garrett took Chloe's hand. He gave her a grin that said he was up to no good and dragged her away.

"Wonder what they're going to do?" Logan huffed indignantly.

"Yeah, well, Chloe went on and on this morning about all of the places they've done it here," Emily shuddered. "They're like animals in heat."

Rainer wondered where Garrett and Chloe had consummated their rather open relationship in Virginia Beach.

They proceeded down the idyllic boardwalk, with Rainer carrying Henry and Logan carrying Keaton. They were both delighted as they pointed toward a clown who was pushing a cart selling stuffed animals.

"Do you want to get one now or after we ride?" Emily asked sweetly.

"Now!" both twins wriggled in their excitement.

"So, I'm going to go with now," Rainer joked.

They stood in line, talking and laughing. Rainer and Logan listened as the boys tried to determine which animal they wanted.

"You could get a sword, instead," Logan urged. He pointed to long, stuffed swords on the back of the cart.

"Logan, no. They'll hit each other with them all day."

"It's stuffed. I don't think they'll do any real harm."

"No. I want a mookey," Keaton announced. His eyes lit up as he pointed to the stuffed monkey on the cart.

"And what do you want, little man?" Rainer asked Henry. He pulled him off of his shoulders and held him in his arms so he could see the different options.

Henry considered for a moment. He was much more thoughtful than his twin. In an effort to tell Rainer what animal he wanted, in secret, Henry leaned his mouth close to Rainer's ear.

Instead of cupping his hand to block his voice, he covered his mouth and shouted, "I want a yi-yon!"

Rainer and Emily cracked up.

"Got it," Rainer assured Henry, who was now beaming over his successful secret telling. After Rainer paid for the toys, they took the boys for pizza.

Logan and Rainer let them pretend to play on the ancient console video games, before they returned them to their high chairs. Emily and Adeline cut the boys' pizza into tiny bites, and by the time everyone had finished, they were covered in red sauce, grease, and pizza spices.

Logan shook his head and proceeded to scrub Keaton down with wipes from the diaper bag Mrs. Haydenshire had packed them. Adeline gazed at Logan with rapt adoration as she watched him take care of Keaton.

He and Emily double-teamed Henry, until he was wriggling furiously but was relatively pizza-free. They stopped at the playground and let the boys down while they sat on the benches to watch them play.

"You're going to be such an amazing dad," Adeline gushed in unabashed devotion. She thoroughly embarrassed Logan. He seemed at a loss for words.

Offering the twins ice cream seemed to be the only effective way to get them to leave the playground. Everyone got a cone and watched as the twins ran around the statues of inventors on display in one of the courtyards near the ice cream cart.

Logan and Rainer chuckled as several Non-Gifted tourists

discussed the brilliance of Edison and Tesla and their discovery of electricity.

"They really were genius," one man vowed to his wife. He was standing near Logan and turned to gaze at him in hopes that he would corroborate his belief.

Logan nodded, then with a chuckle he added, "Oh yeah, definitely very *gifted* inventors."

"See?" the man huffed to his wife.

CHAPTER 27
A RECEIVER

Suddenly, Henry returned to Rainer and held up his arms. He was on the verge of tears.

"What's wrong, buddy?" He scooped him up and gave Emily a quizzical glance. Henry buried his face in Rainer's neck and sucked his thumb.

"Keaton probably pinched him or something." Emily went to retrieve Keaton from a statue of Thomas Jefferson.

They walked on and stopped in a few stores, but Henry continued to fuss and would lean away from Rainer, throwing his body side to side and then rubbing his arms and stomach with his hands.

Rainer tried to determine what he wanted. He set him on his feet, but Henry began crying again, so Rainer lifted him back into his arms.

Everyone studied him to figure out what he was asking for. Finally, Emily glanced around to make sure no one was watching them too closely, other than the private investigator who had been following them all day. They'd taken to waving to the PIs and actually posing for pictures.

Emily placed her hands on Henry's arms and closed her eyes. Rainer knew his energy would be difficult to read in its undeveloped form, but he was desperate to know what it was that had Henry so upset.

Emily's eyes goggled and her mouth fell open as she furrowed her brow.

"What?"

"He wants you to cast him."

"He's scared?"

Emily held Keaton tight and looked around for anything or anyone who might be frightening the twins. Rainer's shield cast formed over himself and Henry.

Henry relaxed. He fell back on Rainer's chest and sucked his thumb again. He rubbed his tiny hand on Rainer's neck tenderly as he let Rainer soothe him.

"Should we take them home?" Adeline quizzed.

"We can't take them home until they've ridden the merry-go-round." Logan shuddered over the fit that would ensue if they left before the boys made it to the rides.

"Well, let's go let them ride and then leave. I've had a weird feeling all day," Emily admitted.

"Maybe we should go," Rainer insisted.

"To ride!" Keaton shook his head at Rainer.

"No, it'll be fine. Let's just let them go a few times and then we'll leave," Logan negotiated.

Rainer handed his wallet to Emily to pay for the tickets as he kept Henry safe in his shield.

"I want Mommy," Henry whispered dejectedly. He buried his face deeper in Rainer's neck.

And Rainer knew instantly as he stared down at Henry and then back to Emily. She smiled at her baby brother and then met Rainer's gaze. She nodded.

Henry was a Receiver just like his big sister. That's why Rainer could pick up on Henry's energy easier than Keaton's. Henry was wide open just like Emily. Receivers were the only Predilect who could access some of their powers before they went through puberty. They would begin to pick up on emotional energy as young children. Receivers were incredibly easy to feel, but extremely difficult to guard. A sudden, overwhelming, possessive need to protect came over Rainer as he followed Logan to get in line to ride the merry-go-round.

It was late afternoon, and they were supposed to meet the rest of the Haydenshires for dinner at Buoy's.

Henry seemed to cheer as they edged closer to the entrance to the ride.

CHAPTER 28
INTELLIGENCE
GARRETT HAYDENSHIRE

"What?" Garrett spat as he jerked his phone from his pocket. He kept his hands tracing over Chloe's exposed breasts as she reclined against him in the bed of the hotel room he'd rented. "This sure as hell better be good." His phone had been ringing for the last ten minutes. Garrett and Chloe had been busy up until a moment or two before.

"Dammit, Garrett, get both of your heads out of Chloe Sawyer! Vasquez followed your family to Virginia Beach. I just got a shot of him on a streetcam on the boardwalk!" Vindico seethed. "I'm almost there. Fitzroy called me this morning. His undercover found out Nic had Vasquez's brother make several appearances for him down in Monterrey."

"What?" Garrett let Chloe fall to the mattress as he leapt from the bed. She huffed and stared up at him to show her disapproval.

"Get up. We have to go!" he commanded.

"I'm fifteen minutes away," Vindico explained. "I've got every available officer with me, but, Garrett, Vasquez is in trouble. Nic's furious that your mom survived. He has to do whatever he's been assigned to do, or he won't be making a return trip home from the beach."

"I'm already on the boardwalk. I got a suite yesterday. I'm on my way. I'll find him before he does anything. Rainer and Logan have the twins out there," Garrett choked.

His mind raced through all of the nauseating scenarios of things that Nic Wretchkinsides could have assigned Vasquez to do, in order to reestablish him back in the Interfeci's good graces.

"I know. And Garrett, Wretchkinsides is going to try to force your father not to run in this election. You and I both know who would be the easiest to attack and the quickest way to get to your old man."

"I'll meet you there." Garrett ended the call and demanded that Chloe get dressed. They were in the elevator a minute later.

"What do you think he's going to do?" Chloe was panicked.

"I don't know, but could you just please shut up?" Garrett sprinted to his car in the parking deck. He pulled his Browning hi-power semi pistol out of his glove box and sprinted toward the boardwalk. He touched Logan's name on his phone.

"Dammit, Logan, answer the fucking phone!" Garrett fumed as he sprinted toward the carnival rides. He was fairly certain that's where they would have taken the twins.

He raced up the midway.

Cal's face, the medevac station in Brazil, the funeral, the phone call, Emily lying in a hospital bed. If she makes it through the night then maybe, the cemetery, the vengeance, it all fed Garrett's fury as he methodically searched for the murderer at hand.

They were not taking another one of his siblings. He wouldn't allow it.

CHAPTER 29
IN THE REFLECTION
RAINER LAWSON

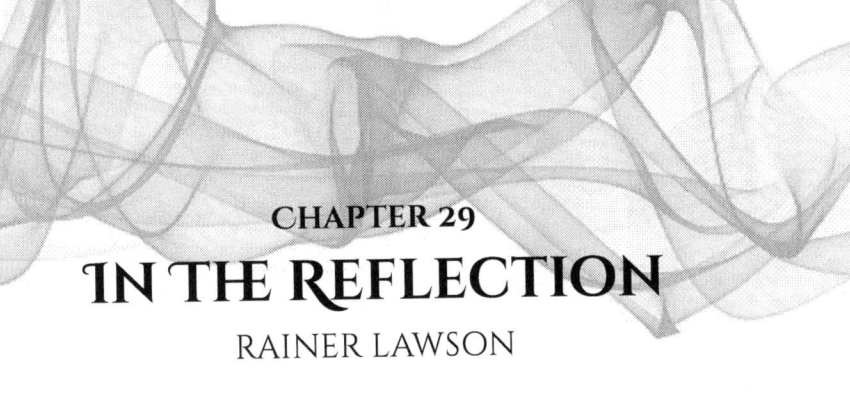

"To ride!" Keaton swung his legs wildly in Logan's arms.

"Okay, we're next," Logan assured him.

They all watched the ride spin with the twins vibrating in their excitement. After several long minutes, the ride slowed and eventually stopped.

Children and parents began exiting and then Rainer and Logan set the twins on the floor of the ride to let them choose a horse.

Logan lifted Keaton onto a large black stallion as Henry pointed to a smaller blue one on the opposite side of the ride.

Rainer lifted him onto it and relaxed as Henry clapped his hands. He looked thrilled. His nerves seemed to have calmed.

The music started, and Henry quickly grasped the pole through the horse. He squealed delightedly.

Suddenly, Emily's entire body pulled taut as she glanced around. She shook her head, and chill bumps charged down her arms. Rainer's cell phone rang. He pulled it from his pocket.

"Lawson," came Vindico's rough voice. "Where are you?"

"I'm on the boardwalk. We're taking the twins on the merry-go-round." He swept the area with his eyes and made certain Emily and Henry were right beside him.

"Stay there. I'm on my way!" Vindico ordered.

"What, why?" The line went dead.

"Rainer, we need to leave." Emily convulsed.

"Okay," Rainer tried to figure out how to get off of the ride without halting it and infuriating dozens of toddlers.

To his relief, the ride stopped of its own accord, but in the split second that it slowed, Keaton slid from his horse and leapt off of the still-spinning ride.

"Keaton!" Rainer handed Henry to Emily and sprinted after him. Emily, Logan, and Adeline were right behind him.

Suddenly several rides stopped at once, and visitors to the boardwalk fair converged onto the midway.

"Keaton!" Rainer screamed, but he could no longer see him.

"Where is he?" Emily panicked.

"We'll find him." He and Logan dodged in and out of the fair guests, both screaming Keaton's name.

"Keaton!" Rainer grasped a toddler dressed in a green shirt and overalls, but it wasn't him. "I'm so sorry, ma'am," Rainer managed a hurried apology to the mother who was set to claw his face off.

"Rainer!" Emily pointed to the ground just to Rainer's left.

"What?" He spun back. His heart sink rapidly to his feet. Violent revulsion washed over him.

There, on the ground outside the House of Mirrors, was Keaton's monkey.

"Rainer, I feel someone." Emily paled and shook in her fear.

"It's Vasquez. He's here!" Garrett and Chloe appeared out of nowhere. They looked terror-stricken and halted beside Rainer and Logan.

"What?!" Logan gasped.

"Vindico just called. He's coming in the gates. Vasquez is here," Garrett shouted.

"I think he took Keaton," Emily sobbed.

"I just saw him. He took him in there!" To Rainer's shock, the private investigator who'd been following them all day raced toward Garrett to tell them where Vasquez had disappeared with Keaton.

"Let's go!" Garrett ran into the House of Mirrors, with Rainer and Logan on his flanks. Fury was armored in Garrett's march. His

Browning was chambered and loaded at his side. They entered the house, and Rainer heard Keaton screaming.

"Let him go, Vasquez! We've got you surrounded! Let him walk away and we'll cut you a deal!" Garrett shouted furiously.

Logan and Rainer edged around the macabre rooms, not certain if what they were seeing was real or only a reflected image. Emily entered behind Rainer.

"Adeline has Henry. They're with the Iodex officers outside." Her voice shook in her paralyzing fear. They could hear Keaton's frightened terror in his screams, but then they were cut off in a chilling, horrific choke.

"Vasquez, let him go!" Garrett snarled.

They continued through the house. They checked every angle and every reflection. They were getting closer. Rainer could feel it.

Emily shuddered. Her entire body faltered as she tried to fight off the dark energy threatening to consume her.

They spun around another corner and caught a glimpse of the tail of Keaton's blanket as it whipped around the next mirror. They stepped carefully. Garrett was the only one with a gun.

As they followed the sight of the blanket, they came face to face with Roberto Vasquez. His filthy hand gripped the terrified toddler's throat.

"EE," Keaton pled in choking terror as he tried to pull his neck away, but he couldn't fight Vasquez's strength.

Emily sobbed. "Please, please let me have him."

Vasquez just laughed derisively.

"Vasquez, let him go," Garrett menaced. He edged closer. Vasquez put Keaton in front of his face and heart, using him as a human shield. Garrett lowered his gun to Vasquez's crotch.

"I don't give a damn how you bleed out just so long as you do."

Vasquez turned Keaton into a moving target, never keeping him over any part of his body for more than a second. Vindico stepped in behind Vasquez.

"It's over, Vasquez. You're surrounded. The governor and the entire police force are right outside. You're done for."

Vasquez spun and spit into Vindico's face. But Vindico was too quick. He reflected it back into Vasquez's mouth.

"Ándate al puto infierno, Vindico," drawled from Vasquez's lips in a hateful snarl.

"Oh yeah, I'll meet you there," Vindico quipped.

"EE," Keaton pled, terrified. Rainer's heart raced. All of his training, all of the hours casting and shielding, could never have prepared him for this.

"Emily," Vindico stated very calmly, "when I give you the signal, I want you to cast only Keaton. Can you do that for me?"

Emily nodded and shuddered in her terror.

Rainer let the stunning realization rock through him. Vasquez wasn't leaving the House of Mirrors other than in a body bag. Vindico and Garrett shared a slight nod, and Rainer's heart hammered.

Vindico would never allow any of Wretchkinsides's men the chance to go back and confirm the power of Emily's ring. Vasquez was a dead man walking. As soon as Keaton was safe, Garrett was going to make certain Vasquez never hurt his family again.

"Good. As soon as she shields him, Vasquez, I'm going to have Officer Haydenshire blow you to hell. So, here's your final warning. Either give the baby to me, and you can plead for mercy in front of the Senteon, or keep this up, and you can tell Satan I said fuck the hell off when you get back home."

Vasquez tried to edge away from Vindico, but found himself backing toward another mirror. With that, Vindico nodded to Emily.

She summoned, and Rainer had never seen anything like it. She projected the brilliant green shield from her left hand using the vast energy contained in the ring.

The illuminating energy was so bright, he had to shield his eyes, but so did Vasquez. He dropped Keaton to block his face.

This was the most powerful shield Emily had ever cast, even when her own life had been in danger. Her inborn will to protect her brothers projected out from her body, and the ring responded to her will.

Keaton ran to Logan, who scooped him up and sobbed.

"Now!" Vindico shouted. He leapt out of the way as Garrett unloaded his pistol into Vasquez.

The echo of the repeated shots throbbed in Rainer's skull. Emily's body gave out, and she collapsed into Rainer. Logan fell back against the wall, unable to believe what had just happened and what he'd just watched his brother do.

Garrett dropped his gun. It tumbled to the floor. He turned and took Keaton from Logan. He held him tight as tears flooded from Garrett's eyes into Keaton's hair.

Vindico led everyone out of the house.

Governor and Mrs. Haydenshire were sobbing as Keaton was passed from Garrett to Mrs. Haydenshire. Vindico gestured into the fun house.

"There's someone inside. He didn't quite make it." The medio medevac team nodded their understanding. As Governor Haydenshire took his turn with Keaton, Mrs. Haydenshire sobbed into Garrett's chest.

"Are you okay?" she stammered.

"I'm fine, Mom," Garrett assured her, but everyone listening knew he was lying.

"How did he get back here? I thought he was in Mexico," Rainer demanded of Dan.

"Yeah, so did I. Apparently, Mr. Vasquez has a twin brother. He made a few appearances for him in Monterrey. He made sure to appear on as many traffic and store cams as he possibly could. Wretchkinsides was pissed Mrs. Haydenshire survived the wedding and decided to play even more cruelly." He shook his head in disbelief. "It's just never enough with him. The only way out is to end him."

Rainer let that information wash over him, and it threatened to make him sick after the afternoon he'd just had. Emily clung to him. She was still shaking in her terror.

"But Vasquez is done for, and he was the only one here. It'll take Wretchkinsides a little while to regroup. So, if you can, maybe try to enjoy the rest of your vacation. You certainly all deserve one," Vindico urged the Haydenshires, who were thanking him profusely.

"I'm not doing this. Absolutely nothing is worth risking my family," Governor Haydenshire choked out his vow.

"Governor, could I give you a police escort home and provide you a broad range security detail? There are some things you need to know," Vindico requested.

Governor Haydenshire nodded. He was still clinging to Keaton who, to Rainer's shock, seemed to be falling asleep tucked in his father's protective embrace.

Rainer climbed into the Hummer and drove Emily, Logan, and Adeline back home.

Logan was a disaster. Adeline constantly tried to soothe him but wasn't having much luck.

Rainer didn't have anything to offer him. It was the most terrifying experience he'd ever lived through, and having watched Garrett come unglued and take out his revenge on his mother's would-be murderer and his baby brother's kidnapper had been a horrifying thing to watch.

As he drove, Rainer kept rubbing his eyes and blinking repeatedly. It wasn't until Emily touched his arm, closed her eyes, and pushed her soothing calm into him that he was aware he was crying. He followed a long line of cars back into the front yard of the Haydenshires' beach house.

Police cars peeled off to the sides to allow the family to park their vehicles. The family was escorted inside, with the media fighting desperately to get shots or reactions from any of the Haydenshires or their guests.

Iodex held them at bay. They screeched at them to get away from the governor's Suburban or be arrested as he and Mrs. Haydenshire rushed the twins inside.

Iodex officers surrounded the house. No one was getting in or out as Vindico rushed Emily inside. He blocked her from the cameras on her right as Rainer blocked the press on her left.

CHAPTER 30
THE PRICE OF THE PRICELESS

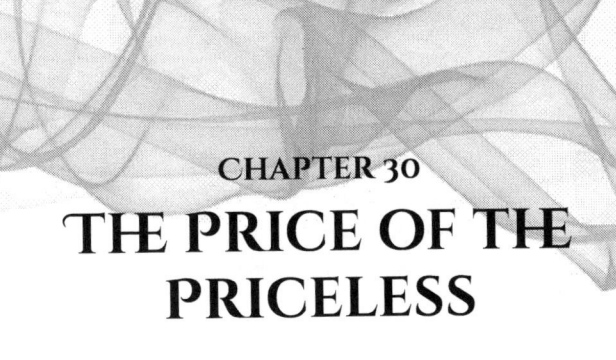

The door was shut and bolted once everyone was seated in the Haydenshires' living room. A shield cast from multiple sources outside the house covered the home.

Vindico accepted one of the beers Will was handing out.

Emily fell into Rainer's lap, and he held her tight as she buried her face in his neck. The world was just too much. He understood only too well. He casted her. He doubted anyone would mind talking to them while they glowed a brilliant green.

Vindico offered him an understanding smile and nodded his appreciation of the gesture.

The twins had both fallen asleep on the ride home and slept soundly, each in one of their parents' arms.

Mrs. Haydenshire refused to allow them to be put in their cribs, and no one argued.

Vindico glanced around the house. He seemed to let uncomfortable memories wash over him. Rainer wondered if he'd ever come to the beach house with Will and Garrett when they were younger. He wondered if Amelia had ever come along.

"It's going to be a media circus for a while," Vindico began morosely. He gestured to the throngs of press agents setting up camp along the Haydenshires' property lines.

"Fine. I'll make the announcement that I'm no longer running for Crown from here," Governor Haydenshire huffed. Fury had quickly replaced his terror.

Vindico looked sickened. "If that's your decision, Governor, certainly the Realm would understand, but before you decide, there are a few things you need to hear."

"Daniel, my wife and two of my children were almost murdered in one week's time. What could you possibly have to say to me that would make me want to continue on with this insanity?" Governor Haydenshire demanded. He stood and handed Henry to Emily as Rainer let down his shield. Emily cradled Henry to her chest as he continued his nap.

Vindico drew himself up to his full height and met the governor's infuriated gaze.

"Lachland Peterson has accepted a $5.2 million dollar campaign contribution from Dominic Wretchkinsides."

"What?" Governor Haydenshire gasped.

Vindico nodded. "I did quite a bit of digging. It seems Wretchkinsides has guaranteed Peterson the win, in exchange for a few favors after he's in office. Samantha was the recipient of this." He pulled his phone from his pocket and scrolled through a few pictures until he came to a photo of a brand-new black Mercedes M-class.

"So, I decided to play private detective myself for a day or two, and I don't know if you want to use these, Governor, but there are plenty more where they came from."

Vindico scrolled to the next photo. It was a relatively close-up shot of Samantha and a few of her friends, along with several men Rainer didn't recognize.

Samantha was taking a drag from a joint. The next photo showed Samantha laid out on the hood of her new car, with one of the men in the previous photo. His hand was up her skirt.

Rainer shuddered as did all of the men in the room.

"Is that...?" Garrett glanced at the phone before handing it back to Vindico.

"Yeah, seems Peterson and Wretchkinsides have played matchmaker. Not sure if that was part of the deal, but that's Adrian

Malicai. He's an up-and-coming player in the Interfeci. Wretchkinsides is personally training him. He's taken a special interest."

Governor Haydenshire looked sick. "I'm not using something like that. That girl obviously needs attention she isn't getting. It's sick and disturbing. It's not political fodder."

"Stephen, you have to run, and you have to win," Mrs. Haydenshire stated firmly. "This is no longer about the better of two choices. All of the shades of gray just turned to black and white, sweetheart. Now, we're fighting good over evil."

"She's right, Dad," Garrett vowed. "If Peterson wins, Wretchkinsides will control the Senate. The Realm will fall right back into the hell it was before you all fought so hard to make it right."

"I will not use photographs of Samantha Peterson being taken advantage of, Lillian."

"Of course not," Mrs. Haydenshire soothed. "But you are staying in this race, and we are going to have to make the Realm see what's going on here."

"Does anyone else have those?" Governor Haydenshire gestured to Vindico's phone.

"She was in the driveway of the Petersons' mansion, and I can assure you, I wasn't the only person parked close enough to see her. I don't know who might have photographs, but if you don't want to use them, I'll never show them to anyone else. You have my word. I will also provide your entire family with twenty-four-hour security, but please, for the Realm, you have to run, and you have to win. You and my dad, Carrington, Crown Governor Lawson, you all fought too hard to let this happen."

"Please consider everything that has happened to me today, Daniel, and don't take offense when I say this, but I believe you were providing Serena Carrington twenty-four-hour security, were you not?"

"I was, but Gallic was not my choice, nor was he my hire. Serena picked him. She liked him because he didn't do his job. He let her be and was off doing other things." Vindico looked sick. "If you're concerned, I will gladly provide you with all of my Elite force throughout the campaign. If we need to hire others, then we'll let Anna Eleanor or your own daughter interview them. Certainly, Emily would have picked up on Gallic had she ever been anywhere near him," Vindico sealed the deal.

An Ioses Predilect who believed in the powers of Receivers was certainly a force to be reckoned with.

"I'll just provide my own security. Thanks, though," Garrett stated.

"I can take care of myself, but I want her watched constantly," Logan gestured to Adeline, who was seated in his lap.

"Done," Vindico agreed. "When Emily and Adeline aren't at work, bring them with you."

"Same deal here," Will demanded. He had one hand behind Brooke's back, the other on her protruding stomach.

"Of course," Vindico agreed. After a few more logistical plans were made, Keaton sat up bright-eyed in Mrs. Haydenshire's lap.

Tears trailed down her cheeks again. He began looking around as every eye in the room was gazing at him adoringly.

"I some juice!" he demanded.

Relief spread through the room as everyone chuckled at his proclamation. Rainer was able to draw a full breath in the light of Keaton's mischievous smile.

Governor Haydenshire fixed him a sippy cup of apple juice, and Keaton scrambled out of his mother's lap. He retrieved his bucket of Matchbox cars and asked Vindico to play with him.

"Come on, Danny. We'll show you how to play." Garrett laughed at Vindico's bewildered expression. Garrett, Rainer, Logan, and Connor left their chairs to sit on the floor and play cars with Keaton, while Henry slept on in Emily's lap.

"Dan, I'm making us dinner, and you're staying. I've been through enough today, and I'm expecting my eleventh child, so turning me down again would not only be rude, it would be cruel," Mrs. Haydenshire demanded.

"Yes, ma'am, of course. Thank you," he offered politely.

"You have to pick a car, man," Garrett urged Vindico.

"I'm really better with a bike."

Keaton ended up selecting a purple full-size Ford van for Vindico to play with.

"A full-size? Really?" he quizzed incredulously.

Rainer and Garrett laughed as they picked their own cars. Henry woke up a little while later and joined the group of fully grown men playing Matchbox cars on the floor with Keaton.

The governor attempted to play as well, though it was very obvious his mind was many miles away.

CHAPTER 31
WHAT REMAINS

The press remained, en masse. They formed a strange sort of intrusive barrier that surrounded the Haydenshires' property on all sides.

Enhanced helicopters circled overhead constantly. They were all desperate to hear from the governor or for a photo of any of the children, especially the twins.

The constant whirring sound was exhausting, and everyone decided to cut the vacation short. Hopes of leaving the house to enjoy the beach, or any other form of entertainment in the area, seemed impossible, and when Keaton had asked to go out to the beach to see the crabs, everyone's resounding "No!" thoroughly confused him.

It seemed best to get the twins back to the farm, where their life could return to normal, for the most part.

Completely exhausted, Governor and Mrs. Haydenshire had gone to bed after they'd put the twins down.

Will and Brooke had retired early as well.

The girls had kissed all of their significant others good night and had disappeared to their room, though they were still talking and laughing when the boys decided they were bored and headed to bed.

Rainer emerged from the shower and pulled on fresh boxers. He'd hoped a shower and clean clothes might wash away some of the anguish the day had held. He climbed into his bunk when there was a knock on the door.

Logan stood and edged it open.

"What's wrong?" Concern filled Logan's tone as he opened the door farther to reveal Adeline. The other ladies were all standing behind her, looking somewhat abashed.

"Emily said she didn't think you all would mind if we decided to invite you all to our sleepover," Adeline explained.

Logan grinned at her. "Anybody here ever not wanted to be invited to a girls' sleepover?"

Everyone laughed and scooted over in their bunks as their girlfriends and fiancées crawled in beside them.

"Hey there," Rainer whispered as Emily scooted in beside him. He wrapped her up in the sheets and blankets and then in his body. She beamed as she wiggled until her back was pressed tightly to his chest with her head under his chin. Her energy spun in jagged, jarring twists, but as Rainer wrapped his arms around her it began to calm.

"I'm scared I'm going to start having the nightmares again," her whisper was barely audible to even Rainer. All of the couples tucked up in the bunks were whispering to one another, with no one paying any attention to anyone but their own bedmate. Rainer nodded. She'd had horrible nightmares for almost a year after Cal's death and her wreck. As Receivers' minds processed the emotions they'd taken on through the day, they'd often have vivid dreams at night.

"Do you want me to go sleep with you in your room, so we won't be in here in case you do?" She smiled but shook her head.

"No, Dad won't mind this, but he doesn't need anything else to worry about, and I think that would bother him."

"I've got you, baby," he continued to soothe her. "I'll hold you all night long. I'll never let anything happen to you."

"I know." She still sounded frightened and uncertain. "I'm a little worried the ring will somehow make the nightmares worse."

He wrapped his arms around her tighter and let his shield cover the two of them. Her body relaxed.

Logan followed suit, and Rainer assumed Adeline was worried as well.

"Do you think the twins are all right?"

"They're in their cribs in your parents' room, and there are Iodex officers surrounding the house. No one is getting in or out."

She nodded and seemed to relax again, but a few minutes later, she turned, burying her face in his chest. "Do you think Samantha will be okay?"

His heart fractured. He knew she was truly terrified for Samantha even after the hell she'd put them through.

"No…I don't."

"Me either," she stated in a choked whisper.

"Try to get some sleep, baby. There's nothing we can do for Samantha tonight, and I have a feeling the next few weeks are going to be rough." He thought again about his idea for her birthday present and the peace it would hopefully allow them, if only for a little while.

Emily was exhausted. He could feel her energy waning rapidly.

"I've got you." He kept his cast surrounding them. He considered the fact that none of her brothers had anything to say about the green glow coming from Rainer's bunk.

Life just wasn't quite as untroubled or carefree as it had been twenty-four hours earlier, when they all would've harassed Emily mercilessly for having Rainer cast her as she fell asleep, and Rainer for agreeing to do it.

Soon she was fast asleep in his arms, and he dropped the shield as he drifted off still holding on to her.

∼

"This really wasn't what I had in mind when I assigned you to separate rooms," Governor Haydenshire's weary voice woke Rainer the next morning.

He'd come to awaken the boys and found everyone in their room. To everyone's relief, he was chuckling and shaking his head.

"Hey, Daddy," Emily drawled. She was clearly hoping to ease her father's discovery.

After giving her a knowing grin, Governor Haydenshire laughed.

"Good morning, baby girl. Please tell me you're both completely dressed under there. I've had a hell of a weekend."

Emily laughed and rolled her eyes. "Of course." She threw back the covers and showed her father that she was dressed in one of Rainer's T-shirts and a pair of knit lace-trimmed shorts with the drawstring still tied tight.

Rainer had pulled his hand away from between her legs before she'd thrown back the covers. She shot him a quick mischievous grin as he pretended to yawn.

∼

Soon everyone was up and packing to head back to McLean in shifts.

"Rainer." Emily looked concerned as Rainer inhaled a bowl of cereal.

"What's wrong?" he mumbled through his Fruit Loops. Emily giggled at his cereal choice. "What? They're still my favorite."

"I know. I just think it's cute."

Rainer washed his bowl out and turned all of his attention to Emily. It was still early. The governor had awoken everyone before six. Rainer pulled her into his chest and wrapped his arms around her. He rubbed his hands from her shoulders all the way to her backside and squeezed it before they made the return voyage back to her shoulder blades.

"I was wondering if you'd walk with me on the beach for a little while before we go home?"

"Of course. But you know we won't be walking alone."

"I know, but I just want to see it again before we leave."

Understanding immediately washed through Rainer.

She needed to walk along the ever-changing, but ever-present shoreline. She needed to stare out at the endless ocean, to let go of a piece of her childhood before she became a married woman.

"Come on." Rainer guided her toward the back door. He slipped on his sunglasses. She did the same.

He decided they would walk for as long as she needed, and he'd wait on her forever.

Everyone deserved those fleeting moments in time when you watched your former self drift away and drown in the restless tide to be replaced with more knowledge, more maturity, and sometimes more pain.

He'd never been given the opportunity to let his childhood wash away to be slowly replaced by his adult life.

In one afternoon, Governor Haydenshire had come to the middle school they'd all attended together, and Rainer had been called from his eighth grade Algebra class.

He'd never forget the long, ominous walk alone down the corridor. He'd known something was wrong since that morning. Emily had clung to him at lunch. She'd just started really being able to fully access her powers, and she felt everything so strongly, especially when it came to Rainer. She'd known as well.

Rainer had almost run into Mrs. Haydenshire as she'd rushed through the front entrance of the school. Governor Haydenshire had flown there from the Senate, and Mrs. Haydenshire hadn't been called until the governor had arrived.

She was sobbing, and Rainer *knew* as she pulled him to her and wrapped him up in a motherly embrace. There, in that moment, in the principal's office with the school counselors standing prepared to tell him about his father's death, Emily burst in. She'd run out of class. She'd sensed Rainer's anguish and had rushed to his side.

He'd spent the rest of the afternoon lying on a quilt, letting her soothe him. He'd shut out the rest of the world that was spiraling wildly out of control all around him.

In one afternoon, at fourteen years of age, his childhood was yanked away. He wanted Emily to have the opportunity to let hers go slowly and delicately at her own pace and in her own time.

He wrapped his arm around her and walked her toward the sand in the hazy morning sunlight. They steadfastly ignored the constant click of the cameras as they walked. Reporters rushed forward as they edged farther down the beach.

"Emily, tell us what you felt facing Keaton's kidnapper."

"Rainer, explain your part as an Elite Iodex officer in taking down Roberto Vasquez."

"Emily, how do you feel this will affect your father's campaign?" The reporters rattled off the same relentless questions.

Rainer narrowed his eyes and clenched his jaw. He kept Emily wrapped under his arm.

"Miss Haydenshire and I will not be answering any questions this morning. Please, I'm begging you to respect her privacy and mine."

To his shock, the reporters backed away slightly.

Rainer and Emily let their feet feel the foaming tide and the sinking sand. The reporters did give them a fairly wide berth. Rainer held Emily's hand as she stared out at the mighty Atlantic.

She stopped walking suddenly and threw her arms around his neck. She buried her face in his chest and hid from the world.

"I've got you, baby."

Her energy was spinning in tightly wrung, nervous twists.

After a few long minutes with Rainer swaying her tenderly and whispering how much he loved her and that he would always take care of her, they walked on.

"I guess we should go back," Emily lamented with a heavy sigh.

"Not until you're ready." Rainer wasn't going to rush her back to the beach house, to the election, to the world threatening to consume her at every turn.

They walked farther. He kept her hand in his own. She drew from him rhythmically. His thoughts turned to all of the things he could do to make the election easier on all of the Haydenshires.

Eventually, with one farewell gaze out at the sea that had raised her, she turned and led them back to the house.

Rainer and Logan packed the Hummer. They avoided reporters and photographers at every turn. Around noon, the four of them headed back to the farm, with Emily and Rainer in the front this time.

It was surreal to leave the beach house before Labor Day. Rainer couldn't recall ever leaving early. They'd always arrived back at the Haydenshires' just in time for dinner Monday night and then all began school the next day.

There was no school to return to this year. They were grown, and life had definitely begun.

. . .

When Rainer pulled into the gated driveway that led to the guesthouse, two of his subordinate Iodex officers waved him through with a warm greeting. The farm would be under constant guard from now until the election for Crown Governor. If Governor Haydenshire won, the family would be assigned security teams for the entire time he held the office.

Emily bristled at the armed guards standing on her family's farm though she would never argue the necessity. Rainer squeezed her hand as he willed his brain to stop recalling the images of Keaton being choked in the hands of Roberto Vasquez. The shots from Garrett's gun still ricocheted in his mind in haunting detail.

Emily would occasionally shudder from the memories. Her energy would tense and churn in sickening twists when she allowed herself to recall.

She needed an escape. Once they'd unpacked all of the luggage they'd taken to the beach house, he grabbed a quilt and guided Emily out to one of the slightly raised hilltops between the guesthouse and the large farmhouse that stood in peaceful reticence in the distance.

Everything about the evening reminded him of the day his father had been murdered. The weather was similar with the hot, liquid, summer air slowly giving way to the cooler fall breezes. Emily had stayed right beside him on a quilt in the back fields that night as well. She'd wiped away his tears and tried to soothe his agony.

This time, Rainer grabbed a bottle of wine and a few glasses to go along with the quilt. Emily beamed at him as he settled her on the quilt and poured her a glass of wine while they watched the sunset.

Rainer held Emily to him. "How about for the next eight weeks or so, if this all gets to be too much, we'll have a night out here, just you and me?"

"You're the best thing ever."

Rainer shook his head. "That's you, baby."

This seemed the perfect solution, until one of the Iodex teams drove by on a golf cart. The governor had ordered them to locate each of his children every hour or so unless they were inside one of the houses. However, as the teams currently guarding Haydenshire Farm were not Elite Iodex, they did have to answer to Rainer who shooed them away.

"I've got it," he assured them. "Don't come back unless I call."

"Yes, sir, Officer Lawson."

Emily giggled. "That's pretty handy."

Rainer grinned at her and pushed a stray strand of her long, auburn hair behind her right ear. He covered her bright red, heart-shaped birthmark that was hidden behind her ear. She hated it, but he found it adorable.

"You know I'm going to have teams following you constantly whenever you're not with me."

"I know." She lay back on the quilt and pulled Rainer to her. She kissed him heatedly. "I don't want to think about the election anymore, or what happened at the beach, or anything at all. I just want to kiss you."

"I think that could probably be arranged." He lay on his side and cradled her close as he engaged her in sweet, lush, tender kisses. They watched the sun set, wrapped up in one another, and as the night grew cooler Rainer folded the quilt back up and led her back to their home.

CHAPTER 32
ONLY JOB

By Wednesday afternoon, Rainer and Logan had a better idea of just what it would mean for Elite Iodex's only job to be to ensure the safety of the Haydenshires.

"I love the little guys and I want them safe, but this feels like skipping out on work," Logan commented as he and Rainer turned on the TV and fixed cups of water for the twins.

"I know, but every time I think about what happened it makes me sick all over again."

After Keaton's ordeal at the boardwalk, Vindico determined that when the twins were out of the care of their parents, Elite Iodex would be watching over them. As the Haydenshires were flying all over the country campaigning, Logan and Rainer's assignment for the next two weeks was to babysit.

"Mommy!" Keaton screeched as Logan summoned to have the large-screen TV in the Haydenshires' living room climb into the Gifted networks.

Logan paused so the twins could watch their parents descend another Gifted jet as they waved to throngs of admirers. They were headed to yet another arena where Governor Haydenshire would vow to uphold the Constitution that he helped write and ratify.

Logan lowered the volume so that the twins didn't hear the

217

comments from the opposition stating that Governor Haydenshire was abusive for dragging his expectant wife to city after city to campaign for him. They would then ask where all ten of the other children were.

Most of the adult Haydenshire children were stepping up and hosting events in support of their father. The press often twisted their efforts to make it appear that they were being coerced into action.

Vindico was just as concerned with Governor Haydenshire becoming the next Crown as he was with all of the Haydenshires' safety. He'd personally scrambled the Gifted jets, and either he or his father, the current acting Crown, had spoken with all of the Haydenshires' offspring's employers.

Currently Levi and Sarah and Patrick and Lucy were disembarking from planes in cities around the country in support of Governor Haydenshire.

Rainer and Emily were hosting a gala ball over the weekend in Boston right after the Angels challenged the Bombers. Governor and Mrs. Haydenshire were planning to attend as a surprise for their fans. Thus far, there were to be nearly fifteen hundred people in attendance.

Henry retrieved his blanket and carried his sippy cup haphazardly as he climbed up in Rainer's lap and sucked his thumb.

"I want Mommy," he fussed. After sharing a devastated glance with Logan, Rainer wrapped Henry up in his arms.

"I know, buddy. She's helping Daddy, and you get to play with me and Logan."

Henry nodded, but Rainer could tell getting to play with all of their older siblings was no longer a highly valued prize to the twins. They wanted their parents, and eventually, no one else was going to do.

Mrs. Haydenshire was coming back to McLean that evening to see the twins, before flying out the next morning to Albuquerque to meet the governor. Logan was going to pick up Emily from practice so Rainer could go over to Will and Brooke's to finalize the arrangements for Emily's birthday present.

Garrett and Vindico would be staying at the house with Mrs.

Haydenshire and the twins that evening. Rainer began rocking Henry as Logan flipped through the Gifted networks.

"Look, *Supernova*," Logan announced with mocked enthusiasm. *Supernova* had the twins out of their doldrums and singing the theme song immediately.

Scully Supernova was a Gifted kids' show that taught Gifted children about all the different kinds of energy. Despite the fact that Scully was a middle-aged man with a pronounced beer gut who wore purple tights and a lightning bolt across his chest, it wasn't too bad. The twins adored Supernova and his assistant, Wavelength. They used energy to solve all kinds of superhero-like problems every day.

It gently guided Gifted children into understanding all that their bodies would be capable of, once they'd gone through puberty, and they were able to harness the energies of the earth and use them in a myriad of ways.

Once the twins were thoroughly distracted, Logan and Rainer picked up their earlier conversation about Rainer's surprise for Emily.

"So, Em has no idea?" Logan grinned.

"No idea." Rainer was thrilled. Keeping things from Emily was next to impossible, but they'd been so busy with the election he'd remained distracted which kept her from picking up on his excitement.

"She's gonna flip."

Rainer laughed. "Hope she's wearing a skirt then."

Logan threw a pillow at Rainer as he laughed. "She's still my baby sister."

Rainer rolled his eyes. "Hey, how's Ad feeling?"

Adeline's appointment with the medio was the next afternoon, and Rainer could tell Logan was worrying. "Worse. The cramps are really bad. I'm more than ready for the energy scans they're going to do tomorrow. She's terrified though."

CHAPTER 33
ESCAPE

By five o'clock, Rainer was antsy. Logan had gone to retrieve Emily, and Mrs. Haydenshire had just arrived home via her security team from the Senate.

The twins were thrilled, but Rainer couldn't leave until Vindico and Garrett arrived for the evening. A few minutes later, they entered the kitchen carrying small duffle bags.

"How are you feeling, Mom?" Garrett quizzed. Concern thrummed in his tone.

Mrs. Haydenshire gave him a weary smile and allowed him to embrace her.

"Just a little tired, sweetheart, but very glad to be home." She moved from Garrett to the twins who were both clamoring to get in her lap so she could continue on with the story she'd been reading them.

"I'm gonna head out." Rainer waved to Mrs. Haydenshire and the twins.

"Hey, Lawson," Vindico called. Rainer spun back as Dan threw him the keys to his custom MV Agusta Brutale 575 motorcycle. Rainer stared at them in stunned disbelief.

"Are you serious?"

Vindico laughed at him outright as he nodded.

"I told you, once you were trained, you could drive it, and you threw me the other day. Not a lot of guys can say that, even in Elite. So, just be careful with her because you may have thrown me once, but if you hurt my bike it won't happen again, trust me."

Rainer nodded his understanding.

"I'll be careful. I'm just going to Will's." Rainer laid the keys to his Mustang on the counter.

"You better," Vindico warned with a slight smile.

"I told you he'd blow his wad," Garrett commented as he pulled a cold Dr Pepper out of the refrigerator.

"Garrett Alexander Haydenshire!" Mrs. Haydenshire scolded from the living room.

"Sorry, Mom." Garrett grimaced as Vindico laughed at him outright.

"Hey, I know I shouldn't ask, and I wouldn't, but this would make his year. Would you mind if I drove by Sam's and let him have a look? He'll flip," Rainer vowed.

"Lawson, I trust you, and I don't care where you take it so long as you bring her back to me looking better and with more gas in it than when you left."

"You got it," Rainer promised as he tried not to sprint out the back door.

~

Rainer couldn't quite wipe the broad, delighted grin off of his face as he slowed the Agusta and drove it into the bay of Sam's shop. Sam was shaking his head and chuckling. He dropped the hood on the Camaro he was working on, grabbed a rag, and began wiping his hands as Rainer pulled off the helmet Vindico had loaned him.

"You trade in your 'Stang, boy?" Sam looked concerned and mildly hurt. Rainer would never have traded in his Mustang, for anything, and most certainly not without letting Sam handle the deal.

"Oh, no way." Rainer shook his head. "This is my boss's. He just let me take it out for tonight." A low, slow whistle slid through Sam's teeth. His contented smile formed on his face. It eased the deep lines etched there and made him appear ten years younger.

"Well, Rain Man, I'd say you better not wreck that, boy, or you'll be out a job."

Rainer chuckled as he nodded his agreement. Sam began inspecting the bike.

"Pretty sweet, huh?" Rainer urged. "You wanna drive her? It's custom. There's only five hundred of them in the world," he reminded.

Sam shook his head. "I've got no need to get anywhere as fast as that thing will take you there. You miss the scenery if you fly by it with your hair on fire."

"The torque and the traction control are epic." Rainer didn't want Sam to miss out on the opportunity.

"Um-hmmm." Sam dragged the rag over the Agusta as he studied the bike. "Let me explain something to you, son, a man doesn't buy a bike like that unless he's looking to spend money he doesn't want and he's trying to escape something that won't let him go. He's trying to tell the world to leave him alone, but that isn't what he really wants. He felt the need to make a gesture to the world, wasn't a nice one either. Brutal indeed."

Rainer's brow furrowed as he considered that. Sam was always right. He was the smartest man Rainer had ever met. Governor Haydenshire had recently stated in the press that if the Gifted Realm wanted the man with the most wisdom and empathy to run the Realm, they should elect Sam.

"Yeah," he finally agreed. "He has had a pretty rough life. His fiancée was murdered several years ago. He's never really gotten over it." Rainer's own comment began tumbling around in his mind.

Sam nodded his understanding. "I don't know that you're supposed to get over that, but that bike isn't gonna drive him out of that graveyard. I'll tell you that. Gotta learn to let the memories live on, even when the body has gone on without you. That isn't an easy thing, but I 'spect you know that." Sam bowed his head to Rainer.

"Yeah," Rainer choked. He'd been having fun on the Agusta. He didn't want to think about his dad. "It's not easy."

"No it's not, but tryin' to drive your motorcycle outta hell isn't an easy thing to do either."

Rainer drew a deep breath and nodded what he supposed was his agreement.

"Now, where's my sweet Emily?" Sam turned his dark, kind eyes back on Rainer and grinned.

"She's with Logan. I'm on my way to Will and Brooke's. They're helping me with her birthday present. This is gonna be huge."

Sam laughed at his exuberance. "I doubt she cares too much what it is so long as you remember her day."

"Oh I know, but she's gonna flip. This may be the best gift I've ever given her," Rainer insisted.

"Best thing you ever gave her was what's right inside there." He tapped his finger over Rainer's rib cage in the approximate location of his heart. "Don't ever forget that, boy. That's all she wants. Well, that and your attention. Flowers never hurt."

"I know, and she knows she has all of me. Trust me. I couldn't make it without her." He smiled as he realized how easily that had rolled off his tongue to Sam, when he would never have said that to most anyone else.

"You got that darn right, boy. Mrs. Rain Man needs to know that too, though." Sam grew thoughtful for a moment. Rainer wondered what he was thinking as he studied him. "Makes me wonder if your boss man there,"—he gestured to the bike—"might need himself his own sweet thang. It seems to me the right woman can make just about everything in the whole, entire world better."

Rainer wholeheartedly agreed, but he had no idea who could be that for Vindico.

CHAPTER 34
EMILY
LOGAN HAYDENSHIRE

"Aww, come on, Em. I'm not so bad, am I?" Logan walked Emily out to the Accord and waved to the Iodex officers who were heading home after watching Emily practice all day.

"No, of course not." Emily shook her head. She looked hurt that Logan thought she didn't want to hang out with him. He knew she would have preferred Rainer to pick her up though. "This whole being watched constantly thing is getting to me," she admitted in a fitful huff.

Logan nodded his understanding. "Let's go to Lesco's. I'll take you out even though you make like ten times what I do in a year," he commented with a chuckle. "We haven't hung out in forever."

"Okay." Emily gave him a sweet grin. "But I still miss Rainer." She seemed to decide to tease.

After giving her an eye roll, Logan chuckled. "But I'll do for an evening?"

"I suppose." She feigned disappointment.

∼

"Well, if it's not the Haydenshire half of the Fantastic Four," Les called as Emily and Logan fell into their usual booth in the back.

"How's it goin', Les?" Logan smiled.

"And where are your better halves this fine evening?" Les pulled the notepad from his waist apron.

"Adeline has to work late," Logan lamented.

"And I don't know where Rainer is because he wouldn't tell me," Emily sassed.

Logan shook his head at his little sister. "But it's for her birthday, and she's being a brat."

Les chuckled. "You two still sound like you're six and seven," he stated with a wistful look in his eye. The Haydenshires had been coming to Les's Pub since long before Logan and Emily had even been born.

"Hey, I saw your dad's running for governor or something?" Les quizzed Logan. Logan's eyes goggled as he shared an uncomfortable expression with Emily.

"Uh, yeah. It's just a local thing. Just to get the issues out there. You know?" Logan scoffed. The Gifted people most often hid themselves right out in the open. The campaign for the most powerful position in the entire world was being run with very little notice from the Non-Gifted.

"He has several signs out on the highway, but you know I don't ever know nothing about who's running for what. If I remember to vote this time, I'll check his box though," Les offered kindly.

Logan studied the menu he'd had memorized since he was ten. "He'd appreciate it."

Emily and Logan quickly placed their order in an effort to get Les to forget the signs he'd noticed on the interstate leading out of McLean.

As Les went to fix Logan and Emily's burgers and onion rings, Logan sighed. "I guess it's good the Non-Gifted don't pay too much attention to who's running for their local offices."

Emily shook her head. "I doubt it's good for them. That seems like a great way to let power get into the wrong hands."

Logan had to agree. "I don't know how to make them understand that."

"Just tell me, please," she begged in an abrupt subject change.

"Absolutely not. Rainer's working really hard to do this for you, and you're gonna flip, so lay off. I'm not telling you." He thanked Les for the beer he placed in front of him, but Emily still looked worried.

"Okay, but it sounds like he's probably spending a ton of money and going way out of his way, and I just...don't feel like I did all that much for his birthday. I don't want him to go to a lot of trouble with everything going on." She blushed.

Logan choked on the onion ring he'd just put in his mouth before Les even had the plate placed on the table.

He drew a long sip of beer to wash down the flaming hot onion ring stuck in his throat. "I do not, under any circumstances, want to think about what you gave Rainer for his birthday, but take it from me, as a guy—that was a huge, massive birthday gift. Like the best ever."

Emily giggled and rolled her eyes. They ate in silence for a few minutes before she started again.

"Okay, but where is he tonight?"

"Nope."

"I know he's spending a fortune on me, and I wish he wouldn't do that."

"Well, it's you, and I've never known Rainer not to spoil you rotten, so I don't know why that would shock you."

"You're in a terrible mood, and you're really nervous and worried. Wanna tell your little sister what's up? She might be able to help."

Logan drew a steadying breath. "I'm nervous about Adeline and tomorrow."

Emily's demeanor turned to deep concern. "What time's her appointment?"

"Two." Logan drew another sip of his beer.

"Garrett's gonna come stay with you and Rainer and the twins while I'm gone."

"Is Adeline okay?" Emily asked in a pained whisper. Logan tried hard not to blush but failed miserably.

He shook his head. "She's in pain, and it sort of seems like she has...uh...her cycle, period, thing, way more often than you're supposed to. I guess. I don't know," Logan choked but then forced himself to continue. "Have you ever had anything like that?"

Emily reached across the table, and he felt her soothing Receiver's cast work through his knuckles and into his heart. "It's okay. You can ask me about it. I know how much you love her. I can feel it, remember? Adeline told me everything, and like you said, you're not just my brother—you're one of my best friends."

Relief flooded through him. There were things he'd wanted to ask, but he'd been afraid he might upset Adeline. "So that's not normal?"

Emily looked crestfallen as she shook her head. "I don't think so, but Mom says she might have a cyst. They're usually kind of easy to heal as long as a medio figures it out in time."

"Yeah, that's what the medio said she thought it was too," Logan's heart raced as he forced out the question he'd needed answered for the past month.

"But that's not something that I caused?"

"No!" Emily vowed. "No, definitely not, and they're not unusual."

"The medio wanted to know if her mother ever had them, or if Ad could get her mother's medical records, but of course Candy told her no."

Emily shook her head in disgust.

"If it is a cyst, what happens?" Logan returned the rest of his burger to his plate. He was too worried to eat.

"I'm not entirely certain, but I think they'll either use their healing rhythms to make it disintegrate or they'll do surgery to remove it. I think it might depend on how large it is and where it's located. She might be in the hospital for a day or two. Then she'll have to rest and everything. Uh, you might have to take a little time off."

"From work? Of course!" Logan was unable to believe that Emily, of all people, would think he would leave Adeline alone to recover from surgery.

"Not from work." She offered Logan a pained expression.

"Oh." Logan nodded his understanding. Though that was the least of his worries, he did appreciate Emily being thorough. "Yeah...uh...I just want her to be healthy. That's fine."

"Right, I know. I was just trying to tell you everything that I know.

Fionna had one removed about a year ago. She's had a few. She couldn't challenge for a week, but she's totally fine now." Emily's voice turned reassuring.

Fionna Styler was the Senior Receiver on the Arlington Angels. She and Emily had become very close friends. They were also gaining quite a reputation of being a Receiving duo to be feared in the world of Summation.

Fionna Styler was also a total knockout. She and Garrett had been in school together and had hung out together often. Logan still got embarrassed whenever he saw her now as he recalled his many fantasies about Fionna in his early adolescence, long before he'd met and fallen in love with Adeline.

"If they do surgery and they get rid of it, then she'll stop hurting and bleeding all the time, and feeling so weak?" Logan loosed all of the terror that had plagued his soul for weeks. He felt some relief just in hearing that other people had suffered the same thing and had been restored to full health.

"Yeah, as long as that's the problem. Once they remove it, she'll be fine." Emily studied Logan closely. "Logan," she soothed as he met her concerned gaze. "If it's all right with Adeline, I could go with you tomorrow. I don't have practice and then you wouldn't have to sit there all alone."

"Thank you for being…pretty much the greatest sister ever." He lambasted himself for all of the hell he'd given Emily her whole life. "I don't think Adeline will mind. Maybe Rainer could come, if Garrett keeps the twins."

"If you want him there, you know that's where he'll be."

"Yeah," Logan nodded. He did know that, and he also knew that everyone deserved a best friend like Rainer Lawson, but that very few people were actually lucky enough to have one.

Emily rode with Logan to pick up Adeline from work. They talked about the election, Adeline, and about the new baby.

Georgetown Hospital was bustling, and Adeline was pale and weak as she hung up her white coat and let Logan guide her out of the hospital.

Emily climbed in the backseat so Adeline could sit beside Logan.

"You don't have to move," Adeline offered kindly. Logan shook his head.

"Yes, she does, and she's pouting. Just ignore her. She used to do this all the time growing up, but it only works on Dad and Rainer," Logan teased.

"Shut up." Emily made Adeline giggle. "Do you know where he is?" Emily quizzed Adeline hopefully. Logan was thrilled that Adeline was still laughing as she nodded.

"Yes, but I'm not telling you either."

"I love you." Logan watched his vow make Adeline beam. "Hey babe, Em wanted to know if you'd mind her coming tomorrow? You know, for your appointment?"

Emily grimaced in the rearview mirror and had Logan thinking he should've waited to ask Adeline when Emily wasn't around.

"But, if you just want me to go, that's fine too."

Adeline seemed thoughtful for a moment. "No, it's fine. I talked to Medio Dawson today, because I was…you know."

Logan gazed at her as his heart shattered. "In a tremendous amount of pain again," he supplied for her.

She nodded. "There's a small chance they'll go on and do surgery tomorrow if it is a cyst. I would feel better if someone was there with you." She sounded relieved.

Logan was dumbfounded. It was so like her to be concerned about him when she was the one who'd been in pain and bleeding for weeks, sometimes so badly she could hardly walk, and she was the one facing surgery.

"I'm not worried about me," Logan reminded her.

"I know," she soothed, "but I am."

CHAPTER 35
TAKE CARE OF HER

As they neared the farm, Adeline smiled at Logan. "Can we go see your mom for a minute? I want to talk to her if she's up for it."

There was nothing in the world he would deny Adeline, so Logan turned down the main cut-through toward his parents' home. He flashed his badge at all of the checkpoints.

"Are you sure you feel up to this? Maybe we should go home, and you should get into bed?"

"I'm okay." Her voice caught in her lie. She was hurting. She was weak, and she was scared. Logan knew it all instantly as soon as he reached and held her hand.

After resigning himself to the fact that his mother always made her feel better, he pulled the Accord in beside Rainer's Mustang.

"Well, look who's here," he teased Emily who was already out of the car before he'd even turned it off. He and Adeline followed Emily into the house and chuckled over her exuberance.

"You see him every day," Logan huffed.

"I know, but I love him, and maybe I can get him to tell me what my present is." Emily sounded like a wide-eyed child instead of a grown woman.

"Doubt it."

Emily's face fell as soon as they entered the kitchen. Vindico and Garrett were seated at the table while Mrs. Haydenshire supplied them with dessert, but Rainer was nowhere to be seen.

"Dan let him take the Agusta," Garrett informed her as he tousled her hair.

"Great, now he'll never come back." She joined in everyone's laughter.

Adeline disappeared to the bathroom. She looked pale and drawn, which made Logan's heart break yet again. Emily and Mrs. Haydenshire shared a concerned glance.

"Hey Garrett," Logan whispered. "Could you watch the twins tomorrow afternoon? Em and Rainer are going to come with us for Adeline's exam thing," Logan hedged uncomfortably. Mrs. Haydenshire patted Emily's shoulder.

"Maybe I should stay home tomorrow. I could meet your father the next day," Mrs. Haydenshire offered.

"Why? Do you think it's that serious?" Logan demanded.

"No," Mrs. Haydenshire soothed. "But I think it might be something you aren't quite prepared to deal with."

"I'll keep the twins. It's no problem." Garrett glanced at Vindico who nodded his approval.

"I can handle whatever it is, Mom. I'm going to marry her, so that means I'm going to take care of her. Whatever's wrong, I'll get her through it." Logan's resolve strengthened as he made his plea.

"Daniel, would you and Garrett mind checking the twins for me?" Mrs. Haydenshire urged. Everyone was aware they were being asked to leave.

"I have no doubt that you'll take care of her, but I want you to understand that she doesn't have anyone else but you two." Mrs. Haydenshire moved her glance from Logan to Emily. "This is not something even Rainer will be able to help you deal with. If she has a cyst, which I'm positive that she does, she could be in a great deal of pain after the surgery. Not to mention the fact that the recovery could be a little gruesome." Logan shook his head and tried not to be offended. He knew his mother was only trying to help.

"I can deal with blood. I'm not a kid anymore. Believe me. I've seen a fair amount lately." Logan choked as the images of waking up with Adeline's abdomen in a pool of her own blood and fluids made him shudder.

"Sweetheart," Mrs. Haydenshire squeezed his hand. "I have no doubt that you'll take the best care of her. I just feel like I'm abandoning you all to go out and tell people I've never even met that they should vote for your father. I shouldn't have to tell them. They should know. His work should stand for itself. My children need me here. It's infuriating."

"We'll be okay. I'll help Logan take care of Adeline. We can do it. Daddy needs you, and the Realm needs both of you," Emily vowed. With a weary sigh, Mrs. Haydenshire stood and planted kisses on Logan and Emily's heads.

"I'm so proud of both of you. In a few weeks, hopefully things will get back to normal. Only I'll be married to the Crown Governor and expecting his eleventh child. I suppose we'll have to see how that will all work."

Logan furrowed his brow. He couldn't recall another time in his life that his mother sounded unsure of anything. Adeline returned. She was looking paler by the moment as she took the seat beside Logan. He instantly reached for her hand. He wanted to feel her energy. It had been growing weaker by the day.

She drew from him, and he closed his eyes to supply her with his strength and love. The sensation of her pulling his energy into her body was heavenly.

"Have you eaten, sweetheart?" Mrs. Haydenshire fussed.

"Not yet," Adeline admitted. It infuriated Logan that she often had to work through meals, but he said nothing.

"Here." Mrs. Haydenshire fixed Adeline a plate of lasagna she'd warmed up for the twins, Garrett, and Vindico.

"Thank you." Adeline dug in. His mother had several words of encouragement for Adeline's exam the next day, and after she'd fixed Adeline a large bowl of ice cream, Logan insisted they head home.

Rainer turned up to thank Vindico for letting him drive the Agusta and to pick up the Mustang before heading home, so Emily rode with him back to the guesthouse.

After bidding Rainer and Emily goodnight, not in any mood to listen to his little sister try and flirt her birthday present out of Rainer, Logan led Adeline to bed. He drew her tenderly to his chest and reached to ease her scrub shirt over her head. She looked devastated.

"Logan, I can't. I'm a mess. I'm sorry." She fussed pitifully and gestured to her abdomen.

"I just want to put you to bed. I know, okay. Please stop apologizing." It broke his heart that she thought she was somehow disappointing him.

"I'm so sorry," she went on again, now apologizing for apologizing. Logan pulled one of his T-shirts over her head.

"No." She pulled it back off. "I don't want to mess another one up, and it's really bad tonight." Her tears finally shattered through her resolve.

He held her close and seated himself on their bed while he pulled her to his lap. She lay her head gently on his shoulder.

"Sweetheart, I don't give a damn how many of my T-shirts get blood on them, okay? We have washing machines. I just want you to be healthy and to feel safe and comfortable." She clung to him with all of the might she could manage which wasn't much.

"I got all of the blood out of the other one," she offered in a terrified plea.

"Adeline," Logan nearly shouted. "Please hear what I am saying to you. I do not care about anything else except whether or not you're okay. That's all that matters to me."

Her body convulsed slightly as her breath stuttered. "I'm so scared, and I shouldn't be scared. I'll be treating this in a few months. Why does this scare me? I know how they heal them. I'm going to be an obstetrics medio," she finally admitted in a heartbroken plea.

"I know, baby." He held her wrapped up in his arms. "But I will be right there the entire time. Whatever this is, I'm not going anywhere no matter what. I will take care of you, and I will get you through this. And taking care of other people is different from you, yourself, having a medical issue. I'm sure every other medio at Georgetown would be scared too."

She was so exhausted her rhythms ebbed just like they did when she slept. Logan grabbed the shirt he'd put on her moments before. He pulled her bra off of her and ignored her weak protests as he slipped the shirt back over her head.

"Come here to me." He summoned heat energy into his hand and ran it over the sheets and quilts on their bed. He laid her gently in the warmth he'd created, as he quickly removed everything but his boxers. He eased beside her and pulled her onto his chest.

"You are not working tomorrow morning."

She put up a weak argument, but he lightly touched her lips with his index finger. "No." He shook his head.

She was making it worse, forcing herself to work through the pain and massive blood loss. He'd suspected it for some time, but she was insistent that work wasn't aggravating the cyst.

"You are staying in bed until I take you to the hospital for your exam tomorrow."

The fact that she didn't argue this time terrified him.

He whispered how much he loved her and that everything would be all right for the few minutes that it took her to fall asleep in his arms.

He offered up a fervent prayer of thanks for her, a desperate plea that she would be all right, and that whatever she might need from him he would be able to supply.

With that, he drifted off to sleep, holding her.

CHAPTER 36
HIS FATHER'S SON

By noon, Logan was distraught. Adeline had been up several times in the night until Logan had finally given her a bath to ease the pain and convinced her to take the pain medication Brad had prescribed.

She'd finally fallen asleep near sunrise. He half walked, half carried her to the Hummer and let her lay her head in his lap as Rainer drove them to Georgetown. Rainer continually gave Logan sorrowful glances, but Logan knew Rainer really had no clue what to say or what to do with Adeline's current condition.

Medio Dawson had agreed to see Adeline early, at Logan's insistence. She'd commented that she could certainly tell whose son he was.

She was referring to the way his father often acted when one of his children or his wife was in need of medical attention. Logan had decided to take it as a compliment since he didn't know anyone who loved his family more than his dad.

Adeline had made it into the hospital and then promptly fainted. Logan caught her as Rainer moved to help him.

"We need a medio, now!" Rainer shouted. As most of the waiting room consisted of Non-Gifted people, they all stared at him like he might be crazy, since they had no idea what a medio was. Logan

237

glanced around frantically. With a slight headshake, he carried Adeline to the nurses' station, and she was taken away on a stretcher.

"I'm sorry, Officer Haydenshire, but you're not related, and you're not married. It's hospital policy. You'll have to wait here," the nurse had rather tersely informed him. It absolutely wasn't hospital policy, and Logan was furious.

"Do you have any idea who I am?" Logan had demanded as Emily and Rainer's mouths dropped open in shock. Logan never played the governor's son card.

"Yes, Officer Haydenshire, I do, but right now I need to go find out what is wrong with Miss Parker. When I know something, I'll be sure that you do as well." The woman turned on her heels and disappeared behind two swinging steel doors.

∼

Logan paced relentlessly. Emily tried to soothe him with her cast, but his internal shield had set and nothing was going to get through to him, nothing but Adeline.

Rainer tried to assure him that she was in the very best hands, but his reassurances sounded distant and tunneled. Logan could hardly hear them. The roar of his own terror was too loud.

An hour went by, and Logan was frantic. Rainer narrowed his eyes as he marched to the nurses' station. The nurse who'd informed Logan that he couldn't go back into surgery with Adeline, even though that was typically allowed during a Gifted surgery, had returned, but she'd refused to speak.

"Look!" Rainer spat. "I know you know who I am and whose son I am. I also know that everyone keeps telling him that you don't know anything. So, listen up! The love of his existence is back there unconscious. No one will tell us anything, and you won't let him back there because he hasn't married her yet. So," Rainer menaced, "you can go find me a minister so that he can marry her now so that you'll let him back there with her, or you can get up and go back and find something out before I get Crown Governor Vindico on the phone and see if we can't get a little information."

Logan couldn't recall another time in his entire life he'd been so happy that Rainer Lawson was his best friend.

"Yes, Mr. Lawson." The nurse slid her rolling chair back and slunk back through the doors that they'd taken Adeline through. Being the son of the most beloved Crown Governor of all time certainly had its perks.

"Thank you," Logan choked.

"No problem," Rainer scoffed. Emily was beaming at him, but he still looked rather put out. To everyone's fury, another hour passed and the nurse never returned to her desk.

No one seemed to know anything about Adeline.

CHAPTER 37
FORTUNE TELLER

While Logan was contemplating marching through the swinging steel doors and demanding to see Adeline, wherever she may be, Brad issued through them. He was covered in blood. Rabid fury blazed through Logan's veins. He wrapped his hands around Brad's collar.

"Where is Adeline?" he growled. Brad looked momentarily terrified, but he placed his hand on Logan's shoulder. He seemed to contemplate the move for a few moments first.

"Get your hand the hell off of my shoulder before I remove it from your body, and tell me where Adeline is," Logan snarled.

"Sit down," Brad soothed. Logan's jaw clenched as he fell into the closest chair.

"I'm sitting!" he shouted. Brad glanced around and took in the waiting room full of people that were all studying the two of them.

"She's all right. Medio Dawson did a vaginal exam first, but there was a great deal of blood and fluid." Brad looked like this information might be more than Logan could bear.

Logan was growing weary of people thinking he wasn't tough enough to deal with whatever was wrong with the very reason for his existence. "I could have told you that, if anyone had let me come back there with her," he fumed.

Brad backed away from Logan slightly before continuing. "So, we did a thermographic scan, and the cyst was rupturing. We had to operate immediately to try and save her ovary. I would have informed you, but it was critical that we get it out as fast as we possibly could. We were locked in an operating room, and I'm sorry no one told you anything."

All of the blood slithered from Logan's head to his feet. Rainer braced his shoulder as he tried to remind himself to breathe.

"They've removed the cyst, and several medios have her casted. They're trying to get the lining in her ovary to heal, but she's going to have to stay here overnight. We're quite concerned the rupture might've damaged part of her left ovary." Brad glanced up at Rainer. He was clearly not certain he should say all of this to anyone but Logan.

Rainer gestured his head to the left. "I'm gonna go over there with Em. Call me if you need me."

Logan could only concentrate on what Brad was telling him.

"What does that mean exactly?" Logan choked.

"It could be nothing. It could affect her menstrual cycle slightly, but I doubt it. If the lining is damaged, it could make it more difficult for her to conceive when you want to have children—not impossible, just more difficult," Brad offered. "I will get you back there once she's back in the room. I didn't know if you wanted me to tell her or if you wanted to, but whatever you want, man, I'll do. I'm really sorry we left you hanging for so long. I know how much you love her, and I would never have allowed this to happen if it hadn't been absolutely necessary we take her to surgery immediately. You should have been in there. She would have healed faster with your shield."

It took Logan a minute to understand why the ground was moving. He stared at his hand. He was shaking.

"She's really all right?" he demanded of Brad.

"She's fine or she will be in a few minutes. She'll have to rest a little. No work for a week, and Medio Dawson will tell you when you can resume sexual activity, but I would say about two weeks. Physically, other than the possible lining damage, she's perfectly healthy now." Since Logan wasn't in any way comfortable discussing their sex life with Brad, he decided to focus on the fact that Adeline was going to be fine.

"I want to see her."

"I know, but the surgery was fairly complicated. We had to sedate her and drain all of her Gifted energies. Then she had multiple casts moving through her, until we reached her ovary. We had to dislodge the cyst, which was rupturing, and force the fluid out of her body. While we were healing the follicle, we noticed the damage. She's probably going to be very weak and very sore for a few days. Let them finish their job, then you can see her. I promise you."

Logan stood and began pacing again. "Don't say anything about the damage. I'll tell her." If anyone was going to tell her that they might have trouble having children, it should be him.

"Okay. I'll come and get you as soon as she's in recovery. She's quite a healer, so her own body should continue to heal the damage. In all likelihood she'll fully recover."

Logan studied Brad for a moment. He knew that Brad either wasn't romantically interested in Adeline or was afraid to mess with an Iodex officer's girl, as he'd stated a few weeks before. Logan still didn't like Brad, but in that moment he extended his hand.

"Thank you. Thank you for taking care of her."

Brad smiled and nodded. "That's my job, and it was my pleasure. She adores you. You're a really lucky guy."

"I know." Logan let his tone sound appreciative with a hint of warning. With a slight chuckle, Brad stood and backed away.

He held up his hands. "Still not interested," he assured Logan.

"Good." His shield was running the show.

"I'm going to go back and check on her. They should be finishing her up soon and setting the pain meds in her IV. I'll come back and get you in just a few minutes."

"Thank you," Logan urged again. His world began to steady. With a nod, Brad disappeared back through the swinging doors.

Logan fell back into the chair and leaned his head against the cold concrete wall. He allowed himself to breathe. Emily made her approach.

"Are you okay?"

"I don't know," Logan admitted. He saw Rainer grin as he followed Emily over.

"Is she okay?" Rainer quizzed.

"Yeah, they took the cyst out. It was rupturing but you heard that, right?" Logan stammered, not certain what Rainer had been privy to before he'd left.

"But it wasn't malignant?" Emily asked in a pained whisper.

"What?!" Logan gasped. "No! I didn't even know it could be that. No one told me that." Emily patted his arm. He felt her trying to cast him discreetly to calm him down, but he was still unreachable.

Cancer was one of the few things that Gifted medios were unable to heal. Cancer forced the body's cells to form incorrectly and quickly. The energy the body uses to heal itself, which is created and stored in the cells formed in the Gifted person's body, couldn't be used to restore their health.

Medios typically tapped into the Gifted person's cells then added in their own ample amounts of healing energies to heal them at a more rapid rate than a Non-Gifted person's body was capable of doing.

It was more physiological than Logan really understood when Adeline had tried to explain it to him. He just knew that cancer was bad, and that Gifted medios and Non-Gifted doctors alike were equally stumped as to find a way to prevent or cure it.

"It would've been very rare for it to have been. I was just making sure."

He forced Emily's question out of his mind. He couldn't go there. Adeline was going to be perfectly fine. Brad had just told him that, and that was what he had to keep focusing on.

"When can you see her?" Rainer seemed to understand that Logan was barely holding on to his sanity. Logan recognized the gravelly tone that Rainer used when he calmed Emily down from one of her signature freak-outs. He drew a steadying breath and swallowed down a great deal of emotion.

"As soon as she's back in her room. Brad's supposed to come get me in a few minutes." Logan tried to sound calmer than he was capable of feeling at the moment.

"Do you want me to come with you?" Emily offered.

"No." Logan shook his head and forced a smile for his sister. She was blinking back tears from just experiencing his emotions. "I mean...maybe you can in a little while...if the medios say it's okay," he faltered. He was unable to reason why he couldn't make coherent statements. "But I need to talk to her first."

He tried to formulate how to tell Adeline that she may have some trouble getting pregnant, and much more importantly, how to convince her that her ability to give him children mattered a great deal more to her than it ever had to him.

"Hey Em, baby,"—Rainer pulled several dollars from his pocket, and Logan knew what he was up to—"would you mind going and grabbing us something from the vending machine?" He winked at Emily. She hugged Logan and then stood.

"Of course." She smiled down at Logan. "Dr Pepper?"

"Yeah, thanks," he replied without any real enthusiasm. Rainer replaced Emily in the seat beside Logan.

"Do you know how you're gonna tell her?"

"I don't even care if we don't ever have kids. It's just convincing her of that." Logan was too exhausted and too worried not to take the opportunity to listen to help when it was readily available.

In Logan's experience, Rainer's advice was always good. He sincerely hoped Adeline wouldn't mind.

"Yeah, I figured. I think I'd just tell her what you just told me, and keep telling her until she listens. You know, that you don't care if you ever have kids and that you just want her."

"That was my basic plan," he admitted. "Is that what you'd tell Em?" He watched Rainer closely. He would know if he were lying.

Rainer slid back in the chair he was seated in and seemed to consider for a long drawn moment. "Yeah," he admitted. "I mean, of course that's what I would say, but I think I'd have to lie a little more than you are." He offered Logan a slight smile as confusion pulsed in his energy. "I do really want kids, but I know that you really don't care. I guess I kind of do. Not that something like that, or anything at all," he vowed, "would change the way I feel about Em, but I guess I'd be a little disappointed." He laid it all out on the table for Logan. That was the way they'd always been.

Trying to envision his life in ten years, or twenty, wasn't something Logan did very often. He lived for the moment, and that had always been the way he'd gone through life. He didn't see the point in trying to predict the future.

Until the night Adeline had decided she was ruining his life and had moved back into her mother's apartment and broken up with him, the future had seemed like an inevitability but always out of reach.

That horrific night had forced Logan to look at his future in blatant acridity, and he'd known that a future without Adeline wasn't anything he wanted a part of. She was all that mattered, all he wanted, or would ever need.

If she was there, he was happy and complete. If she wanted children, then that was fine with him. He would do his damndest to be a good dad, just like his father. All he wanted was to be with her until he drew his last breath. That was all that mattered. Suddenly Logan knew precisely what he had to tell her—the truth.

Emily returned after taking her time with drinks and bags of chips for the three of them. She'd been trying to give them time to really talk.

Logan drew a long sip of Dr Pepper. He was getting anxious again. He needed to see Adeline, to touch her, and to know that she was really all right.

Brad reappeared and smiled at Logan.

CHAPTER 38
ADELINE

"She's back in her room. She's just waking up, and she's asking for you," Brad informed Logan. Logan's heart faltered as he stood.

"Can I see her now?" he begged.

"Yeah, just you for right now though," he offered as an apology to Rainer and Emily.

"That's fine," Emily assured him. "We'll be right here."

"She asked for you the entire time we were putting her under, and she's still asking for you while she's coming out of the anesthesia. I'd say she's just as crazy about you as you are about her." Brad slapped Logan on the shoulder as he made the observation.

Not really interested in a commentary on their relationship from Brad, Logan edged toward the doors. Brad ran a magnetic cast through his hand as he waved his hospital badge over the locking mechanism, which made the doors swing open.

"Come on." He guided Logan through.

Logan ran his hands over his face and willed Brad to walk faster.

"There was a very slight amount of damage from the rupture that we weren't able to heal." He walked and talked slowly. "I don't think it will affect anything, but it could make conception minutely more difficult for the two of you. Medio Dawson and I agree that in time her body will most likely heal it on its own. It's rare for a Valeduto Predilect to have a cyst in the first place, since we heal so readily. We think it's the sheer amount of stress she's been under. It affected her energy and therefore affected her cells' ability to heal." Brad stopped outside of a room with the door closed. "You can go on in. She should be awake by now, and I'd definitely still use the cast until you decide you want kids." Brad tried for a joke, but Logan wasn't really in the mood.

"Thanks." Logan reached for the handle and jerked the door open. She gave him a weak smile as he rushed to her.

"Baby." Logan took her hand and seated himself in the chair by the hospital bed. "Are you okay?" She looked so weak and frail. Adeline turned toward him. She grimaced and clutched her side.

"Don't move. I'll move anywhere you want me." He reseated himself on the bed beside her so she could see him without turning.

"I feel much better actually," she whispered. "I'm sore and weak though, but at least it's gone." Logan brushed a kiss across her forehead. He couldn't stop himself. He needed to kiss her. His lips craved her skin like a parched man craved water.

"Brad said you yelled at him." She was smiling up at him sweetly.

"I didn't yell," Logan stumbled over his lie. She laughed but then grimaced again and moved her hand to her abdomen. She resituated herself slightly.

"I kind of think that's really sweet and really sexy," she informed him in a whisper. Logan gazed at her as a slight chuckle escaped his lips.

"Do you?" He reveled in the sound of her voice.

"I do."

He saw the slight twinkle that he loved returning to her eyes, and he grinned at her as his heart swelled.

"Well then, I did yell, really, really loudly, at a lot of people."

She giggled. The sound righted his entire world. Adeline was quiet for a few long minutes while Logan told her how much he loved her and how worried he'd been.

"Logan..." she urged in a pained whisper.

"What, baby, are you hurting?" He panicked, but she shook her head.

"Will you stay with me tonight? I know I work here, but I'm scared to stay by myself."

Logan rubbed her hand in his own. "They couldn't pry me out of here with a crowbar. I'm not going anywhere. I'll leave this room when I can take you home with me." After giving him a thankful smile, Adeline yawned.

"Do you want to go to sleep, sweetheart?" Logan wondered if he should sit somewhere else so she could rest, and he wouldn't mind putting off the inevitable questions that were going to come. She was an obstetrics medio. She knew. Adeline shrugged but didn't release his hand.

"Maybe in a little while." She seemed to force herself to say whatever was coming. Logan braced. "Did it damage my ovary when it ruptured?" She locked her beautiful onyx eyes on him. She was making certain he wasn't lying.

"A little bit." Logan's heart fractured as tears welled in her eyes. "But Medio Dawson and Brad think that your body will continue to heal all on its own, beyond what they were able to force it to do today. Brad says the effect, if any, will be minute." He took both of her hands in his. He was desperate to soothe her. He reached and wiped the tears tenderly off of her face.

"But what if I can't…?" she stuttered, but Logan shook his head and touched his index finger gently across her lips to quiet every fear of her heart. Logan was certain she already knew everything he was going to say, but she wanted to hear him say it.

"Just listen to me, okay? It's like there's a tiny chance it would affect you getting pregnant but not much at all. My understanding of how all of this works is that you just keep trying until it takes, and if you decide that you really want kids…because you know I don't care. I only want you…" He wiped away more tears before he continued. "Then I am more than happy to repeatedly have sex with you until I knock you up for as long as it takes," he pledged as she laughed through her tears.

"Oh, it hurts to laugh." She winced.

"I'm sorry." Logan regretted teasing her.

Once he'd settled her back down and held a cup of ice water for her to sip through a straw, she still seemed to study him.

"You really don't care?" Disbelief and fear echoed in her tone. He gave her his own version of the signature Haydenshire smirk as he shook his head.

"I don't care at all. I told you if you want kids then we'll have kids. If not, then I'm perfectly happy as long as I get you." He brushed another kiss across her cheek. She let her eyes close in an extended blink as she reveled in his kiss. After he made certain that she believed him, he moved back to the chair beside the bed.

"Why don't you sleep, baby? I'll stay right here, and Em will probably force her way back here to check on you in a little while," he teased again just to see her smile.

Before she could respond, Medio Dawson and a nurse entered after an abrupt knock.

"Feeling better, Adeline?" Medio Dawson moved to the machines at Adeline's head. She seemed pleased with the readings and turned to Logan. "And this must be Logan." She gave Logan an overly appraising huff.

"Yes, ma'am." Logan offered her his hand. She scowled and held up her own hands as disgust etched her harsh features.

"Germs!" She grimaced, as she indicated why she wouldn't shake his hand.

"Right." Logan reseated himself with an eye roll.

"I've never had a patient ask for her husband as many times as Adeline asked for you while we were putting her under. I figured I needed to meet the guy with his claws in our Adeline. Must be quite a man." Her tone bordered on a disgusted sneer.

"He is," Adeline vowed. "But he's not my husband yet."

"If anyone had let me know what was going on, I would've been back there." Logan was still furious with the medio and the nurse for not telling him anything for so long, especially if Adeline was asking for him. The thought of her pleading for him and him not being there made him physically ill.

"See, Erma, I told you he's just like the governor," Medio Dawson huffed. Logan rolled his eyes but then a broad grin spread across his face.

"Oh, that reminds me. Governor Haydenshire phoned from Albuquerque and said that Adeline was to be kept here until Logan was certain that she was ready to go home," Erma informed Medio Dawson.

"Yes, well," Medio Dawson scoffed. "Logan, if you'll just step out, we'll get her bandages changed. You can head on home. She should be ready to leave around noon tomorrow," Medio Dawson directed haughtily. Terror-filled tears leaked from Adeline's eyes.

"No," Logan commanded. He squeezed Adeline's hand and brushed a tender kiss on her forehead. "I'll stay right here while you change the bandages. And I'll stay right here until she's released tomorrow, unless I determine that she needs to stay longer. And in that case, I'll still be right here," he dared either the medio or the nurse to argue with him. He wasn't certain which was more satisfying, the stunned expression on Medio Dawson's face or the adoring one on Adeline's. He crossed his arms over his chest. He wasn't moving.

"Well, that will depend entirely on Miss Parker's wishes. Adeline, I will remind you you're perfectly capable of staying by yourself. You certainly don't need a man to stay with you."

"I don't want him to leave." Adeline clung to Logan's hand. "I mean unless you don't want to see them change the bed pad thing." If ever there was an opportunity to prove to her that he was in this for the long haul, Logan knew this was the time.

"I'm not going anywhere, sweetheart. I'll be fine."

"It's up to you," Medio Dawson quizzed Adeline. She considered for a few minutes as Logan rubbed her hand in his own and prayed she'd let him prove himself.

"It's fine. You can change them."

With a resolute nod, the nurse flung the sheets and blanket back off of Adeline. She began to shiver, though Logan wasn't certain if she was cold or nervous. He moved to the bed as the medio lifted the gown she was wearing. Tears leaked out of Adeline's eyes as they pulled a large square disposable padding out from underneath her. The motion made her wince and gasp in pain.

"Shhh, it's okay," Logan soothed. "Easy, geez, she just had surgery," he spat viciously as he turned from Adeline as the medio rolled her to her side rather forcefully.

The padding on the bed under Adeline was covered in blood—the remnants of the cyst, Logan assumed—but Adeline looked terrified that it would scare him off. As if the fact that she bled was going to make him run from the room and from her.

His only concern was that she wasn't in any more pain and that she knew that he wasn't going anywhere. There was no internal bandaging and, as far as Logan could tell, changing the bed padding was the only thing that would have to be done until her body had dispensed with the blood from the cyst.

Adeline clung to Logan as Medio Dawson pressed around in the general area to make certain that it continued to drain properly. Logan stopped short of screeching at her to get her hands off of Adeline. He swallowed down his fury as he assumed it was necessary and used all of his flagging energies to let Adeline squeeze his biceps forcefully. He whispered that he loved her, that he wasn't going anywhere, and that it would be over soon.

A few minutes later, Logan helped change Adeline's hospital gown. He asked if she'd like Rainer to go home and get her something more comfortable to sleep in. She looked anguished, and Logan knew she'd like that but didn't want to be any trouble to Emily and Rainer.

"Lie back, sweetheart." Logan eased her back onto the pillows stacked behind her.

"It would be best if you slept." Medio Dawson was still glaring at Logan. "The more rest you get, the faster you'll heal, and your Gifted energies will be restored. I'm heading home in an hour or so, but I'll check on you before I go. No work for a week, and no physical strain for the same length of time. You can resume sexual activity once the bleeding has stopped for a full twenty-four-hour period, but take it easy, Mr. Haydenshire." She shot him a cold glare.

Logan ground his teeth and tried to reign in his fury. "Obviously!"

Adeline took his hand and tried to soothe him, but she had no access to her Gifted abilities yet. Medio Dawson made her exit while Erma changed the fluid bags on the IV.

"She hates men. All of them," Adeline explained with Erma nodding her agreement. "She's a really good medio though."

"Yeah, well, the feeling is mutual," Logan huffed. Adeline and the nurse both laughed. Brad made another appearance and asked Adeline if anything felt tender or if there was any unbearable pain. Logan asked if he would send Emily in when he got a chance. Emily appeared a few minutes later and looked anguished. She rushed to Adeline's bedside.

"Are you okay?" As Logan had set his shield cast over Adeline so that she could use his Gifted energy to restore her own, Emily stopped short to keep from intercepting his shield.

"I'm okay." Adeline yawned. She was still clinging to Logan's hand. He lowered his shield, and Emily gave her a tender hug.

"Rainer and I are going home and bringing both of you clothes for tomorrow and you something to eat." She gestured to Logan. "Anything else?"

"Yeah, will you bring her that navy blue Ioses T-shirt of mine from last year?" Logan winked at Adeline. He knew that was her favorite.

"That's my favorite too. It's so soft. I sleep in Rainer's all the time."

"Will you bring my toothbrush and some of those pads in our bathroom? I've seen the ones here, and they terrify me." Adeline explained her request. Emily chuckled and began making a list on her phone.

"Done. Anything else? Can you eat?" Emily took in the IV.

Adeline shook her head. "That's just a bag of fluid. I'm sure they'll be in with broth soon, but that's probably all I can have."

CHAPTER 39
THE PAIN

Logan awoke in the middle of the night. He was stiff from sleeping in a hardback chair against the cold concrete wall. Adeline was shifting constantly and moaning. Logan leapt up.

"What's wrong, baby?" He studied her and tried to locate the source of the obvious pain.

"I think the pain pills wore off, and I don't have enough energy to make it stop hurting." She trembled and writhed in the bed. "Go get somebody, please!" Tears spilled from her onyx eyes.

"I'll be right back!" Logan raced out the door. He frantically searched the empty corridors until he located an orderly.

"Adeline Parker, she's hurting. She needs more pain medication. She should have had it"—Logan rolled his left wrist and took in the time—"three hours ago!" he demanded furiously.

"All right, man, I'll find her nurse, but I can't give out pills." The orderly clearly thought Logan should have known that.

"Quickly! Like now!" Logan demanded. With a shrug, the guy meandered back toward the nurses' station. Not happy with the response he'd been given, Logan continued to search the hospital corridors at three in the morning. He finally located the very nurse who'd denied him access. Logan wasn't taking no for an answer anymore. He demanded her medication.

The nurse followed Logan back to Adeline's room and checked her chart. She proceeded to take her blood pressure and then, to complete Logan's fury, she commented that it was elevated.

"Of course it's elevated! Look at her. She's in pain."

"Logan," Adeline tried to scold, but her body was contorted from the pain in her abdomen.

"I'll be right back," the nurse informed them. To Logan's relief, she returned a few minutes later carrying two pills and some water. Over an hour later, Logan rubbed Adeline's leg tenderly and soothed her back to sleep.

She awoke again several hours later and had improved. Her energy had been restored, and when Logan finally convinced her to let him check the padding on the bed, he found it nearly clean. The morning shift came in, and Brad came to check on Adeline.

"The worst of it seems to be over." He checked Adeline's chart. "Medio Dawson will be in soon. Once she clears her, you can take her home, Logan."

An hour later, Logan had pulled his Accord around. He was thankful Rainer had driven it up for him, when he and Emily had returned with his dinner the evening before. He pushed her in the customary wheelchair out to his car.

"Are you okay?" Logan quizzed as he drove home and tried to avoid potholes or turns. Adeline nodded and gave him her sweet smile, the one that generally made his heart pound.

"You're so sweet, and you took such good care of me. I will never deserve you."

"Stop. You know that isn't true," he informed her for the hundredth time. She rolled her eyes and grinned at him as he drove.

"I'm glad it's over with and that I'm going home. I have so much more empathy for my patients now. Those beds are horrible." Logan chuckled. He was astounded by how much better she was in just twenty-four hours.

"Rainer and Garrett have the twins at our house so I can help watch them and take care of you." He wasn't certain how much of the logistical planning of the next few days she'd actually heard.

"I still feel terrible we're missing Emily's challenge and your parents' big party tomorrow."

"Ad, stop. Believe me, I would so much rather spend the day just the two of us hanging out at our house than stuffed into my tux, smiling until my cheeks hurt, and listening to people tell me how great Dad is, not that I disagree." He was surprised Adeline seemed to believe him.

"But I know you would love to see the Angels and the Bombers duke it out."

"We'll watch it on TV. I just want you to get well." Logan eased the car down the gravel path to the guesthouse. He managed to get the car parked with Adeline only wincing twice.

"I'm sorry," he vowed repeatedly. Rainer and Garrett appeared in the garage as soon as he'd turned off the car.

"Need some help, Miss Adeline?" Garrett smiled as he moved to open the passenger side door for her. He practically lifted her out of the car and eased her into the house. Logan lamented the fact that his big brother's rippling muscles had come to the rescue of his fiancée though he knew he should have been thankful.

The ride home had taken its toll, and Adeline looked exhausted again. Logan settled her in the bed and helped her pull off the sundress she'd worn home so nothing would press against her abdomen. It had been an ingenious idea of Emily's.

He helped Adeline into a T-shirt and covered her up in the quilts on their bed. She fell asleep almost instantly, and Logan tiptoed back out into the living room and shushed the twins.

"How's she doing?" Rainer looked truly concerned.

"Much better." Logan allowed himself to breathe. "She's just really tired. There was a lot of blood loss, you know."

Rainer and Garrett both grimaced.

"So, there's still no way you can come tomorrow?" Rainer asked again.

"No, she'd never make it through a party like that, but if we went she'd try to. She'll be up and around in a few days. We'll be at the debates next week."

"And she'll be good for Em's birthday, right?" Rainer asked.

"Yeah, definitely. That's over two weeks away, and she can't wait. We'll be there. No worries."

Rainer glanced at his watch. "All right, I'm headed to Boston with a plane full of Angels." He chuckled. "So…should be interesting."

"We'll see you tomorrow, man," Garrett pledged. He and the rest of the family were flying up with the twins for the party Saturday afternoon. Unfortunately, the Senate fleet of jets couldn't be used for the family as they were heading to an event for the governor's campaign, so they all had to fly Gifted commercial.

Emily had been planning the epic gala for her parents all week and was having a ball doing it. Rainer had helped when she'd asked. He'd been happy to be doing something to help Governor Haydenshire and to be giving financially to the campaign.

"All right, I'm gone. Tell Adeline I hope she feels better." Rainer grabbed the suitcases and headed to the Hummer.

CHAPTER 40
FIRE WATCH
RAINER LAWSON

Rainer waved to the officers at the checkpoints of the gates to Haydenshire Farm as he headed to the arena to pick up Emily. He stopped briefly at the gas station, raced inside, then jumped back in the car.

Rainer summoned the energy in the air around him and pushed the pedal on the Hummer. The car shot forward. He was late. He made it to Angels Arena in just under fifteen minutes, a new personal best.

He quickly casted the Hummer in the shield cast Vindico had taught him. It continually drew power from the air and gained intensity the longer it was left intact. He headed inside after flashing his badge to all of the security and Iodex officers situated throughout the stadium.

Emily looked nervous as he entered the field. Chloe was giving out boarding passes to the Angels' personal jet to each of the Angels. Rainer joined a cluster of men in the back of the field. They were all awaiting their significant others. The Angels were dismissed, and Emily headed his way. She handed him the boarding passes.

"What's wrong?" He took Emily's hand.

"I'm just nervous. I've never thrown a huge party like this before, and it's so important. And Chloe and Garrett had some kind of a huge blowup, and now she keeps trying to get information out of me."

He guided her back to the Hummer and tried to decide which part of Emily's worries he should delve into first.

"What did Chloe and Garrett fight about?"

"Apparently my brother and Chloe went to a club Monday night for Labor Day, since we weren't at the beach. She saw him flirting with another girl, so she went home with a different guy. He took two girls back to his place after Chloe left. They were still there when Chloe showed up at his house later that night to apologize."

With his mouth hanging open in shock, Rainer had no idea how to respond to that.

"Yeah," Emily sighed. "I love him, but I wish he wouldn't bang my friends."

"I guess that's why Garrett's coming up tomorrow with your family instead of tonight with the Angels."

"You got it." Emily crossed her arms over her chest as Rainer unloaded their luggage and followed her behind the stadium to the Angels hangar, which housed the large, luxurious plane that carried the Arlington Angels anywhere they might be challenging.

"I know he's freaking out about Vasquez. I can feel it whenever I'm near him." Emily's tone turned from frustration to concern. "I just wish he wouldn't drown his sorrows in various, unnamed women." Rainer knew she was right. He just didn't know how to fix the problem. Garrett had been even more brash and wild ever since he'd unloaded his pistol into Roberto Vasquez a few weekends ago.

The many varied Angels pilots and coolant officers began boarding the plane. There were several large closets for the luggage, and the seats were all lambskin leather. They were arranged in small coves for the passengers to tuck into.

"Are you two gonna join the mile high club?" Dana chanted as she passed the seats Rainer and Emily had chosen. Emily looked momentarily confused but then she blushed and shook her head. Rainer waited to see if he needed to tell her what that meant.

"There are three private rooms on the jet. Chloe and Garrett usually take one, but since they're fighting you could probably grab theirs," Dana explained. "We're using that one." She pointed to a closed door labeled suite three. Paran was staring at his wife like he would take a bite right then and there if she offered.

"Uh, well," Emily hemmed. "My dad is running for Crown Governor, and I just somehow think if Rainer and I did make use of one of the suites,"—Emily gestured back to the rooms—"it would somehow make it into every Gifted publication between here and LA, so I'm gonna go with no."

"Maybe after the election," Dana offered.

Rainer's heart raced as he tried to imagine having sex in an airplane with Emily, while everyone in the entire plane knew what they were doing. He shuddered slightly. Emily laced her fingers through Rainer's.

"Maybe," she shrugged. There didn't seem to be anything else to say. As soon as Dana and Paran made their way into the suite, Rainer leaned to whisper in Emily's ear.

"Baby, if you want to join the mile high club, I will rent us a plane so that only you and I, and maybe the pilot, know what we're doing."

"I'm really still pretty new to all of this, and I really like sex on the ground. I don't need it to go to all new heights."

Rainer wrapped his arm around her. "I love you."

The plane taxied away from the stadium and climbed into the sky. Fifteen minutes later, they were landing at Boston Logan. The Angels' jet with its full flight crew of Gifted pilots flew with a great deal of speed.

"Oh, sad for Dana. I guess Paran's a two-pump chump." Emily giggled as Rainer choked on the sip of Dr Pepper he'd just swallowed. After coughing and clearing his throat, he stared at Emily in utter shock.

"Where did you hear that terminology, Miss Haydenshire?" He tried not to laugh as Paran and Dana exited their suite. He looked slightly dazed. She looked highly irritated.

"I have seven older brothers, remember?"

"Who I am apparently going to have to have yet another discussion with over what they say in front of you," he declared as he retrieved their suitcases from one of the luggage closets.

"Rainer, I'm not twelve anymore. I know all about lots of things. I know you're my Shield, but I promise I'm fine."

"Is that so?" Rainer led her off the plane.

"Yes," Emily drawled in a quick retort. "Quiz me!" They walked through Boston Logan Airport following the rest of the team to the vans that would be taking them to the Orange Grove Hotel, where the team was staying in the top floor suites. Governor Haydenshire's gala was being held in their ballroom the following evening.

"Quiz you?" Rainer tried not to laugh but failed miserably.

"Yes, quiz me. I bet I know way more dirty stuff than you think I do. Like I knew what cleaning your pipes meant and Adeline didn't. Remember at the beach?"

Rainer shook his head and continued to laugh. "Just because your brothers are uncouth and say stuff like that in front of you does not mean that I would ever, ever repeat half of the things they say, especially to you."

"I know and that's really sweet, but I just don't want you to think you have to protect me all the time," she lamented as they climbed into one of the vans.

"As you just stated, I am your Shield. Protecting you is the most important thing that I will ever do. I'm sorry if it gets on your nerves, but I love you more than life itself. Keeping you safe is my job. That's how Ioses Shields are wired. You know this." To his relief, she tucked herself up under his embrace as the van driver summoned and casted the engines.

A few minutes later, bellmen rushed out of the front doors to load the luggage onto carts and to welcome the team.

CHAPTER 41
MR. LAWSON

"Okay," Chloe called. "For any of you who might want to see outside of your hotel room and have a little fun, after I get to my room and put on lipstick, we're heading out to party with the Harvard guys down in Cambridge. Just text me if you want to go, but also remember we're the Angels, so everything you do represents the team." She grabbed Fionna and jerked her closer.

Fionna looked highly annoyed. "I'm not going," Fionna said. She also looked begrudged to annoy Chloe, however.

"Why not?" Chloe demanded.

"Because I need some time to myself."

Rainer took Emily's hand and made their way to the check-in desk.

"Are you going to party with Harvard guys?" Rainer teased.

Emily laughed. "Nope, I was kind of hoping to have a party for two with this really good-looking guy from Venton though." She flirted with a hungry look in her emerald eyes. A broad grin spread across Rainer's face as his heart picked up pace.

"Venton, huh?" He smirked. "Tough school. Anybody I know?" He handed the envelope containing Emily's Angel passes and credentials to the clerk.

"You'd probably recognize him if you saw him," Emily assured him with a great deal of sass. Rainer swallowed down raw need as he allowed his eyes to trace down her curves.

The tight jeans she'd worn put her backside on jaw-dropping display, and her ample cleavage had his mouth watering to see more. He took the envelope back from the clerk, and led Emily past the grand staircase and toward the elevators.

"Well, be careful, baby. I wouldn't want anyone to take advantage of you." He shot her a cocky grin. She gave a slight shiver that set Rainer on fire as she pulled him onto the elevator.

"Actually," she whispered in his ear as some of her teammates followed them, "I'm really hoping he will." Her hot breath caressed over his neck in heated swirls that drove him wild.

His mind was full of the many different ways he'd like to take advantage of Emily. Rainer was startled from his fantasies when Chloe moved in front of them as the elevator halted on the top floor.

"Are you coming with?" she urged.

Emily shook her head. "No, I have to get a bunch of stuff done for the security check tomorrow before the party, and then I have a meeting with the caterers, then we're heading to bed."

Rainer was deeply impressed with Emily's resolve not to allow her teammates to talk her in to things anymore. They had indeed learned their lessons, but Chloe wasn't going down without a fight it seemed.

"Oh, come on, Em. Just come have a few drinks first."

Emily feigned regret. "I can't. I have too much to do, but you have fun." She pulled Rainer toward their room.

"We can go if you want," Rainer offered.

"I don't want to go. I'm not doing anything at all that might make Dad look bad. Peterson will do anything to bring him down, and I would much rather spend some time with you. It's been awhile, you know." She looked mildly uncomfortable to be pointing this out.

"I know," Rainer pledged. "Believe me."

"Besides, she just wants me to come because she's hoping that I'll tell Garrett about the guys she's going to hang all over and bring back to her suite."

Rainer was certain she was correct as he lifted the keycard to open the door to their suite. Suddenly the door opened and a maid stepped out.

"So sorry, Mr. Lawson. I was just restocking your towels," she cooed sweetly before pushing her cart out of the room. Emily smiled at her kindly and thanked her for the towels. She started to step in the room, but Rainer grasped her forearm and shook his head.

"I want you to pretend you dropped something, and then we're going to lean down and look for it." Emily stared up at him in wide-eyed terror, but she followed her instructions.

"Oh, my earring." Her fear echoed in her call. She and Rainer knelt down to search for the nonexistent earring.

"What's going on?" Emily pretended to look.

"I don't know, but as soon as our maid turns the corner I intend to find out." Rainer watched the maid as he pretended to expand his search.

"Found it," he called as the maid disappeared. "Stay right here, baby." Rainer took one hesitant step into the room. He cupped his hand and summoned as Emily watched from the hallway. He turned his hand outward, and his heart raced as he scanned the room for energy sources.

He concentrated and picked up on the static electricity in the curtains and sheets. He let his shield flow over the electrical outlets and halted. There were three outlets in the room, and one was projecting vastly more energy than the others. It was the perfect place to hide something that required a battery, as a Gifted person had to be extremely thorough to pick up on the slightly higher level of energy than what would normally be held in an outlet.

He continued his scan over the phone, the clock, the lamps, and then found another source tucked underneath the desk in the room. This one was visible from where Rainer was standing. He pulled his cell from his pocket and moved closer to the desk. He leaned down and peeked around the chair so he could see. He returned to Emily in the hallway and shut the door.

"This is Vindico." He answered on the first ring.

"Hey, it's Rainer."

"What's wrong, Lawson?"

"Just one second, and I'll tell you," Rainer huffed. Vindico waited as Rainer glanced around. A moment later, Fionna came out of her suite.

"Can I use your suite for just a minute, Fionna?" Rainer asked kindly. She looked surprised but nodded.

"Sure, of course." She held the door for him. She and Emily followed Rainer into the suite and closed the door behind him.

"There's a high-powered wire in our room, and there's something else—I'm thinking a camera—in one of the electrical outlets. The outlet is about waist high and situated just to the left of the TV on a dresser, so the camera would cover the bed and most of the back of the room. I didn't scan the bathroom yet," Rainer informed Vindico. Emily gasped as Fionna's mouth fell open in shock.

"Tell me you're not telling me all of this near that tap."

Rainer rolled his eyes. "No, of course not, but if it is a camera, it might've caught me entering the room. I only went in a few steps," Rainer warned. "Is this Wretchkinsides or Peterson?"

"As of right now, I consider them one and the same."

"Do you want me to remove them?" Rainer asked.

"No," Vindico stated readily but then seemed to pause to consider. "Listen to me, and do exactly what I'm about to tell you."

"Yes, sir."

"Has your luggage arrived yet?"

"No, not yet."

"Good. There are hundreds of hotels in Boston. I want you to go back in your suite and wait on your luggage," Vindico instructed. "Act natural. Kiss, talk, whatever. When your luggage arrives, I want you to set the largest suitcase you brought in front of the outlet with the camera, then I want Emily to tell you that she wants to go out. You agree, and then, after you've scanned the bathroom, go in there, and put your toothbrushes and whatever else you'll need for tonight into a bag that Emily can carry as a purse. Then I want you to go downstairs and ask a hotel employee to call you a cab. Do not use an app to get an Uber or anything like that. I want the hotel staff to know you've left."

"Okay."

"Before you leave the suite you're in now, pick another hotel in the city. Don't say it out loud, ever, and don't call me and tell me where you've picked. I'll just trace your phone. Get a room once you're at the hotel that you've picked. Don't call to make a reservation, and use a fake name at the desk," Vindico commanded. "Stay there tonight. Is there a public restroom in the lobby of the hotel you're in now?"

"Yeah, I saw one in the bar."

"Perfect. I want you to take the keycard to your room and wedge it in one of the toilet paper dispensers in the very last stall. Make sure it can't be seen," Vindico ordered.

"Okay." Rainer wondered what Vindico was planning.

"You said there was a TV. Did you turn it on?" Vindico asked.

"No, I knew something was up. I never even let Emily in the room."

"Good man, Lawson, but can you turn on the TV in the suite you're in now?"

"Uh, yeah." Rainer grabbed the remote to the TV and held it up, questioning Fionna who nodded. He flipped on the TV and quizzed, "Okay, now what?"

"Can you access adult channels?" Vindico asked. He wondered why on earth Vindico would ask him that. His boss never joked around, so he flipped to the menu and scrolled to the highest channel numbers.

"I think so," Rainer informed him hesitantly.

"Make certain. If I need to cast a television to show porn, I need to know that before I get in there. I have to know my every move or this isn't going to work."

"Sir, I'm in here with Emily and Fionna Styler. I'm not turning on porn."

"Then ask them to leave because I plan on catching a spy tonight." Rainer ground his teeth and turned to Fionna who was staring at him quizzically.

"I just need to make sure the channel works," he choked. "Could you just go in the bathroom a second please, Em?" Rainer begged.

Emily rolled her eyes. "Not a child, remember?"

"I've seen plenty of porn. It's fine," Fionna assured him. Rainer drew a quick breath and highlighted one of the many adult channels available on the television. He pressed the button and braced, ready to turn it off instantly. A picture of two bleached-blonde, spray-tanned women with enormous chests fawning all over a guy in a lounge chair displayed instantly. After hitting the power button, Rainer assured his boss, "They work."

"Okay, do everything I said, and I'll be on the next flight out."

"Wait, you're coming here now? I thought you weren't coming until tomorrow."

"That was before someone tapped your room, and now I intend to lure whomever did this out. Only, when they arrive, I'll be the one staying in the room, not you and Miss Haydenshire. Just make certain you scan the bathroom and that you block any of the cameras with the luggage." With a chuckle, he added, "You and Miss Haydenshire are going to have a wild night tonight. I feel certain whoever did this is going to want pictures," Vindico completed the plan.

"Ah," Rainer chuckled. "The porn."

"You got it," Vindico assured him. "Hurry up. They're going to wonder why you aren't in the room yet."

"Okay, I'll see you in the morning."

"Yeah, I'll call you tomorrow unless something goes wrong and I need you tonight." After ending the call, Rainer quickly explained what he and Emily were supposed to do.

"How did you know she wasn't a real maid?" Emily asked.

"She might be a real maid, but she called me Mr. Lawson," he explained. "She wasn't even Gifted, and the room is registered to you via the Angels. My name is nowhere on it. Plus, how many hotel maids know the names of the guests in each room?" Rainer tried not to revel at the pride-filled, adoring gaze Emily was giving him.

"Wait, so Dan is coming here to stay the night?" Fionna restated the part of the plan that must've intrigued her the most.

"Uh, yes," Rainer hemmed. "But he'll be trying to catch whomever bugged our suite," he reminded gently.

"Right, I know." Fionna gave him a wide-eyed, dazzling smile. She looked like Rainer had just made her entire evening.

"Are you ready to do this?" he quizzed Emily.

After drawing a steadying breath, she nodded. "I think so. This would be kind of cool if it weren't my life."

CHAPTER 42
THE PERFORMANCE

"Wait. Where are we actually going to stay?" Emily asked as they moved toward the door in Fionna's room.

"I've got it taken care of," Rainer assured her.

He'd been to Boston with his father a few times, but the last trip had been just before Rainer's twelfth birthday. They'd stayed in several hotels while visiting the historical sites in Boston. His dad took Rainer to his lectures to the Gifted people on how each state's governing board should be handled and how important the newly formed Constitution was. Then they would go out and have fun in the city.

Rainer remembered one hotel in particular from their trip. He hadn't thought much of it when he was twelve. He recalled that he thought it was odd their suite had a fireplace and a huge Jacuzzi tub and that his father had commented that it was romantic.

He remembered the comment because his father had never said anything like that before. It had struck Rainer as weird on that warm, spring day that his father had pointed out that a hotel room was romantic.

He realized now that his father had been attempting to teach Rainer a little about women. However, at twelve years of age, his idea of romance meant that he'd taken a shower after playing paintball with Logan, or that he and Emily were on the same team when they went to bowl with the Haydenshires. He'd had no idea how or why a hotel room would be romantic.

With a slight chuckle at his own childhood naivety, Rainer held Emily's hand and slid the keycard through the lock. He guided her into the room ahead of him as he closed the door. She turned and gave Rainer a nervous glance.

"See, I told you the room was nice." He tried coaching her through her lines.

"Yeah, I just had to go to that meeting with Chloe. That's why I wasn't in here earlier." She was overplaying her hand. Rainer moved to flip on the lights in the bathroom and pretended to inspect the room.

"The bath's big enough for two," Rainer flirted. He added a cocky grin to his expression as he walked in front of the outlet that contained the camera. Emily giggled and sounded more like herself.

"Yeah, but we should go out and see the city." She was getting ahead of herself slightly. Rainer moved in front of the camera again and pulled Emily into him.

"Okay, but there's something I want to do first." He hoped kissing might be better than talking since Emily was a terrible liar.

"And what is that?" she sassed as her play-acting improved.

"This," Rainer let his voice take on a lust-filled thrum as he kissed her sweetly. He just brushed her lips with his. He wasn't putting on a show for whomever might be watching them. After a minute or two of fairly mundane kisses, a knock sounded on the door. Rainer pulled away and pretended to be annoyed that they'd been interrupted.

He moved to the door, opened it, and tipped the bellman for their luggage. With determination set in his jaw, he set the largest suitcase on the dresser beside the television and opened it to block the camera completely with the top of the suitcase.

He moved to stand near the microphone. "Here, baby, why don't you unpack? I need to run to the restroom. Then we can go out for a little while if you want?"

A second later, he walked to the bathroom and shut the door loudly. He summoned and scanned the bathroom twice. There was nothing in there that shouldn't be, so he flushed the commode and made his exit. Emily drew a deep breath and began her part. She repacked their toothbrushes and clothes for the next day into her large purse from the bags Rainer had placed in the bathroom.

"You want to go explore for a little while? It's such a cool city," she managed, but she was gnawing her lip nervously. Rainer nodded his approval.

"For a little while, but then I want to bring you back here and explore you." Emily forced a sweet giggle. Rainer grabbed the keycard, shoved it in his pocket, and then opened the door. "Let's go, baby."

Emily stalked out as Rainer let the door bang shut. Air hissed from her lungs as utter relief to be finished with that part of the plan broadcast from her face.

They moved to the lobby and began the second phase. Rainer informed the front desk clerk that they'd need a cab. Then he excused himself to the restroom. After he'd hidden the keycard, he emerged and led Emily outside to await the cab.

"Where to?" the cabby demanded in a heavy Boston accent.

"Uh, I'm sorry. I don't remember the name of the hotel, but it had Roman numerals above the entrance doors?" Rainer stated hopefully.

"The Fifteen," the cabby huffed.

"Yeah, that's it," Rainer urged.

"Nice place. My wife keeps harping for me to take her there." The cabby rolled his eyes.

Rainer nodded. "Yeah, we're not staying there. We're just eating." He didn't want anyone in the city to know where they would be as he held Emily's hand tenderly in his own.

"Hey, I hear ya. Place is outrageous. Outta our price range. Am I right?" the cabby drawled.

"Exactly," Rainer pretended to scoff over the price of the suites. Everything that had been done began to sink into Emily's heart as they rode through the streets of Boston. Her rhythms faltered. She laid her head on Rainer's shoulder, and he wrapped her up in his arms.

Vile revulsion washed over him as he allowed the what-ifs to consume him as well. What might've been caught on camera for someone, had he not realized what was going on, made him sick and clearly terrified her.

"No one will know where we are, baby," he soothed in her ear. He made certain the cabby couldn't hear him. "I'll always keep you safe."

She shrank into Rainer's chest with a slight nod.

"All right, The Fifteen Beacon. Enjoy your meal. Hope she's worth it," the cabby commented crassly as he pulled up to the entrance of the hotel restaurant. Rainer tossed forty bucks through the window in the divider of the cab, then helped Emily out.

As the cab pulled away, Rainer guided Emily down to the doors of the hotel. He moved to the desk, smiled, and asked for a suite, which he paid for in cash and placed under the name Joseph Henderson. He used his father's name and Emily's last initial so he could remember his alias.

"Did you need help with your luggage, Mr. Henderson?" The concierge glanced around for Rainer and Emily's bags.

"Oh no. We've got it." Rainer shook his head and led Emily quickly to the elevators. As soon as the doors shut, Emily furrowed her brow.

"How did you know about this place?" she asked.

"I stayed here once with my dad. It's pretty cool."

Emily looked pleasantly surprised. She smiled and clung to Rainer's hand. His phone chirped in his pocket, and Rainer retrieved it to read the text.

> I'm landing. Nice choice, Lawson. Keep her safe

was the message from Vindico.

"Vindico's here." Not certain how Emily would feel about Vindico knowing where they were by pinging his cell, Rainer decided not to mention the rest of the message to Emily.

CHAPTER 43
THE FIFTEEN BEACON HOTEL

The Fifteen Beacon was a small, quaint, eclectic hotel that held a mix of old world Boston elegance with modern decor. It suited Emily perfectly. Rainer placed the key in the lock and opened their door. He was thankful for the fact that more than just a keycard, or a quick magnetic energy cast, would secure them.

He ushered Emily inside, closed the door, and locked it back. He watched her closely. The suite was much the same as he remembered it. He and his father had been given a different suite, but he supposed they were all similar.

This suite held only one bed. The other had two, but they did both have a fireplace. There was a large, king-sized, four-poster bed complete with heavy white fabric draperies that could be pulled to enclose the space. Dark, wood paneled walls and plush carpeting gave the space a peaceful, intimate feel.

Emily smiled and moved to the bed to run her hands over the down linens and the soft, thick curtains that surrounded the bed. There was a flat-screen TV mounted on the paneling over the large fireplace, and candles stood on several of the shelves and bedside tables in the room. A small writing desk was tucked in the corner by the windows that overlooked Boston Common.

"Wow," Emily whispered. "This is so nice." Rainer was still

watching her take everything in. She took his breath away. He wondered if that would ever stop. He'd been in love with her his whole life, and she still robbed him of breath and made his heart ache just to be near her.

She moved back to him.

"I know it's crazy, but will you scan it please?" She looked frightened again.

"Of course." Rainer summoned. He moved over every space in the room then moved to the opulent bathroom. He shot his radar cast over the large, jetted bathtub and the shower and then scanned the double sinks and even the toilet until he was satisfied there wasn't anything in the room that wasn't supposed to be there.

"There's nothing here, and no one knows where we are except Vindico. I promise, sweetheart." He pulled Emily into his chest and let her bury her head in his shoulder.

There had been a light, drizzly rain falling since they'd landed in Boston, but the storm was gaining in intensity. Thunder clapped in the distance, and Emily shuddered.

Rainer rubbed his hands up and down her back as he cradled her tenderly. "I've got you, baby. I'm right here." He swayed her slightly. Storms had so much violent energy within their atmosphere that they typically disturbed Receivers. Emily was no exception.

"Will you light the fire?" She was biting her lip again as a nervous grin spread across her face.

"Sure." Rainer was pleased she seemed to like the hotel as much as he did. "Why don't you get ready for bed? I'll start the fire, order us some room service, and we can just hang out, okay?"

He told himself he'd be thrilled just to hold her in the bed and make certain she felt safe and secure again. There were other things he would very much have liked, but he doubted she was up for much after all that had happened.

"That sounds perfect." She carried the purse she'd packed to the bathroom.

Rainer moved to the fireplace to inspect it. He turned on the gas and then summoned the radiant heat in the room and used it to light the fire. He lit the candles with his hand as well, then pulled off the polo and jeans he was wearing and flung the covers back on the bed. After grabbing the remote, he flipped through the channels and tried to find something Emily might want to watch.

When she emerged from the bathroom, Rainer quickly shut off the TV. His eyes goggled as his mouth went dry.

"Uh, wow!" His heart picked up pace as his breaths shortened. She was wearing a purple satin slip nightie with dark, cream-colored, lace detailing. The deep V-neck covered her voluptuous breasts, and Rainer panted as he took in her nipples puckered in dark cherry mounds he could see through the lace. The gown barely covered her backside, and the hems, covered in the same lace, cut up to her rib cage on the sides.

"You are gorgeous." He stood and moved to her with greed and lust coursing rapidly through his veins. A soft, sultry half grin spread across her face. Her eyes were dark and hungry as she took him in. He couldn't take his eyes off of her. She was mouthwatering. He wanted to run his hands and his mouth over her soft, sweet skin. He wanted to build a fire inside of her that would consume them both.

He forced himself to stop and use the head above his belt line, if only for a minute. He pulled her to him and whispered softly in her ear.

"Are you sure you want to do this, baby? I know everything at the other hotel was awful. I understand if you just want to go to sleep." He forced himself to make the offer. She lifted her head from his chest and studied him.

"I want you. Please," she whispered hesitantly. Her brow furrowed as she tried to read him.

"Oh, baby, believe me..." He pulled her close enough that she could feel the effect she'd had on him as he pushed his steel hardened length against her silk-covered stomach. "I want you so bad I ache. I want to feel you around me. I want to bury myself in you until I fill you full." His vows made her breath stutter as she trembled in his arms.

"Please," whispered from her in desperate, pleading desire that drove him wild.

"Do you need me to set the cast, sweetheart?"

She shook her head. "I did it already."

He forced himself to move slowly, to relish each and every part of her. He wanted to worship her body that she gave him so freely. He cradled her cheek in his hand and laved her mouth with slow, languid kisses. He reached deeper each time their lips met, until he slipped his tongue in her mouth and let it intertwine with hers as he consumed her.

He backed away slightly and pulled her bottom lip through his teeth, before he moved back in and used every arsenal available to him to set her on one hell of a consuming fire.

He slid one hand to her neck and the other to her backside as he guided her body into his. She reached and grasped him as a heated growl echoed from his lungs and he throbbed in her hands.

"Go get in bed, baby," he soothed "I'll be right there." He watched her turn. Her eyes were dark. Her lips kiss-swollen. Her face flushed as she moved toward the bed. The gown swayed slightly and revealed a peek of her lush backside. He was already aching and thrumming. His entire body was hot-wired for her. He wanted to see more. He wanted to see it all.

He pulled off his boxers and followed her to the bed. He drew the lights from the lamps, so that only the fire and the candlelight illuminated her. She was stunning, and she was his. He was unable to fathom the miraculous truth of that fact.

Her energy was spiraling in heated waves. It gained intensity with each passing moment. Her heart raced. She moaned her approval as the mattress lowered under his weight.

Unable to stop himself, he let his hand drift from her thigh under the gown until his fingers played softly along her slit, and she trembled under his hungry caress. He eased the gown up and revealed more of her. He watched her body flush and pulse for him. A loud groan escaped his lips.

"I want to take this off, baby." He hissed in need. "I want to see you. I want to feel you, and then I want to make you feel me."

A needy, desperate moan escaped her as she waited on him to fulfill his promises. He pulled the gown over her head and threw it off the bed. He tenderly slid his fingertips down her gorgeous curves. Rainer began at her neck. He traced her collarbone and then drew patterns across her chest, circling her nipples as she writhed. He continued on his path down her body and gently moved his fingers over her stomach as it clenched in acute anticipation.

She arched her back. Her breasts were swollen and tender. They swayed from the motion, an intoxicating hypnotic dance all for him. Her nipples pulled taut and strained. He knew what she wanted.

"Tell me, baby." He was suddenly desperate to hear her command him. "Tell me you want me to suck them."

She gasped and moaned as she panted, "Suck me, please." Her body contorted in need. Fervent groans thundered from his lungs as Rainer spun his tongue over one of the swollen mounds.

He pulled her left breast deep into his mouth and let his tongue soothe the strain. She grew frantic as he let his mouth, his tongue, and his teeth bring her the sensations she craved.

He sucked her hard and then slipped his fingers in the swollen wet heat between her legs. She broke almost instantly as he massaged. Her energy spiked rapidly and then quaked as her body flooded hot, wet sex around his hand. He moaned as she bucked and rolled under his touch.

He scooted down the bed and dragged his tongue over her swollen lips to drink what he'd just elicited from her. She went wild. Her energy spun rapidly around him as he built her again. He sucked her lips then reverently tended to all of her magic spots until she was thrusting her hips in the air, desperate for him to tame her.

"Are you ready for me, baby? Are you needy?" His voice was laced with desperate hunger acute to the point of pain. Her eyes flashed.

She grabbed him. She massaged his length, and he gasped from the heavenly sensation. The feeling of her hand on him drove him wild. She pulled him toward her and guided him in showing him exactly what she wanted. He throbbed fiercely as a low, rumbling growl echoed off of the energy that spun from both of them.

"Take it all!" He slipped deep inside of her. She moaned her approval and bucked instantly to take him deeper into the slick, wet perfection between her legs.

He thrust hard as she met his every need and allowed him to move her body and her soul with his own. Her eyes closed in the ecstasy of their energy joining in heated, spiraling twists all around them. None was all hers, and none all his—it only existed in the two of them together.

"That feels so good!" she gasped. It nearly drove him over the edge just listening to her heated pleas. She pulsed and swelled around him. He forced himself to concentrate as he felt her body on the brink of climax. She trembled around him as it began to consume her.

"That's it, baby. That's it," he coaxed her. "Just let it go for me," he urged, and he had her. She screamed out his name. Her body contorted underneath his as her energy seared through him.

Her convulsions pulled him deeper still. He watched her surrender herself to him, with his name reverberating from her lips, and he lost it all. He exploded inside of her. He filled her with all of him as he surrounded her body with his own.

He held her tightly until she stilled. He eased out of her as her breathing steadied, and held her tenderly to him as he rolled to his side but allowed no space between them. She clung to him as he brushed sweet, tender kisses across her forehead and in her hair.

"Are you okay?" He was momentarily concerned something was wrong. She still hadn't spoken. She nodded into his chest. He felt her smile against him. The small motion righted his entire world.

"When you hold me like this, after we do that…" she whispered as he cosseted her closer. "It's like I know everything is going to be okay. I can feel how much you love me." He soared as a broad smile stretched across his face.

"I love you so much, and being with you is the most incredible thing I've ever felt. It somehow gets even better every time I have the pleasure."

She pulled away just long enough to brush a kiss on his jaw. He saw the satisfaction and the peace swirl in her eyes lit by the firelight as she gazed at him.

"Sometimes I just wish the world would go away for a little while. You know?" She traced her hand over his chest as he pulled her in tighter. After considering for a moment, Rainer tenderly brushed a kiss over her lips.

"Why don't we see what I can do about that just for tonight? Stay right here. I'll be right back." He winked at her as she pretended to pout when he climbed out of the bed.

Rainer worked quickly. He drew the heat away from the candles, extinguished them, and then pulled the majority of the heat from the fire. He lowered the gas until it was barely glowing then walked around the bed. He released the curtains, creating a tranquil refuge for the two of them. Once they were sealed off from the rest of the room and from the world at large, he climbed back into bed. He lay back and pulled Emily onto his chest and covered her in the soft down quilts and the cotton bedding.

"Thank you." Contented tranquility moved through her rhythms. He nodded and kissed the top of her head.

"Hang on one sec, baby. I'm not quite finished." With that, he summoned using the heat he'd just pulled from the fire and the candles. He added in his own energy and then casted the bed in his powerful shield. She squeezed him tight.

"You're the best,"—she hesitated—"but I have to go to the bathroom." After chuckling at his fairly shortsighted plan, Rainer nodded.

"Good point." He withdrew the shield cast and pulled the covers back for her. When she returned, he tucked her back in beside him, forgoing the shield this time, as he began using his energy to soothe her to sleep instead.

CHAPTER 44
FIONNA STYLER
DAN VINDICO

Dan discreetly followed a group of Gifted locals into the bar of the Orange Grove Hotel. They were all there in hopes of partying with some of the Arlington Angels. The bartender seemed pleased to have so many patrons.

Dan slipped into the men's room. He stalked quickly to the last stall and locked the swinging door. He knelt down and extracted the keycard from the side of the toilet paper dispenser. He heard the door open again, and he waited, barely breathing and wondering if whoever bugged Lawson's room had seen him enter the hotel.

He summoned, but when the guy began using one of the urinals, Dan released the energy and continued to wait. A minute later, the man exited, and Dan left the stall. He pulled a baseball cap and his sunglasses from his luggage and made his way toward the elevators. He tried to stay out of sight and blend in with the hopeful fans.

He exited on the top floor, removed his sunglasses, and slid quickly toward Lawson's room. Fionna Styler appeared out of the suite across the hall. God, she was gorgeous. Dan grinned at her. If she was going downstairs looking like that, the fans would go wild.

She gave him a tender grin, and he called himself an idiot when his dick stirred from the sight. "I...saw you coming. I thought I'd make sure you could get in. If you need me to, I could tell the front desk that I'm Emily and get them to give me a new keycard."

After giving her what he hoped was a cocky, flirtatious smile, Dan shook his head and held up the card Rainer had left him. It was an ingenious idea though. He was deeply impressed.

"Let's see if this works first. But if not, I'll definitely take you up on that," he assured Fionna with a wink. She swallowed hard and gave him a dazzling smile.

Dan immediately chastised himself. He had no business flirting with Fionna Styler. First of all, she was Gifted, and he didn't involve himself with Gifted women. He reminded himself of this hard and fast rule. Second—Dan allowed himself a moment to let his eyes run the length of her beautiful body—she was the kind of girl a guy could fall in love with. She was sweet, smart, and so fucking beautiful she could make a man believe in a higher power. Falling in love was not something he would ever do again. She waited on him to see if the keycard worked.

Fionna Styler deserved a great guy, one that didn't have even half of the baggage that he did. Dan scolded himself.

"Okay, remember…" He placed his index finger over his lips to make certain she didn't speak. As soon as he opened the door, the wire would pick up any conversation. He allowed himself one more moment to stare at her full lips and to think about what he'd like her to do with them.

She nodded her understanding, and Dan shook himself slightly. Fionna watched as he eased the keycard in the lock and heard the tumblers roll. After giving him another sweet smile, Fionna's eyes lit, and Dan felt his heart pick up pace, though he couldn't determine why.

"Good luck!" she mouthed and pointed back to her suite, letting him know where she'd be. "If you need anything…at all," she whispered.

"Listen, I don't know who might be coming down this hallway. I need to know you're safe." *Stay with me.* He shook himself and refocused. "Are you going down to the bar?"

She shook her head. "No. As much as I appreciate all of our fans, I'm not up to all of that tonight."

"I certainly understand that. Just stay in your room for me. I'd cast the door for you, but then you couldn't leave if you needed to."

She shook her head. "I'll be fine. Don't worry about me."

Dan turned to watch her walk back into her suite. He drew a deep breath and swallowed hard. Fionna Styler had the ass of a goddess. She always had. He remembered admiring it on numerous occasions when they were at the academy together.

He shook himself from his reverie as he realized he hadn't opened the door in time and the lock had reset.

Dan cursed under his breath. He was angry with himself for getting distracted. He eased the card in again and opened the door silently. He pulled a doorstop from his bag and halted the door from shutting as he moved into the room. He glanced around and smiled. Lawson had done precisely as he'd been instructed. Dan congratulated himself on recruiting Rainer to Elite. It had been an excellent decision, and he'd become an excellent officer.

After slipping off his boots, Dan eased into the room without making a sound. He checked the windows and then carefully scanned the parking lot and the adjoining highway. He slunk down on the bed and leaned back. If the camera had caught Lawson studying the wiretap, whoever planted it would be back to retrieve it while Rainer and Emily were out.

He waited and would occasionally ease back to the window to rescan the parking lot he'd memorized. The hours ticked by. Dan checked his watch constantly. He shut out the haunting memories and recollections. He hated being bored.

He allowed himself a few minutes to envision what getting to see and feel Fionna Styler's backside up close and personal might be like. His breath picked up, and his body responded to the lurid fantasies playing in his mind. He shut down those thoughts by reminding himself that she was an extremely powerful Receiver. Being with her would mean she could feel every emotion inside of him. That thought made him sick. No one should have to live his hell with him.

He was fairly certain if he played all of his cards right and said all of the right things, he could get Fionna into his bed though. The fantasies returned in an instant.

With a silent huff, he forced his thoughts to Bridgette. She wanted a commitment. She'd informed him over the phone, as he tried to put off actually going out with her as often as he could, that if he didn't commit, she would stop spying on Wretchkinsides's men for him.

She didn't occupy his thoughts for very long. She never did. He lamented as guilt settled in the pit of his stomach. The fact that she was a momentary distraction from his pain that required very little from him, and that she was one of the linchpins in his catching Dominic Wretchkinsides with the information she was providing, made her the preferential choice.

She won by a long shot. He let the vengeance that blackened his soul push Fionna Styler from his mind.

Dan supposed he'd have to agree to be Bridgette's boyfriend, whatever that meant in her world. He shuddered at the thought. With another glance at his watch, he eased off of the bed. It was two in the morning. He checked the parking lot once again and decided to get the show on the road. It didn't appear anyone was coming to remove the evidence.

He made certain he moved in absolute silence. He stalked to the desk, summoned, and drew the majority of the energy out of the microphone. Then with a taunting grin, he forced the energy he'd drawn along with the ambient sound energy in the air around him back through the microphone at high speed. He couldn't quite halt his broad grin as the microphone squealed loudly. Certain whoever was listening in was currently writhing in pain, Dan moved quickly.

CHAPTER 45
ACTION!

He kept the microphone feedback squealing and turned on the television. He casted the TV and lowered the volume all the way down. He located the adult channels and began to peruse. He moved back to the microphone and raised the energy levels and then lowered them again, with a slight chuckle.

After flipping through the many varied movies available, he found one just beginning with three women and one guy. *Perfect,* he thought, but then grimaced slightly. Watching porn alone in a hotel room that wasn't even his own was a new low.

He released the cast on the microphone and then raced to the door. He pulled the doorstop so that the door slammed shut. He shook the chair by the desk as if someone had stumbled into it. He dropped his keys on the desk just above the receiver, then slowly raised the volume on the television so that even he could barely make out the lack of conversation taking place on the screen.

Dan incrementally raised the volume over the next few minutes until he was certain whoever was listening in caught the porn star informing the women just how he planned on taking care of them in language so filthy Dan blushed.

He pulled all of the electricity from the lights and moved back to the window. Dan waited and watched. He tediously stalked his lured prey.

Ten minutes later, two black cars flew into the parking lot, and Dan had to bite his lips together not to laugh. He raced to the bathroom and edged the door closed, until it stood only an inch from the wall.

Several minutes went by, but he was nothing if not patient. He'd been waiting almost ten years to end Wretchkinsides. This was nothing. A minute later, he heard a keycard slide through the lock carefully. The door edged open enough to get a camera lens through.

"Listen to them. They'll never know. Just step inside, get a few shots, and get out. We'll get the mic tomorrow," he heard someone order in an eager hiss. Wretchkinsides's lackeys stepping inside was precisely what Dan wanted, so with a goading grin he continued to wait.

"Dude, I'm not going in there." He heard another voice in an exasperated whisper.

"Do you hear that? Rainer Lawson is in there with Emily Haydenshire and some other whores. Peterson will flip. This will seal his deal, and Nic will move you up the chain!"

Dan listened and tried to determine the number of his opposition.

"Here, just give me the fucking camera," the first voice ordered, and then the door edged open. Dan watched the cameraman slink along the wall and then turn to aim the camera at the bed.

While using both hands to summon, Dan leapt. He threw the cameraman to the ground and drained the energy out of his accomplice instantly. Utter elation filled Dan as he lit the lamps in the room and realized whom he was holding.

"Well, if it isn't the pride of the Interfeci? What's Uncle Nic gonna do now, Adrian, since you're going to jail?" He glared hatefully at Adrian Malicai, who had been training right under Dominic, lying on the ground in handcuffs.

"And who's this?" Dan moved to the man he'd drained and flipped him to his back with his boot. "Ah, LeCroy." He mocked heartbreak. "Sent you out with a lackey. What'd you do wrong, Adrian?" Dan menaced.

Adrian scowled furiously as Dan forced his way into his energy and kept him from speaking. "LeCroy," Dan called as he handcuffed him and then restored some of his energy.

In a slightly dazed stupor, Marcus LeCroy came to. "You're under arrest, but I'll cut you a deal if you tell me who copied the keycard to the room for you." LeCroy was far from being the sharpest tool in Wretchkinsides's arsenal.

"That girl, Cindy." LeCroy choked to get the information out as fast as he could, though Malicai shook his head violently.

"If you show her to me on your way out, we'll see what we can do. All right?" Dan lied. LeCroy nodded. After thinking this was definitely his night, Dan halted as he heard another voice.

"Ugh, Adrian, what is taking you so long? I thought you just had to take a picture or something."

Dan threw the partially opened door back and gave Samantha Peterson a delighted grin.

"Well, well, well, this just gets better and better." Dan summoned. He was careful to only halt Samantha's escape and get her handcuffed. While he'd love nothing more than to drive his boot through Malicai's rib cage, he had no desire to harm Samantha. She was a pawn in an extremely dangerous game her father had decided to play.

Dan linked Malicai's and LeCroy's handcuffs. He placed them back-to-back and added shackles. Samantha sobbed as Dan called the Gifted police precinct in Boston. He instructed them not to show until seven that morning. Then he phoned the number for the Gifted Associated Press. He informed them whom he was and what would be taking place outside the Orange Grove Hotel in the next few hours.

To Dan's delight, Cindy also grew worried about the men and came around to check on them. After he cuffed her, Dan drawled,

"How much did he give you to do all of this for him?" Cindy scowled. She was clearly more intelligent than LeCroy, but LeCroy came through for Dan again.

"Tell him, and he'll let you go," he urged Cindy.

She considered for a few minutes and then huffed, "Ten K. My kid needs surgery." She didn't lie well.

"Uh-huh," Dan chuckled. "You should've held out for more, sweetheart. He would've given you twice that."

Certain that Lawson was either sleeping or rocking Emily to sleep, Dan waited to text him with his findings.

"You can't just hold us here!" Samantha whined. "Daddy is a governor."

"Uh, no, dear. Your father is no longer a governor, and after this I'm quite certain he won't be the future Crown either. So, you're nothing more than a suspect under arrest for aiding and abetting Adrian here in the wrongful act of invasion of privacy, theft of information, not to mention breaking and entering, oh, and bribery." He gestured to Cindy. "I'd say you're looking at two to five in Felsink. Of course this is Emily Haydenshire's room you two tapped, and as her father is about to be Crown, you could be looking at longer," Dan quipped.

"You can't send us to jail. We're in love. We're getting married."

After taking in the expression on Malicai's face, Dan tried not to laugh. It didn't appear that Adrian knew of his upcoming nuptials to Samantha. Dan released his cast on Adrian's smug mouth momentarily.

"Uh, babe, we are not getting married. We're just hanging out having a good time," Adrian assured Samantha as he opened and closed his jaw while glaring at Dan.

By five thirty, there was a large gathering of press outside the hotel, and officers from the local precincts were awaiting Vindico's orders.

Dan phoned Lawson.

CHAPTER 46
THOSE THAT KNOW THE LEAST
RAINER LAWSON

"Hello?" Rainer cleared his throat and tried not to awaken Emily.

"Sorry I woke you up, Lawson, but you and Miss Haydenshire need to come back to the Orange Grove. I think you're gonna want to see this." Vindico chuckled.

"Okay, sure. Let me wake Em up, and we'll be there." Rainer tried not to lament being awoken at 5:30 from one of the best night's sleep he could remember. He ended the call and rolled back to allow himself a moment to revel in Emily's luscious curves tucked up beside him completely naked.

Curiosity to know what Vindico had found in their room drove him to kiss Emily's cheek and awaken her.

"Baby, wake up," he soothed. She grunted angrily. Rainer tried not to think how adorable she was when she was frustrated, as Emily was definitely not a morning person. "I think Vindico caught whomever tapped our room. He wants us to come back to the Orange Grove." He continued running his hands over her body and trying to kiss her awake.

"No." Emily buried her face in his chest.

"Come on. Vindico sounded thrilled. This has to be good." She let her eyes blink open hesitantly and whimpered.

"Oh, and by the way..." Rainer drawled, "hey there." This got him a broad grin. She sat up with a deep yawn as Rainer stood and pulled the curtain back away from the bed.

"Rainer," she pled.

"Yeah, baby?" He pulled on the jeans he'd worn the day before and the T-shirt Emily had managed to fit in her purse.

"Can we stay here tonight? I don't want to go back to the Orange Grove." She gave a visible shudder.

"Sure, we can come right back here after we throw this big shindig for your parents, and"—he tousled her messy hair—"if you don't tell anyone where we stayed, we could probably have another peaceful night all alone." Her eyes lit. She looked thrilled that they could return to their sanctuary.

∼

Twenty minutes later, they were ordering bagels at a small walk-up shop and then headed to the Orange Grove.

"What the hell?" Rainer spat as they exited the cab into throngs of press. They pushed their way through as the press began to stir with their arrival. Rainer and Emily entered the lobby to find Vindico smiling broadly and talking with several Boston Iodex officers.

"Ah, there you are," Vindico drawled as he spotted Rainer and Emily.

"So, you caught them?" Rainer asked.

Vindico held up one finger and gave him quite a smirk as he pointed to the elevators. Rainer's mouth fell open as Adrian Malicai was escorted out, swearing and trying to jerk away from the officers as he was photographed hundreds of times by the awaiting press.

Another of Wretchkinsides's men exited with two other officers, and Emily gasped as they watched in complete astonishment as none other than Samantha Peterson was brought out in handcuffs and escorted to the waiting police cars.

"Samantha?" Emily turned to Vindico. "Samantha Peterson bugged my hotel room."

While giving Rainer another sly grin, Dan shook his head. "No,

Samantha really didn't have anything to do with this. She came looking for Malicai after I'd arrested him. I'd say her only crime was agreeing to date that scumbag, but I also thought it would make a nice front page to have Peterson's daughter being taken out in cuffs. I thought we'd see if we couldn't shut Peterson up about your family for a little while."

Stunned disbelief etched Emily's entire being. "Dad may not like that you did that."

Vindico didn't seem to mind the assessment. "This was my call, and I wanted to scare the shit out of her. She needs to stay the hell away from Malicai and his kind. She has no idea how dangerous the game her father is playing can become. And your dad may not mind too much once he sees this." Vindico pulled a folded copy of the morning paper out from under his arm and handed it to Rainer.

He flipped it open, and this time Rainer gasped as Emily covered her open mouth in horror.

"Is Haydenshire's son using women to gain access to prescription drugs?"

"What the hell?" Rainer began reading the article.

"Seventh in the long line of Haydenshire sons, Logan Haydenshire, age 21, Elite Iodex officer's longtime girlfriend, Adeline Parker, underwent emergency surgery yesterday. However, it wasn't the patient who was demanding high-powered pain meds. It was Logan. Several orderlies and nurses from Georgetown Hospital in DC stated that Logan demanded pain medication for his recently minted fiancée, and that Logan was extremely rude to hospital staff. One orderly informed the Globe that Logan appeared agitated while staying with Miss Parker after her surgery. His eyes were bloodshot and he seemed to be exhausted, the orderly commented, but during Miss Parker's surgery, Logan was nowhere to be found.

"What?" Rainer fumed. "He was right there in the waiting room. We all were."

"Keep reading," Vindico ordered.

"What will all of this mean for Governor Haydenshire's run for Crown? The Globe caught up with Haydenshire's opponent Lachland Peterson. Peterson 'deeply regrets Logan's drug abuse problem and urges Governor Haydenshire to drop out of the race and help his son seek the help he needs.' The Globe would tend to agree and also wonders if perhaps Logan began dating Miss Parker because of her connection to the drug world at large. Her mother is currently in prison for possession and use of illegal substances."

Fury shot through Rainer's veins. "This is insane!" he nearly shouted. Emily and Vindico immediately tried to quiet him.

"I know, but we can combat this. I'm more worried about Logan and Miss Parker than I am what this will do to the campaign, and I intend to point out to the press that as an Iodex officer, he's tested regularly and has never used." Vindico tried to soothe him, but Rainer was seething.

"They were three hours late with her medication. She'd just had surgery and woke up crying. Logan told me. He was furious! Rightfully so."

"I know. Ramier did some digging for me. It looks like the less than helpful nurse at the desk received a check from the Peterson's. I'm certain she was told to cause trouble and then report everything. But you've got to get it together," Vindico insisted. "You've got a party to throw, and everyone will be looking to you to see how to respond to this." He pointed to the paper. "This, we can clean up, but Peterson is gaining ground with stories like this and the constant bashing of all of you, so we're going to have to fight fire with fire."

"What does that mean?" Rainer asked.

"Watch this." Vindico moved quickly to the front stoop of the Orange Grove Hotel.

The press moved in instantly. "Chief Vindico, can you tell us if you were the arresting officer?"

"Vindico, give us a rundown of exactly what happened?"

"Officer Vindico, does the former governor know of his daughter's arrest?" The questions flew furiously. Vindico held up his hands and effectively hushed the crowd.

"I'll take a few questions." He plastered on his typical irritated façade though Rainer knew he was going to enjoy enlightening the press as to what had happened the night before. He pointed to a man in a cheap suit coat who was standing in the middle of the crowd.

"Can you tell us what Samantha Peterson's part in all of this was?" the man called loudly.

With a single nod, Vindico elaborated.

"Last evening when they arrived, Officer Lawson found that Miss Haydenshire's hotel room had been breached and tapped. After I made certain that Officer Lawson had ensured Miss Haydenshire's safety, I set up a sting and took down two men. They are both known associates of Dominic Wretchkinsides and the Interfeci. After their arrest, Miss Peterson came looking for them. She had been waiting in their getaway car, and she informed me she was planning to marry Adrian Malicai, an underboss in the Interfeci.

"She was arrested as well, but it will be up to the governing board to determine how big a role she played in the attempted information theft," Vindico drawled as the press scribbled furiously. He gestured to a brunette woman on the front row wearing a fierce scowl.

"Could you elaborate on the way the sting operation took place, Dan?" she quizzed haughtily.

"No, I could not, and that's Chief Vindico, thank you," Vindico spat as Rainer tried hard not to laugh in his awe of how Vindico stayed cool under constant pressure and refused disrespect of any nature.

"Next," Vindico pointed to a well-dressed woman in the back.

"You said that Rainer secured Emily. Can you tell us if they're still staying here at the Orange Grove or if they were moved to another location?" she cooed in a heavy southern accent. Rainer clenched his jaw and shot Vindico an annoyed glance.

With a disdainful chuckle, Vindico shook his head.

"I don't really believe that Mr. Lawson needs any interference in keeping Miss Haydenshire safe. Nor do I feel it's anyone's business where they might choose to stay, be it here at the Orange Grove or somewhere else. I will go ahead and let everyone know that they are no longer staying in the city," Vindico lied and never batted an eye as the obvious disappointment washed through the crowd. Vindico pointed to another news reporter near the back.

"Will Rainer and Emily answer a few questions, Officer Vindico?" the reporter asked derisively.

"That's up to Officer Lawson and Miss Haydenshire," Vindico corrected. Rainer stepped forward, but Emily hung back.

"Officer Lawson, can you tell us if this will affect tonight's gala in the governor's honor?" the reporter quizzed. Rainer smiled and shook his head.

"Certainly not. We'll be applauding Governor Haydenshire's efforts in keeping criminal organizations, like the Interfeci, away from the Realm along with giving him our adamant support in his run for Crown Governor."

He pointed to a woman a few rows from the front wearing a stoic, navy blue suit with her hair pulled into a tight bun.

"Emily, could you tell us your feelings on the discovery that your hotel room had been breached?"

Rainer turned to Emily to check before he informed the crowd that she wouldn't be answering any questions, but Emily stepped forward.

She grasped Rainer's hand and drew from his steadying strength. The motion made his heart swell as he gazed at her as she gave the crowd a kind smile.

"This entire process of my father running for Crown has been trying," she stated calmly. "People seem very interested in judging my family by the actions in a brief moment of time instead of seeing my father as the noble and courageous man that he is. His opponents want to isolate an instant in my or my brothers' lives and then, if that isn't enough, they want to put listening devices and cameras in my hotel room. Or they want to use a difficult situation to see if they can trap us into doing or saying something that can be spun into horrendous lies to try and create more drama because people are so eager to judge.

"Rainer's dad used to tell us that everything in life teaches us something, so I guess what I've learned about being who I am and being so deeply in love with the man I'm engaged to marry…"—she turned and gave Rainer a sweet, affectionate smile—"is that it seems the people who know the very least about me often have the most to say. So, I suppose I feel the way any of you would feel if someone tried to force themselves into your life as if it were their own. I feel violated, and hurt, and scared. It seems that my father's run for Crown has brought out the worst in some people, but I guess that's all right because my father is the man that we need to run this Realm. He's good, kind, and wise, and I have faith in the Realm as a whole. Eventually you'll all be able to tell fact from fiction. The Haydenshires are people. We have flaws just like all of you, but we want what is best for this Realm. I firmly believe that my dad is the man for the job, so I'll take the cameras and the wiretaps and the extra security measures, if that's what it takes to give the Realm a Crown Governor like my dad."

Emily smiled to the crowd and then stepped back, still holding tightly to Rainer's hand. Vindico and Rainer stared at her. They were both slightly dumbfounded by her wisdom and her brilliance. While he squeezed Emily's hand, Rainer brushed a kiss across her cheek.

"Wow," he whispered. He watched her beam as the cameras clicked feverishly.

"I don't think I can add anything to that," Vindico admired. He dismissed the crowd as Rainer and Emily waved and then returned to the hotel to begin setting up for the evening festivities.

Tad and Nathan arrived a few minutes later. They were helping Emily with the gala. She was so busy directing the decorators and the caterers for the gala, she didn't have time to get nervous over the challenge until she'd gone to Fionna's suite to change.

CHAPTER 47
CHALLENGE

Rainer decided to forgo one of his Angels T-shirts, with the rather lurid phrasing, and opted instead for a polo with the Angels logo and khakis. He was certain he'd be photographed repeatedly. He walked Emily to the visitors' locker room, and they ducked behind a door in the entryway to exchange the rings.

"Good luck, baby. I know you'll be amazing." Rainer felt her nerves begin to consume her.

"Thank you." She tried to will calm.

"You're going to be great, and I'll be right up there." He pointed toward the stands.

Emily nodded and her lip found its way between her teeth yet again.

Rainer brushed a kiss on her forehead and squeezed her hand. He left her with her teammates and went to find a seat in the visitors' box.

Everyone else was flying in later for the party, so Emily didn't have her normal assembly of Haydenshires there to root for her. Rainer purchased a Dr Pepper from the concession stand and took his seat. As he took in the field configuration, his heart sank.

A Coulomb's web—Rainer recognized it immediately. It would be up to Chloe and Uma to arrange the entire team throughout the web to be able to pass the energy around the energy sinks and then into the iode.

They would have to transfer the energy from one teammate to another, around the energy shields, to get it back through the web until the last person, Fionna, Rainer assumed.

She could certainly convert the energy to electricity and release the iode with the most skill in the least amount of time.

It was an extremely complicated process. If Uma miscalculated at all, it would both eat up the energy in each player's joule meter and eat up their time.

Since every single player would be on the field at the same time, there would really only be one chance to position everyone correctly in order to be far enough away to still access the electromagnetic energy and pass it throughout the team. The process was extremely draining.

The joule meters would empty quickly, and Rainer recalled the number of times when Emily was lead Receiver for the Venton Vixens when there was a Coulomb's web challenge. The Vixens had lost far more than they'd won. Her confidence would be shaken as soon as she saw the course. She hated them.

While letting out his customary wolf whistle when Emily entered the arena, Rainer grimaced. Her nerves were evident from his position in the stands. The refs called Summon and set the field. Every muscle in Rainer's body clenched tight as he watched Chloe and Uma calculate where they would need to position each player to make the web work.

There were six energy drains on each side. If the stream hit one, it would be over. Rainer shook his head. This was much harder than an academy course. It was going to be nearly impossible. The Bombers' captain and Duco Predilect returned to their team and explained their plan. The players moved out.

Uma and Chloe finished a minute later and began positioning the Angels.

"No." Rainer wanted to beat his head against the seat in front of him. His jaw clenched. It wasn't going to work. Dana wasn't going to be able to get the electromagnetic energy past the drain nearest her. She was too close to it and too far from Fionna for her to receive the energy for the transfer.

Sasha wasn't close enough to shield it. Rainer could see it from his vantage point above the field, but the Angels couldn't. His heart sank as he watched Emily summon and make the conversion before she passed the energy to Katie, who reached to pass the electromagnetic charge to Deena Danvor.

After glancing at the other side of the field, Rainer cursed. The Bombers had it. They were positioned perfectly. He turned back to the Angels. His head dropped as Dana realized the mistake. She couldn't pass it to Fionna, and like watching a movie he'd already seen the ending of, Rainer dropped dejectedly into his seat as the Bombers' Receiver released their iode, and the Angels lost terribly.

The crowds went wild since the majority of the fans in Bomber Bowl were, in fact, Bomber fans. Emily was visibly devastated as she went to congratulate the Bombers.

Rainer tried to get on the field, but being Rainer Lawson didn't buy him quite as much in Boston as it normally did in DC. He waited outside with the other family members of the Angels until they'd changed and left the locker room.

"Hey there." He wrapped Emily up in an embrace as she exited.

"Hey," she huffed. "I hate Coulomb. I hated him even when I had to study him in school, and I don't understand his stupid law."

Rainer chuckled and decided against explaining Coulomb's law yet again. He'd tutored her through that particular test in Energy of Physics, Emily's worse subject. Even with all of his, Will's, and Patrick's help, she'd barely pulled a C.

CHAPTER 48
GALA BALL

"Wanna go get something to eat before we get ready for the party?" He hoped she'd take him up on a little break before the evening's events. The challenge had been completed quickly, so they had some extra time. "I bet that I could even locate you a vanilla shake with extra cherries."

Finally getting a smile, Emily hesitantly agreed. He used his phone to locate a nearby ice cream shop that was close enough for them to walk. He held her hand as they walked and steadfastly ignored the cameras following them.

"Rainer, the ring!" Emily gasped. Rainer patted the real Lawson ring on the chain around his neck.

"We'll have to do it at the hotel," he lamented in a barely audible whisper. "There are too many cameras." Not having the ring on Emily made Rainer uneasy, so he rushed through ordering their milkshakes and hailed a cab quickly.

A few hours later, Rainer was pulling on his tux and awaiting Emily. They'd been given the honeymoon suite to use for changing and party planning. The Orange Grove was trying desperately to make up for the fact that one of their employees bugged Emily and Rainer's room. They were thoroughly disappointed when Rainer informed them that they wouldn't be staying there Saturday evening either.

Rainer's phone rang as he was putting on a pair of his father's cufflinks. He smiled when he saw Logan's name.

"Hey man." He began pulling a brush through his hair. "How's Adeline feeling?"

"Better, much better." Logan sounded good. "Of course, I haven't let her see the papers either."

"Yeah, probably best. So you're not still wasted, right?" Rainer teased.

Logan laughed. "I cannot believe that idiot called the papers. I don't know what Peterson's paying these morons, but it must be good money."

"Vindico's going to tell the papers that all Iodex officers are tested regularly, and that you've never used."

"I know. I talked to him this morning. Adeline's taking a bath. I was just calling to see what you and Em were up to. We saw the challenge."

"Yeah, she took it kind of hard." Rainer leaned back to make certain Emily wasn't emerging from one of the two bathrooms in the suite.

"I figured," Logan offered.

"She hates Coulomb's webs."

"Yeah I know. She was doomed from the get-go."

"I don't know about that, but she certainly seemed to think so."

At that moment, Emily emerged from the large, en suite bath dressed in a deep purple, sleeveless, ruched bandage gown that hugged all of her curves deliciously.

Rainer's mouth hung open. "Logan, man, I gotta go," he explained in a thoroughly dazed tone.

"Okay, good luck tonight," Logan called, but Rainer barely heard him as he ended the call.

"Wow! You look great."

Emily spun for him. Her hair was curled and pinned up in a loose French twist with a few sexy tendrils hanging over the sides of her beautiful face. The fabric stretched across her left shoulder and joined at the back of the dress well below her shoulder blades. Rainer's mouth watered as he watched her spin.

"It's Lhuillier," Emily gushed. Rainer had no idea what that meant, but since he was speechless anyway, he just nodded.

"You look sexy as hell. I cannot wait to take it off of you," he growled as soon as he was able to formulate words.

"Thank you." Emily was thoroughly delighted with Rainer's reaction. As she pulled on the pearl and diamond drop earrings that Tad had lent her from his store, she added, "A ball gown I can find. It's my wedding gown I can't seem to figure out."

Though she hadn't had much time to look with all that had been going on, she'd been through several catalogs and even looked at patterns to have a gown made but hadn't come across anything that was what she wanted. She'd lamented this numerous times to Rainer. He brushed a kiss across the bare skin where her right shoulder met her neck.

"You better find something. Because I want to make you Mrs. Lawson as soon as I possibly can." Rainer tried to hide his delighted smirk. He hoped she didn't find a dress. He had plans for that, and he couldn't wait to surprise her with them. Emily looked overjoyed at the thought of being his bride and of changing her name to his.

"Are you ready, Miss Haydenshire?" He grabbed a handful of her backside as he pulled her close.

"Do you have your speech?" She giggled as she shook it for him. Rainer gave her the shuddered moan she was after.

"Right here." He patted the inner pocket of his jacket.

"Then I think we're ready…at least I hope we are."

"You look amazing, and the ballroom is gorgeous. You've completely outdone yourself."

"Are you sure?"

"Definitely." Rainer gave her his arm as they headed to the elevators.

~

303

By eight o'clock, the ballroom was full to bursting with guests wishing to either donate to Governor Haydenshire's campaign or show their support. Everyone gushed over the decorations and the delicious food. Emily had thrown an amazing party.

Rainer moved to the dance floor in the center of the room and magnified his voice. He welcomed everyone and thanked them for coming. He recognized Governors Vindico, Willow, and Carrington, who were all in attendance, along with Jack Stariff and several other key members of the Senate.

He gave what he hoped was a decent speech on Governor Haydenshire's good deeds and ample wisdom to cheers from the crowd.

He then informed the crowd that they had a surprise for them. As the drumroll echoed, he welcomed Governor and Mrs. Haydenshire each carrying one of the twins dressed in tiny tuxedos into the ballroom. Applause broke out, and Governor Haydenshire expressed his heartfelt thanks to everyone for attending.

By ten, the dance floor was crowded. The big band music Emily had selected proved to be the perfect choice for the evening, and everyone appeared to be having an outstanding time. Finally breaking away from the admiring crowd, Rainer pulled Emily in for a dance.

She melted into him and let him spin her around the floor as he whispered how much he loved her, how drop-dead gorgeous she was, and what he wanted to do to her when he got her back to their room.

He kissed her tenderly, well aware they were being photographed, but he was desperate to taste her lips. He didn't want to wait anymore. He broke away as she began to pant. As they were the hosts for the evening, they certainly couldn't leave early.

"So, Fionna's pretty much in heaven right now," Emily whispered in Rainer's ear. Rainer scanned the ballroom and located Fionna dressed in a coral backless halter dress that formed a deep V just over her backside and showed off her olive complexion quite nicely. She was dancing in Vindico's arms.

"Wow, I wonder who arranged that?"

"I don't know, but he's been staring at her all night. I wish he'd ask her out. She's been in love with him since they went to the academy together. She'd be so good for him."

Rainer was beyond certain that Vindico was not the only guy in the room who had been staring at Fionna Styler all evening, so he wasn't sure that was a qualifying factor for asking her out.

"Yeah, he has a pretty hard and fast rule about Gifted women though." He agreed Fionna would be a much better match for Vindico than Bridgette, however.

"Fionna deserves somebody great, you know?"

Rainer smiled at her. "I do, but after everything Dan's been through, Garrett might be right. He may not really be the guy for her."

After considering for a long moment and discreetly glancing Vindico and Fionna's way a few times, Emily nodded her agreement. Although when Rainer allowed himself another glance, he saw something in his boss's eyes he'd never seen before. He saw peace.

By midnight, most of the partygoers had bid everyone farewell. Henry was fast asleep on Rainer's shoulder. He'd removed the jacket to his tux to make the little guy more comfortable. Keaton was tucked up on his father's shoulder, and Mrs. Haydenshire looked thoroughly exhausted.

The Haydenshires stayed to make certain the cleaning crew didn't need any help as they entered the ballroom. Governor Haydenshire thanked Rainer and Emily repeatedly for all their hard work.

"I know it's late, but I don't feel like I've seen any of my kids in weeks. Could I talk all of my sons,"—Governor Haydenshire put his arm on Rainer's shoulder—"into grabbing a beer in the bar before we all turn in? I want to hear about Logan and Adeline and about what happened to your room last night."

Rainer hesitated. He wasn't certain where Emily could go where she would be safe while he was having a beer with her father.

Mrs. Haydenshire noticed his concern. "They've given us one of the suites tonight, and there will, of course, be officers outside the door." She seemed to be growing weary of her vast security detail. "Come with me, Emily. We'll put the boys to bed and talk. I've missed you so much."

Emily looked thrilled, and Rainer smiled. He knew how much she'd missed her mother.

Rainer and Governor Haydenshire walked Mrs. Haydenshire and Emily to the suite. Each of them was carrying one of the twins. They laid the boys in the cribs provided by the hotel.

Rainer kissed Emily and told her he'd be back in a little while.

CHAPTER 49
TELL THE TALES, LISTEN CLOSE

The governor planted kisses on both of the ladies in the room and informed the security team where they would be should they be needed before they headed to the bar.

Vindico was seated in a quiet, dark corner trying to blend in. He was very obviously drowning his sorrows in liquor.

Governor Haydenshire wasn't having that. He pulled Vindico to the tables that Garrett and Patrick were fitting together, and everyone sat down as the bartender supplied numerous pitchers of beer and platters of nachos for the tables.

Several of the Non-Gifted security guards for the Orange Grove blocked the press at the doors to the hotel. This allowed the governor and his sons an evening to relax and chat without interference.

"So, let's hear it, you two. How'd you figure out they'd bugged your room, and how did you catch them?" Governor Haydenshire looked extremely impressed with both Vindico and Rainer.

After Rainer explained how he knew something was up with the room, Vindico nodded his head and drew another small sip of what Rainer assumed was an extremely expensive Scotch, judging by the way Vindico was savoring it.

"They hadn't assigned the keycards to the rooms until you arrived. They only had the short time it took you and Emily to get up to the suites to plant the bugs. That's why the mic wasn't better hidden," he explained.

"Peterson's asking that you and my baby girl drop the charges against Samantha," Governor Haydenshire commented.

"I'll talk to Em, but honestly, she's better off in the holding cells than she is with Malicai."

Vindico nodded his ardent agreement.

Governor Haydenshire considered this for a moment before moving on. "All right, well, since it's been this way since you two were born, I assume you were at the hospital with Logan, so tell me what happened there."

Vindico chuckled as Rainer began the tale.

"I should've been there," Governor Haydenshire lamented as Rainer told everyone about them not knowing where Adeline was or what was going on for hours. After the long, drawn out story, Governor Haydenshire looked devastated. He was shaking his head, clearly mentally reminding himself why he needed to continue to vie for Crown despite the hardships his absence was causing his children.

He moved on to Garrett. "Do I want to know why Chloe Sawyer refused to talk to you all evening but was hanging all over several other men at the party, or why you and Fionna Styler danced almost every dance together?"

Garrett shook his head. "Fi and I have been friends forever, Dad. You know that. As for the other, probably not." He chuckled along with everyone else.

"You know, son, your mother and I wouldn't mind your settling down, getting married, maybe having us a few grandkids."

Garrett looked horrified by the very idea, but a moment later Rainer noted regret playing in his eyes.

"You have ten plus children, so I'd say you're looking to have plenty of grandkids. None of them will, however, be mine." His statement rang with challenge.

With that, he and Vindico clinked their glasses in a fervent toast to bachelorhood.

"Oh, yeah,"—Governor Haydenshire turned to Patrick with a goading grin—"how's married life, son?"

Patrick let a sly grin spread rapidly across his face as he waggled his eyebrows. "Awesome," he vowed with a great deal of lust in his tone.

Everyone chuckled, much to Garrett's annoyance. "Yeah, that whole one woman for the rest of your life thing sounds pretty much like hell to me, so…"

All of the men who were committed to only one woman shook their heads as Vindico and Garrett laughed.

By two o'clock, Rainer was exhausted.

Governor Haydenshire slapped him on the back. "Go get my baby girl, and take her to The Fifteen." He winked at Rainer.

Rainer's brow furrowed as he wondered how the governor knew where they were staying. He was certain Vindico hadn't told anyone.

Governor Haydenshire laughed at him outright. "That was your dad's favorite place in Boston. I knew he brought you here the last trip you took with him. I figured it stuck out in your memory."

Vindico chuckled. "I'd be careful, Lawson. He clearly has your number."

Rainer nodded his agreement, which thoroughly delighted the governor.

It was a testament to the number of beers that Governor Haydenshire had consumed that he added wryly, "Yeah, well, there was another reason I kept you out so late."

The entire table lit with laughter as Rainer debated a comeback.

He decided against goading Emily's father with, *I'm never too tired for that*, so he just shook his head instead.

"Good night." Rainer stood and threw down enough money to cover the beers he'd consumed plus a generous tip.

"Here, I'll head out with you." Vindico stood beside him. He looked relieved to be bowing out of the festivities.

The party broke up quickly after that, and everyone followed Rainer and Vindico to the elevators.

CHAPTER 50
ONLY FOOLS
DAN VINDICO

Dan's shield continued its disconcerting whir against his skin as the Non-Gifted flight made the approach into Dulles. He'd fled Boston at the first available opportunity. He'd had to get out of there, but his escape didn't seem to offer him any reprieve.

What the hell was wrong with him? Several rapid blinks did nothing to clear the imagery of her gorgeous sienna eyes locked on his, of her lips drawn in a delicious juxtaposition that fascinated him. Her smile was somehow innocent and seductive, sweet and sinful, and he knew the taste his shield had craved and his ego had refused would be like sinking his teeth into a forbidden fruit. His shield longed for the nirvana that seemed to exist inside of her, just out of reach.

He'd had a double of a Macallan 25 at that stupid hotel bar. If a four-hundred-dollar pour hadn't satisfied his tongue enough to rid his shield of its longing for her, it wasn't likely anything would. *Dammit.*

He shook himself. With a tight clench of his jaw, he tried to see something in front of him, something that wasn't Fionna Styler's lush curves, or the swells of her breasts so fucking tempting in that damn dress they should've been illegal, or her ass. *God, that ass.*

He rubbed his hands along the front of his tux pants as if that would rid the feel of her curves from his palms.

He closed his eyes and tried to force his Visium bands to push his shield out of the way. Clearly, he needed to reset the fucking thing because it continued to give craving, almost angry pulses. It vibrated against his muscles in protest, an outcry against what he would never allow.

He stood and pushed his way into the aisle as soon as the wheels made contact with the ground. He reveled in the annoyed glances his fellow passengers gave him. He grabbed his bag and pushed past the flight attendants despite their ridiculous scolding.

As soon as the bridge was connected, he was off the plane. He sprinted down the jetway and pulled the cast from his bike when he was still twenty yards away. He had to get out of there. Somehow he had to outrun the memories of the evening.

The first vestiges of sunlight remained locked behind the heavy clouds as he pulled into the apartment complex in Aurora Highlands. His shield seared against his skin. Dan welcomed the pain. He deserved it. But what was happening to him? What was wrong with his shield? Nothing made any damn sense.

He pounded on the door. His muscles cinched against the abuse his own body was wielding.

Finally, she opened the door. "What are you doing here? I thought you were in Boston?"

He pushed himself inside the apartment. "I was." He tried to remember when he'd told her where he was going, but he didn't care enough to try to recall their mind-numbing conversations. He must've mentioned it at some point.

Still desperate to see something, anything that wasn't Fionna, he glanced around the apartment and ordered himself to take in his surroundings. There was a large Gucci bag slung on a chair in the living room and a Louis Vuitton scarf hung with her coat over the coatrack near the door. Clearly she was enjoying the extra paycheck she was earning from the Senate. That was enough to rid him of most of his guilt.

Bridgette stared at him like he'd lost his mind. He was quite certain he had. "Why are you here at five in the morning?" she finally demanded.

He doubted she really needed him to explain it. "I...just thought I'd stop by."

"Have you thought about our last conversation?" she pressed.

He ground his teeth. "Yeah, but we'll talk about it later."

"No, we'll talk about it now."

"Sure. Whatever you want."

"A serious commitment is what I want."

"Yeah. Okay. Fine." His Visium Predilection gave a disconcerting sizzle as if it was taking up arms with his shield.

"Good." Her smile said she was pleased. That made one of them.

Dan fought his eye roll, took her hand, and guided her to the bedroom.

～

Lachland Peterson

He drove his fingers into his eyes and fought to stay awake as the phone rang endlessly. It was the tenth time that day alone he'd called the number he'd been given, the number no one seemed to answer.

He paced in his office. *Dammit! Answer the phone.*

Finally, mercifully he answered.

"Nic!" Lachland demanded. "My daughter has been arrested. Emily Haydenshire's hotel room was bugged and they're blaming Samantha. What the hell happened? You never said anything like this."

Wretchkinsides gave his customary foreboding chuckle that Lachland had learned to expect. "I never said what exactly?" thrummed in his deep Russian accent.

"That Stephen's kids could get hurt. I never intended..."

"Intentions accomplish nothing. I have no use for them. Actions accomplish goals. My understanding was that we shared a common goal."

Lachland's brow furrowed. "Samantha is in prison," he tried again. "Dan Vindico arrested her himself." Wretchkinsides made an odd, almost hissing sound at Vindico's name. "How are we going to get her out? You told me to step down from my office. I have no power in the Senate until I win."

"Then perhaps this will be an incentive."

"Dammit. My daughter is not a part of our deal. I never agreed to that. I'll drop out of the race."

This time Wretchkinsides gave an amused chuckle. "Be cautious. When the king believes himself to be more powerful than the kingmaker, he risks ruling from a stake instead of a throne."

"What the hell does that mean?"

"Precisely what I said. The marionette strings can always become a noose. Never forget that."

"Are you threatening me?! I'm not a puppet." Lachland gasped. "I want my daughter out of prison! Now!"

Wretchkinsides tsked. "All men have a weakness, Lachland. Only fools reveal theirs."

ABOUT THE AUTHOR

J.E. Neal (aka Jillian) vastly prefers coffee to tea, guac to salsa, the beach over anywhere else, and the world inside her head over the one outside her front door. She also loves not having to choose.

Driven by the question 'what if,' J.E. Neal's world began to manifest. What if there were people with powers the rest of us couldn't see? What if the energy of our world could be summoned and used at their will? Characters with these amazing abilities took shape in her mind. She created—and continues to create—an endless number of stories full of delicious escape from our reality where emotions are visible, desire is palpable, and danger is universal.

Learn more about J.E. Neal at JillianNeal.com

        facebook.com/jilliannealauthor
        twitter.com/JillianNeal_
        instagram.com/jilliannealauthor

ALSO BY J.E. NEAL

ENERGY OF MAGIC

Shield and Shattered Cages (Book 1)

Shield and Faltered Steps (Book 2)

Shield and Splintered Oaths (Book 3)

Shield and Humbled Crown (Book 4)

Shield and Vile Serpents (Book 5)

Shield and Coveted Splendor (Book 6)

Shield and Guarded Shadow (Book 7)

Shield and Worthy Sinner (Book 8)

Shield and Sacrificial Heirs (Book 9)

Made in the USA
Columbia, SC
30 August 2023